FINDING
EMMA

a novel by
K. Ryan

ISBN: 978-0692548493

For Andrea, Kristin, Krista, Katy, Elaine, Teah, Lainie, Rachel, Erin, Alexandra, Maggie, Cathy, Kenzie, Kim, Amy, Lindsey, Nicole, and J. Law.

"One must put up barriers to keep oneself intact."
—Neil Peart, "Limelight"

PROLOGUE

It all started with a cat.

Well, to be fair, it technically started over a year ago, but maybe I should back up a little bit first. When I was five, I had the bright idea to corner my neighbor's cat and spray it with a squirt gun and then couldn't understand why the cat clawed and scratched her way out of that damn corner, leaving my five-year-old self bloody and crying. Thus, after that little encounter, my distaste and general indifference to cats began.

They just always seemed like outliers to me: predatory, creepy, sneaky, destroyers of power cords and furniture. The differences between cats and dogs were staggering—take my childhood dog for instance: a happy-go-lucky, tail-wagging, sloppy-kissing, frolicking in the backyard golden retriever. Compared to the anti-social, complicated mannerisms of cats, dogs just always seemed nicer. Easier than difficult-to-please, cagey, and skittish cats.

Not that I didn't think all those cute Youtube videos of kittens were absolutely adorable. I mean, seriously, a cat playing the piano? Making grumpy faces? Sure, they were cute, but that was pretty much the extent of how much I ever even thought about cats.

So, I pretty much kept my distance with a carefully-drawn line in the sand between us, especially since, as I grew older, I'd developed a slight cat allergy—slight meaning I felt my eyes watering and my throat closing within 10 minutes of being in the same room as a cat. No big loss on my part, that was for sure.

I guess I just figured I'd always have dogs. And I guess that was before I belly-flopped off the deep end and landed face-first on the cold, wet floor of rock bottom.

So, like I said, it all started with a cat.

CHAPTER ONE

"Thank you for being a friend...traveled down the road and back again..."

I blew my bangs out of my eyes as I fumbled for my keys and shot a wary glance at the door down the hall from mine. *Must be nice to sit around and watch Estelle Getty verbally abuse Betty White all day,* I mused and shook my head at Mrs. Johannsen's door. Her apartment was technically directly in front of mine with the way our building was structured. Our connecting walls were so paper thin I was beginning to seriously worry about how much more cackling I could reasonably stand.

If marathon after marathon of old lady escapades blaring through my walls was the worst of my problems with Mrs. Johannsen, then I guess I really shouldn't complain. Considering that she never asked any invasive questions and generally left me alone, she was the best neighbor somebody like me could ask for. My eyes landed on the door directly across from mine and a little fluttering of nervousness shot through me. Mrs. Johannsen had not-so-discreetly informed me yesterday that we were finally due for some new neighbors on our floor.

The apartment directly across from mine had sat vacant for two glorious months of silence and disruption-free nights. My last neighbors were nice enough, but given that our patios shared a wall and they *always* had their patio door open, it was difficult to shut out the screeching, ear-splitting crying no matter how loud I turned up my turntable or my TV. The baby was cute. She was really was. Chubby cheeks and pretty brown eyes with little wisps of strawberry-blonde hair.

I still hated her.

All I wanted was peace, quiet, and sleep-filled nights. And all that baby did was cry and cry and cry, making it pretty much impossible for me to sleep or get any work done. I got that babies were difficult, that being a new parent was hard, but that didn't mean *I* had to suffer right along with them too. It wasn't like I could exactly knock on the door and tell them to turn down the noise. I'm sure they would've loved a

1

baby-controlling remote that you could just click to mute the noise and I would've happily bought one for them if a beautiful invention like that actually existed.

Needless to say, I'd done a little happy dance when they finally bought a house and moved the hell out.

That was the scary thing about knowing new neighbors were on their way—you just never knew what you were going to get, but not in that optimistic life-is-like-a-box-of-chocolates way. They could be the nicest, quietest neighbors ever that just kept to themselves and minded their business, kind of like Mrs. Johannsen, minus her tolerable TV addiction, and my upstairs neighbors, who were rarely home anyway. Or they could be loud. Obnoxious. Intrusive. Uninvited. Messy. Annoying.

I blew out a deep breath just at the thought. I was better off just focusing on what I could control, which over the last year, wasn't a whole lot.

After finally pushing through the door, I tossed my keys onto the tiny end table I'd set up right next to the door just for that purpose, kicked off my shoes, and opened my patio door to air out my stuffy living space. I inhaled deeply, my eyes taking in the peace residing in my makeshift backyard. Any kind of tree line in this part of Milwaukee was rare and when I first saw the view in this apartment—thick, green brush and tall trees that blocked everything else out—I knew I had to have it.

This apartment and this city really gave me the best of both worlds: I could get lost in the bustle, but come home to peace and quiet.

Today was really just an average day. My shift at The Corner Café was easy, sort of slow, and uneventful. I had $70 in tips sitting in my purse, which wasn't great for a Friday, but it wouldn't necessarily put me in the red either. Overall, it was a pretty good, quiet day in the city.

As if on cue, my iPhone buzzed in my back pocket. My eyes flew to the digital clock above my stove and then flitted up to the ceiling with a shake of my head. Jesus, it was like damned clockwork with him. Unfortunately, I also knew that if I didn't respond sometime soon, my overprotective-to-a-serious-fault older brother would just keep bothering me until he got what he wanted.

Never should've given that nosy bastard my schedule.

One swipe across the screen told me what I needed to know: *How was ur day?*

Well, I guess I couldn't really fault the guy for trying, so I pounded out a quick reply, telling him what he already knew. Less than a second later, he replied: *Good to hear. Love u, Em.*

There, that wasn't so bad. Pushing aside the nagging guilt tugging at my conscience, I figured my best bet was to just stick with my plan for the rest of my night: eating, watching Netflix, blogging, more Netflix, and last but certainly not least, sleeping. Why was that so bad? Noah knew everything, all the dirty, humiliating details, and he still didn't understand why this was the way it had to be. Why I needed to live this way. Why I needed to separate myself from what he referred to as *actual living.*

His worry wasn't necessarily misplaced, but it wasn't productive either.

Life was just less complicated and less tragic when it was a one-woman show.

With that last thought, I booted up Netflix on my TV and toggled over to the next episode of *Orange Is The New Black.* I needed to write another blog post tonight, this time on the best BB creams to use this fall —compelling stuff, right?—but that still left plenty of time to lose myself in the goings-on at Litchfield Penitentiary and make dinner. Careful to turn the volume up enough to drown out the cackling Golden Girl, I threw a chicken breast on a skillet and let Piper and company give me a little escape.

By the time I was seated on my couch, nibbling away at the chicken and side salad, and engrossed in the middle of an episode, I'd scrolled through emails, made some mental notes about the blog post I had to write, and had a cold glass of Moscato sitting in front of me.

My phone buzzed one more time and my eyes lifted to the ceiling.

Dinner at our house this weekend??

I had to give Noah credit for trying. For *still* trying and refusing to give up on me, even though I turned him and Cristina down almost every time. The last time I'd agreed to a dinner at their house, my mom had shown up unannounced and uninvited.

That pretty much put an end to my desire to travel back to Hickory for any reason. Swallowing back more than a little guilt, I pounded out a quick reply telling him I had to work all weekend and couldn't make it. I would be an aunt in about a month and I didn't want to be anywhere near the town where my soon-to-be niece would live. It was a kick in the gut, salt in an open wound, but it was something I could live with.

Unfortunately.

Pushing aside that gnawing at my stomach, my attention shifted back to my TV and I let fantasy drown out reality for a few blissful, carefree minutes. Just as Crazy Eyes got done throwing pie, I saw it.

Streaks of grey and black. Little flashes of white. All hovering around my patio chairs. What the…

I shot up from my couch and darted over to my patio door. There it was. A stupid, skinny, grey and black striped cat.

"What the fuck?"

The cat was weaving in and around the leg of the patio chair closest to my screen door and his head lifted up at the sound of my voice, giving me a good look at the white patch on his chest and four little white paws. My heart did something I hadn't felt in a long time—it tugged. I swallowed hard in response.

It was the eyes. Soft grey. Glinting almost ethereally in the twilight. It was like someone had taken an Emma-controlling remote and clicked pause. I couldn't move. I couldn't speak. I couldn't think. I just stared back.

As if it could sense it needed to make the first move, the cat ducked underneath the chair, bending and slinking until its nose pressed against my screen door. It sat back on its haunches, opened its mouth, and this little mewing sound croaked out, deep and forceful, like it expected me to understand, to be able to communicate somehow this way.

It stared back at me expectantly as if to say, *Well?*

I just stared back. I didn't know what to do. All my faculties had just sort of left the building. Motor ability. Verbal ability…all vanished as I gaped back at this cat.

Finally, the cat seemed to realize I wasn't going to communicate the way it wanted me to and stood up on all four legs, with its white socks, and slinked down the entire length of my patio door, heading right for my long, rectangular planter filled with rows of little blue and yellow flowers.

Oh shit.

Was it going to…and then its long, striped tail flicked up to reveal the biggest pair of kitty balls I'd ever seen. Okay, I'd never seen a pair of kitty balls before but…Jesus.

So, it was definitely a *he*. No doubt about that.

My attention was too immersed in the logistics of how a skinny little cat like him carried around such massive testicles—bottom-heavy was probably the best way to describe it—that my brain completely delayed when he sat his two front paws on the edge of my planter and then started digging with his right paw.

Oh shit. Oh no…no! No!

My brain was screaming, but somewhere along the way, all the neurons connecting my brain to my voice had completely disconnected. So I watched in complete disbelief and horror as the cat proceeded to

4

use my potted plants as his own personal litter box.

Part of me was a little impressed. At least he didn't piss all over my concrete patio...but my plants. Oh shit. My plants!

Finally, my voice snapped back to life.

"Hey!"

That was all I had.

His head snapped towards me at the sound of my voice and he continued right on pissing, blinking at me as if to say, *Whatcha gonna do about it? Bring it, lady.*

"Stop! That's...don't do that!"

Seriously, this was the best I could do? Couldn't even muster up enough emotion to reprimand a cat anymore...I guess I'd really lost my touch. He glanced at me again from over his shoulder and when he'd finished soiling my bright blue and yellow flowers, promptly resumed digging to cover up his business.

"Yeah, like that'll help. Thanks a lot."

His grey eyes bugged out a little and his mouth curled into a slight O, like he'd suddenly just realized that maybe I didn't want him using my planter as his bathroom. That long, striped tail flicked at the tip a few times and then he hopped down from the planter, heading right for me in slow, leisurely strides. He stopped in front of the screen door again and sat down, his tail flipping up and down on the concrete underneath him.

His mouth opened and let out one long wail, almost like a call, like a plea for me to do...something. That tugging at my heart was right there again, pulling and twisting and digging, and then he leapt up to scratch both front paws on my screen door, mewing and wailing again.

Let me in. Let me in. Let me in.

That's what he wanted.

That wasn't going to happen.

No way in hell.

Even if I wanted to let him in, my apartment complex had a strict no-pets-allowed clause in my lease. So no dogs. No birds. No guinea pigs. And definitely no cats. And most importantly, cats made my eyes itchy and watery. Cats made my throat close and my nose runny. I didn't typically ever want anything to do with them and kept my distance. I didn't know *what* to do with them.

Not happening, buddy, I thought ruefully.

He just kept scratching his paws up the length of my screen door, stretching up as far as he could, mewing and trilling long, throaty sounds. Those eyes...shit, those eyes. Pleading with me. Begging me.

I took a shaky breath and before I knew what I was doing, I backpedalled into my kitchen, keeping my eyes on the cat on my patio the entire time. My mind flipped through the meager supply of food I kept in the refrigerator. What the hell did cats eat anyway? Was I supposed to give them milk? Wait, I didn't have any milk. I hitched my hands on my hips, mentally surveying what little I had to offer.

This was a bad idea.

A *really* bad idea.

I'd always heard that you should never, ever feed a stray cat. They'd just keep coming back. This was probably the stupidest idea I'd ever had, but I just couldn't help myself. He was so skinny...even through the dark fur and even darker night air around him, little bony ribs protruded out of his body. He wasn't skeletal by any means—he just looked like he hadn't eaten much in awhile.

My stomach flip-flopped as I grabbed a few pieces of bread and filled up a plastic bowl with water. When I stood in front of the screen door again, he was just sitting there observing me with those shimmering grey eyes and I swallowed tightly.

The problem was that I had to actually open the door now.

How was I supposed to know what he would do? He could jump at me, bite me, scratch me, try to sneak inside my apartment...I didn't know this cat. Even though he seemed harmless, that didn't mean he'd be friendly once the barriers between us came down. As far as I was concerned, he was just a mangy, wild animal who couldn't be trusted.

He opened his mouth again, this time letting out a long meow that sounded more like a *maawhr* than an actual meow. Then again, what the hell did I know about cats? This was the closest I'd ever been to one in years. And now he was still sitting there, waiting expectantly.

With a deep breath, I slid open the screen door just enough to toss the pieces of bread out to the furthest edge of my patio. He took the bait, leaping up to go after the bread and I hastily stuck my arm out to set the water bowl down a few feet away from me, sloshing water all over the place in the process. Then I snapped my arm back and slammed the screen door shut just as quickly.

There. I did it.

As I watched him wolf down the two pieces of bread, that fluttering sped up again in my stomach. I'd probably just created a huge problem for myself by feeding him, but now that I'd done it, I didn't feel guilty. I didn't regret it. I was just sort of glad I'd been able to help him, even if it was just for a night.

Happiness and relief that he'd have some food in that skinny little body knocked out any other feelings of unease and hesitation.

Happiness and relief were not feelings I was used to having. I wasn't used to feeling like I'd done the right thing. I think I'd forgotten what that even felt like in the first place. But I felt it now. It surged through me, sweeping down from my toes all the way up to the tip of my nose. I took a deep breath and watched him move from the edge of my patio until he sat down right in front of me to lap up some water.

I still couldn't move.

I still stood there, frozen at my screen door, staring at this stray cat.

My eyes wandered over him to take in the details I'd missed before. Patches of wiry, pale whiskers on tiny cheeks. Dark streaks slashed across his face. A brown-tipped nose with pink smudging. Sharp, pointed dark ears. A long black stripe starting in between his shoulder blades running all the way down to the base of his tail, layered with rings of alternating black and grey.

As he lapped up the water like he hadn't seen it in days, which might've been true, the tip of his tail, which looked like it'd been dipped in ink, flicked from side to side. His head popped up once, his eyes boring into me to say, *Geez, lady. Would you quit staring and let me drink this shit in peace?*

In the moonlight, his eyes looked a little more green now than grey. Like sea foam. Sweet. Maybe even a little innocent too.

Where did he come from? Why was he out here by himself? He was obviously somebody's cat, given the way he'd violated my potted plants, so why wasn't he home now? What had brought him here, tonight, to my patio door?

Well, clearly the aroma of chicken brought him to my patio door, but that was besides the point. Did he have a home and just get lost? Was someone looking for him? Hoping he was okay? Or did someone not want him and just let him go?

That last thought seized my heart and squeezed tight. I hoped that wasn't the case. I hoped he had a home. Maybe he was just one of those outdoor cats that roamed around during the day and then went back home at night. I mean, he'd used my plants as a litter box, so I was pretty sure he was at least a *little* house-trained.

Once he'd had his fill from the plastic bowl, his bright pink tongue shot out to tug up the length of his right paw and then he dragged his paw over the side of his head. His dark-rimmed eyes flicked back to me once and a moment later, he was leaping up onto the patio chair closest to where I stood. He reared back on the seat, leaning his body down into his front paws in a long, easy stretch that stuck his butt high in the air then he circled the seat once, found a good spot, and plopped down on the chair, making sure he was still facing me.

He blinked. Then he blinked again. And then he rested his head against a white paw, those grey, sea foam eyes sparkling a little in the darkness.

Huh.

Okay.

I sawed on my bottom lip and frowned back at him.

"I see you've made yourself comfortable," I called out to him softly and narrowed my eyes a little when his head popped up at the sound of my voice. "Well, just...don't get *too* comfortable, okay? You can stay, I guess. But just for tonight. Don't get any ideas."

What was I doing...talking to a cat? Like he could understand me anyway. Still, I felt like I'd made my point and I went back to my plans for the night, finishing my dinner and that episode of *Orange Is The New Black*, my eyes shifting out to the patio every few minutes.

When it was time to start writing my blog post, though, the cat was a distraction. It was hard to focus on whether or not to choose a moisture-based BB cream or a higher SPF formula when there was a wild animal sitting on my patio like he owned the place.

After about 20 minutes of staring at my screen, I figured a little music would do the trick and switched the needle on my turntable to the record I'd lazily left there the night before. Music had long been a source of comfort to me and tonight was really no exception. Whenever I needed to clear my head, or just needed a distraction in general, music had always been there to pick up the pieces, lulling through any pain, any heartache, and anything that ailed me. Whether it was a sad country song or a catchy pop song, the beats never failed to either cure my emotions or enhance them. It was the only form of therapy I could ever agree to and the only thing keeping me sane, in light of recent life-shattering events.

And in light of those recent events, I'd needed music more than ever.

I glanced over at the patio to find the cat watching my every move like he was just sort of...observing. Taking inventory. It was a little creepy. And weird. Definitely weird. Like he wasn't just watching me, but *seeing* me, too.

I wasn't sure I liked it. And I also wasn't completely convinced that my imagination wasn't playing tricks on me right now either.

But when I carried my computer over to the patio and dropped down until my back rested against the wall right next to the screen door, I don't know who was more surprised: me or the cat.

As if on cue, he hopped down from the chair and sat down right across from me until the only things separating us were a few feet and some flimsy wiring.

"Hey," I whispered to him. His ears pricked up and one of them tilted to the side. "You like this song?"

His mouth quirked a little, curling into that tiny O shape again, and he moved a hair closer.

"Hail, hail," I sang softly. *"What's the matter with your head?"*

Those shimmering eyes focused on me and I kept on singing: *"Come and get your love..."*

"Sorry," I told him. "I probably won't be trying out for *American Idol* anytime soon, you know?"

His chest jumped, like he'd hiccuped or something, and he made a noise that sounded like...*meh.* Like a grumble or a murmur. Like he was answering me.

"I gotta get some work done, but I think I'll sit right here while I do it if that's okay with you."

Meh.

My lips twitched at the sound and I shifted my focus back to finishing up this blog post. I had about another two hours or so before I needed to post it, but I still needed to get my ass in gear.

"Can you believe I actually make some money off this?" I told him as I typed. "I guess I've been doing it for so long and enough people started reading it...advertising and all that, you know? You wanna know what my blog is called?"

Meh.

I grinned at him. *"Northern Chic.* Kinda catchy, huh? You know, because we live in Wisconsin?"

Meh.

"Yeah, I started this beauty blog when I was a senior in high school and I just sort of never stopped, even through college and after I graduated. I don't use my real name or anything. No one knows who I am, which, trust me, is a good thing. But it's fun. I like it. I like when companies send me things to try, too."

And I especially liked the extra padding it gave my bank account every month. Between ads and online retailers giving me a kick-back for linking to products on their sites, I had a healthy little side business. It wasn't quite enough to cover my bills every month, but between my blog and waitressing, I was living pretty comfortably, or at least, as comfortably as I could.

"The Smashbox BB cream tends to run a little oily, so if you have combination skin, that might not be the best option for you. When I tested it earlier this week, my cheeks were shiny and greasy enough that I felt like I needed to wash it off *immediately*. This one just didn't work for my skin, but if your skin tends to start to dry out come fall, it might work better for you than it did for me….there, what do you think of that?"

I shifted my eyes back to the cat, whose grey eyes were still observing me intently. That murmuring rumbled from his chest again and I smiled back.

"Now, all I have to do is add some pictures, some purchase links, and I'm all set to post. It probably shouldn't be this easy, but people read it, you know?"

Meh.

My head bobbed a little more to the music as I finished up my post. *"Hail, hail, get it together, baby…"*

Once I had everything all loaded up on my blog, my eyes fell to the clock on my laptop. In my past life, I'd been used to getting my ass to bed by 10 at the latest on school nights, but now that issue was pretty much obsolete. So, when I got the random breakfast shift, my body tended to reject morning-person mode and I usually felt like a zombie for the first hour or so of my shift. It definitely didn't help that this was actually a double shift tomorrow and I probably wouldn't get home until after four.

"Well," I told him and his chin tilted up at the sound of my voice. "I should probably head to bed. I have to get up for work early tomorrow and…um, like I said, you can stay, I guess, if you want to."

His chest bopped and then his mouth opened for one last *maawhr* as I stood up to head into my bedroom and shut the patio door, feeling a prickling of guilt as his eyes stared up at me and his tail flicked up and down on the concrete. It was mid-September, but the air was still a crisp-warm contradiction that was normal for Wisconsin this time of year. Not exactly hot, but not freezing temperatures at night either. My fingers immediately flew to the weather app on my phone and I relaxed a little. Low of 57 degrees tonight. That wasn't so bad.

He'll be fine out there tonight, I told myself as I crept down my hallway, *and this obviously isn't the first night he's spent outside by himself.*

Just as I reached my bedroom door, I glanced over my shoulder to find his dark, shadowy shape perched on that patio chair again.

Maybe he'd…nope. Not going there.

He'd gotten what he wanted from me and he'd be gone in the morning anyway.

CHAPTER TWO

The next morning I rolled out of bed with a little bounce in my step and butterflies playing hopscotch in my stomach. I had a one-track mind as I shuffled out into my hallway until I had a good view of my patio.

Sure enough, there he was. All curled up on the chair right where I'd left him.

The movement inside the apartment must've caught his attention because he lifted his head off a paw, blinking up at me when I moved to stand right at the door. His eyes drooped a little and he yawned, stretching one white paw high up into the air.

My lips twitched in amusement and then my eyes dropped to the plastic bowl I'd set out the night before. It was pretty much all dried out.

I shuffled a little from side to side in front of him, knowing that I had to open the screen door yet again if I wanted to give him any more water...and *did* I want to give him more water? More food? The fact that he'd camped out here for the night had some alarm bells ringing, too. If he actually had somewhere to go home to, it was probably unlikely that he would've parked it on my patio for the entire night.

If I stopped feeding him, if I stopped setting out water, eventually he'd hop off my chair and just go away.

But before I could stop myself, I unlocked the door, slid it open wide enough to slip my hand through, and crouched down so I could snatch up the bowl. The cat's right ear tilted to the side and then he just yawned again as if I was boring him. As if I was somehow inconveniencing him and interrupting his precious sleep.

Still, I dutifully carried the bowl to the sink, filled it up, and scrounged around my cupboards for something other than bread this time around. Hmm...I really needed to go grocery shopping. I didn't know if I should even give him bread—if it was something that would make him sick or not.

At this point, I needed to call in reinforcements and booted up Safari on my phone, doing a quick search for things cats could eat. Okay...something with protein. Boiled chicken, rice, potatoes. I didn't have any of those things. I scrolled through the rest of the article and finally came across some information I could use.

"Fish and cheese," I muttered. "Why didn't I think of that before? Shit."

I had tuna and pre-packaged cheese slices. This was what happened when someone who has never had cats before fumbled through a stray encounter. I just had no idea what I was doing here with the whole damn thing.

Feeding a stray cat. Looking up what to feed said stray cat. I think I might've hopped on the crazy train last night and knocked a few screws loose in the process. But then my eyes flew to my patio, landing right on pointed dark ears, a tiny brown nose, and wide grey eyes.

Shit.

I was carrying half a can of tuna, a slice of cheese, and some more water out to the patio before I could stop myself.

Did you hear that? That was the sound of my sanity flying right out the window. Going...going...gone.

We had to do our little dance again and this time, I tossed the slice of cheese out to the furthest corner of the patio so I could pull the ol' bait and switch, jerk open the screen door, get the tuna and water bowl onto the ground, and slam the door shut again before he wised up.

Satisfied that he was preoccupied, I went about my normal routine to get ready for work: coffee, a light breakfast, quick shower, and then I changed into my uniform. By the time I had my keys and my iPod in hand and was ready to walk out the door, the cat had wolfed down everything I'd offered and perched himself back on the chair, circling around a few times again before plopping down into a good spot.

At the risk of being a little late for work, I strode down my short hallway, grabbed what I needed from my bathroom, and then found myself standing in front of the screen door again.

The cat's head popped up, his eyes half-closed and his ears tilted down to the sides as if to say, *I'm trying to sleep here. Can't a guy get a little peace and quiet? Jesus, lady.*

My lips quirked up as I slid the screen door open one last time and held out the bundle of towels clenched in my hand.

"So," I told him. "I think this might, uh, be more comfortable for you out here. If you could just...I don't know, move for a second so I can..."

He blinked.

Okay, good enough. I guess.

I huffed out a laugh and gingerly set one of the towels down on the chair behind him, careful to keep one hand trained on the door in case he made a mad dash for my apartment. Finally, he got the hint and hopped off the chair, sitting back on his haunches to wait patiently for me to arrange his new makeshift bed. With my eyes darting warily from the cat and the chair, I made quick work of tossing the other towel down and jerked some material into place just enough to form a little bed.

The whole time, the cat waited silently, his eyes flicking in between me and the chair until I snatched my arm back inside the apartment and snapped the door closed again. Then he just leapt back up onto the chair, circled around twice, and settled into the bed, nuzzling the layers I'd set out for him.

After that, I finally felt like I could leave for work, but not without one more glance out towards my patio.

.   .   .

"Are you sure you don't wanna come?"

I sucked in a sharp breath and pressed a weak smile on my face. Mara scrunched her freckled nose and squinted at me. She knew exactly what I was about to say—it was what I said at the end of every Saturday shift we'd worked together and by now, she probably had the exact phrasing memorized.

"You know," I started quietly. "I've got a lot of work to do tonight. It's not that I don't want to. I really wish I could..."

Since I'd moved to the city and started working at The Corner Café —can you believe it's actually located on a corner, of all things?—Mara had been nothing but nice. Friendly. Talkative. Willing to listen if I was willing to talk (which I wasn't) and whenever we worked this shift together, she always asked me to come out with her and her friends afterwards.

This time she was trying to convince me that this micro-brewery, Matthews Brewing Co., was a place I just *had* to try because "they, like, have the *best* microbrews and the *coolest* tasting room with the *sweetest* view of the Milwaukee River." Even if I was interested in the offer, the art of the microbrew wasn't really anything I'd ever been into— blasphemy for a Wisconsin native, but I couldn't help it. Beer tasted like what I imagined piss tasted like.

Mara's eyes narrowed a little and I knew I'd have to give her a little more than my patent excuse.

"I'm not meeting my friends out until, like, 8:00, so..." she made a show of glancing at the non-existent watch on her wrist, "you've got, like, a good four hours to get some work done before coming out with us."

I liked Mara. I really did. She was the best co-worker I could ask for: we helped with each other's tables, shared tips willingly when we needed to, covered for each other when the other took a break, and generally had each other's backs. She never asked too many questions and accepted the little information I tossed out without pressing for more. Most of the friends she routinely tried to get me to hang out with had stopped into the café before, so I wouldn't exactly be going into this thing blind.

But I'd moved to Milwaukee to disappear, to become invisible, not to surround myself with a tight-knit group of dysfunctional girlfriends Lena Dunham-style.

"I know, but by the time I eat, take a little breather, maybe a quick nap, and get my ass in gear with this post, I'll probably only have an hour tops to get some work done and I really don't want to just slap some shit together, you know?"

It was an overly drawn-out, elaborate excuse, but the more she questioned me, the more I felt myself shuffling backwards into a corner. I could post to my blog as often or as little as I wanted; I had enough of a readership at this point that a delay wouldn't really matter in the grand scheme of things. Mara, however, did not need that little kernel of information to chew on.

"Well," Mara sighed and blew some bright blonde hair out of her face. "I really wish you'd come out with us one of these times. I have a hard time believing you need to work on your blog *that* much that you can't take a Saturday night off every once and awhile."

"Every post makes me some money," I shrugged. "The more posts I can get out there, the more money I make."

Mara glanced at me out of the corner of her eye as she reached for her purse. "Alright. I still can't believe you've been in this city for as long as you have and you've never been to Water Street downtown."

I pressed a forced smile on my face and punched my employee number into the Ziosk screen to clock out. "I guess I just haven't gotten a chance yet."

"Well, if you change your mind, you know my number."

"Got it. Thanks for asking though. Maybe next time, okay?"

She just waved me towards the door...she'd heard all my excuses already and I guess I had to give her credit for still trying after rejection after rejection. Someone clearly reaching out to me and wanting to be my friend wasn't necessarily a bad thing in itself. It was everything that came along with it that I wanted to avoid.

So, I just waved goodbye, grabbed my to-go box, pushed out the door, and headed in the opposite direction. The art of keeping people at arm's length was something I'd perfected since leaving my hometown behind and embracing anonymity.

Keep to yourself. Don't ask anyone any personal questions, but listen if they volunteer the information to you. Thank them for their offers, throw out a 'maybe next time' to keep them happy. Let the people you work with know enough generalities about you to make you seem normal enough, so they don't wonder about you, so their gazes don't follow you with narrowed eyes, so they don't dig, so they don't Google your name, so they just leave you alone, and so you become unimportant enough to ignore.

It was how I stayed under the radar.

It was how I maintained whatever shred of dignity I had left.

As I set back out towards my apartment six blocks away from the café, I freed my hair from its rubber band and let my long, honey-colored waves air out some of the grease and salt stench, popped in my earbuds, and breathed the city in. This was the part I loved, the part about my life now that I actually enjoyed.

Cities like Milwaukee made antisocial the new norm. You could literally walk down the street absorbed in music, an email, a text message—whatever your weapon of choice—and you didn't really have to pay attention to anything but what you were doing and where you were headed. So, in this city, no one really noticed me and as long as I showed up for work and paid my rent on time, no one really missed me either.

Stepping inside the middle of a crowded sidewalk, right where I was now, was the next best thing to an invisibility cloak. I could just get lost in it, moving in and out unnoticed, without judgment. Without stares. Without pity. Without disgust. That was exactly the way I liked it.

A rueful smile twisted my lips and I shook my head. It was crazy how different my life had looked in Hickory, where I'd been surrounded by cozy familiarity and careful, detailed plans. I knew every street inside and out, all the 'hotspots' in town, if you could really call them that, the best pizza place, best grocery store, best bookstore, best ice cream...all littered with shades of vanilla-flavored comfort. Hickory was set in its ways, comfortable in its generic, small-town atmosphere—the Maycomb of Wisconsin—where time and tradition seemed to move just as slowly. In Hickory, slow and steady didn't win the race; slow and steady kept you forever miles behind the rest of civilization. Just the name itself bred old-fashioned, Christian mentalities where town scandals gained enough traction to last an entire decade.

It was what I'd always known and where I thought I'd always be.

Of course, that was before my entire life had crashed and burned right before my eyes and the eyes of my hometown.

If someone had told me a year ago that not only would I be working as a waitress in a café, living in a city 100 times the size of what I was used to, where the only person I actually seemed to *want* to be around was, in fact, a stray cat, but the reasons *why* I'd find myself in a such a position—all by my own doing—I wouldn't have known whether to laugh until I puked or curl up in the fetal position and cry myself unconscious.

Life had a funny way of taking the carefully laid plans I'd set out for myself and completely smashing them to pieces.

My mind, thankfully, drifted back to that stray cat. Those sweet, little eyes. There was enough grey and enough green in them...maybe I should just settle once and for all. They were sea foam. Depending on the lighting, they were either green or grey. Sometimes there was more grey, sometimes more green. Either way, every time I looked at them, every time I thought about them, that familiar tugging yanked and tore at my heart.

This was going to be a serious problem for me. Not even a full 24 hours into it and I was sunk already. But still, he had to be somebody's cat, right? He just seemed too friendly, too mild-mannered to be one of those skittish, feral cats that took off before you got within 10 feet of them.

He'd probably be gone when I got home.

But, a tiny voice whispered, *if he's still there, maybe you should think about buying some freaking cat food.*

Maybe.

Maybe I'd think about it more seriously if he was still hanging around tomorrow. If he was going to use my patio as his personal bed and breakfast, the least I could do was act like a decent hostess and offer him something a little more substantial than canned tuna and sliced cheese.

As I rounded the corner to my block, I felt a prickling I hadn't felt in...I don't even know how long.

Hope.

It fluttered and soared and spiked up all the way from my stomach into my throat. Now that hope dovetailed right back down, plummeting into my stomach and knotted into anxiety.

What was the point in hope anyway? Especially hope that a stray cat, who probably wasn't really a stray and would end up leaving me for his actual home, was still perched on my patio?

It was stupid. Nonsensical.

Even if I did like cats, I couldn't keep him.

Still...maybe if he stuck around, *maybe* I'd buy a bag of cat food. Maybe.

The parking lot right in front of my building came into view, but I stopped short. A menacing, over-sized black truck was parked directly in front of the walkway with a U-Haul trailer hitched to the back.

New neighbors. And I knew exactly which apartment they were moving into...shit.

From around the other side of the truck, the passenger side door was wide open and I could see a dark figure hovering around, reaching down underneath the front seats with long arms.

The door of our shared entryway slapped open and a lanky guy with wiry, carrot-orange hair jogged down the sidewalk leading from the door back to the truck.

"Yo, Finn!" he called out to the guy still tucked inside the truck. "What's the hold-up? We still gotta get the TV inside."

"Get it in yourself," a deep, muffled voice yelled back.

"That's what she said."

"Shut up, jackass. I'm pretty sure you can handle your *precious* all by yourself, considering you'll flip a tit if I get my dirty fingerprints all over it."

The lanky guy was standing right next to the bed of the truck now and promptly kicked the other guy right in the ass. He yelped once and then shot up from the passenger side door to fire back, reaching out with a long, thick forearm to sock his friend in the shoulder.

Clad in worn dark jeans and a black T-shirt with a bright yellow neon sign pointing to the words *Mechanical Bull*, the guy just a mere 30 feet away from where I stood was a sight for sore eyes. Devastatingly handsome, even from the short distance away, with his strong jaw, a stupidly perfect nose, and light eyes that crinkled up at the sides when he laughed. Wavy chestnut hair flopped away from his face, curling around his ears and the lower half of his face was covered in thick, dark scruff that looked like it'd needed to be trimmed about three months ago. And that was about all I needed to see to know that all proper mental functioning had vacated.

I couldn't move. I couldn't think. I just stared.

I stood there for a few awkward moments, biting down on my bottom lip, and briefly contemplated backpedalling the way I came just to get myself the hell out of here. The scruffy Greek god's light eyes were on me now and my hands shook around the straps of my purse in response.

It had to be a crime to be that chiseled, that perfect-looking, and just lean against a truck in the middle of the day like it was no big deal.

Like the curveball life had thrown at me last year, I had no idea how to handle the situation I currently found myself in. The guy that inexplicably stared back at me was different than any other guy I'd ever gotten close enough to ogle like this before. Different than he-who-shall-not-be-named and different, than, well just about anyone I'd known in Hickory. And it scared the hell out of me.

My eyes flicked back to him just once as I pulled on my big-girl pants and headed straight for the blocked walkway. He'd tucked his head down, resting it against both folded arms on the bed of the truck while he watched me, like he was hiding, like he thought that if he ducked low enough, I wouldn't be able to see him somehow.

Too late for that.

Now, the lanky ginger waved to me. "Hey! Sorry about the roadblock. We're almost done."

I forced a quick smile on my face and waved back. "Don't worry about it."

Not wanting to give either of them an opportunity to carry this conversation any further, I hustled my ass all the way around the trailer and all but sprinted through the shared entryway, fumbling for my keys and feeling the guy's—Finn's—eyes on me the entire time from his hiding place behind the truck. My heart was still pounding when I scrambled through my apartment door, flipped the lock, and I blew out a deep breath.

Get it together. One glance from an attractive—okay, fine, insanely attractive—stranger shouldn't be enough to send you into cardiac arrest.

And then I remembered something that made that near heart attack-inducing encounter slip to the wayside. I took a cautious step deeper inside my apartment and my eyes landed right on the patio.

There he was, all curled up comfortably around the towels I'd set out for him this morning. His head jerked up as I padded over to the door and pulled it open, leaving just the screen door between us. He blinked at me and yawned wide, stretching his tongue all the way down to the bottom of his chin, and shook his head out like the effort was taking up too much of his energy.

Then, he stood up on all fours, shaking and twitching both hind legs, and hopped down to sit right in front of me.

Maahwr.

"Hey, buddy," I murmured, smiling down at him. "How's it going?"

Meh.

"Well, I had an okay day. I was wondering if you were gonna be here or not when I got home though."

And, deep down, I knew I was glad to see that my hope hadn't been misplaced, even if it was fleeting.

He let out one more long, low-pitched *maahwr* and scratched his thick claws up against my screen door. *Let me in. Let me in. Let me in.*

"Oh no, wait...stop!" my hands immediately flew out to the screen door to gently push his paws away and unhook his sharp talon-like nails from the wiring. Three tiny holes stared back at me. "Oh shit. Thank God for security deposits, right?"

The cat just blinked.

"I bet you're hungry."

More grumbling rumbled from his white chest. I decided it sounded like something between a purr and a mumble. A purrmble. No, that didn't sound right. A purrumble. Sure.

Meh.

"That's what I figured," I smiled back at him and backpedalled into my kitchen. I looked around, hands on my hips, and chewed on my bottom lip in thought. I had one more can of tuna, three more slices of cheese, and half a loaf of bread left to give him.

I guess I was buying a bag of cat food today.

Did you hear that? That was the sound of my willpower flying right out the window. Going...going...gone.

. . .

With *Highway 61 Revisited* spinning on my turntable and Bob Dylan's scratchy voice crooning through my speakers, I situated myself with my back against the wall closest to the screen door again and my laptop resting on my thighs.

I had a glass of wine on one side of me and the cat sitting outside the screen door on the other. Things could always be worse.

An empty plastic bowl sat just a foot away from the cat and I was kind of surprised he wasn't *maawhr*-ing and purrumbling for another helping of store-bought dry cat food. He'd attacked that little bowl of kibble like

19

there was no tomorrow, but then again, maybe he figured, *who knows when I'll see this shit again?* I couldn't blame the guy for taking advantage; I just hoped I wouldn't have a sick cat puking on my patio anytime soon.

We'd done our little dance again of me distracting him with a piece of bread, him jumping off the chair to grab it, me hastily throwing the cat food out there, and then slamming the screen door shut again before he had a chance to get too close.

Even though I was feeding him and letting him crash on my patio, I was absolutely certain I didn't want him inside my apartment. That was just bad news all the way around, not to mention setting myself up for some serious trouble, whether it was from my allergies or my landlord.

Now, though, he was just sitting patiently on the other side of the screen door, watching me type away, drink my wine, and listen to my music.

"*How does it feel?*" I sang along softly, "*To be on your own...with no direction home...*"

My eyes shifted to the cat, whose chest jumped at the attention. *Meh.*

"What do you think of Bob Dylan?" I asked him and his head tilted a little. "He was one of my dad's favorites. I think he had every single album...well, I guess *I* have every single album now, but you get the idea. He's pretty cool, right? With that crazy warble?"

The cat blinked.

"He really liked Rush, too. Liked isn't the right word. It was more like an obsession. A hard-core, unhealthy obsession. He used to say that Neil Peart was the greatest poet who ever lived...I don't know, I guess I'm just partial to Dylan. Anyway, I buy a Rush calendar every year...just because, I guess...and a few years ago, there he was right in the front row on one of the pictures. He was all the way in the corner, but that's not the point. He was there, with that God-awful 80s mullet and everything, and I've got the proof framed right over there," I pointed to the black frame hanging in the hallway. The cat's sharp, sea foam eyes followed the direction of my hand and then darted back at me.

"My mom doesn't like Rush," I sighed. "I don't know why I'm even talking about her. I don't want to talk about her. Talking about her just pisses me off...makes me wanna cry. So, let's talk about something else, okay?"

Meh.

"I'm gonna be an aunt soon," I shifted gears and took a deep gulp from my wine glass. Just thinking about my mom drove me to drink. "Noah—that's my brother—he's gonna be such a good dad. He pretty much was my dad when we were growing up, so I guess he's had a lot of practice. His wife, Cristina, is way too nice for him, by the way. Not that I don't think my brother deserves to be happy or anything. He does; he totally does. He's just always been such a hot-headed asshole most of the time. I don't know how he ever snagged that one, you know? She's either a saint or completely certifiable. Maybe both. I don't know."

My mind drifted back to the sacrifice Noah made for me last year, the risk he'd taken in what he'd believed was the right course of action. It wasn't, of course. And he'd just ended up making everything a million times worse and costed himself thousands of dollars in legal fees all in the name of defending my honor. He shouldn't have done it; I hadn't wanted him to do it and at the time, I'd been shaking with anger when I went with Cristina to bail his sorry ass out of lock-up. Now, I knew he was just protecting me, even if it was wasted effort.

I sighed again, pushing those depressing thoughts out of my mind. No use getting upset over something Noah refused to apologize for.

"What am I gonna do with you, huh?" I asked the cat now and his ears twitched a little at the sound of my voice. "I don't know how much longer you can stay here. I mean, let's face it, you seem pretty settled on that chair. I'm just gonna go right ahead and assume you're planning on crashing here for another night?"

His chest bumped, like he was hiccuping. Purrumble. *Meh.*

"It's gonna start getting cold at night pretty soon," I smiled down sadly at him. "That's no good for you. If you don't have anywhere to go, I'm gonna have to figure something out for you, aren't I? You can't sleep on my patio forever, you know."

A loud knock on my apartment door tore my attention away and the cat leapt up onto his haunches, ears alert and twitching.

"Simmer down, buddy," I laughed as I set my laptop aside and stood to head towards the door. "I'll be alright."

But when I pressed an eye through the peephole in my front door, that goofy guy with that shockingly orange hair stood on the other side of it.

Huh.

And now, yet again for what seemed like the tenth time today, I felt frozen in place. Stunned into immobility. Then just as quickly, I shook myself out of it. He was probably just being friendly. Being neighborly. Being normal. All the things I wasn't.

With a sigh, I pulled open the door and found him grinning back at me triumphantly, his chubby cheeks spreading out right along with that shit-eating smile.

"Hey, neighbor!" he told me and shot out his hand for me to shake.

"I'm Slinger. Me and my roommate just moved in," he gestured behind him to the door literally five feet away from us, "right there."

"Yeah," I replied and carefully slid my hand into his to shake, my eyes watching his every move for some sign of disingenuity. "I figured that. It's nice to meet you. I'm Emma. And you...your name's really Slinger?"

It was such an odd name, I just couldn't help it. Slinger was actually the name of a small town not too far from Milwaukee, so maybe that was some weird nickname? God, I hoped he didn't launch into a 10-minute story I didn't want to hear.

"No, not my real name," Slinger laughed, pushing some wiry hair back on his head, which, naturally, sprung right back into place. "My name's *really* Marshall, but everyone calls me Slinger. And if I told you why, we'd be sitting here for like, two hours, and then I'd just have to end up killing you anyway, so there's that."

I blinked back at him. "Uh..."

"I'm kidding! Shit, I'm sorry. That sounded really bad, didn't it?" he burst out a quick snort of laughter and his shoulders shook.

I didn't really see what was so funny. There was absolutely some sort of inside joke revolving around his nickname, but that didn't make me want to know what it was any more than before. I just wanted to get all the niceties over with.

"Well, look, I just wanted to introduce myself. That's all. Not trying to be a weird creeper or anything. Oh, and I also wanted to let you know we're having a little tailgate/housewarming thing tomorrow for the game. You should stop by and grab a brat and some beers or something. We'd be happy to have ya since we're neighbors now and all."

I nodded slowly. Right. The Packer game tomorrow. I might live under a rock, but that rock wasn't wide enough to drown out football season in Wisconsin. It was like some kind of unofficial state holiday that ran from the end of August all the way through January, if the team did well enough to make it into the playoffs. Even Mrs. Johannsen blared the games at defcon levels and that was really saying something.

You couldn't go anywhere on a Sunday, no matter where you lived, without seeing various green and gold jerseys, T-shirts that read *52 Shades of Clay* and *Drink Wisconsibly*, obese men walking around in nothing but green and gold striped overalls and face paint in 30 degree weather, not to mention assorted paraphernalia like Donald Driver bobbleheads, G-shaped spatulas, cowbells, and buttons that said things like *Da Bears Still Suck, Superman Wears Clay Matthews's PJs,* and *Got*

Rodgers?

I'd seen green and gold cars, full basements decked out as a shrine to former greats like Brett Favre, Ray Nitschke, Bart Starr, and Reggie White, people painting their fences with various cheesy—pun intended —phrases of encouragement like *Bleed Green* and *In Coach McCarthy We Trust*; hell, I'd even seen a green and gold house and someone walking around in a St. Vince—as in Vince Lombardi—pope get-up on game day.

You get the idea. Pandemonium. Epic, die-hard, I-gotta-own-a-piece-of-that-Frozen-Tundra frenzied obsession with professional athletes running around a field in tight pants.

I mean, come on, people went to those games wearing foam cheese on their heads without a hint of irony.

I just didn't get it, but I also knew well enough to never, ever breathe a word of that out loud.

"I, uh…"

Just as I was about to throw an excuse his way, Slinger glanced conspiratorially over his shoulder, leaned in closer, and cupped a hand around his mouth to stage-whisper, "I tried to get Finn—that's my roommate, by the way—to come out here with me, but he pussed out. He's kinda shy around pretty girls, just so you know."

I frowned. "Okay."

Why he'd chosen to share that information was beyond me.

Slinger seemed to sense this conversation was pretty much over, so he leaned away again to shove both hands deep into his pockets and rocked back on his heels. "Okay, then. Well, you know where we live. Feel free to pop over whenever and stay for as long as you want. It's not like you have to go very far to get home, right?"

He paused, like he was waiting for me to laugh and punch his arm like we were old friends. "Anyway, well, it was nice meeting you. Hopefully we'll see you around."

I pressed a quick smile on my face, my hand already gripping the edge of my door so I could close it. "Nice meeting you too. Thanks for the offer, by the way."

That brightened up the dejected smile on his face and he waved goodbye. "No problem. Have a good night!"

"You too."

With that, I immediately shut the door and locked it behind me. It wasn't that I felt unsafe now with these strange guys living so close. The motion of locking the door, of flipping that barrier into place, had become a compulsive habit that a therapist would probably have a field day over.

And seriously, was it a full moon or something? First Noah was on my case yesterday about coming home for dinner, then Mara giving me the puppy-dog sad eyes, and now my new neighbors—the scrawny ginger and his hot-as-shit roommate? Was I walking around with a sign plastered to my forehead that said: *Invite me places, yo?*

When I stalked back to the screen door, the cat was still sitting right where I'd left him, his ears flicking and his ink-dipped tail slapping down on the chair like he'd gotten impatient sitting here waiting for me to come back.

It was also then that I realized Slinger, or whatever his name was, hadn't really given me a chance to turn him down. That probably did not bode well for me come tomorrow.

I put my hands on my hips and glanced down at the cat exasperatedly.

"I don't think I'm going to like the new neighbors."

CHAPTER THREE

On any other day, somebody blasting The Rolling Stones' "Start Me Up" at full throttle would've been awesome. It probably would've been coming right from my own speakers, too, if I didn't have at least a little consideration for the people around me.

My new neighbors, on the other hand, were too busy engaging in tailgate festivities to really give a shit about anyone else.

Their screen door slapped open and closed every few minutes and wave after wave of party-goers poured in and out from the apartment. Pre-game radio interviews were blaring in between songs, some guys were throwing a football around right in front of my patio and making the cat nervous, bottles were clanging, the smell of smoky, greasy brats and charcoal wafted through my screen door, people spilled out from the patio onto the grass, flooding out towards the tree line and taking over pretty much half the apartment building like they'd just started a new frat or something.

Okay, *maybe* that was an exaggeration, but they were still wreaking havoc on what should've been a peaceful day off. Who had a party right after moving anyway? Didn't they have things to unpack? Organize? Make presentable? Then again, my new neighbors were two guys, so they'd probably didn't care—

And then it happened.

Someone starting playing "Green and Yellow", a Packer-themed knock-off of "Black and Yellow" by Lil' Wayne and something dark and sinister twisted all the way down to my stomach. My head turned, glaring at the wall, for all the good it would do, and my lips curled back into a snarl.

I'd been turned into the demon from *The Exorcist* by my new neighbors and Lil' Wayne.

"Hey, Sling!" a deep muffled voice yelled from the other side of the wall. "Jesus Christ, man, turn that shitty song off."

"Hey, step off, Finn," was Slinger's equally muffled response. "I can do whatever I want. You wanna know why? It's GAME DAY, BITCH!"

"Oh yeah? Do you want my foot up your ass?"

"No."

"Then turn it off."

"Fine...shit."

Two seconds later, the music switched to "Mama Said Knock You Out", which was only slightly more pleasing to the ears, but not by much. It might have been a passive-aggressive response to the foot-in-your-ass threat, but I didn't need LL Cool J rapping about takin' the world by storm and makin' the world go boom through my walls.

I think I growled. No, I *definitely* growled. And the worst part of it all was that every time somebody from the other side of the building yelled, screamed, and/or hollered, the cat crouched down on his chair, ears bent back, eyes wide with terror.

They were scaring the damned cat they were so loud.

Now, as I hunkered down on my couch, shooting daggers at the wall, I felt like the Grinch on Christmas Eve as he paced on top of his mountain, glaring grumpily down at the Whos down in Whoville.

If there's one thing I hate, it's all the noise, noise, noise!

Right about now, these last two months or so of peace and quiet seemed like paradise. A blissful dream. A figment of my imagination.

I know, I know. I really should've just shut my screen door. Or at the very least put my earbuds in and listened to some actual good music. But the problem was that if I shut the door, which would effectively drown out a good chunk of the current bane of my existence, I worried I would also be shutting out the cat. The only other times I'd shut the heavy sliding door was when I left the apartment or went to bed.

If I shut the door and just went back to pouting angrily on my couch, two things could happen: he could either paw and *maawhr* at the door with those wide, sea foam-grey eyes of his, making me feel like a pile of crap for doing that to him, or he could just say enough was enough, hop off the patio chair, and disappear into the tree line, never to be seen again.

But I wasn't going to be *that* neighbor either, the one with a stick up her ass that stomped her foot until the people who were actually having fun and enjoying life dialed it back a notch. I didn't think I'd know what fun felt like anymore if it slapped me across the face.

Then, the unthinkable happened: someone, probably that red-haired, apple-cheeked guy with the weird nickname, gave Luke Bryan

26

permission to sing about country girls shakin' it for him by blasting his song through the speakers.

That was it. I'd had it.

I didn't really know how to deal with this kind of crowd anymore. I was used to the hustle and bustle of the city now, where I could weave in and out and then leave it behind me in my apartment, but this was different. This was the kind of crowd I'd thrived on in college. Even before the bomb dropped, I'd enjoyed the random tailgate party or night out at one of the three bars in downtown Hickory. Now, I was lost. Anxiety-riddled and practically shaking with frustration and antisocial grumblings.

This was my life now. Always on the outside looking in. No interest in joining the party.

A loud crash of breaking bottles rattled and split through the walls and I'd barely had time to recover from the abrupt smashing when the cat scurried off the chair and darted right for the tree line, bypassing the patio on the other side of us and sprinting on all four white paws away from me.

Then the panic came, a feeling I was well-acquainted with, and now, the abandonment sent this sharp spike of adrenaline through my body and had me taking off after him.

"Oh no! Wait!" I cried out and scrambled for the screen door. I made it all the way to the edge of my patio before skidding to a stop.

The cat ran right past my new neighbors' patio. It shouldn't have been a big deal. They were just people. It was just a party. But I still stood frozen to the concrete like the coward I was. After peeking around the corner to see if I could catch at least a glimpse of where the cat had scampered off to but coming up empty, I swallowed a hard breath and retreated back into the safety of my apartment.

Maybe he'd come back. After the party died down and everything went back to normal, he'd—

"Hey, miss?"

It was the same deep voice I'd heard muffled through the front seat of the truck yesterday and through the walls about 10 minutes ago. On reflex, I turned on my heel to find the same scruffy, scarily beautiful guy I'd seen yesterday, wearing a forest green Aaron Rodgers jersey to boot, smiling back at me from where he stood on my patio. I might've been completely slack-jawed by his presence alone, but it was what he had tucked underneath his arm that stole all the words right from my lips.

The cat.

The same cat I'd been nervous would try to bite me, scratch me, or anything else a cat could do to attack me. He was just happily nestled in this stranger's arms like it was the most natural thing in the world.

"I think this is your cat, right?" My neighbor grinned back at me a little sheepishly as he held the cat up. One side of his mouth pulled up more to the side in the kind of crooked smile that hit me right in the knees.

I opened my mouth to respond, but nothing came out. My mind had gone completely blank.

"I saw him out here on your patio yesterday," he told me. Then his light eyes widened as he seemed to realize what that must have sounded like to me and jumped to explain. "I, uh, needed to hook up our hose so I could wash off our patio. The tap's over on your side of the building, so..."

He shuffled a little closer and gingerly set the cat down on the chair that held his makeshift bed, glancing up at me with his teeth sawing across his bottom lip.

"Sorry about my dumbass friends," my neighbor went on...and was his voice shaking a little? I was too busy staring at his lips to nail that one down. "I swear we're not gonna be those neighbors that have loud parties every weekend. This one just...got a little out of hand, you know?"

I swallowed tightly and nodded, pressing a quick smile on my face more for my own benefit than his. "It's okay. Don't worry about it."

That smile widened just a hair, but it was enough to propel me closer until I was just inches away from the screen door.

"My name's Finn, by the way."

I found myself smiling back at him. "I'm Emma. It's nice to meet you."

That smile widened until it seemed to stretch all the way across his face, crinkling his eyes and radiating something I couldn't quite place.

"Nice to meet you, too, Emma."

Those eyes...they might as well have been a clear sky reflected back at me. They just about knocked me sideways. And then Finn reached out to scratch the cat behind his ears, making him nuzzle his head against Finn's hand like he was nudging him to keep going. *Oh yeah, right there. That's the spot.*

"He's pretty friendly," Finn was telling me now as the cat purred away underneath his ministrations. "He came right over to me and everything when I went running after him before. Most cats aren't like that, you know?"

No, I really didn't know. I'd never been around a cat, let alone multiple cats, long enough to know.

Luckily, I found my voice. "He's, um...he's not my cat."

Finn frowned at me, perching one hand on his hip and scratching his beard with the other in thought as his eyes roamed from the cat, the chair, the towels, and the little bowls of food and water underneath the chair. As if on cue, the cat glanced at Finn and then his wide eyes shifted back to me, letting out a high-pitched *maaw*. Finn chuckled a little in response and started sawing on that bottom lip again.

"Fair enough," he laughed. "For contraband, I guess he's pretty cute. I promise I won't rat you out, okay? If our landlord shows up asking questions, I know nothing. You should probably get him a collar, though, if you're gonna keep him out here like this. A tag or something like that—just saying."

I guess him thinking my flat-out denial was more about our lease agreement than my actual relationship to the cat wasn't the worst thing in the world.

Finn ran a hand through his hair, pushing the long, droopy pieces of chestnut away from his face, and he blew out a quick breath. "I know things seem pretty crazy over on our side of the wall, but do you wanna grab a beer or something on us? We almost scared your cat away, so it's the least we can do—we've got brats, chips and dip...all that stuff."

I probably should've expected the offer, but I was still unprepared for the hope creeping into his eyes. It was almost a shame to have to extinguish all that hope just as quickly.

"Thanks, but I actually already ate and I've got a lot of work to do today."

His lips curled up again, but this time the smile didn't quite reach up far enough to crinkle his eyes. Despite the hope, I had a sneaking suspicion he'd fully expected me to turn him down.

He shoved his hands deep inside his pockets and now, his lips pulled tightly across his face in a grimace.

"Okay. No problem," Finn shrugged, his eyes falling on the cat one last time. "Well, if you change your mind, feel free to stop over whenever you want."

"Sure. Thanks for the offer. I appreciate it."

I was starting to feel like a robot. Like these excuses were just on auto-loop now. Like I wasn't fooling anybody but myself. Sooner or later, the more I refused people, the more they'd ignore me completely like what had happened with basically everyone from my old life except for Noah and Cristina.

There was a part of me that felt devastatingly pathetic just thinking that.

The other part of me knew it was a necessity.

Finn waved, a pained expression on his face that looked more like a wince than it did a smile, and he shoved both hands in his pockets again with his head down before disappearing around our shared brick patio wall.

.   .   .

Long after the charcoal smoke cleared and the cheers and the jeers from the game faded away, I found myself standing in front of my screen door wearing socks over my hands like the crazy person I'd become.

Let me back up a bit.

I don't know what possessed me to do it. Maybe it was the lingering feelings of unrest surrounding my inevitable fate...you know, the one where the old shut-in dies choking on a piece of chicken because there's no one around to do the Heimlich on her and her body isn't found until the landlord finally investigates the stench? That was my fate. And for a long time, I'd made peace with that fate, or as much peace as a person could muster for something like that.

Maybe I'd decided I didn't want to walk around with a heart two sizes too small.

Maybe I just felt guilty that, even after seeing him tucked under Finn's arm, I was still afraid of a stray cat.

Maybe I'd begun to let myself hope that I could actually keep him, as crazy and idiotic as it was, and even though I had no business entertaining the idea for a second.

Maybe I just wanted to see what he'd do.

Which led me to where I currently stood now with long, wool socks pulled up past my forearms. Between allergies, whatever monstrosities could be lurking on his fur, and the fact that he could still decide to claw my eyes out, I felt like I needed a little protection if I was going to venture out of the safety of my apartment. I didn't know how far socks over my hands would really go in terms of armor, but it was all I had, especially since I couldn't find my winter gloves to save my life.

The strains of *The Cars Greatest Hits* album spun around on my turntable and when "Just What I Needed" crooned through my speakers, I cocked a wary eyebrow at the cat.

"You and I are not going to discuss the irony of this song right now," I told him as his head popped up from where he sat on the chair. "We have a much more pressing matter at hand to discuss instead: I'm gonna open this screen door and walk through it. Then I'm gonna walk real slow and sit down on that empty chair next to you. Let's just see what happens, okay? No funny business. Don't go...you know, attacking me or anything."

The cat's chest hiccuped.

Meh.

I took that as a sign to proceed.

So, with a heavy, anxious inhale, I gingerly slid the screen door far enough to my left so I could sneak through and step onto my patio. To his credit, the cat stayed put, instead choosing to watch me with wide grey eyes—in the fading sunlight, his eyes definitely looked more grey now than green—and his mouth formed a tiny O as if he couldn't believe what he was seeing.

I sort of couldn't believe it either.

My eyes darted nervously from the cat to the chair I needed to get my ass into and I swallowed hard as I sank down right next to him. We sat there like that for a few long beats, both of us staring back at each other, not knowing what to do next, who should make the next move, or what that next move needed to be.

Finally, a beat later, the cat leapt down from his chair, trotted the few paces between us, and hopped right up onto my lap. I froze, stunned into immobility yet again, my socked hands hovering over his little body in mid-air...I just didn't know what to do. He circled my lap a few times, his claws digging into my bare legs the whole while.

"Ow, buddy," I winced and twitched my leg back as a knee-jerk reaction to two pairs of claws flexing into my skin. "Shit, that hurts."

What did someone do about cat claws like that? Declawing? I didn't really know what meant or what it might all entail...and then I realized what had just happened.

The second he'd jumped on my lap, I was a goner. Hook, line, and sinker.

He'd gotten me right where he wanted me.

And for what it was worth, I was sort of okay with it.

I let my socked hands run up and down his back, scratching into his cheeks and under his chin, around his tail as he purred and nudged me right back, and then, I finally let myself hold one of those little white paws, despite the barrier between us.

"You know what's weird?"

Meh.

"I don't feel sniffly at all yet. I mean, I know I've only been out here a few minutes, but still...kinda weird, right? If my throat starts to close and I have to throw you off my lap, don't be offended. It's not you, it's me."

The cat just stretched a paw up at me from my lap like he was saying, *As if it could possibly be me. Have you seen me lately? I'm awesome.*

I don't know what I'd expected, but here I sat, with a stray cat cuddled into my lap as I petted him with my socks over my hands. God, he was skinny. And bony. All elbows and knees as my dad used to say. I needed to start feeding him a little more, get some more meat on his bones, and get him healthy again.

And then my thoughts caught up with me. And then I realized what I'd done. What I was *still* doing and that old, familiar feeling ripped through me.

Cold, hard panic.

It couldn't have come a moment too soon because the cat was getting a little too comfortable on my lap. My hands swiftly dipped underneath his little body to scoop him off my lap and I carried him back over to his chair, holding his body out at arm's length to keep him as far away from me as possible.

Once he was safely nestled back against his towels, I scrambled back inside my apartment and shut the screen door behind me. The cat was already sitting up on his chair, watching me with wide, stunned grey eyes and I couldn't really blame him.

There was no way he'd still be hanging around me if I wasn't giving him food, water, and a comfy place to sleep. I was too neurotic, too screwed up, too set in my ways for anyone—even a stray cat—to look past all my shit, all my heartbreak, all my destruction, and all my damage.

No sane person at least. That went for cats, too.

"I'm sorry," I whispered to the cat, who was still gaping back at me with that stunned expression. "I wish I could be what you wanted me to be, but I just can't right now."

After one last look to make sure he had enough food and water for the night, I turned off the light and shut the door.

Sooner or later, that cat would follow the same path as everyone else in my life, the path that led him right out of it, and now, I found myself hoping he'd just be gone in the morning.

CHAPTER FOUR

The next day, I felt like complete shit during my whole shift. Not because I was sick or hungover or any other logical reason why I might feel this way. No, I felt guilty because of what had happened with the cat the night before. I walked around the café the whole day with a sick, gnawing feeling in my gut that got so bad, at one point I thought I was going to puke all over a customer's French silk pie.

The relief that washed over me the second I saw him sitting there, right where I'd left him that morning, knowing that he hadn't left me, that he hadn't decided to cut his losses and run, even though he probably should, I had to swallow back a thick, heavy lump.

Now that I had the rest of the night, I put on Soul Asylum's *Grave Dancers Union* album on my turntable, burdened by the weight of everything I'd left behind in Hickory...all the bad and what little was left of the good. I'd moved to Milwaukee looking to escape, to outrun the demons chasing me right out of town, hoping that I'd find peace and quiet. All I'd gotten in exchange was loneliness.

I hadn't realized just how lonely I was and how completely I'd screwed up my life until last night. Until I ran away from a stray cat.

Ever since the ashes of my life scattered in the wind, I'd given up on happy endings. I'd given up on fate. I'd given up on the hope that anything, anywhere, anytime, was meant to be. I couldn't accept that fate, that God or whatever force existed out there, had sent my life so disastrously off the rails because it was all *part of the plan*.

That smelled like a heaping pile of cow manure to me.

If this sorry existence in self-induced misery was all *part of the plan*, then I didn't want anything to do with it. I didn't want to accept it. Not anymore.

And then my eyes fell on the cat. With his wide, expressive, sea foam-greyish eyes, his ringed tail that flicked and curled to communicate his moods, those four little white paws...somehow, over these last four days,

I wondered if maybe I'd been wrong this whole time, if maybe there was another reason why he'd chosen this patio on that particular night four days ago and decided to stay.

I was reading too much into things. I knew that, but that didn't stop me from compulsively approaching the screen door again, this time sock-free as another song, "Runaway Train", started playing softly through my speakers.

"Wrong way on a one-way track..."

"I'm sorry about last night," I whispered to him and he promptly hopped down from the chair to sit right in front of the screen door. His front paws latched onto the wiring again as he leaned and stretched against the door. *Let me in. Let me in. Let me in.*

"Whoa, buddy," I scolded gently, reaching down to unlatch his paws as best as I could from the other side of the screen. "Try not to shred my door, okay? I'd like at least a little of my security deposit back."

Maawhr.

"We're gonna try this again, okay, buddy? I can't make any promises, but I wanna try again."

Meh.

That was as good as I was going to get. As I started to push the screen door to the side so I could step through, the cat moved back a hair to give me a little space, but this time I didn't sink down into the chair. Instead, I kept my distance, creeping out to the far edge of my patio. I wasn't ready to go anywhere near that chair yet. My bare hands felt clammy, unprotected, and shaky with nerves. My stomach wasn't much better—rolling and churning and knotting with hot anxiety.

"Somehow I'm neither here nor there..."

The cat eyed me carefully, his head tilted to the side a little like he was trying to figure me out.

Good luck with that, buddy, I thought warily.

Then he was moving towards me while I pretended to inspect the planter he still used as his personal litter box, and I froze when his little body rubbed up against my legs, weaving in and out, taking his time, making sure I wouldn't forget he was there. Like I could forget.

Meh.

His chest kept bumping and hiccuping those little half purrs-half mumbles. We were at a crossroads now, him and me. If I sat down and he hopped up into my lap again, I think that would be it. But if I didn't sit down, if I was too afraid of what might happen if I took the risk, I think that would be it, too. I'd have to take him to the humane society or something, but that would be it. I couldn't keep feeding this cat and letting him sleep on my patio if I couldn't keep him.

The actual act of loading him up in my car, driving him to the humane society, and then leaving him behind, never seeing him again...tears pricked my eyes just at the thought of it.

I wasn't so sure I could do that.

Finally, I took a deep breath and sank down into the chair. Two seconds later, the cat hopped up onto my lap. This time, though, he didn't circle my lap. His talon-like claws didn't dig and flex into my thighs. This time, he sat right down on his haunches facing me and stared back at me. Then his two front paws reached all the way up until they settled onto my shoulders. His head nudged forward, kneading and searching until his little cheek buried itself right in the corner of my jaw.

"Can you help me remember how to smile...?"

I don't know when I started crying. I do know I sat frozen to that plastic patio chair, the music surrounding me and sending me right to the pit of despair, as this cat nuzzled my jaw, my chin, and finally, swept his rough, prickly tongue up the side of my face.

It all just poured out of me. The humiliation. The betrayal. The invasion. More humiliation. The destruction of my life's dreams burning up right before my eyes. The shock. The shame. I couldn't stop it now that it'd started. Wave after wave of horrible, degrading memory washed over me and I was reliving it again, the stares, the whispers, the outpouring of disgust and horror—I thought I'd gotten through that part. I thought I'd gotten past it enough to be able to push it aside...but it looked like I was wrong about that, too.

All I could do was let my hands pull the cat's furry little body against my chest, hugging him to me—or maybe it was the other way around—and hoping that maybe, *maybe*, my life had finally started getting better.

Finally.

I wasn't happy like this. I knew that. Somewhere along the way I'd convinced myself I liked the silence, the solitude, that it was a good thing to just be alone right now and have some time to myself. Tears flowed freely down my cheeks, my shoulders shook with sobs, my hands trembled around the cat's body and the softness I found there was comforting. Reassuring. Soothing.

Maybe I didn't have to be alone anymore.

"I think I want to keep you," I whispered against his head.

It felt good to cry. It felt right to cry. I think I'd earned that right. And the most surprising part of all was that I didn't feel so scared anymore.

.   .   .

About an hour after my cry fest, I was still sitting out on my patio, but this time I had my computer in my lap and a chilled glass of wine at my feet. Music played softly in the background from my music library—the great thing about modern technology when it came to current turntables was that I'd been able to convert all my dad's records into mp4s and then uploaded them onto my laptop. The cat sat on his chair next to me, nestled down into his towels, his ears twitching every once and awhile as he reclined leisurely from his usual spot.

Right now, my focus was trained on a Craigslist search to see if anyone had put out a notice for a lost cat that looked like the one sitting right next to me. If I was even going to attempt to try to keep him, I had to make sure there wasn't somebody out there looking for him, wanting him to come home. If he *did* have a home, which was probably unlikely at this point, I had to make sure.

The last thing I wanted to do was steal someone else's cat. Still, I secretly hoped my search would come up empty.

I wanted to keep him. As risky as it was, with allergies and the whole illegal-per-my-lease-agreement thing, I still wanted him. There was no way I could take him to the humane society and just drive away. That wasn't happening. He was either leaving this patio with his actual owner or he was coming inside my apartment with me.

I knew which outcome I wanted.

Maybe I'd known it the second my new neighbor, Finn, had taken one look at our little set-up out here and just assumed the cat was mine anyway. It was an understandable assumption to make and one I wanted to come true.

I'd be the first one to admit I didn't search *all* that hard on Craigslist and the local humane society's website, but I didn't really feel guilty about that either. Now, I knew what I had to do.

"I'll make you a deal," I told the cat and his ears twitched at the sound of my voice. "I'm gonna make an appointment at the vet for Friday. So that's one week from when you first started showing up here. I know, I know...I'm sure that's the last place you wanna go, but we still need to make sure everything's alright with you before you come inside, okay? No fleas, no worms...all that stuff. If you're still here by Friday, we'll go to the vet and then you can move in. Deal?"

Meh.

If he was still chilling on my patio four days from now, I was just going to take that as a sign he was meant to be my cat.

"This is kinda weird," I muttered to myself and glanced at the cat to find him drowsing again in his chair. "In four more days, I could be a cat owner...who am I kidding? I'm pretty much a cat owner already."

The writing was on the wall the second I bought that bag of cat food. Even then, he'd had me.

Now, my fingers were itching to do something...to call someone and tell them the news, which wasn't really news at all, but still, I wanted to tell someone. My fingers flew across my screen and I hit my speed-dial to call my brother. A few seconds later, all I heard was my brother's clipped voice telling me he wasn't around and would get back to me if he had time. Ever the classy guy, that one...

Of course, now that I *wanted* to talk to someone from back home, it looked like no one was around to actually take my call. Go figure.

Irony, you black-hearted bitch.

It was just my luck that—my thoughts tripped up mid-sentence when my phone rang in my hand.

"Shit, that was quick," I muttered to the cat. "I bet he thinks my apartment burned down or something."

I swiped across my screen to both answer my phone and alleviate my brother's panic. "Hey, brother."

"Em? You okay? What's goin' on?"

Yep. Pretty much what I figured. In his defense, our communication had been relegated to short text message conversation over the last few months, especially after the epic disaster that was our last 'family' dinner, so I couldn't exactly hold his overblown reaction against him.

"Everything's fine," I laughed. "Seriously. I promise. I just...I don't know. I guess I just wanted to talk to you."

"Okay."

Again, I couldn't really hold the hesitation in his voice against him. I never called him and I definitely never called him just because I wanted to talk. This was uncharted territory for both of us right now.

"So...um, how are you guys doing?"

There was a long pause on the other side of the line before I heard Noah take a deep breath. "Are you sure everything's okay?"

"Yes, I'm sure," I laughed again and reached across the short space between me and the cat so I could scratch the top of his head. "I'm okay. Promise. I don't know...I guess I just called because I wanted to tell you something."

"Okay."

I huffed out another laugh. "Geez. Will you cut the gloom and doom shit?"

"Sorry," Noah told me from his end and I could practically see him shrugging his shoulders and mouthing to Cristina, *I don't know what the hell is up with her.* "I've learned only to expect bad things when a woman says she wants to tell me something."

From over the line, I heard my sister-in-law's muffled high-pitched, *What's that supposed to mean?* and then Noah's half-laughing, half-mumbled, "Ow! Jesus, don't hit!"

"Wow," I muttered under my breath. "You two are a walking advertisement for dysfunction."

"Hey, now. That's not very nice. Just because we like it a little rough sometimes doesn't mean—"

"Aaaaand I'm gonna stop you right there," I cut in. "I don't want to hear the end of that sentence."

"Fair enough. So what's up? What do you wanna tell me?"

Now that the opportunity was at hand, I suddenly couldn't find the words to adequately express what I was feeling and what I wanted to say. It was one thing to entertain the idea of keeping the cat and just keeping those thoughts to myself. Admitting it out loud and hearing my brother's reaction was a whole other beast.

"I, um...I sort of got a cat."

Sort of being the operative phrase.

Again, another long pause. "What do you mean *sort of?*"

"Well," I forged right ahead and shoved my nervousness aside for the time being. "There's this cat that keeps hanging around my patio. Well, not around; he's literally *on* my patio. He sleeps in one of my chairs, too. I've been feeding him and giving him water...yesterday I came out by him and he jumped right in my lap, so yeah..."

"Huh."

That was not the reaction I expected. "What do you mean *huh?*"

"I don't know," Noah laughed, relief flooding the deep timbre I knew so well. "I thought you were gonna tell me you got fired or you got kicked out of your apartment or...something."

"Nice," I shot back. "So the first conclusion you jump to when I have news now is that it's something bad?"

Cue the awkward silence. Well, I guess that was my fault too. In light of recent events in my life, my brother had probably learned from experience to just brace himself for the bottom to drop out again. I couldn't really blame him for that either. The last year or so of my life had been nothing but a black parade of tragedy, disappointment, and humiliation, one right after the other.

"Sorry," he muttered. "I didn't—"

"No, it's okay."

Noah took in a deep breath. "Alright. So you're thinking about keeping this cat. What about your allergies?"

"Well, actually, I've had the screen door open pretty much since he started showing up here last Friday and I've been out by him a few times now, but I haven't really had any problems."

I knew just as well as anyone that that alone didn't really say much for what would happen when the cat and I were actually under the same roof, but I was trying to think positive for once in my life. It was new. And weird. Really, really weird. And a little uncomfortable, too, if I was being completely honest with myself.

"Alright," Noah drawled out slowly like he was trying to come up with the best way not to upset me. "So what happens if you bring him in your apartment and you can't stand 10 minutes of being around him without your throat closing or sneezing or your eyes watering...you know what I mean?"

Yeah, I knew exactly what he meant. I think I was just past the point of no return now.

"I know," I informed him. "I just want to try."

"I hear ya, Em. I really do. It's just that..."

He didn't have to say the words. We both knew what he really meant to say. He didn't want me to bring the cat in, get attached, have a raging allergic reaction, and then not be able to keep him. Noah didn't want to see me get my heartbroken again, even if it was at the hands, or paws, of a stray cat. He didn't want to see me set myself up for another disappointment, more heartache, and kicked when I was already down.

"I want to keep him," I whispered into my phone. "But I guess it's really my landlord I'm worried about."

That seemed to break the sad spell cast over us and Noah just chuckled.

"I don't think that's as big a deal as you're making it. People do that kinda shit all the time. You don't wanna know what my roommate in college kept in our apartment—trust me, it wasn't a cat."

"Got it."

"If I were you, I'd be more worried about the allergies, but I guess that's a moot point now. I mean, you get caught with a cat, it'll be one of those *either you go or the cat goes* scenarios with your landlord and I'm pretty sure it won't be the cat who goes."

"So, basically, you're telling me to start packing now?"

"No," he laughed. "You live on the first floor. Your patio faces that kickass tree line. Just keep your blinds closed and you'll be good, Em. I wouldn't worry about it."

"Right. I guess if they do any inspections or anything, they have to give me 24-hours notice, so that'll give me plenty of time to smuggle him out of there."

"Sounds like you've got it all figured out, Em. I take it you checked to see if anyone's looking for him?"

Another moot point, but I relented. "Yep."

Noah just huffed out a laugh.

"I'm going to take him to the vet on Friday. If he's still around by then, that's been a whole week. If he had somewhere to go, he'd go back by then, right?"

"I think so, yeah."

That appeased the lingering panic that I was stealing a cat. Waiting until Friday gave his owners, if he had them, plenty of time to get their asses in gear and do some work to find their cat, if they wanted him back. And that was pretty much what I had to tell myself.

"Well, you know, Em," Noah went on and I could hear the smile in his voice now. "Are you sure it's a boy? If he's been neutered or whatever it's called, you might not be able to tell."

"Oh no," I laughed and shook my head, glancing at the cat with a grin. "He's a boy alright. He's got the biggest pair of balls I've ever seen in my life. And I mean that literally, by the way."

"God, I need to bleach the mental image of cat testicles out of my brain now," Noah muttered. "Thanks a lot, Em."

"You brought it up."

"Yeah, well you didn't have to talk about his—never mind. Anyway, I think it's good you finally have a man in your life with a massive pair of balls. You need that."

"Wow," I shook my head and rolled my eyes up to the roof of my patio. "Anyway...I don't know shit about cats though. What they need, what they should eat. I don't even want to touch the litter box situation yet. He's been using one of my planters as a litter box, so he obviously knows how to use one, but once I have to have it in my apartment...I don't even know where you're supposed to put it. Do you?"

"No clue. But that's what Google's for, right?"

"I guess," I grumbled. "Anyway, enough about me, okay? How are you guys doing?"

"Ah, we're good. Cris is pretty much ready to get my demon spawn out of her body—her word choice, not mine—so there's that."

"Couple more weeks," I told him in a little sing-song voice. "I can't wait to get that call."

That was true, but I was also dreading that call because my niece's birth also meant that in a couple weeks, I'd have to drive into the place I hated more than just about anything and face my mom. No getting around that. And then another spike of panic ripped through me, closing my throat and pricking my eyes. Something that was supposed to be a happy moment for my family would essentially wind up ruined because of me.

And my mom.

It wasn't completely fair to place all the blame for the tension in my family squarely on my shoulders.

As if he could read my thoughts, Noah added, "You're the first one I'm calling when we're on our way to the hospital."

While the sole purpose of that statement was just to make me feel a little bit better about things neither of us could change, I still felt like shit. In the fallout, Noah had been pitted unfairly right in the middle and had, predictably, taken my side, which had infuriated our mom, which was a surprise to no one. Still, it was just one more way my family had suffered because of me. The reminder of that tragic history made me itchy.

"Thanks, brother," I whispered back.

"Gotta keep ya in the loop, ya know? Anyway, while I've got you on the phone..."

I sucked in a deep breath. I knew what was coming next.

"How 'bout dinner at your place this weekend?" Noah didn't even pause to give me a chance to shoot him down. "We can work around your schedule—whatever works for you. We haven't been down by you in awhile and I kinda wanna see this cat of yours now."

Shit. He'd changed tactics on me. It had been awhile since he threw the *if you don't come to us, we're comin' to you, goddammit* strategy at me and I'd been wildly unprepared to deflect him.

"Uh..."

That was the best deflection I had. It sucked.

"You know what?" Noah threw in just for good measure. "You think about it and let us know, okay? If you do keep the cat, maybe this weekend isn't such a good idea anyway. There's always the weekend after that and the weekend after that and..."

"And the weekend after that, I get it," I laughed, relieved that he'd backed off a little for once. "I'll think about it."

It was the best I could give him right now and I crossed my fingers, hoping he'd just accept it already and move the hell on.

"So, other than this cat business," Noah pressed on. "Are you doin' okay, Em? All the way around?"

I pushed out a heavy sigh and glanced back at the cat, who was already dozing in his chair, having long gotten bored with the conversation as soon as the topic shifted away from him.

"I'm okay, Noah. I really am."

That sounded unconvincing even to my ears and I was the reigning queen of self-induced ignorance.

"You need any help? I mean, if you're short a month for rent or something, all you gotta do is ask and we'd—"

"I know," I cut in quickly. I'd heard all this before and I didn't really need to hear it again. "I appreciate it, I really do, but I'm okay."

Or, at least, I think I could be. Maybe not yet, but I could be. And, thankfully, that was enough for my brother tonight.

"Hey, listen," my heart clenched a little at the seriousness in his voice. "I just thought you should know...with school startin' up again, there's been a little activity online. Cris is keeping an eye on it to make sure it doesn't get out of hand, but I don't know. I wanted to make sure you knew in case..."

He trailed off and I didn't need him to finish that thought. *In case something happens...in case you decide to come home for once...*I also didn't need the constant reminder of something that was better left buried in the past where it belonged, but who was I kidding? Running three hours away from my hometown hadn't been distance enough, so why would time be any different?

"I'm sorta nervous about homecoming," Noah added and I could hear the agitation in his voice to prove it. "I just have a bad feeling and look, if something happens, and you feel like it's not a good idea for you to come into town when the baby gets here, I understand, okay? I won't be mad and Cris and I can bring the baby to you. It's—"

"Noah, that's the stupidest thing I've ever heard. Of course I'm coming to the hospital when the baby gets here. I don't care about the rest of it."

I *did* care about the rest of it. I absolutely did, but the lie was for my benefit just as much as it was Noah's.

"Alright," he pushed out a heavy sigh. "I should probably let ya go. I gotta go rub Cris's feet or something before she starts hitting me again. Thanks for calling though, Em. You should do it more often."

"Sounds good," I laughed. "Bye, brother."

"Bye, sister."

I swiped my thumb across my phone to end the call and let out a deep sigh, a light smile still playing at my lips. Now that the call was over,

Noah was right. Calling him tonight was almost like how we'd used to be, just talking and making fun of each other, asking each other for advice. It was nice to have that again, even if it was just for 10 minutes. Even if calling him meant trudging up reminders that I still hadn't shaken off my past, that it was still very much my reality, that my past was still really my present.

Noah could worry about homecoming in October, but I was going to do my best to push it as far back into that little compartment in my mind designated to all the things I wanted to forget.

As I turned the volume back up on my music library, I cast a careful glance back at the cat, who was watching me now with tired eyes.

"That was my brother," I informed him. "You know, the hot-headed meathead I told you about with the smokin' hot wife who's way out of his league? Yeah. That was him. He wants to meet you, but we'll just have to wait and see about that, won't we?"

The cat blinked and then yawned, stretching a little white paw high up in the air.

"You know," I went on with a smile. "Maybe you need a name, huh? I mean, if you're gonna be my new roommate, you should probably have a name."

But what did one name a cat? I could come up with plenty of awesome dog names right off the cuff: Chester, Buddy, Scout, Max, Charlie, Jake, Jack, Cooper...none of those worked for him. He needed something different, a name that fit him, a name that was *him*.

So, because I was feeling craptastically uncreative tonight, I Googled "awesome names for cats" in my browser.

"Yeah," I glanced at the cat out of the corner of my eye. "I'm embarrassed for myself too. Just keep that shit to yourself from now on, okay?"

Meh.

"Whatever. Let's find you a name," I muttered and began the lame process of perusing the list. "Oh...how about Leo? You may not be the king of the world, but you're kinda the king of the castle already, aren't you?"

The cat just yawned again.

"Hmm," this time I was just talking to myself. "I don't know. Do you want to be named after my childhood crush who turned around and crushed said childhood the second I discovered he was just a model-dating whore? Maybe not. Moving on."

My eyes continued their descent down the list and then I saw it. The perfect name. That was it. There could be no other name for him.

"Hey," I told the cat and his chest bopped a little in response. "What do you think of Oliver?"

Meh.

"You know like *Oliver Twist*? Charles Dickens? The little homeless kid who went around begging for some more? It's kinda perfect the more I think about it. Oh...shit, and there was that Disney movie—*Oliver and Company*—about that stray cat and yep. That's it. From here on out, you shall forever be known as Oliver."

Meh.

"Well, Oliver, this turned out to be a pretty eventful night for us, didn't it? You with a new name and maybe a new home and me not being such a spiteful, icy bitch all the time. Progress. That's what this is, buddy."

I was so preoccupied with all this naming business that I didn't realize "Proud Mary", the Creedence Clearwater Revival version, was playing through the speakers on my laptop until I heard the soft guitar strumming along right through my shared patio wall.

It took me a moment for it to sink in that the acoustic guitar I was hearing wasn't coming just from my speakers. Whichever one of my new neighbors it was...he was pretty good. Maybe there were a few flubs here and there, but for the most part, he had the rhythm down and the general gist of the chords.

Then "Hotel California" started and my neighbor easily switched gears, picking right through the famous chords of the song and I found myself bobbing my head along, paying more attention to the acoustic strumming feet away from me than the music coming from my computer's speakers. There was only a 50 percent chance the neighbor giving me this impromptu live performance was Finn, the bearded Greek god who'd returned Oliver to me just the day before, but I still wondered.

It made me a little nervous thinking that maybe he'd been out here this whole time. More than a little nervous—it made me sweaty and itchy. He could've easily eavesdropped on my whole conversation with my brother and all the little interactions I'd had with Oliver in between. That was creepy. And mortifying.

Now, I didn't know which was worse: the idea that my insanely hot neighbor was a creepy eavesdropper or the idea that my creepy, eavesdropping, insanely hot neighbor had been witness to my pathetic evening revolving around a stray cat.

And now, even as the strains of "Baba O'Riley" played from my computer, it was time to get my ass back inside my apartment.

CHAPTER FIVE

Well, it was Tuesday. Three more days until the big C-day...er, cat day. The vet appointment was made after a careful Google search for the best vet clinic closest to me and now, all I had to do was wait.

Waiting around for Friday...I'd be doing some pacing, that was for sure. Wishing and hoping and thinking and praying and planning—I think that was how that song went. At the very least, I only had to wait until Friday morning and yes, I'd asked off for Friday, too, and yes, I was now and forever *that* person.

So when I got home from the café on Tuesday night, I opened my apartment door, hoping against hope, that Oliver was still there. He was. And this time, I had zero issues stepping right out onto my patio and letting him hop into my lap. We were getting comfortable with each other, to say the least, and I kept my fingers crossed that my allergies would stay in check.

Hey, a girl could hope, right?

I was so far down the rabbit hole that I even ate my dinner on the patio and that was probably exactly where I was going to park it for the next few hours until I had to leave Oliver out on the patio and shut the door behind me. It was stupid...I really should just bring him in with me now, but my apartment wasn't cat-proofed yet and I was still stuck on this Friday thing.

Oliver was fine out here on my patio. He had a place to sleep, food to eat, and water to drink. As far as I was concerned, what more could the little guy possibly need until Friday? Of course, there was always the off-chance that he'd up and disappear from my life altogether between now and Friday. *That* particular thought had another fresh wave of panic snaking all the way down to my toes.

My eyes glanced at Oliver, who was currently grooming himself on the chair next to me. "You're gonna stick around, right?"

His eyes widened a little at the sound of my voice and his paw froze in mid-air.

"You wouldn't, you know, abandon me right before I'm about to let you become my new roommate, would you?"

His chest hiccuped and bumped. *Meh. Maawhr.*

"Hmm, I'm gonna hold ya to that, Oliver," I cocked an eyebrow at him just for good measure.

Then with music softly playing from my laptop just like the night before, I turned my attention to my dusty bookshelf. All the books were mainly decoration at this point now as opposed to having an actual function. Most of them were my dad's, just like nearly all the vinyl records I owned, and at one point in my life, I think I might've had the entire library memorized word for word. Now...not so much. Now, they sat on my bookshelf in my tiny living room staring at me like a beacon pointing to all my failures.

But now, *Team of Rivals* sat across my lap, a book I hadn't picked up in years, and I'd forgotten how easy it was to get lost in the politics, the strategy, the genius and foresight of America's greatest president, and the drama of one of the country's most unstable and transformative moments in history. Seriously, *this* kind of drama—the real kind, not the fake reality TV bullshit kind—this was the kind of drama that fascinated me.

I hadn't realized how much I'd missed being immersed in history until I plucked the book off my shelf tonight. It felt exactly like how I'd always felt whenever I came home from college—comforting, easy, familiar, and safe. I picked up the paperback and inhaled must and age and ink. Even the scent was familiar and I squeezed my eyes shut. There were so many things I'd lost, so many things I used to love that I'd tossed aside...some missing piece seemed to slide back into place the moment I picked up that book.

This was good. This was progress. This was me reclaiming something I'd forced myself to surrender, even if it was just a page in a book.

I grinned at my computer because "Moondance" was playing now— not exactly ideal mood music for reading a 900-plus page nonfiction novel about Abraham Lincoln, but that didn't make me enjoy the music any less.

And there it was again.

A guitar strummed lightly along to the music, which was impressive considering this song was heavier on the piano and jazzy saxophone, but the player had the hard staccato picks down pat like he'd played this song a million times before. Granted, I still didn't know which of my neighbors was currently treating me to this little performance, but somewhere, deep down, I hoped it was Finn.

Even if that scared me. Even if part of me wanted to scramble back into my apartment. I still kinda hoped it was Finn.

Now, "Go Your Own Way" was playing and my neighbor easily switched gears, changing up the tempo and matching Lindsey Buckingham's strums tab for tab. After about a minute of Fleetwood Mac, I decided to throw him a curveball and clicked "Any Way You Want It" in my music library and suddenly had images of Rodney Dangerfield dancing with that goofy grin on his face flashing across my mind. Still, impressively enough, my neighbor rolled with the punches and while he couldn't exactly replicate the electric guitar parts on his acoustic, he still nailed those famous duh-duh combos in the stanzas.

After another minute or so, I clicked on "Closer To The Heart", a selection my dad would've wholeheartedly approved of, to see just how deep my neighbor's knowledge of classic rock really was. Again, he riffed right through the opening chords, plucking away at the strings and a slow smile crept across my face as I leaned a little closer to the wall to hear him better.

Once we'd both had enough of Rush for the time being, I moved through my library, clicking on "Hey Jude" next to see if he could pick out the guitar chords through the piano. Sure enough, he strummed easily along with Paul McCartney, finding the rhythm through the melody with practiced ease.

Hmm, I guess I needed to up my game.

I hit my next selection, but when all I heard was Elvis Presley crooning to his mama, my heart sank a little. Maybe he'd decided he'd had enough and went back inside his own apartment. About 30 seconds into the song, the strumming started back up again, this time a little less sure, a little unsteady, but despite the fact that he'd clearly never played this song before, he picked up the chords halfway through the song.

My lips curled up again and I glanced at Oliver out of the corner of my eye, who looked more annoyed by the disruption to his sleep than anything.

"Oh, come on," I whispered to him. "Don't look so pissed. You know you secretly love this."

My eyes went back to my library. What to play next...I clicked my selection and my neighbor easily picked up the strains of "Hold On Loosely" no problem. Okay, that one was just too easy for him. The next one needed to throw more of a challenge at him because other than the Elvis song, he'd pretty much nailed everything I tossed his way.

Ah. There it was.

As the famous 50s chord progression of "Stand By Me" sounded out through my laptop, I waited eagerly to see if he could do it and sure enough, after a good 15 seconds into the song, I heard him strumming along, the soft, familiar rhythm flowing from his guitar. It was nice just sitting here on my patio with Oliver, watching the sun fade out into twilight beyond the tree line, and listening to my neighbor's guitar ministrations.

But when I clicked on "Under the Boardwalk", I finally got the answer I wasn't so sure I'd been looking for. At least 20 bars played all the way through with silence on the other side of the patio before I finally heard a low, familiar chuckle.

"Sorry," he told me through the barrier between us. "Don't know that one."

So. The neighbor treating me to this little show was Finn. Deep down, I'd figured that, even though I didn't know how I could've possibly known...it was just a feeling. Or a hope. Or a fear. I wasn't sure which one of those options made me the most uncomfortable.

"Hey," Finn called out to me. "You got any Kings of Leon?"

My lips pulled apart in a grimace. Did I...? Maybe, but that wasn't really the kind of music I tended to gravitate towards.

"Um, gimme a second."

"Sure," he chuckled. "Take your time. I got all the time in the world tonight."

Smiling a little to myself and sawing on my bottom lip in thought, I scrolled through my library until I came across the two songs I had. When the opening strains of "Sex On Fire" started playing, with its electric guitar riffs rocking back and forth, Finn's grumble was unmistakable.

"Of course. *That's* the one you've got."

"Oookay," I drawled hesitantly and glanced sideways at the wall.

"No, no," he laughed and I swallowed hard at that deep, throaty sound. "Not your fault. Lemme guess, you have one other Kings song, right?"

"Sure do."

"And it's called 'Use Somebody'?"

"That's the one."

"Shocking," he informed me dryly. "You see what most people don't realize is that they've got more than just those two songs and that those particular two songs don't even crack the surface of what that band can do."

Now, I was the one chuckling. "I take it you're a fan."

"Oh yeah. Everything in life is better if the Kings are playing in the background."

I bit down on my bottom lip to keep from laughing out loud. "Okay. So, what song would you play now?"

There was some shuffling from behind the wall and I heard Finn's deep voice again, "Hold on. I got it all on my phone. Just gimme a second."

"Sure."

Then the strains of one of the prettiest country songs I'd ever heard echoed from around our shared patio wall...easy guitar and lazy violin and then, *"Come on out and dance..."*

At this point, Finn was already strumming along with the acoustic in the song and his familiarity with the chords was pretty clear. He'd *definitely* played this one more than a few times before.

"This is pretty," I told him. "I didn't know that band played country music too. I thought they were just a rock band."

Finn's strumming stopped for a second so he could answer me. "Ah, you know, this is the only song they have like this, but it takes them back to their Southern country-boy roots. That's why I like it."

"I like it too. What's it called?"

"'Back Down South'. It's the kinda song that needs to be played when you're just sitting outside having a beer around a fire, except we don't have a fire and I'm pretty sure I'm the only one of us drinking a beer, but you get the idea."

Despite my better judgment, my fingers flew over to the store on iTunes and after a quick search, downloaded the song into my library.

"What else you got?"

"Hmm, let me think," I tapped my index finger across my lips. So, we were obviously taking this little jam session in a more modern direction. Let's see...what did I have that wasn't too old, but would still throw a challenge at him?

I clicked "Snow (Hey Oh)" and as those complicated, rolling chords hummed from my speakers, I heard Finn trying and failing to keep up with the complex melody. For every tab he nailed, he completely flubbed the next one until he gave one last, frustrated drum on the strings with a loud huff.

"Now I'm just embarrassing myself," Finn muttered. "But I'm man enough to admit that song's just too damn hard. How 'bout something else?"

"Sure," I laughed, clicking over to another Red Hot Chili Peppers song. "How about 'Californication'?"

"Yep. Do it."

This time, the slower, simpler chords were a little easier for him to pick up and he strummed along for a few bars until he called out to me, "Hey, how 'bout this one?"

He jumped into something faster, obviously well-practiced, but it was a little more aggressive, a little angrier even, like he was somehow channeling the frustration of the song...whatever it was.

"I don't know that one."

"Gimme a second," Finn called back and within moments, those same acoustic chords played back for me almost exactly how he'd just played it. "You don't know Jack Johnson?"

"Not really."

"Ah, gotta get on that one. He's great. Real chill, too. This one is 'Sitting, Wishing, Waiting'."

It was almost like he knew I was silently taking his suggestions and immediately downloading them into my library. I already had a search for Jack Johnson going before he even told me the name of the song.

"How 'bout this one?"

He launched into another song, starting slow and quiet before upping the tempo, strumming back and forth in a way that had me bobbing my head right along with the rhythm.

"I take it you don't know 'The Pretender'?"

"No, I don't recognize it, but I like it."

"Okay, you go now."

I scrolled through my library, looking for something that would throw him off completely and came across the perfect option. All I heard was silence on the other side of the wall as Finn listened, trying to place the song, and when the singer started in with, *"Gonna find my baby, gonna hold her tight"*, Finn let out a quick burst of deep laughter and I could practically see him throw his head back against his chair with his shoulders shaking as he sang along.

"Aw, man," he chuckled. "I feel like I need to go watch *Anchorman* now."

"Yeah," I laughed. "Me too."

"What about this one?"

His strumming turned into something a little folksier now with a more staccato twang, but I still couldn't place it.

"I don't know that one either."

"'Skinny Love' by Bon Iver," Finn told me as he continued plucking away. "Fun fact: the lead singer of this band, Justin Vernon, is from Eau Claire. This whole album was recorded in a cabin about four hours up north from here in Medford, I think."

"Well, look at you with all your musical knowledge," I laughed.

"Hey, I try. And—that album's actually called *For Emma, Forever Ago.* I'm pretty sure the entire thing is all about one break-up, but still, that's crazy, right?"

It wasn't as if I didn't expect him to remember my name. I just hadn't expected him to...I don't know. This whole thing was starting to make me itchy, my palms were already sweaty, and my heart did a few jumping jacks in my chest to drive the point home. He was being friendly and neighborly by sitting out here like this with me, playing along to whatever I threw his way and tossing a few songs of his own into our little game. That old familiar twitch worked its way down my spine until both my legs jumped with anxiety.

My eyes immediately flew to the time on the top right of my laptop. It was only 9:30 and while I wanted to stay out by Oliver for longer, I couldn't have predicted the turn this night had taken, especially since I still wasn't sure how I felt about said turn.

Now, he was strumming something that sounded a lot like a Radiohead song; I just couldn't tell which one it was. For reasons I didn't quite understand, I found myself scrolling through the few Radiohead songs I had in my library to see if I could place the one he was playing. I tried "Fake Plastic Trees" to see if it matched the acoustic guitar playing from the other side of the wall and all I got was Finn's low chuckle.

"Nope," he laughed. "That's not it. Try again."

The next attempt was "Karma Police", but right away, I knew I was way off-track with that guess. The tempo wasn't even close to what Finn was playing.

"You want me to save you some time?" Finn called out to me.

"I'm no quitter," I shot back. *Yes, you are. Liar, liar, pants on fire.*

"Alright, alright," he laughed right back. "Sorry."

Now, my determination to prove *something* to someone for once dominated pretty much everything else raging around in my mind and I tried "House of Cards" even though I knew I wasn't even in the ballpark.

"Nope."

I shot an annoyed glance at the brick wall even though he couldn't see it. "I know. Just hold on. I'll get it."

"I don't doubt that for a second. Here, I'll start over," he offered and jumped right back into the opening progression again. When he got all the way through the first 20 bars or so, he jumped back into the opening again to make sure I could figure it out.

I listened intently from my chair, head tilted to the side, eyes squinted in thought, and then…

"I got it!" I shouted victoriously and did a mental fist-pump as I clicked over to "High & Dry" to hear the matching guitar chords coming from my computer.

"Nice. I figured you'd get it eventually."

"I think I would've driven myself crazy until I figured it out," I laughed.

Now, I heard some more shuffling and the whoosh of a screen door opening as Finn called out to me, "Hold on. I'll be right back."

So, here I sat, feeling awkward and out of place even on my patio, my gaze darting back and forth to the cat drowsing next to me and the brick wall separating me from my neighbor. When the screen door opened again from the other side of the wall, I sat up a little, my heart seizing at the footsteps shuffling from the edge of his patio and drowning out when he hit the grass.

Finn materialized from around the wall with a bottle of beer in each hand and he stopped short when he breached the threshold of the wall separating our two patios. His light eyes widened, which was probably an understandable reaction given the way I'd frozen still in my chair, eyes wide with terror like he'd morphed into Jeffrey Dahmer or something.

Melodramatic, I know, but the sight of my neighbor—the type of guy only someone as messed up as me would find terrifying—was more than I'd been prepared for tonight. To be completely honest, I hadn't really been prepared for any of it, but my eyes still darted over to the safety of my own screen door and briefly contemplated hauling ass inside before he could get a word out.

Now *that* would be melodramatic. And absolutely insane.

"Uh…" Finn managed to croak out before glancing down at the beers in his hand. "I just wanted to…" his lips pulled apart in a grimace and he shot a quick glance over his shoulder, "I ran in to get another beer and thought I'd grab one for you too, you know, to say thanks for the fun night, but I didn't mean to—"

"It's okay!" I cut in abruptly and I don't know who was more shocked by my outburst: me, Finn, or the cat. I sucked in a deep breath and blew my bangs out of my eyes in exasperation. Now I looked even crazier and more pathetic than I did last night when he obviously overhead me talking to my cat.

"I mean, um, that's really nice of you. Thanks," I tried to press on a smile, but at this point, it probably looked more like a pained grimace than anything. Not attractive.

One side of his face tugged up in a grin and he dared a step closer, like he half-expected me to just up and bolt. I guess I couldn't really blame him. That grin on his face only widened when his eyes flicked to Oliver, who was eyeballing him warily from his perch, and as Finn ventured closer, he held out the beer in his left hand for me to take. I stood to slide it carefully out of his hand and then, kicking myself for my cageyness, still couldn't stop myself from plopping back down into my chair as soon as the beer was in my hand.

Talking to him with a barrier between us had been easy and fun. Now that the safety net was gone, I just didn't know what to do with myself.

To his credit, Finn stepped back until he was leaning against the edge of the wall separating our patios, careful to keep himself as close to his side as possible and out of my bubble. Still chewing on my bottom lip, my eyes fell to the bottle in my hand and I frowned at the label.

"Matthews Brewing Co.," I murmured, still frowning as I tried to remember where I'd heard that name before.

Finn shoved his free hand deep inside his pocket and glanced down at his shoes. "Yeah, it's good stuff."

"I've heard of this place before," I mused, my eyes still on the bottle. "This girl I work with tried to talk me into going there last Saturday."

His eyes widened and he stood up against the wall a little straighter. "Did you go?"

"No, I had some work to do," I shrugged and finally, dared a sip from the bottle. It wasn't so much that I worried he'd laced it something nefarious or anything, but it was beer. The sour taste of hops and barley swirled around in my mouth, but there was something sweet there, too, that I didn't mind...honey, maybe?

"That's not bad," I told him and took another quick pull from the bottle. "I normally don't really drink beer, but I can live with this."

A smile tugged across his lips, crinkling around his eyes, and he gestured to the empty wine glass underneath my chair. "Yeah, I can see that. It's a good thing you didn't spit it out all over the grass because that would've been awkward."

He waited a beat, anticipating my confusion, and unearthed the hand from his pocket to point his index finger at the label on the bottle. "That's my family's brewery."

"No shit."

"Yeah," he laughed and the sight of that wide, happy, almost relieved grin stretching across his too-beautiful face made those butterflies kick soccer balls around my stomach.

"So, you're a brewer? Not like *the* Brewers, obviously, but…"

Finn rubbed the back of his neck and grimaced nervously. "I wouldn't really call myself a brewer. That's more my dad and my uncle. I sort of help out with everything else…marketing, accounting, boring stuff like that."

Hmm, maybe this was the one time where I should've taken Mara up on her offer for a night out.

"Well, I've heard nothing but good things about it," I told him, even though I'd actually only had a conversation about his family's business once.

"That's good to hear."

His eyes fell to his shoes again and I couldn't believe it, but he seemed more agitated and nervous about this conversation than I did and that was *really* saying something. From the stiff posture against the wall, the way one hand buried itself deep inside his pocket as the other clenched around his beer bottle in a death-grip, the way any kind of prolonged eye contact seemed painful for him…all dead giveaways.

I didn't know how this interaction had completely flipped on its head, where *I* was the one feeling more in control, where *I* was the one with the most confidence. But there was something in those eyes, even from the few feet in between us, that I recognized. Something that looked a lot like sadness. There was a hesitancy there that felt familiar—the fear and anxiety wrapped around letting anyone in too close, but needing that human connection just the same.

I recognized it because I felt it too.

"Well," Finn murmured and he pushed off from the wall to pivot back towards his apartment. "I gotta get up kinda early tomorrow. I should let you get back to the rest of your night."

"Okay. Thanks for…" I held up my beer bottle with a small smile.

"You're welcome," he grinned from over his shoulder and kept one hand on the wall to turn back towards me one last time. "We should do this again sometime."

I bit down hard on my bottom lip to keep my smile from getting too ridiculous. "Yeah. We should. It was fun."

He grinned back at me, his shoulders square with the wall now, like indecision wouldn't let him decide whether to head back to his apartment or closer to my patio. "Yeah, it was. Well, have a good night, neighbor."

"You too," I smiled again as he waved before finally disappearing around his side of the wall.

I'd hardly gotten a chance to get a hold of my bearings again before Oliver hopped off his chair, trotted over to me in that lazy gait I already knew so well, and jumped up onto my lap with little regard to the computer still perched across my thighs.

"Jesus," I muttered and managed to put the beer bottle down and grab hold of my computer at the same time before it crashed to the cement underneath us. "Hold on, okay?"

Oliver completely ignored me, choosing instead to circle around my lap a few times before settling in, claws and all. He flexed his paws a few times and I winced, making a mental note to wear something sturdier than just yoga pants next time I came out here by him.

"Were you annoyed you weren't the center of attention for once?" I cocked a faux-stern eyebrow down at him.

His little chest bopped. *Meh.*

He kept right on purring, too, and I reached down to run my hands down his soft fur. My heart was still humming away in my chest, keeping time with the vibrations buzzing from the cat on my lap, but the motion of moving my hands up and down his fur eased some of the nerves to just a distant drumming.

The whole encounter with Finn was just weird. And a little fascinating. For once in my life, I'd actually had some fun in the most unexpected of ways, but that was part of what made it so exhilarating, especially since I wasn't exactly in the market for...whatever that was.

And it was refreshing to see this guy, who was easily the most ruggedly handsome guy I'd ever seen, who also seemed to have no idea just how ridiculously good-looking he was. Even Derek Zoolander would have to agree.

Lumbersexual was a thing, wasn't it?

With his dark, overly-long hair that he flopped away from his face, the unkempt beard, the rumpled KOL T-shirt he was wearing—that was probably a Kings of Leon reference, right?—he was obviously grooming-challenged, but I sort of liked it that way. He didn't seem to care what he looked like or what he wore from the few interactions I'd had with him and there was something about that combined with the shy hesitancy he'd used to approach me that had me reaching for my computer again.

I had my laptop open, balancing treacherously on my knees to make room for Oliver, finger poised on the enter key to Google Matthews Brewing Co., Finn, and everything else in between. And in one brief moment of clarity, whether it was clouded by stupidity or plain old honesty, I just couldn't pull the trigger.

The idea of Googling Finn's name was so hypocritical it wasn't even funny.

All he would have to do was type in my full name, something he could easily find at the front of our building, and he'd learn everything he needed to know about me and then some.

Just the thought of him actually going through with that, of him seeing everything that everyone else had seen, of him knowing all my dirty secrets...it was enough to make my fingers snap my laptop shut, startling the cat on my lap, before I could convince myself otherwise.

I was a lot of things. A liar? Sure. A coward? Most definitely. But a hypocrite? No, that was one of the few things I felt like I actually still had control over.

Well, Emma, I could practically hear my mom's condescending, disappointed voice in my ear, *the reality here is that you have no one to blame for your current predicament but yourself.*

It might be true, but ruminating on that particular reality wasn't going to propel me through the rest of my sorry existence. In fact, it was the very thing that would continue to weigh me down and I was sick of lugging a dead horse around all the time. At some point, I was going to have to start seeing my life here in Milwaukee as a fresh start instead of a by-product of my momentous failure. Sometimes, though, it felt like that day might never come.

Today, though...today felt like that dream of an actual fresh start, of a new, happy life free of drama and chaos, was right on the horizon of my painful reality.

And now, as I glanced at the cat on my lap, whose drowsy eyes had already started to close again, I found myself looking forward to tomorrow more than I'd ever had in a very, very long time.

CHAPTER SIX

Finn

There was nothing more relaxing than polishing a stainless steel 150-quart brewing kettle. The running joke between anyone in the microbrewery business was that the business is 90 percent cleaning and 10 percent paperwork. That was pretty much my life, but the cleaning part of the job had become a necessity to my sanity.

The act of physically smoothing my microfiber rag up and down the inside of the kettle had become almost meditative, soothing, easy, and numbing. Just the way I liked it. Now, at the end of my work day, this was the thing that needled everything else away, that allowed me to exorcise some demons in a way that didn't involve me putting my fist through someone's face. Next to strumming on my guitar, nothing else really seemed to calm my nerves.

Everything else I did at the brewery—whether it was balancing the books, meeting with a new buyer, leading customers through the tap room, or helping my Uncle Kurt fix whatever random pipes broke that day—cleaning was the thing I wished I could do all day. So, it really was too bad that, because of everything else I had to do during a given day, I was lucky if I got to spend an hour inside one of the used, empty kettles.

It was so damn hard to go anywhere in the brewhouse, and especially the office, without being surrounded by people. Here, inside the kettle, the only thing I heard was the muffled hum of the kettles brewing around me. It was a sound I'd grown up with my entire life and it was just as comforting and familiar as the nutty, airy scent of fresh barley.

"Hey, Finn? You in there?"

I blew out a deep breath and fought the urge to pound my fist against the steel. So, scratch that about peace and quiet.

Guess I can't hide anywhere in this place without being found.

"Yeah, Dad?"

"You almost finished up?"

"Almost got all the deposits scrubbed out, so yeah," I called back. "What's up?"

"Come on outta there when you're done."

Great. This had all the makings of every other pep talk he'd sat me down for over the last three years and I wasn't really in the mood for another today. At this point, I had the monologue memorized: *Finn, you're turning into me. I don't want this shit for you, son. I want you to live your life and find some damn happiness. You're too young to be so old.*

He'd even gone so far to tell me once that if finding happiness took me somewhere outside of Milwaukee, away from the brewery and our family business, then...that would be okay too. I didn't know how he'd managed to choke out the words, but he did it. I guess I had to give him credit for that.

"So how's the new apartment?"

Shit. I shook my head, glancing up the kettle's opening irritatedly even though I knew he couldn't see me. He couldn't even wait for me to climb out of the kettle to start the latest round in this pity party.

"Ah," I managed to croak out and hide my annoyance at the same time. "It's fine. It's an apartment, you know?"

"Yeah, yeah, I get it…" he trailed off like he was trying to sort out his thoughts and part of me just wished he'd get this over with already so I could go back to polishing out my frustrations. "So, Slinger had a lot to say about the girl livin' next door to you boys now."

I rolled my eyes up to the ceiling. Jesus, what were we, 14-year-old girls? I'd managed to go a full six months this time around without any of those three douches—my dad, Uncle Kurt, and Slinger—trying to push me towards some chick. I didn't need any help; I just wasn't interested and they just didn't get that.

We'd had this conversation already—monogamy, relationships, commitment...that shit was overrated and a pain in the ass. My dad was the perfect example. He'd spent the majority of his life toiling away in this very same brewhouse, determined not to only put food on the table, but to get my mom everything she'd ever wanted: the perfect house with the white-picket fence, the fancy clothes, the expensive vacations, the luxury car.

The bullshit American dream.

All that got him was hours and hours of hard, long work inside the brewhouse to make it the success it was today while my mom lived in that perfect house with that white-picket fence with her new husband and my sister, who'd chosen sides and who'd, naturally, chosen to stay with my mom.

So, the fact that history had inevitably repeated itself hadn't sat well with him and I could understand that. I was living that. But I also didn't need him butting into my life, thinking he knew what was best for me, and trying to save me from his own empty existence outside of the brewhouse.

Monogamy, relationships, and commitment had done nothing but bulldozed right through my life. Falling into that again ass-first wasn't something I was keen on doing anytime soon.

So, in regard to my new neighbor, the best course of action was just to say, "She seems alright."

Nobody needed to know I'd been thinking about Emma Owens since I woke up this morning and that she'd never drifted far from my thoughts since. I'd looked at the names on the buzzer outside our building just because I couldn't help myself. People who'd been court-ordered to stay x-amount of feet away did shit like that. At least I'd been smart enough to make sure Slinger was long gone for the night before I went on that little recon mission.

My dad huffed out a laugh. "Sling seemed to think she's more than just alright."

"Yeah, well, that's his problem."

"Alright. If you say so."

At least he seemed to know when to back off.

On that note, I climbed up the ladder, swung my legs around the side of the kettle to plant both feet down on the metal walkway. Without so much as a glance over my shoulder, I shut the kettle and programmed the system to run through a cleaning cycle to disinfect the steel I'd just left.

"Got it all?" my dad called out to me and from the corner of my eye, I could see him leaning against the metal railing with eyes fixed squarely on me.

"As much as I could," I shrugged.

"Everything else squared away for the day?"

I flipped the soiled rag over my shoulder and finally glanced at my dad. "Yeah. Why?"

"Good," he lifted a shoulder and then gestured with his head towards the doors leading to the tap room. "Then I think you should take off for the night. And, just so you know, I don't wanna see your ass back in here until Monday."

A bitter laugh pushed its way from my chest and I crossed my arms defiantly. I knew where this was going and I didn't like it. "Not happening, Dad. Besides, we're meeting with the guys at Bluestone Lounge next week and I gotta—"

"We both know you've got that pitch all set and you're gonna nail that meeting just like all the others. I want you to take a few days off," he told me, holding up both hands in defense before I could pounce. "You've been working too hard, putting in too many hours lately, and I don't think there's anything wrong with slowing down. You look tired, Finn. You should take a break."

"Where the hell is this coming from?"

This was the first time in...I don't even know how long...that he'd thrown this particular curveball my way. Three years ago, sure. I could see it. But now? I didn't realize I was such a pathetic asshole that my own father had to kick me out.

My dad just stared me down, hands on his hips, not budging an inch. "It's just four days, Finn. Thursday through Sunday. This place isn't gonna burn down if you're not here. You can take a few days off. Unwind. Drink some beers. Finish setting up your new place. Whatever you gotta do."

I pushed out a rough sigh and clamped down on my bottom lip.

"And if you show up here tomorrow, I'm just gonna toss you out on your ass. And if you show up Friday, I'm just gonna do the same thing again, too."

Now, my eyes lifted up to the ceiling again and I tugged a hand through my hair to push it off my face.

"I know I've said it so many times you've probably started tuning me out," my dad pressed on and I knew what was coming next. "But you're turnin' into me, son. You're married to this job and that's not a good thing."

I winced at the poor word choice and he held up a hand.

"It's been three years, Finn. Gotta move on sometime."

I huffed and gestured between us, "Pot. Meet kettle. Seriously, Dad, you sound like a broken record."

"Yeah, well, maybe I'll shut up when it starts sinking in."

This time, I hitched both hands on my hips and cocked an eyebrow at him. "If I agree to this bullshit, will you start shutting up about everything? I know you mean well, Dad, but I'm 29-years-old. I'm not a kid. I don't need you fighting my battles for me and I *definitely* don't need you following me around waiting for the other shoe to drop."

My dad threw up his hands before landing them right on the metal railing in front of us. "Serves me right for givin' a shit. If you take a break, if you start slowing down, if you start *living* a little, yes, I'll back off."

"Sounds great," I snapped back, pushed off the railing and stalked across the walkway to get my ass out of the brewhouse.

I'd made the mistake of actually telling the truth before and since I legitimately had no reason to stay here any longer, I actually did have to sulk over to my truck and drive away. At least I had the satisfaction of ignoring both Slinger, who was already behind the bar for the night, and Uncle Kurt, who'd practically chased me down from the brewhouse, on my way out.

That would show them.

I fisted my hands around my steering wheel and blew out a frustrated breath. My dad obviously had my best interest in my mind, but that didn't mean I appreciated being all but tossed out of the brewhouse. Now, the real dilemma: what the hell was I going to do with four days off? Yeah, I had a few episodes of *The Walking Dead* to catch up on and some unpacking I could do, but after that? I'd drive myself insane.

Restlessness was a feeling I knew too well. I wasn't the type of guy who could just lay around and sleep all day. I had to *do* things. Fix things. Clean things. Make things. I don't know what my dad really expected me to do with this time off, but I would probably end up scaling the walls before I figured it out.

I trekked through the downtown sector, narrowly sneaking through a yellow light so I could speed out towards the on-ramp I needed. Sometimes all these one-way streets could be lethal if you weren't paying attention, even for someone like me who'd spent nearly every day of my life out by the myriad of traffic on Water Street.

The song blaring through my truck's speakers right now really shouldn't have surprised me, but I still rolled my eyes at the irony. If there was one Kings of Leon song I could've played the first time I saw my next door neighbor, it would've been this song, "Temple". In reality, it pretty much summed up everything I didn't want to feel, but just couldn't help. Hands in my pockets, crossing my fingers for something so ridiculous it wasn't funny.

So I probably shouldn't have been all that surprised either when I parked in front of my apartment building, slid out of my truck, and glanced over my shoulder, I found my new neighbor rounding the corner and heading straight towards me.

From my vantage point, all I could do was watch helplessly and slack-jawed as she stopped short mid-step. Dressed in a black T-shirt and jeans with an apron wrapped around her waist, the girl standing just out of my reach was the most arrestingly beautiful woman I'd laid eyes on in a long time.

When her lips curved up in a barely visible, hesitant smile, my chest stuttered for a few beats and somehow, my hand lifted up to shoot her a quick wave. How long had it been since anything made me feel like this? Loneliness, combined with a severe deprivation of genuine female company, had completely warped my brain, but right now, I couldn't give a shit.

Like a breath of fresh air, I was suddenly reminded of who I'd used to be, the cool confidence I'd once had, and the swagger I'd once carried in my walk. And now I remembered the effect I'd always known I had on women...I just hadn't really cared too much about that effect lately.

Seeing that subtle curve of her lips snapped some lost piece of myself right back into place and that simple reaction made me decide to try something I hadn't done in awhile: I grinned at a beautiful woman and laid on the charm.

Her lips curved up again and she bit down shyly on her bottom lip, quickly shifting her eyes back down to the concrete at her feet. As she shuffled towards our building's main entrance, my feet practically tripped over themselves to match her stride. Running a hand through my tangled hair, I scrambled to round the side of my truck to beat her to the door.

When her steps slowed, I echoed her gait and shoved my hands in my front pockets, letting a slow, lazy grin spread across my face. Her eyes brightened and as she got closer, I still couldn't tell whether her eyes were green or blue, something I'd tried and failed to figure out last night. As her pace quickened back up, I sped up one last time, smirking at her over my shoulder as my hand shot out to pull the heavy glass door open before she could reach it.

Swinging it open—God, what was I doing?—I waved an arm playfully out in front of me. "After you, neighbor."

Finally getting to see her up close was almost too much. The problem was my senses didn't really know where to focus first: her apple-round cheeks, her light caramel-colored hair flipped up in that messy knot, the way she blew her bangs out of her eyes, which only made me focus on her lips. But in that split-second, everything else fell away and all I could zero in on was her aquamarine eyes. Not quite blue, but not exactly green either, they practically jumped out at me, just bright enough to make me wonder if this was all some sort of dream or if I'd jerk awake to find myself alone again.

"Thanks," she exhaled, her voice low and breathy, as if she was struggling to catch her breath. The huskiness there caught me off guard and it took me a moment to recover.

"You have a good day?" I asked her, despite the fact that I sort of wanted to kick myself for acting like such an idiot.

Here I was, *flirting* with my gorgeous, skittish neighbor. The game I'd had in college was rusty and dusting off the charm sitting on that proverbial shelf felt awkward and stiff...but she was still smiling up at me, so maybe I was actually doing something right.

"Yeah," Emma lifted a shoulder as she stepped through the threshold, still smiling when I fell in step next to her. "I did. You?"

"It was alright."

My hands shoved deep into my front pockets. I was like Ricky Bobby —I just didn't know what to do with my hands right now. And before I knew it, we'd covered the short distance from the entrance all the way to where our paths forked in the hallway. She'd head to the left and I would head to my door on the right. Now I was just trying to come up with something that might keep her out here a little bit longer with me, but I kept coming up empty.

She had me tongue-tied, tripping over myself, and stammering like a horny teenager who'd never talked to a pretty girl before. I might as well have been that horny teenager, starting from scratch and fumbling through an attraction I never saw coming.

I paused in front of my door, daring a glance her way to find her chewing on her bottom lip in thought.

"So, um, maybe I'll see you outside tonight?"

My eyes widened at the suggestion, something I'd told myself not to waste time hoping for. Now, for lack of a better, more articulate response, one of my hands unearthed itself from deep inside my pocket to smooth some long strands away from my face.

"Yeah," I nodded finally and smiled right back when her lips curved up. "I think so."

"Good," Emma told me as she turned to put her key in the lock. "I'm looking forward to it."

I felt just like the first time I saw her, when I had to cower behind my truck, scared stupid and stunned into silence, except this time, I had no safety net. No place to hide. Thankfully, she waved and then disappeared inside her apartment, leaving me standing alone in the hallway, grinning at the door across from me.

.   .   .

Times like these, I was really glad Slinger worked nights in the tap room. That way, he wasn't around to see me haul ass onto our patio with my guitar in one hand and two beer bottles in the other. Sling didn't need any ammunition. God, I could already see him, playing air guitar and banging his head to music only he could hear, singing, *Go for it, go for it.*

Bringing two beers out with me was presumptuous, I knew, but she'd taken one from me last night and I wanted to be prepared in case the opportunity presented itself again.

Jesus, forget the horny teenager act. I'm knocking down 40-Year-Old Virgin *territory now.*

So, as I sat down on a chair on my patio, listening for the telltale sound of that screen door swooshing open and close, my mind went through a mental list of everything I'd brought outside with me. Guitar? Check. Beers? Check. Pathetic, wishful thinking? Check. Blatant disregard for my own well-being? Check.

Looks like I got everything I need minus the girl.

This was a bad idea, not to mention potentially setting myself up for something I wasn't so sure I wanted. Yet here I was, sitting out on my patio, waiting for my neighbor to join me.

I strummed a few lazy strains of "Fans", flubbing some of the chords, which sucked because I'd played those same chords a thousand times before, and in my frustration over something that should be so simple, I missed the sound I'd been waiting to hear.

"Hey," Emma's voice called out to me and a moment later, she hesitantly peeked around her side of the wall. "That sounded pretty good. Is that Kings of Leon again?"

I laughed, grateful she'd either missed my epic screw-ups or chosen to just ignore them completely. "Trying to be, yeah."

"I liked it."

Now, as I rested both hands against my guitar, I found myself grinning right back at her. "Good. That's what I like to hear."

It was crazy how just a few conversations, a few interactions, and I was shuffling, a little aimlessly, with my hands in my pockets, crossing my fingers, and hoping for the best. In spite of everything. In spite of the fact that I'd promised myself I'd never go down this road again.

*Here I go again...*that sounded like a Whitesnake song. A pretty crappy one, too.

She chewed anxiously on her bottom lip and then her head jerked down by her legs. "Hey, Oliver. Just hold on. Don't go out on the grass, buddy."

Then she glanced back up at me, venturing a little further out onto the grass herself. "Sorry about that. He's getting a little fidgety."

"Cats will do that. You can't tell them to do anything they don't wanna do."

"Yeah, I'm starting to figure that out."

"You're finally admitting that he's your cat?"

Emma lifted a shoulder, this time rounding the corner of the wall until I could see her whole face. "It's not official until Friday."

"Friday?"

"Yep," she nodded and then she was sawing nervously on that bottom lip again. "It's kind of a long story. Do you want to...I don't know..."

I had my guitar in hand and was reaching for the two bottlenecks before she could even finish that suggestion.

"I'd come over to your neck of the woods, but I think the cat would get all messed up with me being on the other side of the wall and I don't wanna scare him off, so—"

"No problem, Emma," I shook my head, already heading her way.

I pivoted around our shared wall to set my guitar and the bottles down, then grabbed a chair from my own patio to find Emma gingerly moving the cat's chair closer to her own to make some space. At this point, I knew I should just be grateful for the invite. I wasn't going to give her any shit for keeping a buffer between us, even if it was a cat. So, I settled in next to the cat and passed Emma the beer I'd brought for her.

Pretty much the second I sat down, Emma launched into the story of how the cat, Oliver, came to live on her porch. Every part of it, her being nervous around him, reluctantly deciding to feed him, to him jumping right up on her lap...I could practically picture it all happening exactly the way she described it. I barely knew this girl, but there was something about her—maybe it was the quiet strength underneath that blanket of hesitancy she seemed to use as a shield—but whatever it was, I found myself listening to her with rapt attention, hanging on every word, and wanting to know more about my neighbor, who was so taken by a stray cat that just the thought of leaving him at the humane society made her tear up.

"So Friday's the big day then," I surmised.

"Yep," her eyes fell down to the cat and the soft look in her eye was one I knew well. "If he's still hanging around, that is."

"Oh, I'm sure he will be. If he had somewhere to be, I think he'd be there by now. You know," I told her, gesturing to the tiger-striped little guy sitting next to me. "This dude looks just like one of the cats my sister had when we were growing up."

"*One* of the cats?"

"Yeah," I chuckled and took a quick pull from my beer bottle. "She was kind of a cat-hoarder...always bringing home strays and wanting to keep them. My parents gave in most of the time, but after we had five cats living with us, they started to put their foot down, you know?"

She was still smiling at me, so I kept on talking.

"They made her start bringing them to the humane society, so then she started volunteering at the humane society, which meant she always wanted to bring all of *those* cats home with her, too."

Emma laughed and shifted in her chair to face me. "Yeah, I guess I can relate. It sounds like you're close to your sister."

I just shrugged. "I was, yeah. Now, I'm lucky if I even see her on the holidays."

"Oh," her smile faded. "I'm sorry. I didn't—"

"Ah, it's not a big deal," I told her and now, it was more about getting that smile back on her face than anything. "It's not like we live that far away from each other or anything. I guess we just kinda grew apart after my parents got divorced when I was in high school. She went to live with my mom and I stayed with my dad. That was kinda it, you know?"

I had two nephews I hardly ever saw, but my sister and I had never really been the same once we'd had to take sides.

"I'm sorry," she murmured softly and probably because she didn't know what else to do, reached out to scratch the top of the cat's head.

"What about you? Brothers? Sisters?"

"Older brother," she told me and frowned as her phone beeped underneath her chair. Sweeping it off the ground, she muttered something under her breath and then held her phone up to me. "Speak of the devil. You'd think I wasn't a 26-year-old grown woman perfectly capable of taking care of myself."

"He's a little overprotective, huh?"

Emma huffed out a laugh as her fingers flew over the keys to pound out a reply. "You don't know the half of it."

"You're living by yourself in a big city. He probably just wants to make sure you're okay."

I was making a few assumptions here, but I wanted to keep her talking and I wanted to keep her *willing* to talk to me, too.

"Something like that, yeah."

"Does he live here?"

She shifted anxiously in her chair and I could tell we were edging towards some uncomfortable waters. At least, for the most part, I hoped

I'd be able to read her well enough to know when to back off.

"No," Emma answered finally. "Him and his wife live back in my hometown. I know they'd like to see me more and honestly, I'm kinda surprised he's not showing up here every weekend pounding down my door. I'm glad he's not though, especially because that would mean he'd be dragging my eight-months pregnant sister-in-law along with him, too."

"Yeah, probably a good choice," I grinned back. "So where are you from then?"

It was a perfectly normal, average question to ask someone you were trying to get to know, but judging from the way that smile slipped right off her face, I knew I'd somehow crossed into more than just uncomfortable waters now.

She shifted around on her chair again and, as if the cat could sense her obvious distress, he stood up on his haunches, stretched a little, set his two front paws on the armrest, and then launched himself into Emma's lap. She caught him easily, yelping softly in surprise as he circled around her lap before finally settling in. Now, with her hands running up and down his fur, whatever had hitched her up before seemed more settled and less rocky.

When Emma finally spoke again, her eyes landed squarely on me like she was summoning the strength she needed, and her voice was quiet, but firm, "I'm from Hickory."

I didn't really see what was so monumental about that. Hickory was one of those blink-and-you-missed-it type of towns up north, the kind that was right next to a bunch of other equally tiny towns and when you passed from one to the next, you barely even noticed a difference. So, I figured the only real way to play this, since it was obviously out of the realm of what she was willing to tell me, was just to act like Hickory was any other town in Wisconsin. No big deal.

"Oh sure," I told her easily. "I've heard of that place."

It was right on the tip of my tongue to ask her for more, how long she'd been in the city, why she wasn't in Hickory anymore, where her parents were, but I had a sinking feeling those kinds of questions would feel more like an interrogation to her. Since she'd almost clammed up completely on me with just one simple question about her hometown, now was probably the time to back off.

With that last thought, I lifted my guitar up onto my lap and started strumming the first song my fingers remembered. After a few bars, her shoulders started swaying a little from side to side as she listened and I waited, curious to see if she could place it.

Her eyes squinted a little in thought and she murmured, "Coldplay?"

"Yep," I nodded and continued plucking away. "You got the song?"

"It sounds like 'Yellow'."

"That's the one."

Maybe it was a subconscious choice, too, considering the lyrics waxed poetic about how the stars shined for the girl Chris Martin wrote the song for, and maybe it mirrored a little of what I was feeling around this girl right now, even if I had no business trying to insert myself into her life.

"You're pretty good, you know," she went on. "Do you play in a band or something?"

I laughed and cast her a sideways glance. "Nah. I don't think I'd do so well on a stage in front of a crowd. I just like to play."

Her lips curved up in that soft grin and I was starting to wonder if maybe that song had been written about her after all. "There's something to be said about just doing something because you enjoy it."

"Yeah," I grinned back at her. "There is."

It was also right about then that I realized I'd smiled more around this girl than I probably had the last year or so combined and I'd only known her for a few days. Now, she was taking another pull from the beer I'd given her and a swell of pride rushed through me.

"I see you haven't gotten sick of our beer yet," I nodded my head to the bottle still in her hand.

"No, it's good. I normally go for wine, but I don't mind this. So...you're not the one who makes this though, right?"

"Nope," I took a pull from my own bottle just for good measure. "This one's my uncle's recipe. He typically oversees the lighter ales and my dad's more about the darker lagers."

"I have no idea what you just said."

The words came tumbling out of my mouth before I could stop them. "Well, maybe you'll have to swing by our brewhouse one of these days and I could show you the ropes."

Her eyes widened at the suggestion and I mentally kicked myself right in the ass for overstepping—seriously, I didn't know her and she didn't know me and what little game I had left clearly wasn't enough to carry me through that awkward, probably pretty damn creepy, outburst.

"Or," I scrambled to save face. "You could just forget I ever mentioned it."

My lame attempt at recovery sounded stupid even to my own ears and I cringed down at the bottle in my hand. The sad reality was that I just didn't know how to do this anymore...talking to members of the opposite sex, flirting with a beautiful girl, figuring out how to turn on the charm. I wasn't just rusty. I was out of practice. Exhausted. And getting too old for this shit.

"Maybe I will. Swing by, I mean."

My eyes flew back to Emma and found her watching me with a hesitant smile playing on her lips. Maybe I wasn't quite as pathetic as I thought I was. Jesus, maybe there was actually hope for me yet. It felt foreign, but yet, now I felt lighter, too. Optimistic and excited for the first time in a very, very long time.

"Well, I'd be happy to show you around, show you how everything works."

She smiled again and I think my chest might have seized a little bit. "I can't believe I'm saying this, but I think that actually sounds fun."

"What?" I cocked an eyebrow at her and some of that charm I'd been groping for slid back into place. "You mean a brewery tour doesn't sound like the best thing ever?"

"I don't know," she laughed. "It wouldn't necessarily be my *first* choice for a good time, but I'll give it a try."

"That's what I like to hear."

She shifted in her chair again, rearranging the cat on her lap, but this time, it wasn't because she was uncomfortable. This time, it seemed like it was just because she wanted to keep talking to me. Because she'd given me an opening now, I decided to surge ahead.

"I actually have the rest of this week off," I swallowed back as much awkwardness as I could manage and hoped I sounded at least *a little* smooth, but not like a creepy, stalkery psycho who lured little kids into their vans with promises of puppies and candy. "So, if you've got any free time or anything, we could…"

Definitely not smooth. Not even close.

That hesitancy she'd had when she first popped her head around the wall crept back into her eyes and once again, I'd overstepped. Too forward. Too much. Too soon.

"Maybe I'll have to get back to you," she murmured, some of that quiet confidence quickly fading. "I, um, have to work tomorrow and then I have to get Oliver to the vet on Friday."

Still, despite my better judgment, I pushed just a little further. "That still leaves us Saturday and Sunday, right?"

My persistence might've paid off because her lips curled up into that smile again that sent something warm rushing down to my stomach.

"Right."

"So where do you work?"

Another harmless, normal question and I crossed my fingers that this question wouldn't have the same reaction as the last personal question I'd asked her.

"The Corner Café," she told me easily and I let the breath I'd been very aware I was holding. "Have you ever been there?"

"Nope, but I've heard of it. That place is supposed to have the best homemade pie in the city, right?"

"Oh yeah," she grinned. "The best..."

She trailed off like she'd been about to say something else, but clammed up again. Then she surprised me by switching gears completely. "I actually write a blog, too."

My lips pulled apart in awe, with more than a little curiosity thrown in there. "Really? What do you write about?"

She cringed and sank down into her chair as best as she could, considering the cat in her lap. "It's kinda stupid."

"Come on. Tell me."

"It's a beauty blog," she must've seen the flash of confusion on my face because she jumped to explain. "I write about trends, tips, products to use, things I've used and liked or didn't like. It's, um, called *Northern Chic*. I've been doing it since I was in high school so..."

"Cool," I just shrugged. The pink coloring her cheeks was cute, but wasn't necessary. There was no point in being embarrassed over something you enjoyed. "So how do you get all the stuff then? Do you have to buy it yourself?"

"Sometimes," she shrugged. "But there are some companies who send me products. I get a kickback if readers turn around and click on the links I put in some of my posts."

My eyebrows lifted in impressed surprise. "You make money, too?"

"Sure," she shrugged again like it was no big deal. "There are ways you can monetize your blog with ads and kickbacks. It's not enough to make a living, but it helps."

"And you like it."

Her smile was more careful this time, but it was still there and that was all that mattered. "Yeah, I do."

"Good."

With that, I could tell a change of pace was in order and I picked up my guitar again, pointing at the cat. "This one's for you, buddy."

The chords buzzed out from the strings, my shoulders swaying a little bit with the beat, and searching for just a little bit of courage to sing along with the music so she could figure the song out. Finally, my humming turned into quiet, slightly off-key rasps.

"*Whoo whoo whoo whoo whoo,*" I sang, trying to remember the words as I went along.

She was already laughing, but I decided to lay it on thicker just because.

"*Why should I worry? Why should I care...I've got street saviore faire.*"

"Oh, I haven't heard that song in forever!" she laughed and reached down to hold the cat tighter to her. "I need to watch that movie now. You know, I'm pretty sure *Oliver and Company* was the first movie I ever saw in the theatre."

"Of course," I shook my head and kept right on strumming. "It was fate then. Obviously."

"Obviously."

For the next few hours, this was my night: a beautiful, crisp September night, a bottle of beer, my guitar, music, a stray cat, and my captivating neighbor. We traded songs, starting with the classics like The Beatles and The Doors before moving to music that was more contemporary like Green Day and Foo Fighters—I still couldn't believe she didn't know "The Pretender". Every once and awhile, she threw in something off the wall, like Michael Jackson or Miranda Lambert, of all choices, and while I didn't always get all the chords in the right progression, I was able to keep up long enough for her to either laugh or listen with admiration.

That was good enough for me.

So, at a certain point, long after the sun faded into the tree line and long after the four beers I'd run back to my apartment for had emptied, it was time to call it a night. I didn't really want it to end and I didn't really want to head back to my apartment alone when I knew she was right across the hall, also alone, minus the cat. But, as I swept up some of the empties underneath my arm and reached for my guitar, she called out to me one last time from behind her screen door.

"Hey, if you don't have anything going on tomorrow, seeing as you have the day off and all, you could stop by the café for lunch or something."

Because I was tossed in the scatter of expectations, anxiety, and trying not to look like an idiot, I stood there, gaping openly back at Emma like the asshole I was trying to avoid being.

"I could save a piece of pie for you. On the house," she offered shyly as her fingers picked at the screen in front of her.

Finally, I felt myself coming back to life again and this time, the smile I shot her was more confident and, hopefully, more charming than anything I'd sent her way before. "You guys have banana cream? That's my favorite."

"Absolutely we do," she bit down on her bottom lip to hide her smile.

"You sold me, Em."

Something flashed in her eyes and it probably had everything to do with me calling her Em. But at this point, even though I could count on one hand the number of times we'd interacted, I felt like I'd known her for longer. Like, somehow, we were old friends who'd reconnected and picked up right where we left off. I couldn't apologize for something like that even if it meant that I'd overstepped again.

"Okay," she murmured and waved to me. "I'll see you tomorrow."

Yeah. Tomorrow was looking pretty good.

CHAPTER SEVEN

"More coffee, Ed?" I asked, lifting the coffee pot up to him.

The café's gruffest, yet most loyal regular customer, just grunted in response and held up his empty coffee mug. Biting my bottom lip to keep the surly old man from seeing my knowing grin, I quickly obliged him by filling the mug to the brim.

"Food should be out shortly."

I knew better than to expect actual words in response, but whether it was out of stubborn relentlessness to break down his hard exterior or just plain old fashioned manners, I waited a few beats at the edge of the table before finally giving up, throwing Ed a quick smile, and heading back by my station to get my side work finished. I still had three hours left of my lunch shift and since Ed was currently the only customer sitting in my section, if business didn't pick up, I'd probably find myself cut for the day soon anyway.

With that last thought propelling me forward, I got down to the business of rolling forks and knives into paper napkins. It wasn't the most stimulating work by any means, but if anything, it was better than nothing to pass the time. Casting a quick glance into the kitchen's window to check on Ed's food, my eyes fell back down to the work at hand as Mara flitted past me with a tray hitched on top of her shoulder.

"Everything alright, Emma?" Mara asked me from over her shoulder, pausing just long enough to get an answer.

"Yeah, I'm fine. Why wouldn't I be?"

"I don't know," she shrugged. "You're just quieter than usual. And normally, you're pretty quiet anyway, you know?"

I guess I hadn't realized it was that obvious.

"I'm fine," I told her and hoped that would appease her for the time being.

When she just shrugged again and headed towards her table, I blew out a deep breath, grateful I had something to distract myself. The problem was, with only one customer and mindless side work in front of me, my mind had no problem wandering to how I'd spent the previous night. And the night before that.

My mind flashed to the way I'd easily fallen into something that ran just a little bit deeper than mere conversation with my neighbor. The way he'd smiled at me like I was the most interesting girl he'd met in a long time, the way he'd hung on every word, the way he'd carefully led the conversation away from topics that made me uncomfortable just so he could stay on my patio a little bit longer...it was all hard to forget and it was seriously clouding my judgment.

I knew better than to let myself get too close, to let him in, to tell him anything slightly personal. There was only one way that could end and we were neighbors for God's sakes. The worst idea ever in the history of terrible ideas was to get even remotely involved with your neighbor.

So, I tried to tell myself that it was just because the situation was convenient and easy. All either of us had to do was walk five feet across the hall or across the grass for easy access to companionship. That was all it was. Loneliness. A cliché need for connection. The irony, of course, was that I'd run away to the city to escape those connections, to become anonymous, to blend in with the crowd, but I hadn't been able to escape a stray cat or my next-door neighbor.

Because, let's face it, I never would've been sitting out on my patio that night if it wasn't for the cat.

So, really, this was all Oliver's fault.

Considering that I'd completely lost my mind by even suggesting he come into the café today...careless with no thought to consequence, pulled in once again by another pair of light eyes, the last thing I needed was to invite Finn into my life right now. This flirtation, this interest, this attraction, whatever *this* was, it wasn't good for me.

It was too bad, at least I thought it was, that my gut didn't really agree with my brain.

So maybe it was serendipitous or just sheer bad luck that the moment I padded back into the dining room with Ed's food was the same moment the door swung open so Finn could come shuffling through. Everything seemed to freeze. I stopped short, mid-stride with the plate still secured in my hand, and gaped openly, my eyes wide and disbelieving.

Despite the fact that I'd literally just seen him the night before, I was so inexplicably happy to see him again it had to have been written all over my face. Maybe it was just because I hadn't really expected him to take me up on my offer. Maybe it was simply because he was the mirror image of the way I felt. So world-weary. So exhausted. Lost, even. And despite all that, just as happy to see me as I was to see him.

There was nothing I could do but smile as I moved towards him. His eyes glowed as I approached and he met me halfway.

"Hey, Emma," he greeted me softly and shoved his hands into his front pockets as he lingered around the doorway.

"Hi, Finn," I exhaled.

We stood there like that for a few long moments, staring back at each other with crazy-stupid grins on our faces, until I remembered the food in my hand and flushed red as I waved my free hand to an open booth on the other side of where Ed sat.

"I just have to…" I gestured with my head to the food in my hand. "Um...have a seat. I'll be right back, okay?"

The lopsided grin he shot me just about sent the plate tumbling out of my hands and I hastily moved back to Ed's booth in order to preclude any other embarrassing reactions. Ignoring Ed's stink-eye and gruff grunt when I practically threw the plate at him, I couldn't get back to Finn's booth fast enough. My feet slowed just enough to keep me from looking ridiculously over-eager as I re-approached the booth, that happy, easy smile creeping back across my lips.

"I'm so glad you're here," I blurted out the second my feet stopped moving. "I mean...uh…" I shook my head, already feeling a traitorous rush of heat flooding my cheeks, "I'm glad you decided to stop in for lunch."

Okay, so that wasn't much different than what I'd said before, but it was still true. And now that his grin seemed to reach all the way up to the excited glimmer in his light eyes, I didn't regret it for a second.

Seeing him shuffle through the door was like something out of a surreal dream. What happened from here on out wasn't even on my radar, at least not yet, because all I could focus on was that the only reason he was sitting in a booth in this café right now was because of me.

And the warm feeling that realization created spilled right over all my hesitations and all my reservations, saturating everything my mind screamed at me.

"I'm glad I decided to stop in, too," Finn was saying now, his eyes trailing up and down like I was a real sight for sore eyes.

The heady combination of warmth, excitement, and that glint of something else radiating from his eyes needed to be shelved for later. I could sort through it then, but for now, staying calm and collected in his presence was going to prove difficult enough.

"So...um…"

He grinned at my hesitation and rested an elbow good-naturedly on the table. "Well, seeing as how this is my first full day off in way too long, what I really want right now is a nice, fat slice of that banana cream pie. You think you could make that happen for me, Em?"

"So you're skipping the meal altogether and going straight for the pie?" I hitched a hand on my hip and now, there was really no point in trying to mask my smile.

"Yep," Finn grinned back brightly. "Pretty much."

"Let me go grab a nice big one for you, okay?"

The wink he shot me as I backpedalled towards the kitchen managed to hit me all the way down to the pit of my stomach, taking over every one of my senses and filling me near to the brim with feelings I'd long-believed would forever lay dormant. It didn't help that I just couldn't reconcile what he was even doing here in the first place. Sure, he might not have considered it if I hadn't thrown the invite his way, but that didn't explain why he was actually here.

I'd long been resigned to my role as an observer in life. Someone who was inconsequential and immediately forgotten once you passed by. Frankly, up until about a year ago, it was a role I'd played so often it'd become second nature. So the fact that he was here now, that he was obviously here to see *me*, didn't quite gel with all the other moving parts that made up the mess that was my life.

He was just being nice. Maybe that was it. Or maybe he legitimately just had nothing better to do with his day off and wanted a piece of pie. Even worse, it was just as likely that he felt sorry for me, that he saw how pathetic I was to the point that my only real friend was a stray cat. Maybe it was just for the best that I start mentally preparing myself for that now.

It was a good thing, too, because Mara had already passed right by the booth and her eyes flew directly to me. So, I made sure to keep that slightly faux-smile plastered on my face as I re-approached Finn's booth just for good measure. If anything, I figured my best course of action right now was just to act like everything was fine and that I wasn't keeping a freakout at bay. *Yeah*, I mused ruefully, *that's gonna be super easy to hide.*

When I set the plate down in front of my neighbor, I could only hope he was none the wiser to my current frazzled state. Thankfully, the moment his pie appeared, all his attention focused squarely on the creamy folds of banana goodness in front of him and he licked his lips in anticipation.

"Jesus," he muttered under his breath. "I think you might need to grab a wheelchair to haul me out of here, Em, because I think I need at least two more pieces of this before I get out of your hair today."

"Wow," I shook my head with an amused smile on my lips. "Men and their pie."

Finn barely wasted a moment before digging his fork into a corner and shoveling as much as his fork could carry into his waiting mouth. Pausing only to point his fork at me, he somehow managed to garble through a full mouth: "Hey, I will have you know that I'm completely committed to pie. The love and understanding between us is unrivaled, Emma. *Unrivaled.*"

With that, he shot me yet another wink—this time with a glint of mischief—and scooped another whopping portion into his mouth. There wasn't much I could do other than shake my head to laugh off the tongue-in-cheek insinuation.

Something had changed since the last time I saw him...while the shuffling, hand-in-his-pockets, shy nature was still there underneath the surface, he'd brought an air of confidence with him today, too. The flirtation seemed to roll right off him now like second nature, where last night, he'd seemed to fumble a little for the right words. There was no shortage of charm now and whether I liked it or not, he was most definitely hitting his target.

"Well, I'm pretty sure I only promised you *one* piece on the house. You want any more, you're on your own, my friend."

His low chuckle followed me back to Ed's booth, which incidentally, was right next to Finn's.

"How is everything, Ed?"

If I was friendly and paid him a little extra attention, a decent tip from Ed might not be totally lost. He grunted, shoved some fries in his mouth, and barely cast me a glance. Alright then. Ed *used* to leave halfway decent tips for me as a café regular...I guess the way I'd tossed his food down on his table and hightailed it back to Finn hadn't gone over so well.

I blew out a deep breath. "Can I get you anything? Another refill?"

Ed just grunted one last time, gesturing with his head towards his empty coffee mug in a not-so-articulate way of affirming what I already knew. I dared a glance to my left only to find Finn observing the exchange from his respective booth with his lips pulled apart in a grimace.

"*He's friendly,*" Finn mouthed to me.

So, although it was bad form to laugh at the expense of a customer pretty much anyway you looked at it, I just couldn't help it. The laugh burst out of my throat and I immediately bit it back. Happiness sounded foreign and uncomfortable to my ears, especially when it was coming from me.

With both men's eyes on me, Finn watching me with amusement and Ed glaring at me like he would rather drive his fork into my hand than use it as a utensil, I decided now was the time to get my ass off the floor. Ed needed his third cup of coffee, you know?

I managed to get all the way to the kitchen with a hand reaching for a fresh coffee pot, when Mara murmured in my ear: "Looks like your shift just got a little better."

"Something like that, yeah."

"You know him, right?" she pushed on, reflecting all the excitement I was trying and failing at concealing. "I mean, the way he was looking at you and waving at you...please tell me you know him because if you don't, I'm stealing your table."

"He's my neighbor."

Mara's bright blue eyes widened with glee and she bounced on her heels, clapping her hands together in front of her like a little kid. "Of course he is. Oh, Emma, he is easy on my contact lenses that's for sure. And he's got that messy, unshaven hunter thing goin' on. Like a Browning Adonis."

I wanted to roll my eyes, but there was no use. *Can't deny the facts.*

"Why didn't you tell me you were seeing somebody?"

That snapped me back to reality. "I'm not seeing him."

Mara's eyebrows lifted high into her forehead. "Sure. Whatever you have to tell yourself, Em."

"Come on, Mara. I think you're making this a way bigger deal than it has to be."

"Well, all I know is that this is the first time I've ever seen anyone come in this place specifically to see *you*, so I'd say it's pretty damn monumental. Now, give Ed his coffee and take your break."

"It's not time for my break yet."

She arched an eyebrow at me and leaned in closer. "Emma, stop making this so hard. It's actually very simple: give Ed his coffee and go sit by your smokin' hot neighbor already."

More like long-legged guitar pickin' neighbor, as June Carter Cash would say, but that was besides the point. Mara was the closest thing to an actual human friend I had and not only did she obviously have my best interest and well-being in mind, but she was right, too. To make her point, she practically shoved me back out onto the floor.

Coffee sloshed at my feet and I scowled at her over my shoulder, but as my shoulders squared and I got a good look at the scene in front of me, my steps skidded to a stop. I couldn't believe what I was seeing. Ed was laughing. Not just any old chuckling, but heavy, belly-shaking, rip-roaring laughing. Finn had shifted around in the booth, one forearm slung along the divider between the two booths and his head tilted over the side as he murmured something to Ed that made my normally grumpy customer's shoulders shake.

"Holy shit," Mara whispered behind me. "He's the Ed whisperer."

There was no rhyme or reason to it. Had I suddenly fallen into the Twilight Zone? How did that go—something about a fifth dimension as vast as space and as timeless as infinity? That's exactly what this felt like right now. It couldn't be real.

Now, as I ventured closer, I heard different music in my head. This moment was like something from a Taylor Swift song...

When I filled up Ed's coffee mug, he was still grinning back at Finn, but managed to spare a second to gesture to Finn and say, "I like this one. Keep him around, ya hear?"

I shot him a quick smile, eager to get back to the booth next to him. "Do you need anything else right away?"

Ed waved me off with his fork. "Go ahead and see your fella. I'll be fine."

It took a moment for his words to catch up with me and I found myself glancing back nervously at Finn, hoping he didn't read too much into Ed's off-the-cuff remark. The last thing I wanted was for Finn to get the impression I had some sort of revolving door of guys showing up at the café to see me. That was definitely the opposite of my reality, but I could also count on one hand the number of truly personal things Finn knew about me. Ed's assumption that Finn was my 'fella' didn't quite sit well with me either...and judging by the way Finn's eyes lit up at the comment, he'd heard every word.

Still, that Taylor Swift song grew louder in my head, drowning out those pesky insecurities, and I found myself standing in front of Finn's booth, feeling like I was really standing at the edge of a limitless precipice, teetering on the edge of something I used to think I'd never wanted again. Part of me wanted to cut and run, to hold him at arm's length and keep my distance, but here I was, blowing my bangs out of my face and gesturing towards the empty seat across from Finn, watching it all begin again.

"So," I started unsteadily. "I'm on break now. Is it alright if I sit?"

"Of course, Em," Finn held a hand out across the table. "Have a seat."

Now that I had permission, I swept one leg underneath the other and settled back into the squeaky, worn pleather bench. "Man, it feels good to sit."

"You look tired," he told me. "Late night?"

And just like that, he had me laughing again. "Yeah, I've got this really loud, annoying neighbor who thinks he's this awesome guitar player, but all that awful picking is keeping me up at night."

There was a glimmer of mischief in his eyes that I think I liked a little too much. "Ah. I see. Need me to go over there and put the asshole in his place?"

"Nah," I batted a hand his way. "I think I can handle him."

His entire face brightened and it was like he was lit from within, his sky-blue eyes glimmering and shining. Those eyes...they were thieves. Stealing my breath, stealing my resolve to keep my distance, stealing the axis my world rested on and tipping it sideways. Right about now, I didn't know which end was up.

"I read some of your blog last night," Finn informed me and that playful glint in his eyes just wouldn't let up.

I cringed a little at the admission. God, I could only imagine what he thought of content like, "How To Prep Your Skin For Every Season" or "Which Toner Is Right For Your Skin?". High-quality literature at its best.

"Great," I managed to croak out.

"What do you mean *great*?" he laughed, leaning his elbows on the table to get closer to me. "It was interesting."

I shot him a withering look, cocking both eyebrows at him and everything. "Right."

"Yeah. I learned a lot actually. I feel like I should start exfoliating or something now," he ran a hand through his scruffy beard just to reiterate his point. "Ah, but then again, I'd have to shave and that's not happening."

"Oh boy..." I groaned. "You don't have to lie. It couldn't have been *that* interesting to you."

He held up his hands in defense. "Okay, okay. Maybe some of it wasn't...exactly my thing, if you know what I mean. But your writing— that was what was interesting to me. Your tone, your voice...you really seem to know what you're talking about, but you're not condescending or weird about it though, you know? Some of it was pretty funny, too."

I still felt myself cringing with embarrassment. "Thanks. I guess."

"I'm serious," Finn pressed on. He was still grinning, but his voice was firmer this time, like he really wanted me to believe this. "Judging by all the comments and all the follows you have, your readers really like what you have to say. They seem to listen to you. That's really cool, Emma. *And* you get paid for it, too. Doesn't get much better than that."

"Yeah, I guess you're right about that."

I'd never really thought about it like that before. My blog, at least up until now, had always been a fun hobby that let me play with products I was interested in and sometimes get a little extra money on the side. The idea that my writing—not just the content, but the actual form itself —had any impact with my readers beyond beauty advice was a brand-new and strange concept. Most of the time, my blog was more my excuse to get out of doing things than anything.

"I noticed you don't use your full name on your blog though. Is that just a privacy thing? Or is it about branding?"

I sucked in a harsh breath. In the beginning, I'd chosen to stay anonymous mainly because I was just a senior in high school at the time and then after college, I'd wanted to keep my online life separate from my real life. Now, I might as well have been hiding behind it, too.

"Um, you know, it's just a personal choice," I offered lamely. "I guess I don't really see the need to put *all* my information out there, you know? I don't think anyone needs to know my last name in order to get the content."

Finn just shrugged. "I can see that."

My palms were getting sweaty and I needed to shift the conversation away from myself, so I fumbled for something that had been right on the tip of my tongue ever since I found out his last name. "Can I ask you a weird question?"

"Shoot."

"Your last name is Matthews, right? Like the name of your family's brewery?" I paused long enough for him to nod and seeing how his eyes narrowed ever so slightly, he probably already knew where this was going. "Isn't there a Packer player with that last name? Are you related to him or something?"

His eyes lifted to the ceiling and then he blew out an exasperated breath before finally, hilariously, glaring back at me with hooded eyes. "You mean Clay Matthews?"

I was almost afraid to answer. "Yeah...?"

"No, Emma," he pushed out roughly and it was clear this was a conversation he'd had many, many times before. "I'm not related to Clay Matthews."

"Geez," I laughed, lifting my eyebrows high into my forehead.

"Sorry. It's not *that* big a deal, is it? Isn't he a pretty good player?"

Finn just lifted a nonchalant shoulder. I'd clearly hit a nerve. "I guess. He's no Rodgers, but yeah, he's alright."

And then all the pieces flew into place.

"Oh my God!" my mouth dropped open with evil delight and I shot forward in the booth to jab my finger at him. "You have a man-crush on Aaron Rodgers! That's why you hate when people ask about your last name! That's so sad and beautiful and awesome all at the same time."

"I do not have a..." Finn's voice dropped an octave and he glanced over his shoulder to make sure no one was listening, "*man-crush* on Aaron Rodgers. Keep your voice down, alright?"

My shoulders shook with laughter and I clamped down on my bottom lip to mask as much as I could. Finally, my hand slapped over my mouth.

"Stop laughing."

That, unfortunately, only made me laugh even harder. I think I snorted I was laughing so hard.

"I'm sorry," I managed in between unabashed giggles. Yep, I was giggling. The whole thing was just weird. "I can't help it. I mean, if only your last name was Rodgers, right? Then everything would be perfect for you."

Finn's lips curled back into what I knew was a playful, albeit frustrated, snarl and he leaned forward against the table. "I have a deep respect for him. That's all. He's the best player in the league. He was the MVP last year for Christ's sake. The dude has a 5-year, $110 million contract with the Packers. Why *can't* I secretly wish I had his life, huh? What's wrong with that?"

"Oh God," I had to hold my stomach now. "You're just making it worse."

"You know what really sucks?" Finn scowled. "Sling got me one of those personalized jerseys a few years ago just to be a dick and rub it in my face. I literally own a Packer jersey with the number 12 on it and the name Matthews on the back. I can't wear that in public because I'd look like a complete tool. It's terrible."

"That must be really hard for you," I don't know how I was able to form a coherent sentence while laughing so hard and I wiped some tears from my eyes.

"It is."

All that got from me was another sputtering of laughter.

"Well, I'm glad you're enjoying this," Finn crossed his arms sullenly across his chest. If I didn't know any better, there was a hint of a smile there, too.

"I'm sorry," I held up a hand and shook my head. "Seriously. I didn't mean to lose my shit like that. I just didn't expect...*that.*"

Oh boy. My shoulders were shaking again and I squeezed my eyes shut to get a handle on myself.

"Yeah, I can see that," Finn tossed back lightly. "Hey, now that you're done humiliating me—"

My eyes rolled right up to the ceiling. "Oh, come on."

"Okay, fine," he amended with a slight bow of his head. "Now that I'm done humiliating *myself*, I think we should talk about your cat."

I had to swallow back the shot of panic that ripped through my stomach. "What about him? Did something happen? What—"

"Relax," Finn fanned out both hands across the table to appease me. "He's fine. I peeked over by your patio before I left and he was still there. No worries. I was just really wondering if you're gonna cave tonight or not."

I frowned. "What do you mean?"

"Really?" he smirked. "Come on, Em. You got that vet appointment right away in the morning tomorrow. There's no way you don't cave and let him in tonight."

My mouth opened to protest, but all I could come up with was: "I don't know...I don't have anything for him yet."

Finn just shrugged. "You gotta get stuff eventually. Might as well do it today so you're all set for tomorrow. And then, since you'll already be set, you'll cave and let the little dude in. I know it."

"Oh yeah?"

"Yeah," he nodded easily. "I'll bet you a whole pizza."

"A whole pizza?"

"Yep."

"Huh."

His angle wasn't really that difficult to decode. Regardless of whoever lost the bet, I assumed we'd still be sharing that pizza. Who paid for said pizza still remained to be seen. I had a feeling that had been his plan all along.

"Okay," I agreed. "I'll take that bet."

Besides, it wasn't like I could really say no...who could possibly turn down the Browning Adonis? Nobody. That's who. Not even an icy, closed-off girl like me could find the willpower to say no. From over Finn's shoulder, I could see Ed getting a little fidgety in his booth, clearly needing his waitress, if not most definitely his bill and then my break was pretty much over.

"Hey, so, I gotta get back to work," I told Finn as I started to slide out from the booth. "Thanks for letting me crash your table."

"Anytime," Finn smiled back at me. "Thanks for the company. And you were absolutely right about this pie. It's honestly the best thing I've eaten in a long time. I'm definitely gonna need at least one more piece before I go."

"I think I can make that happen," then I pivoted on my heel to turn back to him and leaned down to lower my voice so my only other customer couldn't hear. "Hey, just curious...what did you say to Ed? Before I sat down for my break?"

The smile that touched Finn's lips gave me the sudden urge to launch myself into his booth and...I didn't know what else I'd do.

"I just told him spending time with a beautiful girl and having a piece of banana cream pie wasn't a bad way to spend a day off," he shrugged. "And he agreed. That broke the ice pretty quickly."

Something warm lodged itself in my throat. Even as I waved to him to head back to my shift, I heard Taylor Swift's voice in my head, singing about how she used to think all love ever did was break and burn and end.

It wasn't a Wednesday in a café though. It was a Thursday in a café, but I still watched it begin again.

CHAPTER EIGHT

When I had my apartment door closed behind me, my eyes fell on Oliver, still perched on his chair, waiting for me to come home. He stretched one lazy white paw up in the air and shifted onto his back with half-closed, sleepy eyes as if to say, *Oh, hey. It's you again.*

My heart tugged and warmth spread out through my chest.

I was going to lose Finn's bet. It was pretty much a foregone conclusion at this point.

The problem, I realized as I surveyed the space in my tiny, one-bedroom apartment, was that I had nothing for this cat and no idea what he even needed in the first place. Food bowls and toys I could probably figure out. But litter boxes and everything that went with it? I didn't even know if I was feeding him the right food. There had to be something better out there than what I'd grabbed in a rush from the store last week. Should I be giving him wet food or dry food? What kind of treats did cats get anyway? And carriers! I needed something to smuggle him out of my apartment, but...I felt like a chicken with its head cut off.

My other problem, of course, brought me to why I was currently standing a foot away from Finn's door. Sure, I could look all that up online. I could even wait and ask the vet all those rookie questions tomorrow, too. But no, I was standing outside Finn's door, telling myself the only reason I stood here right now was because he'd mentioned growing up with cats in the house.

It was lame, but it was my excuse.

My fist lifted up to the door, ready to knock, but fell to my side just as quickly. Something as simple as knocking on a door shouldn't be so difficult, but the reasons holding me back weren't easy or simple by any means. Yet, I still wanted to knock on the door.

It was a beautiful, confounding feeling.

For all my misgivings about being here, the aura of peace

surrounding the little time I'd already spent with Finn tempted me to knock on the door. But would doing that send me falling face-first into something I wasn't quite ready for? Was I just setting myself up for yet another failure and yet another epically tragic disappointment? Wasn't I better off in the long run if I just turned around right now and headed back to the safety of my own apartment?

Of course, the answer to all those questions was a resounding yes. If I knocked, this was a slippery slope I might never be able to find my way out from. If I knocked, it was just going to be that much harder to keep my carefully constructed walls in place. If I knocked, I'd essentially be inviting him into my life. I wasn't sure I wanted or needed to do that.

I knocked on the door anyway.

It only took Finn a few moments to swing open the door, but when he did, happy surprise flickered across his handsome face.

"Hey," he greeted me, leaning into the doorjamb as he spoke, "What's up?"

I blew my bangs out of my face...God, I really needed to start growing those things out already.

"So, I owe you a pizza."

A satisfied smirk worked its way across his face. "I knew it."

"But," I added. "Just so you know, I'm gonna be using that $20 you left on my table. So, *you're* really the one buying the pizza."

Both hands shoved sheepishly into his pockets. I'd told him not to leave any money at the table, that the pie was on the house, but I guess I shouldn't have been surprised he hadn't listened to me either.

"I can live with that," he allowed.

Now came the part I was already embarrassed to ask.

"So, I gotta get some stuff for the cat, but I have no idea what I really need and I feel like I'm just going to be wandering the aisles of PetSmart like an aimless idiot if I don't have any help."

Finn nodded knowingly and crossed both arms over his chest. "I see. Well, my sister *was* a crazy cat lady when we were growing up. I suppose I could offer some assistance, if you want."

He'd obviously seen through the paper-thin excuse and was game for a trip to the pet store, even though I hadn't exactly come out and asked. Just as I opened my mouth to invite him along, a flash of bright orange, wiry hair appeared at Finn's side.

"Hey there, neighbor," Slinger drawled, his eyes darting to Finn and then back to me again. "What brings your lovely self to our door?"

The exasperation, not to mention borderline mortification, that crept across Finn's face was enough to set aside my own slight embarrassment at his roommate's forwardness. Slinger didn't really let up either, lifting his eyebrows suggestively one after the other Jim Carrey-style as his gaze swept over the awkwardness.

"I was actually just about to ask Finn if he wanted to take a little shopping trip with me," I offered, trying to at least appear calm and collected.

Slinger balked at the suggestion, his eyes widening as he stared back at me. "Finn doesn't go shopping. I mean…" he gestured to the wrinkled mountain-print T-shirt that said *California Waiting* and the well-worn, slightly frayed jeans Finn was wearing, "You've seen him, right?"

Finn's head turned slowly towards his roommate, like all this was happening in slow motion, and his face darkened as his lips curled back into the same playful snarl I'd seen at the café earlier today. "Hey. No one asked for your opinion, Sling."

Slinger's hands shot up in defense. "Geez. Bite my head off, why don't you. I was just stating the obvious. But maybe you do need a chick to take you—"

"We're not doing that kind of shopping," Finn cut in sharply and then his eyes flicked back to me apologetically. "I just gotta grab my keys. I'll be right back."

He jabbed a finger at Slinger as he turned on his heel to disappear in the apartment and told him: "Behave."

Slinger just shrugged, moving to the side so Finn could glide past him, and then his twinkling green eyes shifted slyly back to me. "You can come in, you know."

"Nah," I batted a hand into the empty space in front of me. "I'm good."

"Sure you are," Slinger tossed back good-naturedly with a grin. "You and Finn seem to be hitting it off nicely."

I sucked in a breath, searching for some way to respond to that, but came up empty. What a shocker.

Now, Slinger glanced conspiratorially over his shoulder, mimicking his actions outside my door almost a week ago, and leaned in to whisper, "I think he likes you."

I huffed out a laugh, despite the flurry of butterflies kicking soccer balls around my stomach, and shook my head. "What are we—12?"

Slinger's head fell back, his shoulders shaking with hearty laughter, and he waved his index finger at me. "I need to get to know you a little better, but I think you just might be perfect."

My eyebrows lifted into my forehead and I chewed on my bottom lip, hoping Finn showed up soon. Luckily, not even a moment later, Finn appeared at the door and face-palmed Slinger to push him out of the way so he could shut the door behind him. Without room for any hesitation, Finn gestured out to the hallway to signal it was time to get moving. I could've sworn I felt his hand ghost over the small of my back as he led me down the short hallway, but that could've easily been wishful thinking, too.

His black, massive Ford truck loomed out in front of us and after opening the passenger door for me, Finn scrambled to clear off the seat, tossing some of the trash into the back before I even had a chance to look inside. When we were both seated inside the truck and he was backing us out of our building's parking lot, the intimacy of the whole thing suddenly struck me. Finn in the driver's seat of his truck, me sitting close, breathing in the masculinity that lingered in the air, taking in his personal space, and still feeling comfortable with him even in the confined space.

Just the admission that I felt comfortable this way with him made me uncomfortable. God, feeling uncomfortable because I felt comfortable? This was a new low.

Those conflicting emotions raged war in my mind, twisting and pulling until I finally had to stare blankly out the passenger window to clear my head.

"Sorry about Sling," Finn's deep voice called out to me as he turned onto the street. "I've been trying to house-train him for years, but I've still got a lot of work to do."

"It's alright," I laughed. "He seems nice enough. What's up with that nickname though? When he came over last week, he told me his name is actually Marshall, but…"

I trailed off, looking to Finn to finally fill in the blanks for me, which he obliged with a sly grin.

"Ah, now that's a good story. So, me, Sling, and a bunch of our other friends all went to high school together, right? Our sophomore year Sling was the new kid. He shows up the first day of football practice that August with these crazy thick glasses on that look like magnifying glasses, he's got this 'fro of clown-orange hair, freckles all over the place, but he's cool, though, you know? Really funny. Easy-going. And he was a helluva a wide receiver, too, quick, good hands—"

"Let me guess," I cut in with a knowing grin. "You were the quarterback?"

I wasn't stupid enough to comment about the brand of truck he drove. You know, the one Aaron Rodgers was the spokesperson for?

Finn's eyes narrowed sharply. "Is it that obvious? Never mind. Don't answer that. *Anyway*...so by the time school started back up again, he'd just sorta fallen pretty easily into my group of friends. Then, the first day at lunch, he launches into this elaborate story about how his parents used to be U.S. ambassadors in Europe who'd just retired and moved back to the States and that was why he'd transferred in that year. So, naturally, everyone had questions—where did they live? What kinda shit did he see in all those different countries? He rolled with every question, telling us all these crazy stories about getting caught drinking in the embassy and making out with all these chicks from Amsterdam and Brussels and Munich and finally, by the time my head stopped spinning, I said, 'I thought Coach said you were from Slinger'."

"Oh no," I half-groaned, half-laughed. I could already see where this was going.

"Yep," Finn shot me a quick grin. "Good ol' Marshall was just a transfer from Slinger. His dad's a dentist and his mom's a paralegal, by the way. I don't know, I guess he thought telling us all those crazy stories would make us like him more or make him seem cooler. Needless to say, from that day on, everyone, even our coach, has always called him Slinger."

"Poor Marshall," I cringed. It was really too bad...I'd probably seen a hundred kids play that game in my past life and every time it hurt my heart. "You guys probably would've liked him anyway, huh?"

"Ah, it wasn't that big of a deal," Finn just waved a hand in the air. "He was embarrassed, sure. And he got ragged on for it, definitely, but honestly, I think we liked him even more after that because who comes up with that kinda shit, you know? Besides, that was...what, almost 15 years ago? Wow, that makes me feel really old."

"Sounds like you guys had a decent group of friends," I mused. "You know, if something like that happened now, I doubt he'd come out so unscathed. Kids can be so mean and just...diabolical, you know?"

When Finn just frowned at me, cold hard panic crept down my spine. I'd just violated one of my cardinal rules: never give away any information. I'd said too much. I'd made him wonder why I'd even have an opinion like that. This wasn't even the first time I'd given too much away with him, too. And now, I had to scramble.

"I mean, I can think of a million ways kids could use social media to torture him now," I went on, feeling my palms grow clammy with each word. "That story would've been all over Twitter or Snapchat or something like that within minutes. He never would've lived it down. Probably would've ended up switching schools, too."

"Yeah, I guess you're right," Finn offered thoughtfully as he pulled us into the store's parking lot. "I never thought about it like that before. I guess Sling's lucky we weren't a bunch of assholes back in the day and just gave him a little shit for it and moved on."

"Minus the nickname," I reminded him with a weak smile. The turn this conversation had taken made me queasy.

"Right. Minus the nickname. There's no way around that."

Luckily enough, he'd already parked his truck in a space and had turned off the ignition, so it was time to leave this conversation behind us.

Finn gestured to the main entrance of PetSmart with a bright smile, "Let's go cat shopping."

I laughed, letting him sweep away the tension that coiled its way through my body. It was time to have some fun for once and time to actually get excited about something, too.

. . .

"Well, I think that's everything," Finn surmised, his hands on his hips as he surveyed all the plastic bags sitting in my living room.

As it turned out, Finn was way more knowledgeable about all things feline-related than I'd ever given him credit for. We'd grabbed a cart and he'd easily led me around the cat section of the store, filling me in on foreign concepts like catnip, litter that clumped, and dust-free litter, which he informed me would be easier on my allergies, as well as the fact that my best bet was to find a place for Oliver's litter box in my bathroom, which did not appeal to me at all.

Within a half hour, we had everything I needed: a collar, fancy ceramic bowls that Finn rolled his eyes at, a plastic pet carrier, a litter box complete with liners and that dust-free litter, a pooper scooper, an assortment of cat-friendly toys and treats, higher-quality dry food (apparently, according to Finn, the brand Oliver currently ate was, and I quote, "shit"), a scratching post, a brush, some waterless shampoo, and a tiny nail clipper.

"Yeah, I think so," my eyes lingered on the shopping bags in a vain attempt at my mounting anxiety over Finn's presence in my apartment. "I didn't realize cats were so expensive."

Finn laughed, dipping his head down in a nod. "Oh, just wait 'til the vet bills start popping up. That'll be fun."

I grimaced, my eyes falling to the reason I'd just dropped over $200 at a pet store. "I don't think fun is the right word for it."

"Maybe not," he allowed and ducked his head down to get a better look at the cat who was still perched leisurely on his chair out on my patio.

"So should I order that pizza?"

"You know what?" Finn cast me a quick glance over his shoulder before turning back to grin at Oliver. "I think you two need some time to figure each other out. You don't need me hanging around, crowding your big moment. Let's do the pizza tomorrow night."

There was something about the prospect of having the rest of the night with Oliver, let alone that Finn recognized this actually *was* a pretty significant moment for me, as sad as that was, that had my lips curling and my chest warming.

I wasn't going to argue with that logic, especially since he wasn't exactly reneging on our bet either.

"Okay," I exhaled and followed Finn's gaze out to the patio. "I'm not really sure what to do though."

"You'll figure it out," he told me and I hoped his confidence bled into my reality. "And, if you need some help, I'm right across the hall. You sure you still don't want any help tomorrow?"

"Yep," I nodded firmly. If I was going to take responsibility for this cat, I was going to do it all the way. Go big or go home, you know? I'd told Finn as much during our shopping trip and while it would probably be smart to let him help me smuggle Oliver out of my apartment, I needed to do this on my own.

Finn just held up both hands, clearly resigned to his offer being cast aside. "Alright. You know where to find me tomorrow though if you change your mind."

"That I do. Thanks, though. I really appreciate your help. I probably would still be at the store right now huffing into one of those treat bags because of a nervous breakdown."

"Oh, come on," he laughed. "You're doing just fine. Why don't you stop over when you're done at the vet, let me know how everything went, and then we can go from there."

Suddenly, I didn't mind his presence in my apartment so much anymore.

"That sounds like a plan."

Finn gestured with his head towards my front door and I followed his lead, trailing after him until we stood at the threshold between my door and the hallway.

"Well, this is where I leave you," he exhaled dramatically and put a hand on my shoulder. "I've taught you everything I know, so I think you can take it from here, Emma."

"Wow," I rolled my eyes up to the ceiling. Through the light material of my T-shirt, my skin felt on fire underneath his light touch. "I'm sure I'll be alright."

It didn't help, of course, that Finn's eyes dropped to my lips for just a split second and he lingered a moment too long. With that, he snatched his hand from my shoulder like he was the one who'd been burned and slapped that hand against the door on his way out.

"Night, neighbor," he called out to me and waved over his shoulder as I shut the door behind him.

Now I had a new problem on my hands. I was grateful for the space, appreciative that he'd sensed my need for a little independence here, and looking forward to finally letting the cat in my apartment, but now...I sort of wanted Finn here, too.

Pushing that terrifying thought aside, I settled on the matter at hand and shuffled around the shopping bags until I stood right in front of the heavy patio door. Oliver's little head peeked over the side of his chair and then he hopped down onto the cement, probably expecting some food.

Man, was he in for a surprise.

My heart drummed in my chest, thundering hard, staccato beats and my teeth sawed across my bottom lip as I reached for the door handle. This was it. No going back now.

With a deep breath, I pulled the heavy door open and my fingers nimbly closed around the handle for the screen door. At this point, the cat was on to me and he sat back on his haunches, patiently waiting for me to make my move. But when I finally pulled open the screen door, he just stared back at me.

Maahwr.

Are you serious? Is this for real?

"Oh yeah, Oliver," I told him, smiling down at him and gesturing one last time inside. "Time for you to move in."

Meh.

He didn't need anymore convincing as he glanced up at me one more time and then trotted inside, taking his time to cover the length of my living room carpet to get acquainted. I trailed after him, following his lead, as he went right for the shopping bags, rubbing up against them and dipping his head inside the one that held his treats.

"Of course," I laughed. "How did I know that was the one you'd find first? You know what? I should probably get your litter box ready. This should be interesting, huh?"

He sat back, watching me carefully while I sifted through the larger bags for the plastic litter box and grabbed the huge tub of litter Finn had lugged inside the apartment for me.

"So, I'm going to go set up your litter box. Wanna come with me?"

Maawhr.

"Okay, then. Let's go," I waved him down the hallway and he padded after me all the way into the bathroom.

Luckily, I had a big enough space that there was room for the whole thing, even though I was going into this blind. As Oliver sat patiently waiting, I got down to the business of getting his litter box ready, trying my best to follow Finn's instructions to the T: lay down the mats first, litter box against the wall, put the liner in for easy clean-up, a little bit of that freshening sprinkle he'd told me to buy, and then I poured the tiny little pebbles into the plastic pan. I stepped back to survey my work, satisfied with my first effort at litter box prep, but Oliver didn't waste any time marking his territory and was already right smack in the middle of it, pissing away like he owned the place.

In fact, he even had the nerve to glare up at me as if to say, *A little privacy please...come on!*

I held up both hands, wincing sheepishly and tip-toed out of the bathroom to give him his private time. This was going to be a challenge with his litter box there. Between that strong ammonia smell, the way he already sprinkled litter everywhere the second he jumped out of the box, I already had a mess on my hands.

Oh well. Like Finn had said, there really wasn't a better place to put it that would contain the shit and contain anything that might affect my allergies. Whatever I had to do to keep that problem at bay...which reminded me...

"Shit," I muttered under my breath. "Goddammit. I can't believe I forgot."

I marched right into the kitchen and popped a 24-hour allergy pill. That was probably the only way I would ever survive this, so even if I had to pop one of those little white pills every day, that was what I was going to do.

Since I was already in the kitchen, I got to work unpacking all of Oliver's new things, set up his fancy ceramic food and water dish with the cartoon cats on it, put away all his treats in a cabinet, and tucked everything else away underneath my sink to keep it all hidden as much as possible. Oliver, again, waited patiently.

"Should we put your collar on?"

Meh.

I grinned back at him and held out the collar, a thin, structured tan band with plaid squares of brown, blue, and orange. Very manly.

"Finn said this was a fancy-boy collar," I told Oliver, who'd moved a little closer to me now at the sound of my voice. "I like it. I think it's you. A fancy new collar for a not-so-fancy life, huh?"

I held the collar out to him and his hind legs hit the floor right in front of me. With quick movements, I snapped his new collar around his neck and straightened it just enough so the little bell sat right at the center of his white chest. It all felt very official and final. He was mine now and from a certain point of view, I was his now, too.

You know what they say, Finn had told me at the pet store as I'd perused the toy aisle, *you don't own the cat, they own you.*

It was only our first night in this thing, but it looked like that he wasn't too far off with that particular sentiment.

"So," I told him with my hands on my hips. "What should we do now? You wanna watch something on Netflix?"

Meh.

I took that as a yes and plopped down on my couch, reaching for my remote and nearly jumped out of my skin when Oliver leapt up over the side, landing right on my stomach. He circled around a few times—I guess I shouldn't have been surprised seeing as how we'd done this dance before—until he found a good spot and settled into the fabric of my T-shirt, nuzzling my arm until my hand started stroking his soft fur.

It was probably a few hours later when I jerked awake with a random episode of *Orange Is The New Black* playing on my TV. Oliver cocked one eye open at me from his little nest on my stomach and yawned, stretching one tiny white paw up until it gently tapped my cheek. I slid up against the couch, prompting the cat to scoot off my stomach and jump over the side.

As I moved down the hallway towards my bedroom, I glanced over my shoulder to find Oliver crouched down over his water dish and figured that was probably as good a time as any to get ready for bed. But when I stepped out of the bathroom, I stopped short to see Oliver lying down right in the middle of the hallway, waiting for me.

"Hey," I murmured.

Meh.

"I'm gonna go to bed now, okay?"

Meh.

I chewed on my bottom lip. I didn't really know what I was supposed to do here. Did I run into my bedroom and slam the door in his face? Did I let him in and risk waking up a sniffly, snotty, stuffed-up mess?

What if he didn't even *want* to sleep by me? That was probably the worst option of all and I knew just how pathetic *that* was.

Finally, I chose not to decide. That was still a choice, right?

I left my door open, opting to let him do whatever he wanted to do and see where that landed. And as I climbed into my bed, it took about 30 seconds for a tiny grey and black striped cat to jump up onto the bed, step around my limbs and all my pillows, and finally settle right against my stomach, purring away as I stroked his fur.

"I think I might love you," I whispered to him in the darkness. "Night, Oliver."

Meh.

CHAPTER NINE

"Goddammit, Oliver," I grunted, pushing both hands into his little body in a vain attempt at shoving him in the plastic carrier. "Get. In. There. Now."

He had both front paws planted on the sides of the carrier's mouth as I struggled—sweating and everything—to get his furry ass inside. Well, wasn't this just a marvelous failure. This was pretty much what my morning had consisted of: chasing after a cat, not to mention being woken up at 4:00 in the morning by a pair of sharp claws kneading into my shoulder and Oliver meowing in my face.

I pressed on his butt to push him in the carrier, but his super-feline powers of strength held out until he managed to flip himself away from the mouth of the carrier, vaulting in the air and using my bare arms as his launch pad.

"Ow! God!"

Both my arms now had angry crimson claw marks running up the sides and I cringed at the sting. There was no time to be a baby. I had a cat to wrangle.

Unfortunately, that little reprieve had given Oliver ample time to scamper down the hallway so he could throw himself under my bed. Right in the middle. Just out of my reach. At least he wasn't hissing at me or anything...the scratching I might be able to live with. Hissing, not so much.

Now, I found myself on my stomach with half my body lodged underneath my bed, trying and failing to coax my cat out from under it.

"Come on, buddy," I pleaded. "We have to go. We're gonna be so late."

I'd totally underestimated how long it would take to actually shove the little guy in that equally tiny carrier. Finn hadn't mentioned that getting cats inside those crates was a next to impossible feat. He'd probably conveniently left that part out...all the better to torture me with. What a jerk.

Finally, my last resort was sticking a broom under my bed to literally force Oliver out the other side. Then I had to chase after him yet again when he made a beeline for the hallway, not that I could really blame him. I'd probably run for my life, too, if some crazy lady was trying to shove me into a cage.

Now, I set the plastic carrier on top of my bed with Oliver squirming under my arm.

"I'm going to get you in this stupid thing if it's the last thing I do, cat," I told him firmly, dead set with resolve.

His sea foam-grey eyes widened in panic. *Maawhr. Don't even think about it, you bitch!*

With the carrier lying flat on my bed, I switched up tactics, holding the edge of the carrier with one hand as I simultaneously shoved the cat in head-first and slid the carrier towards the edge of the bed. Oliver was defenseless against the trick, outdone on all sides, and helplessly skidded right inside the carrier until he'd cleared it enough that I could snap the metal door closed.

"Ha!" I pointed in his caged face. "Take that, sucka! In your face! I win!"

Oliver stared up at me from the edge of the bed, his eyes round and devastated as if to say, *How could you do this to me? I thought we were cool.*

"I'm sorry," I whispered quickly. "I didn't mean it. Okay, maybe I did, but I'm still sorry. We really do have to get going though."

Which reminded me...how in the hell was I going to smuggle him out of my apartment and into my car? If the wrong person, like my landlord for instance, happened to walk by at the wrong moment, they'd see everything and I'd sink before I even had a chance to really swim. Taking him through the hallway was a bad idea, too. While Finn wouldn't care if he heard some suspicious animal sounds coming from outside his door, Mrs. Johannsen and the couple that lived right in front of Finn's apartment or anyone who lived upstairs might. I definitely didn't know Mrs. Johannsen well enough to expect her to turn a blind eye and right about now, I really wished I wasn't such a hermit and had actually made an effort to at least be neighborly towards her.

Any way you looked at it, I'd sort of screwed myself.

So, with a deep breath in a fruitless attempt at calming my thundering heart, I wrapped Oliver's carrier in a blanket—that wasn't at all suspicious, right?—and stepped out onto my patio.

As the opening trill of the *Mission: Impossible* theme played in my head and that syncopated, disjointed two-bar riff took off, I tip-toed around the corner of my building with the blanketed cat carrier tucked underneath my arm. I heard one painful *maawhr* and then a high-pitched yelp, like Oliver was in actual physical duress just being in that stupid carrier.

"Knock it off, you big baby," I murmured harshly down to the large, not-so-inconspicuous rectangular box in my hands.

I rounded the front corner, my eyes frantically scanning the near-empty parking lot for tell-tale signs of life. Luckily enough, I'd had the foresight to make the appointment after I knew everyone who lived around me would have already left for work. Practically sprinting to my car, I skidded to a stop as one hand reached for the passenger door handle on my beat-up Corolla and the other haphazardly balanced Oliver, er, I mean the box, against my hip. Once the *box* was secured, I jogged around the front of my car, hopped inside, and got us the hell out of there before we got caught.

And of course, the entire ride over to the vet, my cat treated me to the most horrific sounds I'd ever heard in my entire life.

Maawhr. Maooow. Miaaaooow.

Oh my God, he was *howling*.

Howling, I tell you.

"I'm so sorry," I murmured to him when we finally pulled into the vet's parking lot. "We're there, buddy. Geez...I don't know who that was worse for—me or you."

Oliver glared back at me from his tiny cage to say, *You really wanna go there right now, lady?*

"I'm sorry. I'm sorry. I'm sorry," I murmured down to him again as I pushed through the clinic's double doors and hurried to the front desk.

The receptionist sitting there looked a little too much like that crazy clown lady from *The Drew Carey Show* with her heavy-handed bronze eyeshadow and sky-high hair that had been tortured and teased with hairspray fumes. I sneezed right when I sidled up to the desk, but I couldn't really be sure if it was due to animal dander or a natural reaction to the sticky hairspray stench.

"Hello!" the lady greeted me brightly as she stood up from her chair to peer over the side of the desk with her hands clasped in front of her. "And who is this handsome little man?"

"This," I gestured down to the carrier in my hand, "is Oliver."

"Oh, hello Oliver!" the lady cooed down to him.

All she got was silence. Oliver, it seemed, wasn't having it.

"So, you're Oliver's mom then, I take it?" the lady looked to me now for confirmation.

My heart seized. I swallowed hard, glanced down at the cat in the carrier, who'd somehow wormed his way into my life and in the process, thawed out a piece of myself I'd thought would sit in ice forever, and nodded.

"Yeah," I smiled back. "I guess I am."

.   .   .

As luck would have it, smuggling Oliver back into my apartment was way easier than smuggling him out of it. Of course, it probably had something to do with the fact that once I had the cat, I mean, the *box*, tucked underneath my arm and took off for the side of my building, I couldn't see anything but brick and the tree line.

Out of sight, out of mind, right?

Just as I'd jostled the blanketed box against my hip, much to Oliver's vocal dismay, Finn appeared from around his side of our shared wall with eyebrows raised and a wide, goofy smile on his face.

"How did it go?" he asked, quickly jumping in front of me to slide my patio door open so I could step through.

"Well," I exhaled, relieved that it was over and more than happy to finally be back in the safety of my apartment. "Oliver's got an ear infection in both ears, so the vet gave me some drops for that and apparently, he probably has worms, too. And...he has to get his balls chopped off next week, so there's that."

Finn winced and bent down to get a glimpse of the cat before I let him out. "Sorry to hear that, contraband. Well, it could've been worse, that's for sure."

"The vet said all that was pretty normal for strays, so I guess it's not so bad," I sighed and reached down to release the metal clamp on the carrier's door to let Oliver out.

As he scampered onto the carpet, it took me a moment to realize what had Finn's shoulders shaking with laughter. That little shit's hind legs were completely soaked...

"Oh, no!" I groaned and squeezed my eyes shut. "You pissed in your carrier! Oliver, you rat bastard!"

Oliver glanced over his shoulder at me as he took off down the hallway, shooting daggers at me to say, *This is what happens when you shove me in a cage, you heartless bitch.*

"He is *not* happy with you," Finn mused. One hand rubbed across his mouth, but that didn't do much in the way of masking his obvious

99

amusement over this little hiccup.

"You think?" I laughed. "Between the shots, getting poked and prodded, and shoved in a car, I guess I'd be pissed at me, too."

"Yeah, but he gets to go home to his new apartment now, so I'm pretty sure he'll get over it."

"Right," I shook my head and then headed down the hallway to catch that little butthead before he dripped piss all over the carpet. "When should we get that pizza?"

Even while wrangling a piss-soaked cat, I apparently couldn't go another minute without making sure Finn hadn't forgotten about our vague pizza plans.

"It kinda looks like you've got your hands full right now," he laughed heartily, watching with a little too much levity for my taste as I gripped Oliver underneath his shoulder blades and held him out in front of me at arm's length to keep that wetness as far away from me as possible. "Besides, it's pretty early for pizza anyway. Why don't I come back in a couple hours...around noon?"

At this point, I already had the pissface back in the kitchen and rummaged around for the waterless shampoo. "Yeah, that sounds good."

When I turned around, Finn was holding Oliver up in the air in between his shoulder blades, mimicking the way I'd carried him from the hallway, and gestured with his head towards the cat in his hands.

"Go for it," Finn nodded to me. "Hurry up before the little RB starts fighting me."

I laughed, even as I got to work spraying Oliver's butt with the waterless shampoo and wiping him down with a towel as fast as I could. "RB?"

"Yeah, rat bastard."

"Oh God," I just shook my head.

"You started it."

"Oh boy," I murmured as I toweled the cat off, rubbing him down as best I could. "Good call on this shampoo, by the way."

Finn just shrugged, flipping Oliver around so I could get at his stomach. "That's what I'm here for."

Once the cat was back on solid ground, twitching his hind legs to shake out the leftover moisture, Oliver glanced up at both of us with malice in his sea foam-grey eyes and the side of his lips curled up in a snarl. *Maawhr.*

"I think he just called me an asshole," Finn mused.

Yep. That was my cat.

* * *

. . .

I sighed heavily and took a step back, surveying the contents of my tiny closet once more. It felt like I'd been standing here, staring at this space for the last few hours, and still came up empty.

"I've got a closet full of clothes and nothing to wear," I muttered under my breath. "Figures."

Feeling soft fur brush against my bare leg, I glanced down to find Oliver standing at my feet, staring up at me with an exasperated expression as if to say, *Just make up your damn mind already.*

To add insult to injury, he curled his lips back and let out one of those patent, snippy little mews I'd quickly become familiar with to show me just how annoyed he was with my current state.

"Oh, shut it, Oliver," I batted a hand down at him and turned my attention back to my closet. "You're not helping, you know."

He responded by simply lifting his two front paws up to my shin, stretching himself up until I finally relented, dipping down to give him what he wanted. When I scooped him up, nestling him in my arms, he nuzzled his cheek into the side of my face to show his appreciation.

"Love you too, buddy," I murmured and kissed the top of his furry head.

There. I'd kissed a cat. It had only been a few hours since Finn retreated back to his apartment, but already, I couldn't remember a time when I *didn't* have this cat in my life. Where I didn't have his little soft mews and purrumbles adding music to my life. I didn't even feel moderately pathetic about that either.

With another fruitless glance into my closet, I started my inevitable retreat back into my bedroom and sank down on the mattress with Oliver still snuggling in my arms. When my eyes landed on my closet yet again, my gaze lifted to the cracked ceiling and I groaned, running my free hand over my face.

This was so stupid. Talk about making a big deal out of nothing...God, I was totally blowing this way out of proportion. It was just pizza. Finn was just my neighbor. When my anxious eyes fell to the digital clock on the nightstand, I practically leapt off the bed, sending Oliver flying towards the opposite side of the mattress, snippy little mews and all.

It was 11:30. Which meant I had exactly 30 minutes until Finn came over to my apartment for pizza.

"Stupid, stupid, stupid," I murmured under my breath.

The first morning I'd had off in a long time had mostly been spent furiously scrubbing my apartment from top to bottom. Some kind of demonic fervor had taken hold and I just couldn't stop compulsively cleaning and vacuuming every inch of space, like Finn hadn't literally been in my apartment just a couple hours before and already seen it for the disaster it was. Hell, I'd even rearranged the furniture in my living room, too, with Oliver looking on in confusion like, *What is with you, lady?*

If I wasn't embarrassed with my nervous antics before, that moment was definitely the tipping point.

Now, with time ticking steadily away, I reached for my phone and hit the speed dial. Unfortunately, if I even had a prayer of getting my shit together in time before Finn showed up, I needed to call in some reinforcements.

Before I had a chance to change my mind, that familiar voice with its soft Latina lilt sang into the phone: "Well, hola, Tia Emmie. I was wonderin' if I'd hear from you this week. How you been? Wait a minute, wait a minute...it's Friday. What time is it? Oh shit, you're not working today? Really? Finally?"

I rolled my eyes at the greeting; as usual, my sister-in-law talked so fast I'd be lucky to get two words in before Cristina sniffed out the real reason I'd called.

"Hey, Cris," I laughed and shook my head. "Wow. Yes, it's Friday. How are you feeling?"

"Oh, you know, like a fat whale, but I'm just trying to enjoy it and get as much as sleep as I can. How's that little kitty doing? I can't wait to finally meet him. You're gonna send me some pictures, right?"

"I will," I laughed again. I'd missed this...we used to talk all the time, but, in my self-imposed exile, I'd put distance between us, just like I did with Noah. Now, I was starting to see just how unnecessary that distance was. "Look, I don't have a ton of time to talk; actually, I have like 10 minutes tops——"

"You okay, Em?" Cristina cut in abruptly. "You sound weird. And nervous. What's goin' on?"

"Wow," I huffed out another laugh. "Gimme a second, okay? Alright. So, I'm having...."

Oh shit. How did I explain this?

"Having....? What? A heart attack? An aneurysm? Oh God, are you pregnant? What's goin' on with you, Em?"

"Jesus, settle down, Cris. I'm fine. Okay? I'm fine," I blew out a deep breath and decided to just come out with it. "I'm sort of having a guy—a friend—over in about, crap, 20 minutes and I need you to tell me what to wear."

There was a long pause from the other end of the line and finally, Cristina let out a clipped, albeit relieved, chuckle.

"Oh, thank God," she sighed.

Here it comes, I thought ruefully, *the Puerto Rican Inquisition.*

"Okay," Cris pressed on. "So, lemme get this straight: this guy—sorry, *friend*—is coming over to your apartment. Who is this guy? Where did you meet him? Why haven't I heard about him before? Why didn't you tell me you were seein' somebody?"

"Sorry, Cris," I shrugged, even though I knew she couldn't see me. "Don't really have time for that right this second, but I promise I'll call you tomorrow and give you the details, okay?"

Okay, so maybe I'd stall for as long as I could on that last part, but she didn't need to know that right now.

"Fine. So, where is this mystery *friend* takin' you, hmm?"

Seeing as how that seemed to appease her for the time being, I pressed on. "He's coming over to my apartment. It's just pizza."

"What do you mean it's just—you know what? Never mind. Okay. So is this your first date?"

"It's not a date, Cris," I cut in a little too sharply. "He's my neighbor."

"*Sure,*" Cristina chuckled over the line. "Keep telling yourself that. This neighbor obviously knows a good thing when he sees it. Anyway, just wear something comfortable. A nice, tight pair of jeans. Show off your assets without giving away too much, ya know? And I think you should wear that long black tank top, you know the one with that stitching on the front pocket? And that silver necklace we gave you for Christmas last year. You'll look put together, but not dressed up, ya know?"

Mentally clicking the outfit into place, I nodded into the phone. "Yeah, you're right. I think that'll work."

God, that was easy. Way too easy. I'd spent too much time wringing my hands over something my no-nonsense sister-in-law had solved in half a second. If anything, this whole debacle just shined a nasty light on how rusty I was about all this.

The last time I'd 'hung out' with a guy I just met was seven years ago. Only that time I'd invited, unbeknownst to me, the asshole who would eventually set my life on fire. If only I knew then what I knew now, I would've slammed the door right in his face or maybe pawned him off on my psycho roommate. In retrospect, they would've been absolutely perfect for each other.

"Look, Em," Cristina was saying now, her voice losing the playful edge from before and now, seeped with a sincerity that scared me a little. "You don't have to tell me anything you don't wanna tell me about this...*friend*. I know you'll tell me when you're ready to give me some dirt, but just have a good time today, alright? Have some freaking *fun*. Let loose and just enjoy it. You deserve it."

At this point, I didn't know whether to laugh or cry. If anything, this was all one big, fat reminder of the current status of my life, where one guy—scratch that, one *friend*—taking pity on me and actually wanting to hang out with me was an event with a capital E, where I stood in front of my closet for more time than I was willing to admit, where I stressed over something as simple as a stupid outfit. This was the state of my life now and maybe it was about time I made peace with it.

"Okay," I replied finally, trying to infuse as much confidence into my voice as possible, even if I didn't really feel it. "I will. You're right. This is my first full day off in a really long time and you're right—I need to have some fun for once."

"So, go out, have fun, and don't worry about anything else, okay?"

"Yeah, I will, Cris," I told her, this time feeling the confidence I'd attempted to feign before. "Can you do me a favor and just...don't say anything about this to Noah?"

The short pause on the other end had me jumping into damage control.

"I just know exactly what's going to happen if you turn around and tell him that I'm seeing my neighbor today. He's gonna be blowing up my phone every hour on the hour, hell, probably every *half* hour, and that's exactly the kinda thing that's gonna ruin my day, Cris."

The reality was that I just wanted to keep whatever this was with Finn untainted for as long as I possibly could.

Cristina sighed like she could hear my thoughts and blew out a deep breath. "Alright. Whatever you want, Em. I won't say a word unless you tell me to."

"I just don't wanna make a bigger deal out of this than I already am, okay?"

"Alright, I hear ya. Oh, you don't have much time now. You'd better get going, but just tell me one thing..." Cristina's voice dropped into a half-whisper. "On a scale of 1 to 10, 1 being butt-ass fugly and 10 being Calvin Klein underwear model hot...how hot is he?"

I barked out a quick laugh, but when I glanced at the digital clock on my nightstand one more time, my eyes widened. Time to wrap this shit up and get on it with already.

"Uh," I laughed into the phone and shook my head, shimmying into a pair of tight jeans as I spoke. How did I even begin to classify the unassuming masculinity Finn exuded, that sexy, but shy crooked grin, the way he could make me feel safe yet frazzled all at the same time, the way he tugged a hand through his unkempt russet-colored hair and shoved both hands in his pockets when he got nervous, the way his whole face seemed to light up every time I took a step towards him...

So, I went with the easy answer: "I'd say he's a 12."

"Shit!" Cristina howled from the other end. "Well, when you put it like that, maybe we need to rethink our definition of *fun*, huh?"

"I wouldn't go that..." the sudden knock on my front door gave me such a jolt I nearly dropped the phone. "Oh shit! Cris, he's here. What...he's 10 minutes early! And I'm standing here in skinny jeans and my bra! Shit!"

"I don't know," Cristina laughed. "Maybe that'd be a good way to break the ice, ya know? Maybe you should—"

"Can it, Cris. I'll call you later, okay? Bye!" I didn't even give my sister-in-law the opportunity to respond and promptly swiped across the screen to end the call, tossing my phone haphazardly on the bed to turn back to my closet.

After frantically attacking my closet in search of the black tank top Cristina had instructed me to wear, I tugged it over my head, cast a quick glance in the mirror to tame my long waves and tousle my bangs, and practically tripped over my feet all the way from my closet to the front door.

By the time I threw the door open, I was out of breath, my nerves a tangled mess at my feet. And now, met with smiling sky-blue eyes and a devastatingly crooked smile, my heart melted into a puddle right next to my knotted nerves.

"Hey, Em," Finn greeted me, that grin curving up both sides of his lips now and all rational thought left the building. How the hell was I supposed to get a handle on this when all it took was one look, one smile and I was a sputtering, frazzled mess?

"Hi, Finn," I finally replied, wincing a little as soon as the words left my mouth at how breathless I sounded.

We stood in my threshold like that for a few moments, with Finn lingering near the hallway, waiting to be invited in and my fingers gripping the edge of the front door because once my brain short-circuited, I didn't know what else to do.

When I felt the tell-tale light brush of fur against my jeans, I couldn't have been more grateful that my cat seemed to be overly curious about what was happening. In fact, he was already heading right towards Finn with those little purrumbles like he was saying, *Oh hey. I remember you.*

It was the excuse I needed to break this spell and that sent me rushing forward to scoop Oliver up in my arms before he could venture out into the doorway much further.

"Careful there, you little RB," I murmured and then looked up to find Finn watching the two of us with a bemused grin sliding up his lips.

"You look nice," he told me, gesturing to the outfit he didn't need to know I'd inappropriately agonized over.

"Thanks," I grinned.

I was painfully aware of how overeager I sounded right now, but there wasn't much I could do about it. The Browning Adonis had arrived. All mental functioning was shot now.

He just winked back at me and as he took a few unsteady steps to the middle of my kitchen, I found myself running an anxious hand through my hair, watching Finn survey my little cardboard box of an apartment.

"So you cleaned up a little, huh?" he cast me a knowing glance from over his shoulder.

"Don't worry," I shook my head, gesturing into the open air between us. "This isn't for you. You saw this place before. It looked like a tornado ripped through here."

"Nah," he just batted a hand. "It wasn't that bad. You've obviously never seen my place after a game day."

I could only imagine...and then I realized I still wasn't completely ready. Ugh. This was just pizza. That was it. And here I was, over-analyzing and freaking out over nothing more than a shared pizza between neighbors.

"Um, I just, uh...still need a few minutes," I told him sheepishly, already feeling a slight flush creep across my cheeks in embarrassment. "I was on the phone with my sister-in-law before and I wasn't—"

"I know," Finn cut in with that sexy, sly grin that threatened to buckle my knees. "I'm early. Sorry about that. I just...well, I guess I just didn't wanna wait another 10 minutes, you know?"

And with those words, all the doubt lingering over what this was, my own hang-ups, Finn's intentions...everything...it all just slipped away.

"So, take your time," Finn went on, leaning an arm against the dividing wall between my kitchen and my living room. "I can wait."

There was something about the way one side of his lips rolled into a soft curl that told me those words might have a deeper meaning. If I stood there for too long, I had a sinking feeling I might do or say something I'd kick myself for later, so I gladly took the out he'd given me and retreated to the bathroom to put the finishing touches on my hair and my makeup.

Now, as I stood in front of the mirror with a tube of mascara in my hand and Finn Matthews waiting in my kitchen, I couldn't help but feel like a complete idiot. There was a kind, generous, patient, funny, and devastatingly handsome man in my apartment and here I was, locked in the bathroom because I didn't know what else to do. Because I was nervous. Because I was scared.

This was beyond stupid.

Laughing to myself, I swiped another layer of mascara on, passed a brush through my long, caramel-colored waves, tousled my bangs, spritzed a dab of perfume on just for good measure, and took one more glance in the mirror. There was a man out there I wanted to spend time with and I was just getting in my own way. Cristina's words of encouragement echoed in my ears, but it was more than just that.

In spite of the short time I'd known him, and in spite of the sudden frenzied feelings of chaos he inspired in me, there was also an inexplicable aura of calm around him, too. Acceptance, even. Like nothing I'd done before meeting him, no place I'd been, and no ugly, pain-leaden past following me from Hickory really mattered all that much to him.

I could do and say anything in front of him, embarrass or lay myself bare, and he wouldn't care. It was as if the past didn't exist and with him, there was only now. It was as if he'd judged me from the moment we met, but hadn't found me wanting...hadn't tried to push me into anything I wasn't ready for. He'd given me space, followed my lead, but shown me a different path at the same time. A new possibility. A new chance.

There was a safety in Finn Matthews's presence I never thought I'd ever feel again.

It was liberation. It was a rediscovery. It was a door opening. It was that elusive second chance I'd been chasing since the moment I left my hometown without looking back. It was the possibility, the real, honest-to-goodness possibility, that everything might be okay now.

I glanced back at my reflection again and shook my head, a mirthless laugh escaping my lips. Turning this into something it wasn't would only end up hurting myself in the long run. And while the idea that redemption, forgiveness, and second chances were irrevocably intertwined with a man, especially a man I barely knew, flew directly in the face of being the independent woman I'd once prided myself on being, maybe that was something I could live with.

That last thought was enough to propel me from the bathroom and back towards my poor excuse for a living room and I found Finn leaning against the wall with Oliver tucked under his arm and his free hand scratching underneath my cat's chin.

Something clicked into place for me then and the time for second-guessing and overanalyzing was over. My feet padded over to him and the sight of that bright smile curling into his handsome face, the smile that was all for me, only spurred me towards him. Just as he pushed off the wall and turned to face me, my hands slid over both his cheeks to bring in him closer and then I pressed my lips against his mouth.

It only lasted for a moment, but when I pulled back, Oliver abruptly dropped to the carpet. Finn's lips curved and his free arm snaked around my waist to pull me in as close to his chest as possible as his head dipped lower to capture my lips.

This time he didn't let me pull back so easily. This time his lips parted, sealing his mouth over mine, taking the control and pressing me even deeper into his chest. My hands trailed down his cheeks to his neck, finally resting over the hard, sinewy muscles over his worn T-shirt.

His lips continued their ministrations and my feet lifted up onto my toes, Finn pulling me along with him as he leaned back. Then, he settled me back onto my feet, placing sweet, feather-light kisses against my lips and the hand around my waist drifted a little further down, curving down the side of my hip.

That was a little more than I felt ready for and when I pulled back just enough, Finn didn't miss a beat, sliding his hand back up to its original resting place.

"Sorry," he murmured against my lips.

I laughed and he quickly caught it with his mouth.

"It's okay," I managed to get out in between kisses with another laugh.

There was something about how careful he was being with me that told me pulling back and pumping the brakes was absolutely fine with him. No pressure and no need to rush something that just felt so *good*.

Finn's rough fingers squeezed my shoulders and I shivered a little under the light touch. His lips brushed my forehead, moving to the side of my head.

"Damn, you smell good," he murmured. His nose dipped into my neck, running along my skin and sending another round of shivers ricocheting down my body. Almost as suddenly, his head lifted and he leaned away, taking a full step behind him to literally hold me at arm's length.

"Sorry, Em," Finn exhaled. A beat later, he leaned forward again to kiss me, pulling me right back against him and catching my laugh yet again with his mouth.

My hands skimmed over his shoulders and around his back, reveling in the feel of him under my touch and Finn abruptly pulled his mouth away to rest our foreheads together.

"Sorry," he muttered. "I guess I just can't help myself."

"You don't have to stop, you know," I told him.

Finn blew out a deep, tortured breath and lifted the hand from my shoulder up to my cheek. "No, I really do. Trust me. I mean, I just got here, you know? Our date hasn't even really started and here I am, mauling you up against a wall. That's not really how I saw this playing out today, Em."

Everything he'd just said swum around in my brain as I tried to pin down one thing to focus on. It was all just so...*sweet.* Finally, I found something to zero in on.

"So," I cocked a playful eyebrow at him as I wrapped an arm around his neck. "This is a date, huh?"

He frowned down at me. "What did you think this was?"

"I don't know," I shrugged. "I thought we were...hanging out?"

Finn's eyebrows rose. "Hanging out? No. I'm sorry if you're confused, Em, but lemme clear this up for you. This," he gestured between us as he spoke, "is a date."

"Oh," I leaned forward to peck him on the lips and it felt like we'd been doing this forever. "Okay. Thanks for clearing that up. Should we still order that pizza?"

A wide grin spread across his face as his eyes shone down at me. "Absolutely, Em. We've got all the time in the world today, don't we?"

CHAPTER TEN

"So we're all in the tap room," Finn told me in between bites. "It's my buddy Chase's five-year anniversary with his company and all our friends, his boss, and his co-workers are there. And I guess, before I get too into the story, you should probably know that Sling's got this inferiority complex when it comes to being around people who've got a college degree and a successful career."

I laughed, grinning back at him from my spot on the couch. "Right. College isn't for everyone."

"It's hard to put my finger on, but he wasn't exactly a straight-A kinda kid in school, you know? I mean, I definitely wasn't either, but Sling *really* had a hard time even sliding through with Ds. I think the only reason he graduated was because Coach would quiz him on the ride home from away games and made him come in after school during the off-season."

"Sounds like your coach was a good teacher, too," I smiled wistfully.

What I didn't say was that it also sounded like Slinger was someone who might have an undiagnosed learning disability...possibly. Sharing that suspicion would once again throw me into the deep end of the pool and sooner or later, I wouldn't be able to float through on Finn's politeness alone.

"Yeah, he was the best," Finn affirmed, none the wiser that I'd just drifted off into that dark territory. "So, everybody's there and things are starting to go downhill once the beer taps start free-flowing. Sling is just blitzed out of his mind, and I don't know how he even made it over to the other side of the bar without falling on his face, but he marches right over to Chase's boss, completely unprovoked. Picture the most polished, regal, stick-thin, polite as shit, blonde business woman you can imagine and that's Chase's boss. The head of the company and everything."

I covered my mouth as my shoulders shook with laughter. This was not going to end well.

"So, Sling marches right up to her, jabs his finger right in her face and says, 'I bet you think I work at Wal-Mart, don't you?'"

My shoulders were still shaking as I leaned back against the couch, just enjoying being here like this with him, in my apartment, listening to him talk. "Oh no…"

Finn just shook his head, that sly grin playing on his lips as he leaned forward to grab his beer from the coffee table. "That poor woman…she didn't know what hit her. She's just standing there, completely in shock, and she's saying, 'Sir, I'm sorry. I don't know what you're talking about. Why would I think you work at Wal-Mart?' At that point, I've got Sling around the shoulders, I'm pulling him back, and Chase is just white as a sheet, absolutely mortified, and he's waving his hands at his boss going, 'I swear to God, I don't know that guy!'"

I had to cover my mouth yet again, laughter shaking my entire body, and I shook my head as the whole scene flashed through my mind. "Poor Slinger. I barely know him, but I feel so bad for him."

He scoffed and batted a hand at me. "Trust me, he brings a lot of it on himself. And he's not exactly short on, uh, female company, if you know what I mean. Whatever he lacked in high school, he's more than made up for since."

"I can picture exactly what you guys were like…" I started, fumbling for the words as I realized I was about to tell him something I'd never intended on revealing, at least not yet. "You know, I probably had at least a hundred students just like you two."

Finn's head snapped towards me, shock and surprise flickering across his face. Now he would have questions and I already knew where those questions would lead. Just great. I'd opened up the floodgates now. No going back…

"You were a teacher?"

Were. Past tense. Hearing it out loud hurt a little more than I expected.

"Yeah," I nodded weakly. "I was."

His brow creased in thought and I could practically see the wheels turning in his head, trying to put it all together without overstepping.

Yeah, I thought ruefully, *good luck with that, Finn.*

"So…" he hesitated, chewing on the inside of his cheek and I waited for the inevitable question I just wasn't ready to answer yet. *Why aren't you teaching anymore?*

"What did you teach?"

The deflection had me moving closer to him now, and out of sheer gratitude, I kissed him. I pulled away just as quickly, just needing to thank him, and the soft grin that curved up his mouth told me he understood.

"I used to teach social studies."

Used to. Talking about it in past tense was worse than hearing it said out loud.

Finn's eyebrows flew up into his forehead at the admission. "Social studies? Like history?"

"Yeah, like history. Well, actually, I was teaching civics and U.S. history if you wanna get all technical about it."

"Huh. I gotta say...that's not really what I would've expected."

"What's that supposed to mean?" I laughed, swatting him on the shoulder.

"I don't know," he chuckled and ducked when I wound up one more time to hit him. "I guess I just would have figured you'd teach music or art or English or something like that. You know, all the classes I never took or paid attention to. Actually, I can't say I really paid much attention in history class either."

"Too boring?"

He smirked. "Yeah. I paid a little more attention in math and science class, which definitely paid off for me in the long run."

"Trust me, I hear that all the time...well, *heard*, I guess."

I had to look down at my hands on my lap, momentarily overwhelmed by the depth of my failures and shortcomings and humiliations and all the things I just couldn't tell him.

"But," his strong, deep voice jerked me right out of my negativity. "I gotta say, Em, if I'd had a history teacher that looked like you...let's just say I would've paid a helluva lot more attention, you know?"

I knew that comment was supposed to distract me and take my mind off the painful memories, but all it really did was sting. He had no way of knowing, of course, what he was really saying, what that really meant in the grand, epic failure that was my life and the end of my teaching career, that encompassed all the reasons I just couldn't let myself do much more than kiss him.

How could he? I hadn't told him anything.

He must have sensed there was something very wrong with what he'd said, so he gestured with his head towards the bookshelf leaning next to my TV.

"I take it that's why you've got all those books?"

Finn pushed off the couch and ambled over to the bookshelf until he peered down at the titles. Following his lead, I rose from the couch and padded across the living room, stopping right next to him.

"Team of Rivals. People's History of the United States. Killing Kennedy. 1776. Unbroken. Diary of a Young Girl..." he trailed off and glanced at me, one side of his face pulling up in that crooked grin that sent shocks down my legs. "You're kind of a history nerd, aren't you, Em?"

I rolled my eyes. "I think history *buff* is the correct term you were looking for, thank you very much."

His hands flew up in defense. "Sorry. History *buff.* So, tell me, oh wise history buff, what does history have that say, English and art don't?"

"Wow," I laughed. "Okay. Where to even begin?"

He grinned back at me. "Oh, I'm sure you'll figure it out."

"Sure. I guess the simplest answer is that history is like a great book: larger-than-life characters doing either insanely heroic or insanely deplorable actions no normal person would think of doing. Except the difference between history and a great book is that it really happened; everything those people did impact us today one way or another, whether it's where we live, what we eat, how we speak, the laws we live under...it can all be traced back to those great historical heroes."

Finn's eyebrows rose, but this time the amusement in his eyes was more affectionate than anything. "Historical heroes? Like JFK, who... did what in office? Sleep with Marilyn Monroe?"

"Yeah," I chided him. "JFK gets a bad rap—cheating rumors aside. He played a big part in getting the Civil Rights Bill passed, just so you know."

"Okay, okay," he held his hands up in defense. "So who would you consider a 'historical hero' then?"

I just shrugged. "An ordinary person doing extraordinary things. I think people who are remembered in history for good reasons are the ones doing the things no one else wants or even has the strength to do just because it's the right thing to do. They're not *trying* to be a hero, you know? That's what makes it heroic."

He nodded, admiration shining in his eyes. "So, like Martin Luther King, Jr.? Abe Lincoln? Nelson Mandela?"

"Sure. Or people like Susan B. Anthony, for example, or Eleanor Roosevelt or Harriet Tubman—no one would've ever looked at them and thought they'd be capable of doing what they did, but they did it. I don't think most people know what they're capable of until their backs are against a wall. *That's* why I love history...all these fascinating stories that are so much better than fiction, you know?"

"Shit," Finn muttered under his breath. "Now I feel bad for making fun of you for having all these books."

"Well," I just batted a hand at him and gestured to a particularly yellowed copy of *Night.* "A lot of these older ones were my dad's. He was a history teacher, too. We actually taught at the same high school...not at the same time though. He, um...he died when I was 10. Car accident."

Again, past tense still didn't hurt any less. Even though I hadn't meant to share all this with him today, this minuscule step forward, rather than all the steps backward I'd seemed to have taken over the last year, felt like something had opened up inside me, cranking its way free, stubbornly unwilling to go unnoticed anymore.

Finn's face softened with remorse.

"It's okay," I shrugged. "It was a long time ago."

"So you taught back at home?" Finn was asking me now, his eyes filled with empathy and understanding.

"Hickory," I corrected quickly. "I wouldn't really call it home anymore."

He nodded tightly, his Adam's apple bobbing up and down enough to let me know he understood just what thin ice we treaded on now. "Do you ever miss it?"

I noticed that since we'd been standing next to each other, we'd systematically, unconsciously inched closer and closer to one another, so much that all I'd have to do was lean a hair to the left and my shoulder would brush against his.

"Teaching?" I frowned. "Or Hickory?"

Finn just lifted a shoulder. "Both."

Considering the severity of the question, I didn't know how else to answer other than with as much truth as I could muster. "I don't know. Sometimes I do. I mean, my brother and sister-in-law still live in that area, so I miss seeing them, especially now that Cris is about to pop soon."

I gestured to a picture frame resting on the top shelf. "That's Noah and Cris."

Finn tilted his chin up to get a better look and his eyebrows rose a little. "Your brother looks like a badass. Was he a wrestler or something?"

"Baseball player."

"Ah," he nodded. "I guess that explains the arms on that guy. And, let's face it, your sister-in-law is *way* out of his league."

I laughed and shook my head. "Yeah, I make sure to tell him that every time I see him."

"Do you get to see them a lot?"

"Not as often as I'd like. And now with the baby coming...I guess there'll always be a part of me that wishes I could live closer to them. They're the only *real* family I have."

Please don't ask about my mom, I pleaded inwardly, *please don't ask about my mom.*

To deflect any other questions about my family, I quickly changed gears. "And teaching? I don't know if I really miss it. I mean, there are some things about it that I definitely *did* like. Summers off, for instance. Snow days were always a huge plus, too."

He huffed out a laugh and bumped my shoulder.

"I liked basically being able to plan out my own day. The curriculum wasn't always mine or what I would've chosen, but I was still the one dictating what the lesson was and how I delivered it. That part I didn't mind. I liked the actual teaching part of it, too—telling stories from history, figuring out what lessons we're supposed to learn from it, you know? But the rest of it...the politics, the grading, the stress, the 30-plus kids crammed in a room who are too busy playing on their phones to listen...honestly, I'm sorta glad I'm not doing it anymore. Okay, not sorta glad, I *am* glad. I loved history—I still do—and I think I was good at teaching, but I never really loved it. Most of the time, I didn't even really like it. Teaching, at least for me, was one of those things where everything looked great on paper, but the reality was so different from what I thought it would be."

"What do you mean?"

I lifted a shoulder. "I don't know...you think you're gonna change lives and inspire all these kids to better themselves like Hilary Swank in *Freedom Writers* or Michelle Pfeiffer in *Dangerous Minds.*"

"Or Jack Black in *School of Rock*," Finn added.

"Right," I laughed, but my face fell just as quickly. "But then you get there and it's real and you're lucky if two kids in the class even really care all that much. The other 20 are just taking it for the graduation credit and the *other* ones are doing everything in their power to waste time, distract their friends, or give you shit and make your life miserable because they think it's funny. Not to mention that getting them to put their phones down for even a second is like asking them to chop off a limb. I don't think ever I loved it, not even on my first day. I don't know...maybe I never should've been a teacher in the first place. I did it for four years and I was miserable for nine months out of the year for all those years."

I hadn't realized I felt that way until I finally said it out loud. It was an ugly truth, but it was still *my* truth.

"So, this was a good change for you then, huh?" he asked, smiling sadly like he could read my thoughts.

Well, it brought me to you. And Oliver. So yeah, maybe it was a pretty good change. And that was the first time I'd ever seen anything positive about what had happened to me.

"Yeah," I modified.

"What's the worst thing a kid ever did in one of your classes?"

Dread washed over me...and here I'd been actually telling the truth. Well, it wouldn't be quite a lie. I could give him something that actually happened. But the worst thing? That I couldn't tell him. At least not yet.

"Well, I've been flipped off before. Called a bitch. Some kid gets pissed off because they're not getting their way or they just want attention. Oh, and there was the time a girl called me the c-word because I took her phone away in class. That was a fun phone call home."

Finn cocked an amused eyebrow at me. "The c-word? You mean cu___"

"No!" my hand flew out to cover his mouth. "Don't say it! That's the worst word ever!"

His fingers reached up to coax my hand away from his mouth, his shoulders shaking with laughter. "The worst word ever? I think I've just made it my personal mission in life to get you to say it."

"No."

"Yes," Finn laughed. "Mark my words, Em. Sooner or later, I'm gonna get you to say it."

I just rolled my eyes at him. "Oh boy."

"Hey," his expression had turned softer, more apologetic now. "That really sucks. I mean, I wasn't crazy about all my teachers when I was in high school either, but I *never* would've called one a cu...sorry, the c-word. I might've flipped one or two off behind their backs, but I never would've gone *that* far. Especially not if it was a teacher like you. You're just...the nicest person I know. I can't imagine anyone ever saying that to you."

"Well, if makes you feel any better," I added. "That girl was suspended for a couple days. It was more of a three strikes and you're out sorta thing, but anyway, it's not like that happened all the time. I think I could count on one hand the number of times I've actually been called a name at school. It's just that...for every 10 nice kids in the class, there's always that one who ruins it for everyone else and that one is pretty much the only one you remember."

Here I was talking about it like it was still present tense, like it was still my life, when it just wasn't. And besides, I was really speaking from experience before the bomb went off. After, I'd been called every name in the book to my face and otherwise. Not like Finn exactly needed to know that right now either.

"Still sounds like you were surrounded by assholes, Em."

He didn't even know the half of it.

As if he could, once again, sense my thoughts, Finn's attention shifted to my turntable and record collection on the other side of my bookshelf.

"Wow. This thing is pretty cool," he murmured, leaning down with both hands on his thighs to hover over my state-of-the-art turntable with its digital volume settings and recording capabilities.

The whole thing was one giant contradiction, playing old school, out-of-date music recordings on a high-tech, modern, digital machine.

"I used to use my dad's ancient one, but it broke a few years ago."

Finn cast me a sideways glance. "So you traded up, I see. Do you mind if I...?"

He trailed off, gesturing to the crate of worn records next to the turntable and despite my hesitation at letting him see deeper into my world, I couldn't deny him. Especially not when he was looking back at me so hopefully and so patiently—all my defenses were no match for him.

"Sure," I nodded carefully. "Go ahead."

Now that he had permission, he didn't waste any time crouching down for a better look with both hands flipping through my collection. It was a leisurely perusal though, like he was taking his time, trying not to rush, and just letting himself enjoy the experience.

"Ah, sweet!" Finn murmured, more to himself than anything. "Pink Floyd? The Who, The Rolling Stones, Crosby, Stills, & Nash, The Police, Triumph, The Doors, Cream, Van Halen, Foreigner, Blue Oyster Cult...look at all these vintage Zeppelin records...this is crazy. Were these all your dad's, too?"

"Yep," I shrugged. "Noah grabbed all the sports stuff. I took the books and the records."

He nodded, his fingers still nimbly flipping through the records. "Sounds like a fair trade."

Oliver chose that moment to brush up against Finn's legs, rubbing his head into his jeans, and finally staring up at him with a long *maaahwr*.

"Oh hey, contraband," Finn murmured down to my cat and I watched, my heart fluttering and skipping and tugging in every direction, as Finn bent down to lift Oliver's front paws up to the front of the crate. "What do you think of all this?"

Oliver leaned forward on both white paws, sticking his head right into the crate, and sniffed the musty records with mild curiosity. He sneezed once and then turned to Finn, his mouth curling up into an affronted snarl as if to say, *What the hell is this? I don't like it.*

"Alright, alright," Finn laughed and lifted Oliver's front paws down so he could scamper off before turning his attention back to the contents of the crate. "Wow, this has gotta be every single album Rush has ever made, huh?"

I laughed, inching closer and closer to him until our shoulders brushed. "My dad was a Neil Peart fanatic. Best drummer in the world. Greatest poet who ever lived. The whole thing."

"I can see that."

"Actually..." I nudged my head towards the hallway and waved Finn along with me. "I gotta show you something."

He followed my lead, trailing after me through the short distance from the living room to my hallway where the framed calendar page sat until we stood shoulder to shoulder in front of the wall.

I pointed to the far corner of the page and turned to Finn with a wide grin, "That's my dad."

Finn squinted to get a better look, leaning closer with his hands on his hips, and then his head tilted towards me, his light eyes shimmering and pulling me in.

"My dad would always buy a Rush calendar every year," I explained softly. "So after he died, I started buying one every year instead. One year, I'm flipping through the pages and there he is...right in the corner, mullet and everything, having the time of his life."

Finn's hand ghosted around my waist to tuck me into his shoulder, his eyes silently asking for permission to keep touching me. He must've seen my soft smile as the confirmation he needed and his fingers squeezed my hip in response.

With his free hand, he pointed his index finger at the frame. "This is really cool, Em. What are the odds, you know?"

I smiled sadly, my eyes pulled right to the corner of the frame, taking in the image I'd seen millions of times: my dad with both fists raised high in the hair, in his prime and screaming at the top of his lungs. Finn had a point—what were the odds that this picture would end up in a calendar? One that I, out of obligation to tradition, would end up buying? It really was pretty crazy. Maybe fanciful, intangible things like fate really did exist.

"Do you have any newer records or is everything all from your dad's collection?"

My face brightened, grateful for the change of pace, and I shot him a playfully exasperated look. "I do, actually."

To be fair, I only owned two records that I'd actually purchased myself, but I did, in fact, have records that were made after 2000. Once we hovered in front of the plastic crate again, I plucked them from the back, holding them up proudly for Finn to see.

Finn's eyes widened, zeroing in on the record in my left hand, and grimaced like he was about to be physically ill. "Taylor Swift? Oh, Emma. No. Just...no."

"What?" I glanced at the *Red* album in my hand and shrugged. "I love her. She speaks to me."

He scrubbed a hand melodramatically over his eyes and gestured to the other record in my hand. "Amy Winehouse is fine. I bet that album sounds great on vinyl, too. But Taylor Swift I cannot abide by. I just can't do it."

"Why? She writes songs that might as well have come out of my diary, if I kept one. She's the best."

His eyes might as well have popped out of their sockets. "The *best?* And here I thought you were perfect..."

I had to bite down hard on my bottom lip to keep from reacting too much because Finn was already grinning back at me sheepishly and shoving both hands deep into his pockets like he just didn't know what to do with his hands. At this point, it would probably be okay if he put those hands on me, but that would be getting a little ahead of myself.

He probably wouldn't be saying that if he Googled you.

No. I didn't want to do that. Not today. Not when I was actually enjoying life for once. Not when I just wanted to spend more time with him.

"I don't think you're being very fair," I announced diplomatically and held the *Red* album right in front of his face just to be a brat.

"Please," he swatted down the square album. "All she does is write the same thing over and over again. Same song, different breakup."

My eyes lifted to the ceiling and I shook my head exasperatedly at him as I slid the vinyl from its sleeve so I could set it up on my turntable. "Yeah, you would think that, but I will have you know that she is an excellent storyteller, which is the best kind of music in my humble opinion."

Finn's upper lips curled up comically. "You're going to play me a song, aren't you?"

"Yep."

"Shit."

"Suck it up, my friend. You don't have to be a baby about it. This is just Taylor Swift we're talking about here, not a torture chamber," I chided, lifting the needle to place it against the vinyl and let the strains of "Everything Has Changed" hum from my speakers.

I turned, only to find Finn sprawled out on the carpet behind me with his hands folded across his chest.

"Are you sleeping or listening?"

He sighed dejectedly. "I'm listening."

My legs folded down underneath me in silence, suddenly feeling exposed and laid bare next to Finn. I really wasn't kidding before about these songs being like my diary and I wondered if, underneath the sweet acoustic strumming and Taylor's earnest singing, Finn was able to read in between the lines. I'd just set the needle right to this song thoughtlessly, not realizing that I'd accidentally chosen the one song that described the way I felt almost perfectly. Lyrics about holding doors, walls standing tall painted blue, wanting to know him better, and eyes that looked like coming home floated around us in the stillness.

The sublime lyrics had me squirming a little and the weight of their meaning seemed to pin me right into the carpet.

"You know," Finn murmured as he cocked one eye open to glance up at me. "It's not terrible. I'll give you that."

"I'm glad you gave her a chance," I laughed.

"I wouldn't exactly say I'm ready to drink the Taylor Kool Aid," he cast me a sideways glance before rolling onto his side to face me and propped his head up with an arm. "That was Ed Sheeran she was singing with, wasn't it?"

"Yeah, it was."

"You got anymore of his stuff?"

"Other than 'Thinking Out Loud', nope."

"Well," he drawled, flipping around to his stomach and rested his chin on his folded hands. "Let's get that computer going and fix that, huh?"

I sighed dramatically, reaching around him to slide my computer out from its hiding place underneath my coffee table and promptly booted it up. Once iTunes was up and running, I relinquished my computer to Finn, pushing it towards him with an eye roll.

He propped himself up on his elbows and rubbed his hands together like a little kid. "Alright. Let's do this."

Less than a minute later, Ed Sheeran's acoustic stylings sang out from my computer. I recognized the song as "Give Me Love" and the longer it played and the longer I listened to the lyrics, the more I wondered if maybe this was Finn's answer to the song I'd just played for him as Ed

Sheeran crooned about wanting her to give a little time to him and how all he wanted was the taste that her lips allowed. Whether it was intentional or otherwise...I wasn't really sure I wanted to know. All I knew was that music seemed to be communicating all the things we weren't sure we could say and all the things we maybe weren't ready to say.

I wasn't sure how I felt about that. My emotions were too scattered to be able to pin a solid one down.

Finn abruptly paused the song and clicked over to my library, scrolling through it to take in my selections. "You definitely need to broaden your music horizons, you know?"

"What's that supposed to mean?"

"Well, Emma, there is more to the world of music than classic rock, Amy Winehouse, and goddamn Taylor Swift."

"Wow," I laughed. "Cut out my heart, why don't you."

Oliver skimmed past us, walking in between us and stepping right on my computer, taking his sweet time as he ducked underneath the coffee table to disappear around my couch.

Finn cocked an eyebrow at me. "I hope you know that cat already owns you."

"He had me wrapped around his tiny white paw the second he showed up on my patio," I sighed. "You're preaching to the choir."

He just laughed and shifted the computer closer to him so he could type in another search. "How about more Kings of Leon? If I had to listen to Taylor-boring-Swift, you can tolerate a little of my music, don't you think?"

"Shut up," I swatted him playfully on the shoulder. "Stop knocking Taylor. She's my girl. Like I said, she speaks to me. And I don't recall ever saying I didn't *like* Kings of Leon. I just don't really *listen* to them. There's a difference, you know."

He held both hands up playfully in defense, his eyes smiling. "Whoa. Relax there. Just let me play you one song and then we can move on, okay?"

"Fine."

Strong percussions drummed through my computer's speakers before rolling guitar chords kicked in and I listened, bobbing my head to the beat until the lead singer sang a line that had my eyes widening in horror. Finn, on the other hand, had his head buried in his hands, his shoulders trembling with barely-concealed laughter.

"Is he saying what I think he's saying?"

Finn's lips curled up in evil glee. "Oh yeah. He's saying 'cu—" my hand flew out to muffle the word and he promptly batted it down, "'—nts watch their bodies'."

"That's terrible. I don't even know what that means, but it's terrible."

"I don't know what it means either, but I like it."

"Turn it off."

"Oookay," his fingers lifted up in the air. "No more 'Taper Jean Girl'. How about some Alabama Shakes then? I think you might like 'Always Alright'."

The next song that played from my speakers had a similar new-school-yet-retro feel to it as the Kings of Leon song that I liked. This one was a little funkier though and sounded like something that people would've been making out to, among other things, at a club in the 70s. I figured that was probably why he'd played this for me...already figuring out my tastes.

"I like it," I nodded to him with approval.

"Really?" he squinted at me. "You won't listen to a song with the c-word in it, but you're fine with the f-word?"

I waved a hand at him. "Not the same. The c-word is just ugly. Pure, unadulterated ugliness and it should only be said when someone—not necessarily a woman—is being a complete, no-holds-barred, insensitive, and all-around asshole douchebag."

"Alright," he laughed. "Whatever you say. I can't argue, I guess, considering you're down with Alabama Shakes now. You've got pretty good taste in music, not including the Taylor Swift debacle of course. You know, my ex-wife wasn't into..."

He trailed off and stared blankly at my computer screen, his eyes wide and disbelieving. I couldn't help the way my head snapped to turn towards him—how else was I supposed to react? At least I wasn't the only one compulsively sharing without realizing it. So, I waited. He had to have known he needed to explain now—not that it mattered. Not that it would change anything, especially since I couldn't imagine anything that could possibly trump the dead horse I dragged around everywhere.

"Sorry," he muttered before rolling onto his back and scrubbing both hands over his eyes. "It's not like I wasn't gonna tell you. I just...I didn't plan on doing it today. Especially not like that."

"It's okay," I whispered. "I understand."

I slid my legs down to mimic his posture and propped my head up on an elbow so I could give him my full attention.

He blew out a deep breath, readying himself to tell me whatever it was he had to say. "We were together for almost ten years, married for five...started dating when we were 17 and I don't know why we stayed together as long as we did, maybe it was just because neither one of us knew any better or didn't know anything different. I just kinda thought that's what you did when you were with someone so long, you know? You got married. So we did."

Finn rubbed his eyes and shook his head, as if he was trying to shake off the memories. "And somewhere along the way, we grew up and grew apart, the way most people do. She thought I worked at the brewhouse too much, which was and is still true, and I thought she spent too much money on shit we didn't need. She wanted to go out and do things, see things, go places...I guess I was so tired from work all the time that I never wanted to do any of that. I was perfectly fine just being at home or going to the tap room if she wanted a night out. I guess it's safe to say we didn't really see eye to eye on a lot of things. One night, I came home early from work—I'd wanted to surprise her, take her out to dinner or something to show her I was gonna try to be home more, and she was screwing one of the guys she worked with in our bed."

My breath came out in one long whoosh. "I'm sorry."

Finn just lifted a shoulder from his spot on the floor. "It's okay. It wasn't the drawn-out drama like you see in the movies. It was pretty quiet, actually. I just turned around, went to my dad's, drank a whole bottle of Cuervo, and passed out on the kitchen floor. The next day I called a lawyer. That was pretty much it."

I needed a few moments to absorb everything. What kind of idiot was this woman? Who in their right mind would throw away a relationship —a *marriage*—with someone like Finn?

"Did she...?" I couldn't even bring myself to say the words out loud.

"Yeah," Finn exhaled. "She gave me all the lines: it was a mistake, it just happened that one time and would never happen again, we could go to couple's counseling. She tried everything."

"And you didn't—"

"No," Finn cut in tightly. "I didn't. It's kinda hard to forget seeing your wife getting railed by another dude in your bed, you know? You can't really come back from that."

"Yeah, I guess I can see that."

"Looking back on it, we never should've gotten married," Finn shook his head. "We both knew it, too. We were both just too stubborn to admit it. Everything looked good on paper, like you said before, but the reality just...wasn't."

His eyes squeezed shut and he rubbed his eyes again, almost as if he was reliving the memory and I had a sudden urge to do something to make that harshness, that anxiety disappear from his beautiful face. So, once again, I found myself compulsively telling him more about myself than I'd told anyone the entire time I'd lived in the city.

"I almost got married last year," I told him quietly and his eyes snapped open at the revelation. Because I had a sudden need to be closer to him, I lowered down to his level, lying close enough to be within reach, but still leaving both of us enough room to breathe.

"I met him my sophomore year in college. We were together, what, six years? Yeah...six years," I shook my head, whispering, "Wow. I wasted so much time on him."

"What happened?" Finn's soft voice called out to me.

I pressed a weak smile on my face. "I had a pregnancy scare last year. I just completely freaked out about it and pretty much lost my mind thinking about how my life would've been over, how I didn't want a baby, wasn't ready to be a mom and all the responsibility that came with it and then I realized that while all those things were true, it all boiled down to the fact that I just didn't want *his* baby, if that makes any sense. I didn't want to be tied to *him* that way and that's why I'd freaked out so much."

I paused long enough to see his head dip down in a tight nod, his eyes fixed on me intently.

"How was I supposed to marry someone I didn't want to have kids with?" I pressed on. "I just couldn't imagine marrying him after that, so I called it off a couple days later."

You know how everyone thinks *The Little Mermaid* ends all happy with Ariel finally landing her prince and keeping her human legs just because Disney says so when, in the original story, the prince marries someone else and the mermaid kills herself and turns into sea foam?

I'd given Finn the Disney version. The real story, grounded in actual facts instead of fantasy, was much darker and uglier. It wasn't necessarily a lie; I'd just let him believe the story ended with me calling off my engagement.

Finn's hand grazed my shoulder and trailed lightly down my forearm. "So is that why you moved here? Why you're not teaching anymore?"

I looked down at the carpet and chewed anxiously on my bottom lip. He was giving me an opportunity to tell him the whole story, the unedited version of the story, but I just couldn't do it.

"That's part of it," I modified.

When he opened his mouth to respond, I had to scramble.

"I'm not ready to talk about the rest of it yet, okay?"

That was the best I could give him. The *most* I could give him. I just hoped it was enough for now.

He nodded and the light touch on my arm drifted up to my cheek. Then he shifted closer, sliding across the carpet to close the short distance between us, and kissed me. His lips were gentle and careful like he didn't want to scare me away, but needed this intimacy at the same time.

We inched closer until our chests pressed together and both my hands skimmed down the thin material of his worn T-shirt, curling around his shoulders to draw myself closer to him. It was slow and lazy, like we had the whole rest of the day ahead of us...and we sort of did, too. This was what I needed. Easy. Patience. Time. Restraint. All the things he was already giving me, but I had to make sure he understood.

"Finn," I exhaled against his lips. "I need to take this slow. I want to tell you why. I really do; I just can't right now. I'm not..."

The words just wouldn't come: *I'm not what you think I am. I'm not good. I'm not clean.*

And in doing this, in asking for patience, I'd also inadvertently promised to tell him, eventually, everything I'd never said out loud before. I'd also inadvertently admitted I wanted him in my life, even if those terms were undefined right now. It was terrifying.

"Okay," he murmured and his thumb rubbed across my cheek. "I promise I didn't come over for..." he glanced down between us, "*this* today. Just being here, talking to you, listening to music with you, that's enough, Em. It really is. I can do slow. Slow is perfect."

An easy smile curled my lips. "Thank you."

He rolled onto his back to put a little more distance between us again and that was okay. He'd clearly sensed that was what I needed right now and the fear of sending him mixed signals was the only thing keeping me from rolling onto my stomach so I could kiss him again. I didn't want to hold him at arm's length anymore, but I couldn't completely wrap myself around him yet either.

"You wanna turn off the music for awhile and watch something on TV?"

He'd already been in my apartment for a few hours and my whole body warmed and fluttered because he obviously didn't want our time together today to be over yet.

"Have you ever watched *Arrested Development?*"

He frowned and shook his head.

"What?" I immediately hopped up onto my feet and grabbed the remote. "How is that possible? We need to fix that."

His laugh followed me all the way to my couch.

* * *

.   .   .

A few hours, pieces of leftover pizza, beers, and episodes of *Arrested Development* later, Finn glanced at the time on his phone and blew out a deep breath. My eyes immediately flew to the clock over our heads and felt a little disappointment creeping my way. He'd basically spent the entire day over here...it was really amazing how time flew when you were having a good time.

"I should probably get going," he told me dejectedly, unwinding his arm from around my shoulders. "I don't want to, but..."

I nodded, not wanting him to leave yet, but our time together today had to end sometime. It wasn't like I'd exactly planned on him spending the night or anything.

"It *is* getting late," I admitted and pushed off the couch to grab the few empty beer bottles on my coffee table.

Finn followed me into the kitchen with the pizza box in his hands. "So...are you working tomorrow?"

"Yeah, I've got the lunch shift," I nodded, adding quickly, "but I have Sunday off."

"Hmm," he rubbed a hand over his mouth and then shoved that hand into his pocket. I half-expected him to offer up that brewery tour again, but he surprised me when he finally asked, "You wanna come over to my place for the game on Sunday?"

I saw exactly what he was doing here. Not only was he giving me a little breathing room, but he was drawing me out of my comfort zone, too. Getting me out of my apartment. Away from my safety net. One step at a time.

"It'll just be me and Sling," he explained right away. "No loud party this time around."

"Not gonna lie—that *was* pretty annoying. Especially since you guys literally just moved in."

Finn grimaced and pushed his floppy brown hair back from his forehead. "Sorry about that. It was all Sling's fault, I swear. I didn't want that many people at our place, especially since, like you said, we just moved in, but he doesn't listen to me. As I'm sure you've figured out already."

"Well, I suppose you're forgiven."

"Thanks," he laughed. "Now I'll be able to get some sleep tonight."

"Oh, good."

He leaned back on his heels, hands still in his pockets, and chewing on the inside of his cheek. "If you want, I can text you tomorrow and give you the details for Sunday."

I had to bite down on my lip to hide my smile. "You could've just asked for my number, Finn. You didn't have to try to be sneaky about it. You know I'm going to give it to you."

His eyes squeezed shut as a wince worked its way across his face and he blew out a frustrated breath. At this point, I liked to think I knew him well enough by now to know that his exasperation was directed at himself, not me.

"Okay," Finn exhaled, but that shy smile still lingered. "I'll try this again. Emma, I'd really like to have your number. So...can I have it?"

"Sure, why not?"

He cast me a sly, sideways glance as he passed his phone to me so I could type in my digits. "I had a good time today."

"I did too. I'm looking forward to Sunday."

"Good," he grinned. "You have no idea how hard it's gonna be to wait 'til Sunday to see you again."

"Well, I don't know. Maybe, after my shift tomorrow, I'll find myself out on my patio—the cat will have to stay inside this time—and maybe I'll want some company."

Now, that bright smile reached all the way up to his eyes, crinkling the edges and I had to clasp my hands in front of me to keep them to myself. He gestured with his head towards my front door. As we lingered near the doorway, Finn reached for me, letting his thumb brush across my cheek and then he leaned forward. His lips easily found my mouth like we'd been doing this for years. My hands slid up his chest and finally wrapped around his neck just as both his arms curled around my hips to pull me in. Everything felt hazy as heat pooled from my chest down to my stomach, igniting something I thought had died a long time ago.

Finn backed me up until my hips hit the door. One of his hands flew out to plant onto the door, easing off me just enough to keep me from being smothered completely against my front door. Finally, he pulled away and pressed his forehead into mine.

"Sorry," he murmured, backing away from me completely with both hands in the air. "I didn't mean to take it that far. I guess I just couldn't stop myself."

I kinda wished he would stop apologizing for kissing me.

"It's okay," I whispered. "I don't mind."

Finn blew out a deep breath and he reached for the door. "I should probably go now. If I stay any longer, I'm gonna…"

He swallowed hard, casting me a quick, embarrassed glance over his shoulder. "Have a good night, Em. Maybe I'll see you tomorrow? If not then, Sunday?"

"Yeah," I laughed softly. As if there was any question about Sunday in the first place. "Night, Finn."

And as he walked out into the hallway, I knew his earlier assumption about my move to Milwaukee might actually be true. It was crazy how something so humiliating and devastating to my life could eventually lead to something that was the complete opposite of everything I'd suffered. Something positive. Something *good*.

This was a good change.

This was the *best* change.

And for the first time in a very long time, I didn't feel completely owned and conquered by the past that clung to my legs, trailing after me and haunting every move I made.

Now, the present looked pretty good. The hope of a real future, that elusive dream of getting to start over, of getting a second chance…that hope rekindled as I watched Finn wave to me one last time before disappearing inside his apartment.

Now, that hope burned bright.

I glanced down at Oliver, who sat right next to my feet. "What do you think, buddy? Should we go to bed now?"

Meh.

I waved him into the hallway and he trailed after me, that little tinkling from the bell on his collar following me all the way into my bedroom.

CHAPTER ELEVEN

Well, I thought to myself as I surveyed the spread in front of me, *they really have all their bases covered when it comes to tailgate food.*

And then I realized that I'd just made a baseball reference, albeit internally, during a football game. Oh well. No one had to know but me.

Now, looking at the contents of Finn and Slinger's kitchen table, I wished I'd brought more than just a pie from the café. Granted, that was exactly what Finn told me to bring, but still...I felt just as underprepared as I was underdressed.

"Here you go," Finn's voice called out to me from over my shoulder and I turned to see him holding out a blue and yellow throwback Rodgers jersey to me. "It's gonna be huge on you, but it's better than nothing."

Apparently, I'd committed the cardinal sin of showing up to watch a Packer game without—gasp!—wearing a Packer jersey. Finn had, naturally, informed me of this egregious error the second I stepped foot in his apartment and set out on rectifying said error immediately.

"Don't spill anything on it," Slinger told me from the living room. "He will literally chop your balls off if anything touches it. I'm telling you, Emma."

Finn cast an irritated glance over his shoulder and then shook his head at me, mouthing, "*No.*"

As far as I could tell, the only person—sorry, cat—getting their balls chopped off around here was Oliver, but that wasn't happening until Wednesday. So, with that thought, I slipped the jersey from Finn's hands, shaking out the light shiver that rushed up my forearms when our fingers brushed, and promptly tugged the jersey over my head. I held my arms out and grimaced at just how oversized the whole thing was—the hem skimmed my knees and the extra material pillowed out around my chest. I might as well have been wearing a tent.

"I didn't realize you were such a fatty," I informed Finn and the sly grin that slid up his lips hit me all the way down to my jersey-covered knees.

"I didn't realize you were so tiny," he laughed. His hand rested on my shoulder, lingering just long enough to warm the skin underneath his touch and he murmured, "You look good in my jersey."

Suddenly, he turned me around to face the table again and with one hand lightly pressed into the small of my back, he gestured to the spread. "Grab some food, Em. Seriously. We've got enough here to feed a small army. I guess we got a little overzealous at the grocery store. Sling's eyes are a little bigger than his stomach, I think."

"Oh, sure," Slinger shot back from the couch. "Blame it all on me. You were the one freaking out over the food, not me."

Finn's head snapped to the side and glared daggers over his shoulder, but Slinger just shrugged it off. When Finn finally turned to face me again, his cheeks were already burning red. So, to save him from himself, I gestured down to the spread.

"All this looks pretty good," I smiled. "I don't know how I'm going to decide."

Some of the color had already retreated and Finn flashed me a warm grin. "Just pile as much onto a plate as you can. You can always come back for more."

I glanced at the table, which held three large plastic bowls of assorted chips, two smaller plastic deli packages of potato salad, salsa, French onion dip, a slow cooker wafting the mouth-watering aromas of little smokies and meatballs, some cheese and summer sausage slices, crackers...for lack of a better option, I took a little bit of everything to start out with.

"I'm gonna go check on the brats," Finn told me and his hand brushed the small of my back one more time before taking his leave out onto the patio where the smoky grill sat.

By the time I turned to face the living room with a heaping plate secured between both hands, I found Slinger perched on the couch, leaning towards me with an impish grin. He looked downright giddy and that made me downright anxious.

He patted the spot next to him on the couch. "Come on over here, neighbor. Have a seat. I won't bite."

Rolling my eyes up to the ceiling, I shook my head and against my better judgment, dared to take the seat next to Finn's roommate. Slinger hitched an elbow against the armrest, a movement that gave me a little more space on the couch, and cocked an eyebrow at me.

"So," he started good-naturedly. "I see you'll take Finn's invitation for football festivities, but not mine, hmm? That cuts me deep, Emma. It really does."

"Sorry," I shrugged. "You did come on a little strong the first time we met."

Slinger frowned back at me and tapped his chin in concentration. "Did I? Oh well, what can you do? Besides, Finn saw you first, so you were already off-limits as far as I was concerned."

My mind flashed to that first day in the parking lot—which was, God, only a week ago—and I smiled, remembering the way Finn ducked into his truck, trying to stay hidden, but watching me just the same.

"You two have been spending a lot of time together these last few days, huh?"

"Yep."

"And I heard you guys out on your patio last night, too. Finn had his guitar and everything."

True to my word, I'd immediately texted Finn when I got home from the café the night before and within minutes, he'd plopped himself down in Oliver's old chair, plucking away on his guitar before I even had a chance to change out of my work clothes.

"Yep."

That was the best I could do. Weak, right?

Slinger's eyes flicked to their patio for just a second to check on Finn before he leaned closer to me and confided lowly, "Between me and you, I haven't seen him show this much interest in a girl in a very, very long time."

My eyes must've widened the size of footballs because Slinger's grin spread to Joker-esque proportions.

"Don't act so surprised, Emma," Slinger gestured with his head towards the patio. "That dude has it bad and he's known you, what, a week?"

"Something like that, yeah," I mumbled.

"Trust me, neighbor, this is a good thing, but," he leaned his head in closer again and his voice dropped to a serious tone, "all I ask is that you be gentle with him. Please. Just be gentle."

I opened my mouth to respond, but came up empty. I'd never considered the possibility that I might not be the only one with something to lose here.

Slinger smiled sadly with a slight nod. "I heard he told you about Claire. The ex."

All I could do was nod tightly.

"He never talks about it, so the fact that he even told you...and how *much* he told you...I don't think you know how huge that was for him," he went on, his eyes darting to the patio again just for good measure. "I think he just kinda decided he never wanted to go anywhere near all *that* again, you know? But, I don't know, I think you might've made him a convert and you guys barely know each other."

Once again, I had no idea what to say.

"So," Slinger told me, his voice turning just a notch tighter. "I just want you to know that that guy out there is the best person I know. I'm not just saying that because I wanna see the two of you run off into the sunset together and all that shit—he was the first real friend I ever had and he's got the biggest heart out of anyone I've ever met. When he cares about you, when he's serious about wanting you in his life, he doesn't do it half-assed. He's all in. And he never should've had to put up with all the shit Claire put him through at the end. So, if you're just looking for a good time, if you're just looking for a casual hook-up or something, Finn's not your guy. He deserves better than that and he's gonna want more than that from you, too, so if that's what you're here for...I don't know, I guess you know where the door is."

I blinked back at him. The fact of the matter was I just didn't know Slinger well enough to know how to digest all this information. My eyes flicked to their front door and immediately shook my head.

"I don't know how to do casual," I admitted finally. "I haven't known Finn for very long, but I want to get to know him better. That's the best I can give you right now."

Slinger studied me for a few long seconds, as if to determine whether or not that was a line of bullshit, and he must've seen whatever he needed to see because he nodded. "Good. I was hoping you'd say something like that. Look, I didn't mean to be a jerk or anything, but I had to put it out there. He's too busy seeing stars when it comes to you and there was no way he'd ever tell you any of that himself, but I thought you needed to know before you two took things any further."

"I'm glad he has a friend like you," I smiled wistfully. "He's really lucky you've got his back like this."

Must be nice.

"Thanks," Slinger grinned back and just like that, the mood shifted. Gone was the tense, awkward atmosphere and in its place was something lighter that made it a little easier to breathe.

"And just so you know," I patted his forearm. "I would never look at you and think you worked at Wal-Mart."

Slinger's eyes rounded, popping out just enough to tell me I'd hit a nerve, and his gaze snapped to Finn, who was stepping through the patio entryway with a steaming plate of fresh brats in his hand. Finn froze mid-step, glancing uncertainly between the two of us on the couch, his lips pulling apart in a wince at our current seating arrangement.

"What?" Finn frowned.

"Don't what me, Finn—or should I call you Brett?" Slinger shot back.

Now I was lost. "Why are you calling him Brett?"

Slinger crossed his arms sullenly over his chest, shooting daggers at Finn. "As in Brett Favre. Vile betrayer."

Finn pointed a pair of greasy tongs right at his roommate. "That's going too far! I don't even know what I did, but—too far, Sling. Too damn far!"

I turned to Slinger, still baffled by the strange argument happening before my eyes. "I don't get what's happening here. Why is Finn like Brett Favre?"

Slinger chose to ignore me, opting instead to hook a thumb my way. "This one says she would *never* think I worked at Wal-Mart."

It took Finn a moment to catch on, but when he did, the edge of his lips quirked up in an amused grin. He used the back of the hand holding the tongs to rub his forehead and shrugged. "Oh right. So what?"

Now Slinger jabbed a pointed finger at Finn. "How dare you use my shame to impress a pretty girl, Finnegan!"

My eyes flew to Finn, mouthing, *"Finnegan?"*, but he just shook his head.

"Can someone please explain what's happening here?" I spread my hands out in front of me.

"Sling thinks I'm Brett Favre because I—"

"Betrayed the team," Slinger cut in abruptly as he sprung up from the couch, turning on his heel to head towards the hallway. "You know, when Favre said he was gonna retire for like, the 100th time, so then the Packers decide to move forward with Rodgers and then when Favre, big surprise, decides to come out of retirement yet again, the Packers have already moved on. So what does he do? He throws away years of hard-earned legacy to go play for the *Vikings* because he's a bitter, betraying asshole. He might as well have driven a knife in my heart and twisted it around—just like your boy, Finn, here."

With that, Slinger stomped down the hallway and disappeared behind a closed door.

"Wow," I exhaled.

"I guess he showed me," Finn laughed as he crossed the living room to put the plate on the kitchen table.

"I thought people were kinda cool with Brett Favre again these days, or at least, not cursing his name and burning his jersey anymore," I wondered out loud.

"Let's just say Sling knows how to hold a grudge," Finn explained and gestured to the table. "You still hungry? We've got about 50 brats that gotta go somewhere so..."

Finn trailed off as Slinger reappeared in the living room, this time, having swapped the Jordy Nelson jersey he'd been wearing for a green Rodgers jersey instead. Judging by the fury creeping into Finn's cheeks, I had a pretty good idea which jersey it was, too. And sure enough, Slinger flashed us the back just in case we weren't sure—good ol' number 12 with the name Matthews stitched onto the back.

"Where did you find that?" Finn growled, clenching those tongs a little too tightly.

"Oh, you know," Slinger shrugged and dropped down into the reclining chair next to the TV. "Just somethin' I found in your closet, collecting dust. Such a shame, too, because whoever gave this to you is a freaking genius."

"Take it off," Finn demanded hotly. "*Now*."

Slinger just shook his head with a satisfied smirk.

"Is genius a euphemism for something?" I chimed in from the couch.

Finn's lips curled up into a proud grin while Slinger blinked back at me like I'd just told him the Bears won the Super Bowl before throwing his head back into the chair with laughter.

"Whoa!" Slinger laughed and wiped his eyes. "Where did that come from? I like you. Did you hear that, Finn? I like her."

"Yeah, yeah," Finn called from the kitchen. "Heard you loud and clear, Sling."

That was enough to deter whatever animosity lingered between the two of them and before long, Finn was seated next to me on the couch with a plate of food in one hand and a beer in the other. But the real fun, at least for me, began with the kick-off: both Finn and Slinger rose to their feet as the kicker punted the ball high in the air across the stadium and when a Packer player caught it to run some yards, they both threw their heads back and howled.

They were howling, I tell you.

Howling.

"What in God's name..." I muttered, shaking my head. "Is that some kind of weird kick-off ritual or something?"

"It's hardly weird, Emma," Slinger told me from his chair. "You're just jealous you didn't get in on the action with us."

"Yep. That's it. Totally."

Finn cast me an amused sideways glance as he took his seat on the couch again. He winked at me and then leaned forward with his elbows on his knees, rubbing his hands together anxiously. The offense was out on the field now and I had the sudden urge to elbow him right in the shoulder and say, *"Look! Your man-crush is on TV!"*

That probably wouldn't go over well, so I opted to keep my mouth shut.

And forget the game. It was way more entertaining to watch my couch companion instead—Finn leaned forward just a hair as Rodgers called a play at the line, pointing to one receiver, then another, before finally hiking the ball. Finn's entire body seemed to tense in anticipation, his eyes glued to the screen, none the wiser that I'd pretty much foregone the game entirely now.

My focus was on him. The way his eyes squinted in concentration, flicking from side to side as he watched the quarterback's every movement with razor-sharp precision, and when Rodgers sent the ball sailing high over the heads of just about everyone else on the field, Finn sat up in mid-crouch with both hands rising in anticipation.

When the ball landed right into the hands of the wide receiver, who leapt into the end zone, Finn bounced up from the couch, hollering at the top of his lungs, "Whoo! Yes!"

Slinger hopped forward so they could high-five, but this wasn't just any high-five. No, this was the high-five of two best friends who'd been watching this game and playing it together for years. Slinger held his hand up high, Finn met him all the way up to the top, they smacked hands, whooshed their hands down low to smack hands again, and then wiggled their fingers together—all the while swiveling their hips and singing, *"I don't wanna work...I just wanna bang on this drum all day!"*

I blew out a stunned breath. I honestly didn't know whether to laugh with them or cackle at their expense.

"You guys are *weird*," I mumbled under my breath and took a long pull from my Matthews Brewing Co. beer bottle.

That beer nearly spilled all over Finn's jersey when he jerked the bottle out of my hand and promptly set the bottle and my food on the end table so he could yank me off the couch and into his arms. He lifted me right off my feet in a tight bear-hug and when he set me back on solid ground, both hands closed around my cheeks so he could press a hard, elated kiss into my mouth.

"We scored, Em!"

Oh my God, *we?* Yep, he'd definitely said *we.*

"I know," I laughed, acutely aware that his hands still lingered over my shoulders.

I liked this football-obsessed side of Finn. There was no pretense here. No putting on a show or trying to impress me. He'd invited me into his home to spend time with him and his best friend watching a game he obviously loved, completely uninhibited. Completely himself. In the middle of it all, I felt completely welcome, too. I wasn't in the way. I wasn't an afterthought. I wasn't there just to make food and serve his friends. I was there to be part of it, to share in the thrill of watching the game *with* him, instead of just sitting next to him.

It was safe to say I'd never been kissed like *that* after a touchdown before.

Now, the hands burning holes through the jersey I was wearing skimmed down to my waist and pulled me against his chest. My heart thundered, my stomach warmed, and little tendrils of fire snaked around the side of my hips, resting right at Finn's fingertips. I chewed on my bottom lip as Finn grinned down at me, his sky-blue eyes melting into pools of something I knew I wasn't quite ready for.

A throat cleared behind us.

"Get a room," Slinger coughed into his shoulder.

Finn's hands flew up in the air, backing away from me and sinking down into the couch, but that grin never left his face. In fact, that grin was pretty much mirrored on Slinger's face, too, albeit with a slightly smug variation.

So, by the time I situated myself back down on the couch, this time a few inches closer to Finn, the game was already on a commercial break. This must've been the opportunity Slinger was waiting for because the second that first commercial started, his bright green eyes darted right to Finn.

"Emma," Slinger called out, his fingertips wiggling together like a Bond villain, or better yet, Mr. Burns from *The Simpsons*. "My sweet, darling, gorgeous Emma…"

"You better be going somewhere with this, Sling," Finn shot back and it was no accident that his arm curled around my shoulders at that exact moment.

Slinger completely ignored Finn and instead, leveled his mischievous gaze right on me. "Did Finn ever tell you about his bathroom escapades back in the day?"

My eyes snapped to Finn, who'd gone still next to me. Horror and mortification flicked across his face and suddenly, that arm around my shoulders unwound itself so he could scrub both hands across his face.

"Don't do it," Finn pleaded and shook his head at his roommate, who was practically salivating at his humiliation. "I'm begging you, Sling. I'll do anything you want—I'll do your laundry for a month, whatever you want. Just...don't."

"Bathroom escapades?" I rose my eyebrows playfully at Finn. "There are a lot of ways a girl could take that, you know."

Immediately, Finn had his hands in the air. "It's not what you think —"

"No," Slinger interjected with a cackle. "It's better. Soooo much better. And *you*," he pointed at Finn, "you have this coming and you know it."

"Oh shit," Finn mumbled as he sunk down into the couch and lifted the collar of his jersey to cover the bottom half of his face.

"So," Slinger wiggled his fingers together again with devilish glee. "Back in the day, when our little Finnie here was in college at good ol' UW-Milwaukee, all our friends would hit the bars downtown on Water Street. After bar close, we'd usually hit up some sort of late-night food joint to grab a bite before heading back to our house. So, one time, we're sitting at a booth, eating our subs, when Finn comes back from the bathroom and says, 'Guys, we gotta get outta here.' And we're sitting there like, 'Why? We just got here.' Finn's still insisting, 'I'm serious, guys. We *gotta* get out of here.' And now I'm pissed because we just got our food and Finn's still freaking out saying, 'I don't think you understand. We *have* to leave. *Now.*' All of a sudden, we hear this chick yelling, 'The bathroom's flooded! What the hell!' So I look over and sure enough, there's water pooling out from underneath the door into the hallway. Finn is beet-red, nervous as shit, running his hands over his face, and going, 'We gotta go, we gotta go'. So we left and it was only *after* we left that your boy finally admits he didn't just flood the bathroom, but *broke* the damn toilet—on purpose!"

My hand slapped over my mouth to muffle my laugh, but my shoulders were already trembling uncontrollably. Finn, on the other hand, mumbled something inaudibly, sunk down into the couch even further, and covered his face with his hands.

"It takes some serious planning ahead of time to figure out how to do that shit when you're wasted," Slinger carried on, his evil grin widening by the second. "I mean, he had to have been doing some research, watching Youtube videos, I don't know...*something* to figure out how to completely unhook and unscrew everything in the tank and get it to flood like that. So, for the next couple weeks, every time we ended up at a place like that after bar close, Finn's running out of the bathroom, guilty as all hell, and going, "We gotta go, we gotta go!'"

"Oh no," I laughed and leaned to the side until my head rested into Finn's shoulder. "What in God's name possessed you to do something like that?"

"It was fun at the time," Finn mumbled.

"But why?" I shook my head, biting my lip at the image of Finn bent over a toilet in some bar, fiddling with all the knobs until the spray broke free.

"Ah," he rubbed the back of his neck with a wince. "I'm pretty sure it started when some bartender pissed me off. I don't even remember why I was so pissed in the first place, but I remember thinking to myself, 'I'm gonna fuck with their toilet now.'"

I covered my mouth with my hand to muffle my laughter.

"And then you got addicted to the rush, the thrill of the crime," Slinger swept his hands out dramatically. "His bathroom escapades finally came to an end the night we ended up at Miko's. I was just sitting there, happily eating my monstrous gyro at three in the morning, when Finn skids back over to the table, completely drenched head to toe in water. All I need to see is the water streaming into the hallway and I knew what went down. The manager's already out there with those caution cones, but the water just keeps right on coming. Then they're waving people out of the restaurant and Finn's sitting at our booth, soaked in water and sweat and redder than a tomato, going, 'Guys, seriously. We *have* to go'. They had to close the restaurant for two days for repairs, too."

"What?" I practically shrieked, clapping my hands on my thighs.

"Oh yeah," Slinger nodded wickedly. "Two days. And the worst part about the whole thing was that I didn't get to finish my gyro. After that, little Finnie knew it was time to retire from his devious, criminal ways and finally go straight."

"I never got caught though," Finn wagged a finger at Slinger.

Slinger shook his head, raising his beer bottle high in the air. "No, my friend, you did not and for that, I salute you."

Finn followed suit and lifted his own beer up to toast him before wrapping his free arm around my shoulders again.

"To be fair," Finn explained with a sheepish grin. "I was a drunk idiot with a fake ID. Drunk idiots with fake IDs think they can do anything, apparently."

"And just look at you now," Slinger nodded to us from his chair. "All grown up with skills and responsibility and shit. You know, Emma, your boy's got a big presentation on Thursday with the guys at the Bluestone

Lounge."

"The Bluestone Lounge?" I shot Finn an impressed glance. Even I'd heard of that place before—Mara had been trying to convince me to go there with her pretty much since our first shift together at the café.

"Yep," Slinger answered for him. "He's gonna nail it, just like all the other ones before it. You know, Finn's a regular Don Draper, well, without the womanizing and the smoking and the drinking and the self-loathing...anyway, Finn's gonna give them the best damn presentation they've ever heard. It'll be so good, they'll be begging us to let them sell our beer at their place."

"Just relax, Sling," Finn chided and his eyes darted back to me. "No pressure, right?"

I smiled, shifting on the couch to face him. "He sounds pretty sure of you."

"That's right," Slinger assured me, nodding to both of us. "His dad and his uncle already have a little celebration planned for Thursday night at the brewhouse because they know he's gonna nail it, too. You should swing by if you're not too busy and celebrate with us," and now he was wiggling his eyebrows at me, "and if you, uh, have any female friends who would like to come along, feel free to invite them, you know?"

"I think you're getting a little ahead of yourself," Finn called out, exasperation with just a hint of hesitation creeping into his voice, and he turned back to me with a shy smile, "*If* everything goes well, and that's a big if, I would love to have you there on Thursday—if you want to."

I didn't even have to think twice about it and that only scared me a little bit. "I'm working the dinner shift, but I'm sure I'll be able to switch with someone."

Finn's eyes widened. "No, Em, you don't have to do that. It's really not—"

"I want to be there," I insisted and squeezed his hand. "I'll make it happen. Don't worry about it," I glanced at Slinger, "And maybe my friend from work would want to come, too."

Slinger's eyes sparked with slightly scary anticipation—maybe asking Mara to come with wasn't such a good idea if he was already looking like *that*. Not to mention the fact that I'd basically fibbed my ass off just now when I'd called Mara my friend. But, I couldn't imagine myself actually showing up at the brewery on Thursday alone. I'd just feel uncomfortable and out of place, even though I'd been invited.

But the grin Finn flashed me told me everything I needed to know and sent all those worries right out the window. It was pretty simple: he wanted me there on Thursday just as much as he'd wanted me here today and that thought alone had me pressing myself even tighter into his shoulder. The last thing I wanted to do was send him mixed signals just days after telling him I needed to take this slow...but I just couldn't help it. I just wanted to be as close to him as possible without embarrassing myself in front of his best friend and roommate.

The rest of the game pretty much went like this: Finn and Slinger jumping and hollering at the awesome plays and the not-so-awesome plays, more high-fiving, more food and beers, and more time spent being tucked underneath Finn's shoulder.

So, after the Packers triumphed over the Seahawks and all the excess of leftovers were shelved away in their refrigerator, Finn led me out into the hallway with his hand carefully pressed into the small of my back. When we crossed the short distance between his door and mine, I gestured down to the blue and yellow jersey I was wearing.

"I still need to give this back to you."

My fingers lifted the hem, but Finn's hands ghosted over my shoulder to stop me, smoothing the soft material down.

"You can hang onto it for next Sunday. I don't mind. It looks better on you anyway."

As if my limbs had minds of their own, I found myself trailing both hands up his chest, slipping around his shoulders to curl up his neck, and finally, I tugged his lips to mine. His strong arms wrapped around my waist, pressing me into the door and flush against him at the same time. Our lips melded together, exploring and tasting, and somewhere along the way, my left thigh lifted just enough to hitch around his hip and let him in a little deeper.

He groaned into my lips and the hand melting into my thigh grazed higher, slipping up my jeans and curving around the base of my—

"Ahem."

Finn's lips halted and we both turned at the same time to see Mrs. Johanssen in her fuzzy pink pajamas, both hands on her hips, and her mouth set in a firm, appalled line.

"Excuse me," she snapped. "But I think maybe you should take that somewhere else. Somewhere *other* than the hallway!"

I winced as my left leg hit the ground again. Finn backed away from me, tucked his hands behind his back, and shot our elderly neighbor a quick, pained look over his shoulder.

"Sorry, Mrs. Johanssen," I called out with a grimace.

"Yeah, uh, sorry," Finn added.

Mrs. Johanssen narrowed her eyes at him. She was not convinced.

"It won't happen again," I tried lamely.

"Actually," Finn scratched the back of his head as he spoke, a sly grin crossing his face. "It probably will happen again."

I smacked him on the shoulder and turned back to Mrs. Johanssen, but she was already batting a hand dismissively at us as she disappeared inside her apartment. Before I had a chance to do much else, Finn was backing me into my door. So, on pure impulse alone, I gripped his neck and pulled him to me again, smiling into his kiss.

It had been so long since I'd done this...just kiss like this. Maybe I'd never been kissed like this up against my front door either, but this was so nice. Going slow, taking our time, it was right. There was no need to hurry. No need to rush and whip our clothes off like there might not be a tomorrow.

I had a pretty good feeling there would be a tomorrow with him. And a day after that and after that and after that.

"I really should get going," Finn murmured against my lips now. "Especially before you attack me again."

"Hey, I can't help it," I laughed. "Sorry."

"Trust me, Em, you never have to apologize for attacking me. Anytime. Any place. Do it. Seriously. Do it."

My shoulders shook with laughter and he cocked an eyebrow at me.

"You think I'm joking? I'm dead serious, Em. I mean it. Attack me. Get all up on me."

Now, my head fell back against the door, laughing as his words washed over me. Oh God, if only...if only...

"But seriously though, Em, let's face it, if we keep this up, I'm never leaving and I'm gonna end up coming inside your apartment and I don't know if..." he trailed off, searching for the right words that wouldn't offend or embarrass me.

"If I'm ready for that?" I offered with a smile.

"Right," he exhaled. "But, before I go, what do you wanna do tomorrow?"

My eyebrows lifted. "Tomorrow? What makes you think I wanna see you tomorrow?"

"Emma," he levelled that sexy, crooked grin on me and I leaned my hips into him a little more, unable to control myself. "You wanna see me tomorrow."

"Yeah," I murmured. "I wanna see you tomorrow. But I have to work the dinner shift tomorrow night and I probably won't be home until at least 10:30."

"Okay," he shrugged. "What about Tuesday?"

"Tuesday I've got the lunch shift."

His lips curled victoriously. "Tuesday it is then."

"Hmm, what should we do?"

"I don't know. What's something you haven't done in awhile?"

There he went again, drawing me out of my safety net and pushing me back out into the real world.

"Let me think. I haven't seen a movie in a theatre in a while. I used to really like doing that…"

A wistful smile crossed his face and I knew he hadn't missed the words *used to*. Past tense.

"A movie it is. What do you say we head over to the theater at around 5:30? You'll be home from work by then, right? We could just pick the first thing that's playing at that time and go with it?"

My lips curved up into a grin. "Yeah, let's do it."

I'd never really been that spontaneous before, but with Finn, I found myself doing and saying a lot of things I might not have, if not for him, and that was probably more significant to my life than I was ready to admit.

"Okay," Finn leaned in to kiss me one last time. "It's a date."

CHAPTER TWELVE

I tapped my chin and squinted at the marquee in thought. "What do you think? Crappy sci-fi action movie, crappy romantic comedy, crappy zombie movie, crappy superhero movie, or crappy family-friendly animated movie?"

"Hmm," Finn hovered over my shoulder and rested a hand on my hip. "I'm gonna have to veto the crappy romantic comedy and the crappy family-friendly animated movie. Crappy superhero movie or crappy sci-fi action movie?"

"Let's go with the crappy superhero movie. I'm kinda sick of the crappy sci-fi action movies."

"Got it," he grinned.

He shot me a wink as he dipped into his back pocket for his wallet to pay for our tickets with one hand and kept the other firmly lodged onto my hip. I couldn't remember the last time something as simple as a guy taking me to a movie with his arm wrapped around me felt so *good*. Made me feel so *happy*. So *alive*.

In reality, it was just a crappy movie. Just greasy movie theatre hot dogs. Just salty popcorn. Just sweet hand-holding as Finn led me to a bench in the lobby. But I guess in *my* reality, it was everything. Acceptance. Ease. Butterflies. Fun. Warmth.

Being with Finn was effortless. I didn't have to worry about anything. I wasn't looking over my shoulder. I wasn't stressing out about what someone might be whispering in his ear about me. I was just in the moment, just happy to be there.

"I forgot how much I loved these things," Finn mumbled in between bites.

I don't know how he managed it, but he still kept his arm around me even as he attacked the hot dog in his other hand. We still had a half an hour until our movie started, but at this point, who cared if we made it into the theatre or not? Just sitting out here on this bench with a guy who was so beautiful it hurt to look at him sometimes, a cheap hot dog in my hand and a tub of buttery popcorn in the other, that was enough for me tonight.

"So tomorrow is poor contraband's big day, huh?" Finn was asking me now.

"What?" I'd been so lost in my dream world that it took me a second to register the words. "Oh. Yeah. Tomorrow's the big snip-snip."

Finn winced and shifted stiffly on the bench, like just the thought alone caused him actual pain.

"That poor guy. You're gonna have him emasculated before he's even been living with you for two full weeks."

"Oh, come on," I laughed and tossed a piece of popcorn in my mouth. "The sooner we get it over with the better. I still can't believe that little shit pissed on the carpet literally *right* before we left."

"Aw, I think that was just his way of saying he didn't want you to leave," Finn shrugged and proceeded to shove the rest of his hot dog in his mouth.

"Yeah, well, I think the two of you had a little too much fun watching me scrub cat piss out of my carpet."

Finn just smirked and tucked me tighter into his shoulder. "I *did* have a pretty good view."

My eyes narrowed, remembering the way I'd been on my hands and knees on the carpet in front of him while he held a smugly indignant Oliver underneath his arm. Yeah, he'd probably liked that a little too much.

"Right," I allowed, twisting my lips in annoyance. That pretty much disappeared when Finn's warm fingers curled around my shoulder and sent little icy-hot chills down my arms.

"You can't really blame me, can you?" Finn murmured in my ear. "Don't answer that. So, anyway...declawing, yay or nay?"

I shook my head vehemently. "Nay. Definitely nay. Did you know they cut off the cat's first knuckle?" I stretched my fingers out to demonstrate a chopping motion against my own knuckles and shuddered. "That's so terrible. It seems more like torture than anything —I can't even imagine doing that to him and letting him run around with only part of his front paws."

Finn tugged me closer to him and kissed the side of my head. "He made the right choice picking your patio that night. It was like he took one look at you and thought to himself, 'Now here's a girl I can con into letting me live with her. Maybe I'll have to get my balls chopped off, but at least I won't lose my paws.'"

"Oh no," I laughed. "When you say it like that it doesn't sound so good."

"Nah, you're doing everything right, Em," Finn smiled warmly. "He's lucky you didn't ship him off to the pound."

"Well, we're in this together now, him and me," I shrugged and took another handful of popcorn just for good measure. "I'm attached. What can I say?"

"Allergies still holding up?"

"Yep. I still can't believe it. I've had cat allergies for almost 15 years of my life—this stray cat with a double ear infection and worms shows up on my patio and, two weeks later, I'm cured? I mean, I still pop a 24-hour allergy pill every day, but...I just don't get it."

Finn's eyes shimmered back at me with warm admiration. "I guess he was just meant to be your cat."

"Maybe."

And maybe this whole fate thing wasn't such bullshit after all.

"Come on," he gestured with his head towards the hall. "We got a crappy movie to see."

By the time we settled into our seats in the back row, the previews were already playing. We got comfortable, situated all our snacks, and Finn had his arm wound around my shoulders just as the opening credits started. The movie lamely attempted to get the party started with a bang. Well, a shoot-out. Big deal.

"You know, I think this movie isn't just gonna be crappy," I whispered to Finn. "It's gonna be shitty."

Finn barked out a laugh, prompting the guys two rows ahead of us to turn around and shoot him the stink-eye.

"Keep it down, Finnegan."

"My name's not Finnegan," he muttered back to me. "It's just Finn. Sling only calls me that to piss me off."

"I guess that's only fair."

"I guess you're right."

We turned our attention back to the movie for a few seconds and that was about all it took for my boredom to set in.

"You know," I leaned in closer to his shoulder to keep my voice down. "Where are all the women superheroes? It's just not right."

Finn chucked under his breath and the closeness, the tingle of his breath so close to my ear made me momentarily forget where I was. "In these movies, the women are usually either the sidekicks, the brains, or the damsels in distress. There's not really an in between."

"You're absolutely right," I shook my head and waved a hand at the giant screen in front of us. "It's complete bullshit, too. Why can't a woman ever be the hero of her own story? Why does it always have to be the *man* jumping off buildings and stopping the villain from world domination?"

"Fair enough," Finn laughed lightly as he reached over to grab a handful of popcorn from the tub in my lap. "I'll give you that."

"And you know what else really pisses me off?" I didn't give Finn a chance to answer, but still managed to keep my voice down to a harsh whisper. "Women are always the ones that end up getting hurt, kidnapped, and/or murdered in these movies. The men either end up defending them, saving them, or mourning them. Women should be able to save themselves...the whole thing is so stupid."

"You know, some of them *can* defend themselves," Finn offered. "Black Widow in *The Avengers* for instance. Catwoman. Batgirl. Any of the chicks in *X-Men*. Elecktra in *Daredevil.*"

"Right, but did any of them get their own movie that people actually *liked?*"

"I see your point," Finn laughed, muffling as much of it as he could. "Nobody and I mean nobody liked the *Catwoman* and *Elecktra* movies."

"Even Michelle Pfeiffer in *Batman Returns* is bullshit," I huffed. "Nobody notices her until she gets all sexed up in that DIY plastic catsuit. Then all of a sudden she's this sex kitten—pun intended—and everybody's panting after her. Her entire identity in that movie completely revolves around the way men see her. And! And! By the end, she's so hung up on Bruce Wayne that she completely foregoes the whole reason she even became a crazy sex kitten in the first place—to get revenge on crazy-haired Christopher Walken! Even when they're bad, they still end up being good—all for a man. Don't get me started on Anne Hathaway in that last *Batman* movie either. Why does it always have to revolve men and sex? Why can't women just save themselves *for* themselves?"

Finn's eyes bulged out a little in his head and he leaned back in his chair, his lips curling up as he drank me in before dipping his head down to my ear to murmur, "That was the most awesome movie tirade I've ever heard. Please don't stop. Tell me everything. Lay it all out there, Em."

I might've been laughing, or at the very least, doing everything I could to stifle the noise as best I could, but deep down, I knew all that tirade really amounted to was one big, fat projection. The only way women could defend and stand up for themselves in superhero movies and in real life was if they had the strength to do it. The follow-through.

The ambition and the motivation. The grit and the backbone. I didn't have any of those things and if the last 26 years of my life was any indication, I probably never would.

Finn bumped my shoulder, shaking me out of my reverie. "Hey. You okay?"

I nodded a little too quickly. "Yeah. I'm fine."

He might've nodded, but Finn's eyes watched me a little too carefully with a little too much concern and that made me a little too panicked. Questions would come next and even though it was probably inevitable, I wanted to put off answering those questions for as long as humanly possible. I just wanted us to stay like this, happy and enjoying each other's company with Finn looking at me with respect and admiration instead of disgust.

Was I always going to feel this way? When was I going to stop allowing myself to be ruled by the way other people saw me? Was I always going to be this frustrated and disappointed in myself? Was I always going to feel this...unworthy?

"This is my favorite part," Finn leaned into me now, once again drawing me away from my thoughts as he grabbed another handful of popcorn. "The unveiling of all the gadgets...fancy guns, high-tech suits, invisibility cloaks, robotic implants. God, I wish I was a superhero sometimes."

"You mean when you're not secretly wishing you were Aaron Rodgers?"

Finn shot me a wary glance out of the corner of his eye, but the sly smile was still there.

I nudged him with my elbow. "Then you'd be able to save the world and all the damsels in distress, huh?"

Finn just batted a hand out in the air. "Maybe the world, but I'll let the damsels save themselves for once."

"Good call," I nodded. "They can do it. They just need the opportunity, you know?"

"Yeah," he told me softly. "I think you're right about that."

The guys two rows ahead of us abruptly turned around in their seats and glared menacingly at us.

"Would you guys shut the hell up?" the balding one whispered furiously. "Some of us are actually trying to watch the damn movie here!"

Finn sprung forward, nearly dumping the whole popcorn tub into the aisle, and had a hand on the seat in front of us before I could stop him. "Hey—"

My free hand shot out to his chest. Now, I was the one almost dumping all the popcorn into the aisle and I pushed him away from the chair. "Finn, don't. Just let it go, okay?"

All my anxieties, my insecurities, and my past came raging back at me at once and my mind flashed to Noah, sitting in a jail cell with his head in his hands and his knuckles torn to pieces. While the two situations couldn't be more different and even though I honestly didn't believe this particular situation would escalate to that point, I wasn't about to let Finn head down that road.

Luckily, Finn didn't need anymore convincing and he dropped back in his seat as I waved to the guys in front of us.

"I'm really sorry," I whispered to them. "We'll shut up now. I promise."

They grumbled something I didn't catch and shifted forward in their seats, finally putting the matter to rest.

"Sorry, Em," Finn mumbled to me and wrapped his arm around my shoulders again to tuck me in closer.

"It's okay," I whispered. "Maybe we should just watch the shitty movie now."

Finn cocked a devilish eyebrow at me and tugged the popcorn tub out of my hands to set it down on the floor. His lips grazed my ear and my eyes fluttered shut at the contact.

"We're already the noisy couple in the back row," he murmured in my ear. "We might as well be the couple making out in the back row, too."

"Oh, I see how it is," I snickered and had to chew on my bottom lip to keep from jumping on him right there. "So *that's* why you were all about seeing a movie tonight, huh?"

Finn just lifted a shoulder and then practically tugged me all the way across the armrest. "I saw an opportunity and I took it. Can you blame me?"

He didn't give me a chance to answer because his lips had already sealed over my mouth, stealing the words away from me, and gingerly slipped his tongue in between my lips. Here we were, making out in the back row of a movie theatre like a couple of teenagers. It was beautiful. And fun. And by sheer willpower alone, most of our limbs stayed in our seats.

We didn't see the rest of the movie.

.   .   .

"Here you go, Ed," I told him brightly as I poured him another cup of coffee.

Despite the grunt I got in return, my grin didn't falter once. All morning I'd been walking on air, flitting around from table to table, and smiling like an idiot. Mara was already onto me, but I didn't really care.

I guess I just couldn't help the easy elation that had me practically skipping around the café.

The night before kept flashing through my mind and that silly grin was almost permanently plastered onto my face. Popcorn, greasy hot dogs, two Mountain Dews, a crappy superhero movie, Finn kissing me through half the movie...all the makings of a perfect date.

It was the best date I'd ever had. Simple, easy, and fun as hell.

And, the second I entered the kitchen, Mara was on me like a cheap suit.

"What has gotten into you today?" she whispered, her voice dripping with excitement. "I've never, and I mean *never*, seen you like this before. Oh—is it your neighbor? The Browning Adonis who came in here last week to see you?"

I knew she wasn't going to let me get away without some sort of explanation. "We went to a movie last night."

Mara's whole face lit up. "That's great! I mean, it obviously went well. Look at you, you're practically glowing."

"And," I figured I might as well get this over with. "I've been meaning to ask you...Finn actually works at Matthews Brewing Co., well, he doesn't just work there, his family owns it, but they're having this little party there tomorrow night and they said I could invite a friend, so I was wondering if you wanted to go with me."

She reared back, shaking her head at me like she couldn't believe her ears. "Wait a minute, wait a minute...let me get this straight. *You're* inviting *me* somewhere?"

"Yep. So, do you wanna go? I already got Nicole to switch shifts with me and I figured since you're off tomorrow night anyway—"

"Oh my God, Emma, I'd love to go. I just can't believe—you know what? Never mind. I can't wait! And...your sexy neighbor, sorry, your sexy boyfriend has got some seriously awesome connections. I just went to that brewery and let me tell you. It. Is. Beautiful."

Unfortunately, I was only able to zero in on one part of what she just said. "Can we not refer to him as my boyfriend?"

I didn't need her blurting something like that right in front of Finn or worse, Slinger, his dad, or his uncle. Our relationship, our friendship...whatever it was, the undefined lines between us were already so blurry, I didn't need to add any confusion to the mix, too.

Mara, on the other hand, cocked an eyebrow and swept her eyes over me skeptically. "Sure. Whatever you say. So, are you going there with your boyfr—neighbor? Should I meet you there or come to your apartment? What do—"

Luckily, my phone buzzed in my back pocket at that exact moment and rescued me from having to finish that conversation with Mara for the time being. I glanced at the number flashing across my screen and gestured towards the back door with my head. I'd had the foresight to clue Mara into Oliver's little operation today as soon as my shift started and she'd agreed to cover for me whenever the vet called to check in. She waved me to the door and I swiped the screen to answer.

"Hello?"

"Hi, Emma, this is Dr. Gentry at Bayview Veterinary Clinic. I was just calling to talk to you about the results of the tests we discussed when you dropped Oliver off this morning."

"Right," I nodded to myself as I stepped outside through the café's back door. I couldn't remember what those tests even were—she'd rattled them off so quickly I hadn't been able to keep up.

"He tested negative for feline leukemia, but he did test positive for FIV."

The vet kept talking—she said something about a low white blood cell count, but I barely heard her. All the air whooshed out of my lungs. My eyes stung. My legs felt anchored to the pavement. My heart skidded to a stop.

"Wait—what?" I shook my head. There was no making sense of this. "FIV? Like HIV?"

"Well," Dr. Gentry explained and her calm, laid-back tone just did not match what she was telling me. "Feline immunodeficiency virus affects the body similar to HIV, but unlike in humans, it'll never turn into full-blown AIDs."

Just hearing that acronym had my body seizing in shock.

"What...I don't understand."

"It's very common in strays, unfortunately," she went on, clearly oblivious to the fact that I was practically hyperventilating into the phone. "And it is absolutely *not* something you could contract. It's a strictly feline to feline disease. If you have any dogs in the house, they wouldn't be affected either. It's mainly transferred from saliva, so he probably contracted it through a bite wound from another infected cat."

That still didn't make me feel any better or really answer any of the questions I just didn't know how to ask. All my brain seemed to hear was *disease*.

"Oh my God," I whispered. "Does that mean...does he need to be put down?"

It was like I was in some sort of nightmare. There was no way I'd just said those words out loud. It didn't compute. My brain and my heart wouldn't accept it. Numbness had the rest of my body on ice and I couldn't have moved if I tried.

"I wouldn't jump right to that," Dr. Gentry asserted quickly. "There's no need to go doom and gloom right away because there's no way of knowing how or when the disease will impact him. He could easily live for years with the disease if it's managed properly, just like a person with HIV."

My lungs still heaved. My eyes still burned. My heart still tangled and spliced.

"So it's like HIV or it isn't? I don't understand," my tone was sharper than I'd intended, but I didn't really have the capacity for politeness right about now.

"Like I said, it's similar. It'll affect his immune system the way HIV would affect a human. He'll be more prone to things like ear infections, dental issues, and upper respiratory problems because his body won't be able to fight those issues off as easily the way an uninfected cat could."

"So...he's not going to *die*, is he? I just don't—"

"I wish I could give you a better answer about longevity, Emma, but there's just no way to know. He's still young, all his organs look fantastic —his kidneys, his lungs, his heart—everything looks great. He's going to need special care, potentially a special diet, but I've seen plenty of cats with this disease live for years with proper care."

Years. She'd said *years*. She'd also said *disease* in the same sentence. My brain just refused to digest it.

"So, that being said," Dr. Gentry concluded, still in that easy, light-hearted tone that made me want to shove my fist through the phone and punch the woman in the face. "I still feel comfortable with moving forward with the surgery today. We won't give him that next round of shots like we'd planned and with your consent, I think it would be best to do the procedure by laser instead. It's a little more money than we previously discussed, but the recovery time is faster and healing is—"

"Yes," I cut in abruptly. "Whatever you think. If it'll be easier on him, do it."

After Dr. Gentry promised to call me after Oliver was in recovery, I swiped across my screen to end the call and covered my face with my hands.

A pair of grey, sea foam eyes flashed through my mind and the dam broke right along with my heart. Hot tears rushed down my cheeks and I somehow managed to muffle a loud sob with my hand. Words like *disease, illness, white blood cells, infection, organs,* and *longevity* rushed across my mind and another sob erupted from my throat.

I was losing my shit right behind the café...I was supposed to be *working,* goddammit, but instead, I was crouched down against a wall with my face splashed with tears, weeping over a cat.

Just a cat.

Even thinking that sentence fragment had me convulsing in tears.

He wasn't just a cat. He was *my* cat. He was my *sick* cat. Or at least, it seemed that way. Devastation didn't even begin to round the corner of what I was feeling right now. I was demolished. Heartsick. Completely ripped apart.

Somewhere in between worrying about allergies, whether or not he'd attack, scratch, or bite me, and getting caught with contraband in my apartment, this had never, ever crossed my mind. The possibility that he could have a disease that would be detrimental to the course and longevity of his life just wasn't on my radar.

And now that he was in my life, I couldn't imagine being without him. I couldn't even imagine what my life had been like before he showed up on my patio...that was how deep I'd fallen. The one thing I thought I'd never want in my life had somehow become the one thing I didn't think I could live without. Trust me, the irony wasn't lost on me.

The idea that he could suddenly just disappear, that he could just be gone—I couldn't go there. I just couldn't.

Tears streamed down my face. There was no point in even trying to stop it. And before I could stop myself, my fingers swept across my phone and hit dial. My phone kept ringing and I just kept on crying until a familiar deep voice finally answered.

"Hello?"

"Finn?"

I couldn't fake calm if I tried. The panic practically oozed from my pores, so it was no wonder Finn picked up on it instantaneously.

"Em, what's wrong? Are you okay? You're at work, right? What's goin—"

"I'm fine," I whispered into the phone and squeezed my eyes shut. "I just talked to the vet and..."

I couldn't say the words. I just couldn't do it.

"Emma, slow down. Take a deep breath. Tell me what's wrong."

My breath heaved in and out and I tried to follow Finn's instructions, I really did, but I just couldn't.

"Oliver has FIV."

That reality, served with a fresh stream of hot tears, did nothing to alleviate this frenzied terror shooting up and down my body.

"Okay."

Okay? That was all he had to say?

"I mean, he's gonna be sick, right? How long can he live with that? I just don't—"

"You know," Finn cut in thoughtfully. "I think one of my sister's cats had that."

"Really? Is that cat...still alive? God, what am I saying? Of course the cat's dead. That was, what, fifteen years ago?"

"Yeah. She's dead. I think she was about eight or nine when she went."

I sucked in a breath. I don't know why, but that made me feel better. The vet thought Oliver was a year old at the most, so that meant he still had time, didn't it?

"Was she sick?"

"Nope. I'm pretty sure my mom accidentally ran her over with the car."

"Oh," I exhaled and then that exhale reshaped into a breathy laugh. "*Oh.* That actually makes me feel better. Is it terrible that it makes me feel better?"

"No," Finn laughed and I could practically see him tugging his hand through the long floppy pieces that always hung in his face. "It doesn't. It really doesn't. So, is the vet still doing the surgery today?"

"Yeah."

"Then he's not in bad shape, Em. There's no way they'd do surgery if they didn't think he could handle it. He's gonna be okay."

I swallowed hard as his words gradually sank in. "Okay."

"You're doing everything right, Em. You're taking good care of him and you're gonna keep taking good care of him. That's all you can do."

"Thank you," I whispered and then, I stepped out of my self-involved bubble for just a second. "Oh my God, I just called you at work. I'm so sorry. I didn't mean to interrupt—you were probably right in the middle of something, weren't you? And you have your presentation tomorrow! I completely—"

"Don't worry about it, Em," he chuckled. "You can call me anytime. You know that. And I'm glad you called—you sounded like you pretty much lost your shit before."

I ran a hand over my face and wiped my eyes. "Yeah, pretty much."

"You're picking him up after work, right?" He didn't give me a chance to answer. "I'll meet you there. Just tell me where to go."

"No, you don't have to do that. It's fine. Besides, Finn, you'd have to leave early and—"

"Em, it's not a big deal. Family business, remember? I'll be there. Just tell me where and when."

I guess I had two choices: I could tell him to just stay at work and that I'd see him later or I could stop fighting and let him be there for me...and Oliver. The reality, served with a plate of fear and panic on ice, wasn't just the fact that I didn't want to go alone. I didn't want my brother there or even Cris.

I wanted *him* with me.

True to his word, Finn met me at the vet and wrapped me in a tight hug as soon as he was close enough to touch me. He kissed the side of my head and held my hand when the receptionist took us back to a consultation room where a vet tech was already waiting for us. He held my hand all the way through my crazy, helicopter-esque, frantic questions and the vet tech's patient, thorough responses. And finally, when the vet tech brought Oliver out, safely tucked away in his little carrier and wearing a plastic cone, Finn was still holding my hand.

Oliver lifted his tiny head and blinked at me from behind the metal gate separating us. Invisible strings rolled out from Oliver's carrier, wound around my heart, and tugged.

After 26 years of going through the motions and heartbreak after heartbreak, I'd finally come face to face with true love...with a cat. And I was finally ready to admit it.

CHAPTER THIRTEEN

I reached out a hand high in the air, stretching it up and over my head, only to have a white paw press into my cheek.

"Oh, okay," I laughed and turned to kiss the top of Oliver's head. "I'm sorry I'm not paying attention to you."

His tired, glazed eyes blinked at me before he nuzzled my neck, settling back against my chest so I could continue rubbing the spot in between his shoulder blades that had those vibrations in his chest rumbling like crazy.

"You're funny," I smiled down at him.

Since his little surgery the day before, this had pretty much been his life in between eating and me forcing his pain meds down his throat. The second he'd stepped out of his carrier when Finn and I brought him home from the vet, the only time he left the comfort of the couch was to eat or use his litter box. I guess if I'd had my balls lasered off, I probably wouldn't move around too much for a while either. At least he got to have his cone of shame off as long as we were snuggling on the couch together, not that it was much of a consolation.

"I have to leave pretty soon, you know," I told him.

Meh.

"I'm a little nervous," I went on.

Oliver's head turned warily to face me, one side of his upper lip curling up into a kitty snarl, probably because I'd stopped touching him for just a second. As soon as my fingers slipped to the top of his head and down his back, the purring picked up again and my anxiety waned a little.

I'd spent a whole year in Milwaukee reveling in the crowds and the city life that allowed me to blend in, to get lost, to be anonymous, and now, I was about to throw that anonymity away. Tonight, I would have to step inside a crowd and allow myself to be seen.

The prospect was absolutely terrifying.

So, obviously, I wasn't just a little nervous. Petrified was probably a better adjective.

Because I'd invited Mara to the brewery tonight, I'd felt responsible for picking her up at her apartment, a move that surprised her just as much as it surprised me. At least I wouldn't have to walk into the brewery by myself. So there was that. Going over to Finn's apartment to watch a Packer game with him and Slinger was one thing...that was easy. That was the type of social situation I felt equipped enough to handle. But I wouldn't have my usual fallbacks tonight: wine, my blog, and Netflix. This was on a whole other scale. This was meeting his family. This was meeting his group of friends—people he'd known for years. People who would be scrutinizing me closely, as they rightfully should if they gave a shit about Finn at all, considering Finn's history.

But what about *my* history? What if one of them sniffed it out? What if one of Finn's well-meaning friends did a little research on me or God forbid, recognized me?

At some point, I would have to tell him.

We couldn't stay in this wonderful bubble I'd purposefully kept us in for much longer, at least not if I wanted to keep him in my life, if I wanted this to move further. Although Finn and I were undefined, we were still *something*...I wouldn't have been invited to the brewery tonight if we weren't.

I just wasn't ready.

I wasn't ready for the judgment. The disappointment. The disgust. The shock. The inevitable withdrawal that was bound to happen as soon as he knew.

I felt safe with Finn. I really did. I felt like I could be myself...but I couldn't look him in the eye and tell him. Fear crippled me emotionally, socially, probably financially, too, if you really wanted to dig in there and psychoanalyze, and I knew it. I just didn't feel like there was anything I could do about it.

Once again, those familiar tingles of everything I'd tried to push away —self-loathing, dread, panic...it all came rushing back. My old, dysfunctional friends were all here for the party and what a dismal, pathetic party it was.

"Ugh," I groaned when my eyes fell on the clock. "Crap. I have to go or I'm gonna be late."

Oliver yawned. That's all I got from him.

"Thanks for the vote of confidence, buddy," I told him as I leaned down to kiss his head one more time before scurrying out the door. "Love you too."

* * *

. . .

One would think going to a small party to celebrate my maybe-probably-boyfriend's success at work would be enough to lift me up and carry me through a case of cold feet.

Nope.

My feet wouldn't move.

And now, Mara stared at me like I'd just told her there would be no available men at this little shindig.

"Uh, Emma? Everything okay?"

How to answer that question without looking like I needed to be committed? I guess the answer was in the question, so I took the easy way out.

"I'm fine," I started a little too unsteadily. "I'm just a little nervous, you know?"

Understatement of the year.

Luckily, Mara took that to be just a normal amount of nervousness, not an intense, crazy-person amount that was bound to have me sinking faster than the Titanic.

"Oh, it'll be okay, Em," she wrapped an arm around my shoulder so she could tug me closer to the brewery's entrance. "It's just like ripping off a band-aid. You only have to go through the obligatory meeting of his friends the first time and then after that, it'll get easier every time."

"Yeah, but it's not just his friends. His dad and his uncle will be here, too," I reminded her.

"Right, right," she waved a hand. "You're beautiful, you're funny, you're smart, you're kind—just remember that and you'll be fine. Promise."

I didn't like the sound of that. In fact, it sounded like bullshit to me. Mara clearly had me confused with someone else. But, sooner or later, I had to step inside Matthews Brewing Co. and set aside as much of my own bullshit as possible. So, I let Mara lead the way and push us through the double doors to step inside the main entrance that opened up right into the tap room, where the party had clearly already started.

As we made our way through the crowd, my eyes wandered around the space, taking in every crevice with the little time I had to really enjoy it. The entire room looked like the inside of a garage with polished, shiny cement floors. Directly to my right, the horseshoe-shaped bar wrapped around the length of the room with a few bartenders flitting back and forth from the stack of taps at the center of it. The entire beer menu was hand-written in chalk on boards on the fire engine red walls and from the corner of my eye, three oversized garage doors separated the tap room from the brewhouse, where gigantic iron kettles with long pipes attached to them sat.

There was a decent-sized crowd pushed up against the bar and the only thing I recognized was Slinger's carrot-orange hair moving around behind the bar. We must have walked in at the exact right moment because Slinger's eyes shot up from what he was doing at the bar and he flashed me a smile, but when he caught sight of Mara at my elbow, that smile brightened mischievously as he waved us over.

"Hello ladies," Slinger greeted us from behind the bar and it was then that I finally took in the bright red Matthews Brewing Co. T-shirt he wore.

"Hey, Slinger," I told him and pointed at his attire. "I didn't know you were a bartender here."

"Correction, milady," Slinger told me, leaning both palms onto the bar top, but his eyes darted suggestively to Mara as he spoke. "I'm the *head* bartender and bar manager."

I blew out a breath and lifted my eyes to the ceiling. "Oh boy."

Mara, on the other hand, leaned into the bar ever so slightly with a coy smile playing at her lips. At that point, I pretty much rolled my eyes at her, too.

"Mara," I gestured towards Slinger as I spoke. "This is Finn's roommate, Marshall, but everyone calls him Slinger. Slinger, this is my friend, Mara. I work with her at The Corner Café."

As the two shook hands, I felt like I'd stepped out of my body and was somewhere on the ceiling, watching myself introduce my co-worker and Finn's roommate/best friend like I'd known them for years, like they were actually my friends. It was pathetic and unsettling all at the same time. Finn...he didn't really count. What we were wasn't the same as friendship.

The only real friend I had right now was a cat. That counted, right?

On cue, a familiar warmth caressed my back and I turned to find Finn grinning down at me like the night was somehow complete because I'd arrived. That was just as difficult to wrap my head around as the pretense of having normal friendships with anyone who wasn't a feline.

"You made it," he told me as he wrapped an arm around my waist. The happiness and the pride radiating down at me was infectious and all I'd done was just show up for a party.

"I did," I laughed and quickly gestured to Mara to deflect the intense giddiness threatening to topple the little control I had left. "This is Mara, my friend from work."

Finn and Mara dutifully shook hands and even though Finn appeared genuinely interested in making small talk with my co-worker, Mara quickly turned her attention back to the *head* bartender, who was currently leaning so far over the bar to whisper in her ear he was practically lying across it. Clearly, our presence was no longer necessary and Finn made a show of rolling his eyes at me to signal as much.

I nodded my head towards the small crowd behind us. "So, I take it the presentation went well?"

"It did," Finn confirmed, even though no confirmation was really necessary. "The Bluestone guys were all for it. We're doing the official roll-out next month at the lounge."

"That's great," I smiled proudly. "As if it could've gone any other way."

One side of his face pulled apart in a playful wince. "Well, I don't know about that, but thanks for the confidence."

At least I was capable of brandishing confidence to someone else, even if I didn't quite feel it myself.

"Come on," he whispered in my ear. "Let me show you off."

My eyes reflexively drifted down to my outfit, a Cristina-approved ensemble of dark skinny jeans, an off-the-shoulder black top, and some dangly jewelry. Half a second into my indecision, Finn's warm breath flooded my ear again.

"You look beautiful, Em," Finn stated matter-of-factly. "Let me introduce you to everyone, okay?"

I couldn't have denied him even if I wanted to. With his warm hand putting just enough pressure on my back, I had to put one foot in front of the other. No getting around it now. Time to put on my social butterfly face, one I used to wear so easily, even if it wasn't 100 percent genuine.

Tonight, I was lucky if it was even 50 percent genuine and, I guess, I had no one to blame for that but myself. I was just a walking, talking bundle of nerves that only spiked when Finn led me deep into the abyss of my social anxiety. The only thing keeping me from turning and bolting was Finn's hand planted firmly in the small of my back and I had a sinking suspicion that was exactly why his touch hadn't left me yet.

"Hey guys," Finn started as soon as we joined the small circle and he gestured to me. "This is Emma."

I waited for the inevitable awkward pause: 'this is Emma, my...' but it never came. I was just Emma and that was okay.

I waved a little awkwardly and finally let myself take a good look at the people important enough to Finn to be here for him tonight. They were all in various degrees of casual dress, one in dress pants and a tie, and they all looked so friendly, inviting, normal...exactly the kind of people I would've expected Finn to surround himself with.

Finn started rattling off names, pointing to each one to help me remember who was who, and when each name was called, the name's owner waved in greeting.

"This is Alex and his girlfriend, Heather, that's Ethan, and Tyler and his wife, Amanda, Colin, Chase, Nick and that's his girlfriend, Megan, and Tanner."

"Hi everyone," I waved again, albeit pretty awkwardly, and did my best to put on my friendliest, bravest smile despite the fact that I was two seconds away from pulling the ol' cut and run.

Be normal, I told myself. *For the love of all that's holy...good God, just be normal.*

"It's nice to finally put a face to the name," one of Finn's friends told me...what was his name? Tyler, maybe? "We've heard a lot about you —all good things, of course."

"Good," I laughed and it actually felt genuine, too.

"Well, it certainly doesn't look like anything Finn told us was an exaggeration," Finn's friend in the tie—Chase, I think—acknowledged with a grin.

"Finn said you work at The Corner Café?" Amanda asked me. "I love that place! The pie is absolutely to die for."

"Yes, it is," Finn added and rubbed his stomach a little like he was picturing a piece of that banana cream right there.

"Yeah, it's great," I laughed. "I actually, sort of, write a blog, too."

"What do you mean *sort of?*" Finn grinned down at me and then shifted his attention to his friends. "Your blog has, what, thousands of hits a day, right?"

I shrugged sheepishly. "Something like that. It's, um, *Northern Chic.* I don't know if you've heard of it—"

"Oh my God!" Heather cried out. "I love that blog! I seriously check it almost everyday to look for new posts! I swear to God I won't buy anything unless you recommended it. This is crazy!"

Oh God. Now, I was beginning to feel cornered, not to mention startled by all this sudden attention.

"I've actually read some of it, too," Finn admitted with a shrug as Heather's eyes just about popped out of their sockets.

"You got Finn to *read?*" Heather asked me in a low whisper.

Finn shot her a playful, exasperated look. "Hey, now, I read. Sometimes. And Em didn't get me to do anything. I did it on my own, okay?"

Heather's eyes only widened the size of the beer glass clutched in her hand and then her gaze flew back to me, her expression shifting between awed and disbelieving in alternating strokes.

I wished it could've been left at that. Things were going so well...but then Finn's friend, Chase, just had to keep staring at me, watching me, appraising me, trying to place me. I could almost see the wheels in his head turning, *where have I seen this chick before?* But too polite to say it out loud, at least right now. Fortunately, I think I was also the only one to realize that Chase just couldn't tear his eyes away from me and not in a flattering way either.

Swallowing tightly, I did my best to turn my attention back to the rest of the group, who were too busy asking Finn for the details about his presentation. I tried to listen, I really did...I *wanted* to hear all the details about Finn's slam-dunk today, too, but Chase's dark eyes still hadn't moved on. This was deeper than scrutiny and more sinister than curiosity.

This wasn't just my paranoia manifesting itself and playing tricks on my mind.

He recognized me. That was all there was to it.

Even if he hadn't put all the pieces together yet, that awareness, that acknowledgment that he seemed to know me from *somewhere*...it was only a matter of time before all the puzzle pieces slid into place for him. Hot fear slipped down my back, turning icy cold right where Finn's hand rested on my lower back, and even the best actress in the world couldn't turn off the heat that burned into my cheeks.

"Well," Heather was saying to me now. "I'm really sorry you have to live right across from this loser," she gestured with her head towards Finn, "I can only imagine—is it football non-stop, 24/7 over there?"

At this point, I could have kissed her I was so grateful for the distraction.

"It's not quite that bad," I laughed and glanced at Finn, who was currently shooting that playful snarl Heather's way. "I *did* see their obsession first-hand though on Sunday. It was...interesting, to say the least."

"Oh, just wait until they all get together," Amanda added and rolled her eyes at her husband. "This one is absolutely intolerable about the whole thing. And don't even get me started on what happens when they all get to Lambeau. It's chaos."

"Embarrassing chaos," Heather nodded ruefully. "Just you wait, Emma. You won't want to take Finn anywhere in public on game days after you see him at an actual game. Trust me on this one."

Finn just shook his head at me and I finally remembered what being included in a group felt like...an odd sense of deja vú clouded over me and I was suddenly transported back to how much fun I used to have with people who cared about me, with people who were my friends, back when I still had them. Back when I was still normal and able to handle these type of social situations without feeling like I needed to heave into a paper bag.

And it was somewhere around this time that I realized they'd all assumed I was Finn's girlfriend, or at least, nearly there. Surprisingly enough, *that* didn't make me want to cut and run.

"They're exaggerating a little," Finn murmured in my ear. "It's not that bad."

I cocked an eyebrow at him. "I don't know about that. I *have* watched a game with you, you know."

He grimaced. "Yeah, I guess you're right. I apologize in advance for anything I might do or say to embarrass you whenever I get you to a game."

"Okay," I laughed. "So you're serious about taking me to a game?"

The thought of being thrust into yet another social setting, this time with tens of thousands of people sent another wave of panic flooding through me. It was so irrational it wasn't funny...like anyone in those tens of thousands of people would pay any attention. For all intents and purposes, going to a Packer game wouldn't be that much different than walking in the crowds here in Milwaukee, but still...

"Of course," Finn grinned down at me and equal parts of excitement and dread shot down my arms at the same time. "We're actually trying to get tickets to the next home game in two weeks. It shouldn't be a problem though, so mark that on your calendar, Em."

I just shrugged and tried to play it cool, if that was even possible. "Okay."

And against my better judgment, my eyes flicked across from me to find Chase's dark, calculating gaze locked right on me. Now, my mind was pulling out all the stops to convince myself that I'd been way off-base before, that this was all in my head, that I was just being paranoid.

It had been so long since I'd stepped foot in a public place and been recognized that I'd forgotten what it felt like...no, that wasn't true. I would never forget what it felt like as long as I lived. That little prickle of awareness, that cold panic sliding down your spine—there was no mistaking it.

Paranoia. That's all this was. I was projecting. Seeing things that weren't really there. Over-reacting and over-analyzing. Just an overactive, unhinged imagination. That was it.

Stop getting in your own goddamn way.

I just had to keep telling myself that until I actually believed it.

Finn's touch drifted to my elbow to, thankfully, get my attention. "Hey, why don't we head back over to the bar, okay?"

He was already leading me over there before I had a chance to nod and Finn tapped the bar top with two fingers in an attempt to draw Slinger away from my co-worker. Finally, he smirked at me and cupped his hands around his mouth.

"Yo, Sling! You gonna do your job tonight or what?"

Slinger barely cast a glance our way, but Mara at least had the decency to flash me an embarrassed wince.

Finn blew out a deep breath and lifted both eyebrows at me. "Ooookay. I guess I'll be our bartender tonight then."

He walked around the length of the bar, rounding the corner until he was facing me from the other side of the bar top. With a flick of a wet rag over his shoulder, Finn leaned both palms against the edge of the bar, taking the bartender role pretty literally now, and winked at me.

"Since this is your first trip to our fine establishment here," he started with a wide grin and gestured dramatically to the tap room around us, which I had to admit, really did have a breath-taking view of the Milwaukee River. "I think a tasting sampler is in order."

"Oh, I see," I nodded, doing my best to stifle a laugh. "Let's sample away."

He ducked underneath the bar for a second, clinking some glasses around, and materialized again with three smaller tasting glasses in one hand and two in the other. With a practiced flourish, he set each glass out onto the bar in a careful line then grabbed the one closest to him to fill up from the tap. He repeated this movement with ease, tipping each glass at just the right angle to keep as much foam out of the top as possible, until all five glasses stood full in front of me.

"Let's start with something easy, something light," Finn smiled knowingly and it probably had something to do with the uneasiness on my face at seeing all this beer lined up in front of me. He pointed at the thinnest looking beer at the end of the line. "Try this one first. It's our pale ale."

Was it bad form to tell him that his pale ale looked like pale piss?

Probably best not to go there. Still, I thought it was best to warn him, so I leaned my elbows on the bar, mimicking Mara's posture just at the end of the bar, and lowered my voice low enough so only Finn could hear.

"Do I have to drink all this?"

Finn's lips quirked up and he shifted his weight on his elbows so his mouth grazed the side of my cheek. "No, Em. Just do whatever you can handle."

Those words alone had my eyes flicking back to find Finn staring back at me with soft, understanding eyes and if the words weren't enough, the light, tender tone in my ear told me everything else. He understood. He felt my anxiety. He'd brought me over here to the bar not just to spend time with me, but to give me a chance to adjust to my environment.

He didn't know any of the details, he didn't know what the last year of my life had been like, but yet...he saw me anyway. All I'd given him was a Disneyfied tale riddled in half-truths and fantasy. And he knew it. He felt it. He didn't push. He didn't hover. He just let me be me at my own pace.

I think I would've done anything he asked in that moment. I would've given him anything, told him anything he wanted to know, if only he'd just keep looking at me with this acceptance. In that moment, I felt free of everything. In that moment, I knew if I pulled him aside right here in the tap room and told him everything, it wouldn't change anything. Well, it *would* inevitably change somethings, but it wouldn't change the way he was looking at me now. The way I knew he felt about me, even if it didn't make any sense to me.

Finn gestured with his head to the small sampler glass of pale ale in front of me, that smile still playing at his lips and sending me nothing but warmth. "Well, go on now. Give it a try. See how it feels."

So, with a deep breath, I slipped my fingertips around the glass and brought it to my lips. Cold, crisp liquid poured down my throat and from what I could tell, this one had hints of a bitter, citrus undertone I wasn't sure I liked. When I set the glass back down, Finn cocked an eyebrow at me, waiting for my reaction.

"It's not bad," I lifted a shoulder. "It's actually pretty good. I don't know if I like the citrus and that bitter taste together though. I still like whatever we've been drinking at the apartment better."

"Fair enough," Finn shrugged. "That's the honey ale. It's one of my favorites, too, and it's actually the first one we started bottling."

My eyebrows lifted playfully. "I see. Should I keep going?"

A large hand clapped me on the shoulder and I jumped at the

contact. "Absolutely. I'd love to hear your thoughts."

I turned my head to see an older, worn, and greyed version of Finn grinning back at me and the man thrust his hand out to me with Finn's identical light eyes twinkling. "I'm Finn's dad, Max. Please tell me you're Emma."

"Yep," I nodded shyly and shook his hand. "That's me."

"Fantastic," Max clasped his hands together in front of him as he slid into the bar stool next to me. "I'm glad that old stick in the mud over there invited you out here. We've got a lot to celebrate tonight."

Finn just rolled his eyes and shook his head at his dad. "I am *not* a stick in the mud."

Max shot me a wry glance. "Don't listen to him, Emma. I'm glad to see you've brought him out into the real world for a change. I don't know that he would've even shown up to his own party if you weren't here."

Even through the dim lights, the flushed embarrassment coloring Finn's cheeks was unmistakable. Once again, that warmth leapt through my stomach and into my chest, spreading over my shoulders and down my arms. It was only this public setting, not to mention the fact that Finn's dad was standing right next to us, that kept me from leaning over the bar and kissing him.

Max's gaze shifted to the end of the horseshoe-shaped bar, where Slinger and Mara still had their heads bent close together and he cocked an eyebrow at his son. "So is Sling takin' the night off or what?"

"I don't know," Finn sighed and rested his hands on his hips.

Max jerked his thumb over his shoulder at Slinger and shook his head, telling me, "Can you believe I took mercy on that skinny kid over there? Hired him as a bartender right outta high school, made him my bar manager two years later, and this is the thanks I get?"

"Sorry," I grimaced and lifted my shoulders. "I brought the girl he's talking to. That's my friend from work."

"No, no," Max batted a hand at me. "Don't take the bullet for that jackass. It's not your fault he spotted a pretty blonde and suddenly forgot he's on the clock. So, did Finn fill you in on our brewhouse?"

"A little bit."

"Ah," he shook his head reproachfully at his son, who just rolled his eyes. "I see. I'm not going to bore you with all the details, but we've been operating since 1980. Me and my brother Kurt have always been head brewmasters and Finn's been working odd jobs around this place since he was...12, I think. He started bringing Sling around in high school, so like I said, I took mercy on him until he got that," he paused to make air quotes, "'big' promotion, so I kinda feel like those two boys have grown up here, you know? Every year we experiment a little or add another brew into the mix, and every year, now thanks to your boy right there and all his marketing wizardry, we're slowly gaining more traction."

I glanced back at Finn with a small smile and found him leaning his palms into the edge of the bar with an exasperated expression.

"Now," Max continued, pointing to Finn. "Let's keep this tasting going, huh? So, I take it you liked the pale ale?"

"Yeah, it was good," I nodded.

"Most people agree," he went on and swept a hand out to Finn to signal it was his turn to take over.

Finn exhaled deeply, lifting his eyes agitatedly to his dad just once before picking up the next glass and sliding it to me. "This one is a little different than the pale ale. My Uncle Kurt calls this our 90-minute double IPA because, like the name, we hops it for 90-minutes."

I grimaced a little with a laugh. "I have no idea what any of that means."

"It's okay," Max assured me and even put a hand on my shoulder for good measure. "This one has more hops in it—meaning it's got a more bitter taste and more alcohol content. The IPA means that it's an india pale ale, but it's made differently than the pale ale you tried before. Give it a try and see what you think."

He gestured to the glass and now, I really had no choice but to take the glass and give it a try. God, it was bitter. And really, really sour. How did people drink this all the time? Ugh. I needed a wet towel or something so I could wipe off my tongue. However, I didn't want to offend the brewmaster sitting next to me either, so I put on the most diplomatic face I could manage.

"That one's not my favorite."

Finn burst out laughing, ducking his head underneath the bar as he leaned all the way back, and his eyes flicked to his dad, whose twinkling light eyes smiled back at me.

"Oh, you should've seen your face," Finn heaved as he swept some dark hair away from his forehead. "God, it was priceless. Where's a camera when you need one?"

"You *did* pucker up like you just swallowed a whole lemon," Max told me matter-of-factly and promptly took the glass with its disgusting beer in it from me to hand to Finn. "Here, take this one away. Now, are you ready for another one?"

What had I gotten myself into? At this point, I was feeling more than a little green from that last IP whatever it was, but I couldn't back down now. So, I dutifully endured two more tastings, a stout that Finn informed me was barrel-aged in oak that tasted like sweaty, dirty socks and a brown lager that was tolerable, but its sour aftertaste overwhelmed the malty flavor I'd initially enjoyed.

"We're striking out here, Dad," Finn surmised with a laugh as he took the lager glass away from me.

"Trust me, it's me, not you," I shook my head. "I've never really been into beer and all these fancy beers might be a little more than this wino can handle, you know?"

Max laid one hand over his heart and the other on my shoulder. "Did you hear that, Finn? Your girl here called our beer *fancy*. Thank you, sweetheart, that's the nicest compliment I've heard about our brews all day."

Once again, the slow, tender smile that slipped across Finn's face sent another wave of heat flooding down and over me.

"Now," Finn leaned into his elbows to get a little closer to me, completely ignoring his dad's presence, and tipped his chin towards the last beer I'd yet to taste. "I think we saved the best for last. This last one is a specialty beer. We used to just bring it out for the holidays, but people kept requesting it throughout the whole year, so we caved. Let's see what you think of this one."

My stomach still swirled from the last two tastings, so I put on a brave face and grabbed the glass, but I wasn't prepared for the decadent amber liquid that poured down my throat. It was sweet and velvety, creamy chocolate with a nutty, vanilla aftertaste. I almost downed the whole glass right there in one sitting it was so delicious.

"Oh my God," I practically moaned into the glass. "Forget wine. This is the best thing I've ever tasted."

"It's our vanilla porter," Max nodded proudly. "Customer favorite."

"Uh, yeah, I can see why. This is amazing. It doesn't even taste like beer. It's like you just melted chocolate into my glass and added alcohol, vanilla, and almonds or something to it."

"That sounds about right," Finn smiled. "I'm glad we finally have a winner."

"Absolutely," I agreed and lifted my glass up to toast him before taking another sip.

Sex in a glass. That's what this was. All that rich, savory chocolate laced with alcohol in liquid form felt a little naughty and more than a little inappropriate to drink in front of Finn's dad, so I allowed myself just a sip at a time to not look so greedy.

"So," Max started, leaning against the bar top as Finn discarded my other tasting glasses. "Finn tells me you used to be a history teacher."

My heart seized. My lungs froze. My eyes flew to Finn, who was observing me with careful, slightly narrowed eyes, and in *that* moment, I knew I'd officially given myself away. Finn's dad might be able to overlook my hesitation and fear and write it off as just catching me off-guard. But Finn...I'd only known him for two weeks and he already knew me too well. He'd caught on to all my tells, even if he didn't know the reason why.

The suspicion clouding his sky-blue eyes was undeniable.

"I, uh...yeah, I used to teach."

That was the best I could do. It was pathetic.

Max nodded, lifting a shoulder, and I braced myself for the inevitable question. It came half a second later. "So, why did you stop teaching?"

I didn't like having to lie, but the lie was the only defense I had.

"I just needed a change," I offered quietly, purposefully averting my gaze to focus solely on Max instead of Finn. "Teaching wasn't going to be a lifelong career for me, you know? It was stressful and frustrating..."

I trailed off, figuring I didn't need to elaborate and Max nodded sympathetically as Finn continued his quiet observation of our conversation.

"I can understand that," Max allowed easily. "I can't imagine these last few years have been very good ones to be a teacher. All that Walker business had to have made things even more stressful, huh?"

Somehow, this conversation had taken a political turn and pretty quickly, too.

"Yeah," I laughed. "It definitely made it worse. Suddenly, teachers are the bad guys now and I've always thought it's the opposite."

There it was again. Present tense. I needed to do a better job of getting a handle on that.

"It's really too bad things had to go that route," Max nodded soberly, his eyes flicking to Finn just once before settling back on me. "It was ugly, to say the least. And unfortunate. I've always thought teachers deserve more credit and more money than they get."

"There was definitely a decline, for sure," I explained, my mind sifting through the memories and I had to fight back a shudder. "Every year since Act 10, everything just got harder. I had less money, less respect from my students, more expectations with less clarification, less resources to actually do my job, more students crammed into every class, not to mention colleagues losing their jobs because of budget cuts, and somewhere along the way, those kinds of things really make you start to resent your job."

"I'm sure you don't think too highly of our governor then, huh?" Max asked and this time, that twinkle gleamed from his eyes again.

"What gave me away?" I laughed and shook my head. "Seriously, every time I see that weasel with his beady little lazy eyes on TV, I shudder and grind my teeth. I can't stand the sight of him."

"And," Max smiled. "I'm sure with your background, all that really killed you, huh?"

I laughed good-naturedly, enjoying this conversation more than I expected. "You have no idea. Basically, he set our state back about 50 years in labor and union rights, so yeah, it really killed me."

"I should probably admit right now—and please don't hate me—that I voted for him all three times," Max admitted with a shrug. "We're small business owners, you know? My hands were tied."

I just batted a hand and took another sip from my devilishly delicious chocolate beer. "Don't worry about it."

Finn leaned forward and smiled wistfully. "I think people have a tendency to just look out for themselves when push comes to shove. It's not personal, but at the end of the day, everyone wants as much of their money to stay in their own pockets as possible."

"You're right," I agreed and felt my lips lifting to match his smile. "But let me be the first to say that it's all gonna come back and bite everybody in the ass sooner or later."

"Absolutely," Max shook his head. "The way the whole system is changing, it's just gonna keep driving out young, dedicated teachers like yourself until all we're left with is people who barely have a degree, if they even have one at all, and then we'll all be sitting around wondering why the hell our kids can't read or do basic math and think that Africa is a country."

"I couldn't have said it better myself," I told him, even though he wasn't even close in his assumption about why I no longer taught.

Max winked at me and clapped a hand on my shoulder again. "I think you and I are gonna get along just fine, Emma."

"I think so, too."

"Now," Max pointed a finger at Finn. "I've taken up enough of your time tonight. Why don't you take this lovely lady on a little tour of the brewhouse? Show her how we make all that beer we just made her choke down?"

"Hey, I really loved that last one," I reminded him. "Do you guys bottle that? I'd seriously buy it in bulk if you did."

Max tapped his chin in thought while Finn looked on with a grin.

"That's not the first time someone's suggested that. Maybe we need to think more seriously about it, huh, Finn?"

Finn just shrugged and tossed the towel flung over his shoulder back down onto the bar top.

"Hey, I have a question," I interjected.

"Shoot," Max replied and I grinned at the similarities between him and his son.

"What's the difference between the brewery and the brewhouse?" I asked, my eyes falling to Finn, who was watching me with a smile. "I think I've heard both of you refer to this place as both those things and I don't understand the difference."

"Well, now," Max explained easily. "That's a fair question. The brewery is a reference to this whole building, you know? The brewhouse is where, well, we house our brews; that's where all the magic happens."

"Ah," I nodded. "That makes sense now."

"Good," Max clapped me on the shoulder one more time and gently pushed me to his left. "Now, I think you two kids need to get out of here for a little while."

Finn motioned with his head for me to follow him and I moved down the length of the bar with him still on the opposite side until we finally met at the end. The second he stepped out from behind the bar, his hand found my back and his lips grazed the side of my head.

"Have I told you how pretty you look tonight yet?" Finn murmured in my ear.

"Uh huh."

"But just the once though, I think," his warm breath was still in my ear and I shivered at the contact. "So, in that case, let me just say that you look absolutely beautiful and I'm a lucky bastard because you showed up here tonight for me instead of some other guy."

"Oh boy," I laughed lightly. "I wouldn't go that far."

"I would."

I was still shaking my head when my phone buzzed in my purse. With an apologetic wince at Finn, I slipped my phone out and glanced at the caller ID.

Frowning, I swiped across the screen to answer. "Hey. What's up?"

"Em?" The frantic, frazzled tone in Noah's tone told me everything I needed to know. "We're on our way to the hospital. Cris's water just broke."

My hand shot out to grip Finn's forearm. "What? But it's...she's okay, right?"

I couldn't let the words, *it's too soon*, fall from my lips. That wouldn't help my brother right now.

"Well, she's in labor, so I'm sure you can imagine how she's feeling right now. We'll be at the hospital in a few minutes. I just wanted to let you know."

"Right. Thanks for calling. I'll be there as soon as I can, okay?"

"I know," the panic in his voice still hadn't subsided. "Hurry...if you can, okay, Em?"

"I will. I promise."

My thumb swiped over the screen to end the call as Finn's arm slipped around my waist and lifted my eyes to find him watching me worriedly. "I'm so sorry, but I have to go. My sister-in-law is in labor and they're on their way to the hospital right now."

"Is everything okay though?"

"I don't know...I think so," I swallowed hard. "Noah sounded pretty freaked out because it's a little early, but she's only a few weeks before her due date. They weren't in an ambulance, so I'm sure everything's..."

I trailed off and sucked in a deep breath. Everything was going to be fine. Noah was a first-time dad who was basically losing his shit on the way to the hospital. That wasn't really anything out of the ordinary in terms of real life, but for Noah, whose normal reaction was fists over tears, even I had to admit this was a little alarming. This panicked, terrified version of my usually tough-as-nails brother was not one I'd ever seen before, at least not like this, and that was enough to send *me* into panic-mode right along with him.

"You're gonna be an aunt," Finn grinned down at me and gently pushed me in the direction of the exit. "You gotta get going, Em."

"I know, I know...I'm so sorry. I wish I didn't have to leave and you were just about to show me the brewhouse."

"You'll just have to come back," Finn laughed. "Trust me, that's not a bad thing."

My hand flew over my mouth when I remembered. "Oh my God! Oliver! I have to leave, but I can't really take him with me...and Mara! I can't just leave her here."

Finn's hands settled over my shoulders to calm me. "Don't worry about it. I got this, okay, Em? You get your ass on the road and I'll take care of your cat and..." he pointed to the bar where Slinger and Mara still had their heads bent in close, "I don't think Mara's gonna have any problems getting herself home."

Now, I just couldn't stop myself and wrapped my arms around his neck to tug him in close. "Thank you."

"I know you probably don't want to leave him after…" he caught himself from saying that three letter acronym that would probably have me bursting into tears again just from the stress alone. "But he will be fine. He's gonna be so doped up the next few days he won't even know you're gone."

Something about that hit a nerve and my lips dipped into a frown. The idea of Oliver forgetting about me completely didn't sit well with me.

"Okay, well his food is—"

"I know," Finn cut in with a grin. "Underneath the sink. Three scoops a day. Got it, Em."

"And his pain meds are—"

"In the cabinet *above* the sink," he finished for me. "Did you forget I helped you bring him home yesterday or what?"

"No," I laughed nervously and played with my purse strap for lack of anything better to do. "I didn't. I'm just trying not to freak out here."

"It's gonna be okay, Em," he reassured me, squeezing my shoulders to really drive the point home. "Your sister-in-law and the baby are gonna be okay, too."

Instinct and reflex took control and I leaned forward to kiss Finn in front of his family and friends. Both his hands closed around my cheeks and he kissed me deeply, putting just enough pressure against my lips to tell me one more time everything I needed to know, everything we weren't quite ready to say.

When I opened my eyes again and he pulled me into his chest for one last quick hug, I didn't even care that all eyes, at least where his friends were concerned, seemed to be on us. In fact, two of Finn's friends, Tyler and Ethan, were openly gaping at Finn like their eyes were about to roll right out of their heads.

"Don't mind them," Finn whispered in my ear. "It's been awhile, you know?"

"Yeah," I nodded into his chest. "I know."

I pulled away gingerly, eager to get on the road, but decidedly less eager to leave Finn and Oliver behind. So, in an effort to deflect the whirlwind of emotions whipping through me, I turned to his group of friends with the most apologetic smile I could manage.

"I'm really sorry, but I have to go. My brother and his wife are having a baby and I have to get to the hospital—it's a three-hour drive, so…"

"So what are you still doing here?" I heard Max call out to me from behind Finn. "Get going!"

"Call me when you get there and whenever else you need to, Em,"

Finn's voice was in my ear again. "Stop at your apartment before you leave, grab whatever you need, leave your key under your mat, and drive safe, okay?"

"Okay."

That was really all there was left to say. I trusted Finn to take care of everything else.

CHAPTER FOURTEEN

When that "Welcome to Hickory" sign came into view, panic seized hold of my throat. Up until that moment, I'd been able to push it away —out of sight, out of mind, you know? Now that the sign literally passed me by, no amount of denial could hide the truth: I was back in my hometown.

I swallowed hard, but the panic wouldn't subside. In fact, it multiplied the deeper I drove into Hickory, the town of my nightmares. I'd even had to pull over to dry-heave on the side of the road about 40 minutes into my drive. It was like my body physically rejected the prospect of stepping foot in this town again.

This was exactly what I'd always feared and exactly what I'd always tried to avoid. On the outside, the town felt ageless. Like it was stuck in some sort of time warp where time never actually moved forward. Everything looked exactly the same. Everything remained exactly where I'd left it. But my mind couldn't trick itself into believing that I'd been the one to move forward, that I'd changed for the better since leaving this town in my dust.

If anything, I'd only regressed more.

Then the visions started. Little bright images of my past life flashed before my eyes—shopping at Mike's Market, the smallest, sparest grocery store I've ever seen, going to movies at the only drive-in theatre left in Northern Wisconsin, meeting my friends at Jessie's Coffee Shop for scones and lattes or Luigi's for some of the most savory Italian pasta I've ever had in my life, family dinners at Noah and Cristina's—the normal life I used to know...I squeezed my eyes shut before those visions turned into something more insidious.

It wasn't like I could exactly turn my car around and head back to Milwaukee. Come hell or high water, I was getting my ass to that hospital, even though my mind screamed every obscenity in the book every step of the way. My mind knew this was a terrible idea, knew this wouldn't be doing myself any favors, but this was also not a time for selfishness.

My brother and sister-in-law were having a baby, goddammit.

Even when I pulled into the hospital's parking lot, I'd almost convinced myself everything was going to be okay. I'd almost forced myself to focus solely on Noah, Cristina, and the baby—they were why I was even in this goddamn town anyway.

My hands shook as I walked through the hospital's sliding doors and even now, at a hospital of all places, that old familiar paranoia stifled any hope that I'd be able to move around here unnoticed and undisturbed. It crept down my spine, slid over my arms, and all but suffocated me. I could barely tell the nurse at the front desk who I was looking for. All my normal body functions were lost to me—my mind, my voice, my limbs, nothing seemed to work properly.

"Emma?" The nurse asked impatiently. "You're here for Noah and Cristina, right?"

That snapped me out of it momentarily and I shook off as much craziness as I could. "I'm sorry...I'm Noah's sister and—"

"Yes, I know who you are," the nurse informed me curtly and pointed down the hallway. "They're in room 1311. Second to last on the right."

My heart sunk deep into my stomach as the nurse promptly returned to the paperwork in front of her, choosing to ignore my presence rather than assist me any further. I sort of wanted to crawl into a hole and stay there forever and this was really only the beginning.

Be strong. Be normal. Don't yell at this nurse. She doesn't know you.

Easier said than done.

As if on cue, my brother materialized in the hallway, stepping out of room 1311 to check his phone.

I cupped my hands around my mouth to call out, "Noah!"

His head snapped up at the sound of my voice and his face broke out in a brilliant, mega-watt smile. With his arms spread out wide, he waved me down the hall towards him where he met me halfway. His clothes were rumpled and a little off-center, his dirty blonde scruff reflected that 5 o'clock shadow I knew so well, his cropped hair looked mussed, like he'd spent the last few hours tearing his hands through it and he probably had, and his green and blue eyes—the mirror image of my own—were somehow exhausted and elated all at the same time. That was my brother, though...hard and soft, tired and refreshed, violent and gentle...a bundle of opposites just like me.

As soon as I was within arms' reach, Noah pulled me into a tight bear-hug and kissed the side of my head.

"I'm so glad you're finally here, Em," he told me. "I've been going a little crazy without ya."

"I drove as fast as I could," I laughed and leaned into him.

It had been a few months since I'd actually seen this guy in person and it wasn't until I finally saw him up close that I realized just how much I'd missed my big brother, the one person who'd always stuck by me like glue. Distance helped me push him away, but now, I couldn't deny that I'd made a mistake in systematically shutting Noah, as well as Cristina, out of my life.

"Well, I'm glad you made it here in one piece. Now...I have someone I'd like you to meet. Are you ready for this?"

I bit down on my bottom lip, my eyes already burning with tears. "Ready as I'll ever be, I think."

"Come on," he chuckled and rested both hands on my shoulders to steer me into room 1311.

Noah pushed open the door and it was like an unveiling—angels were singing somewhere above me, airy clouds carried me through the room, and a spotlight shone down on the figure lying on the hospital bed just feet away. Cristina, although understandably worn, slightly disheveled, and a little puffy, beamed at me from the bed. That fresh maternal glow seemed to just radiate from her and that blissful, gorgeous smile beckoned me closer to the bed so I could finally see that little pink bundle snuggled protectively in her arms.

"Hola, Tia Emmie," Cris whispered to me as I stepped over to her, my eyes already stinging with fresh tears.

I covered my mouth with my hand and leaned down just enough to see the baby Cris lifted up in her arms. There she was. My niece. Her skin was flushed an odd crimson and lavender hue, her dark eyes were a little cloudy, her patchy black hair was matted, sticking up around her forehead, and she was perfect. Absolutely perfect.

Love at first sight. Once again, I'd been knocked sideways by a pair of eyes.

"Tia Emmie," Cristina cooed breathily. "This is Maria."

"She's so beautiful," I murmured, wiping a tear from my cheek. "Oh...she looks just like you, Cris."

"Yeah, she does, doesn't she?" Cristina laughed as she shifted the baby to gingerly place her into my waiting arms.

Once my niece was nestled in my arms, I felt Noah hovering over me, his hand on my shoulder, and Cristina's fingertips brushing the arm that held her baby, but all I could see was Maria.

"*Maria,*" I sang softly to her. "*I just met a girl named Maria...and suddenly that name will never be the same to me...Maria."*

"I knew you'd throw a *West Side Story* reference in there," Noah grumbled behind me.

"Can't help it," I smiled down at my niece, not bothering to give her dad a glance. "It was just too perfect...just like you, Maria."

"Oh boy."

"You shut it," Cristina laughed and swatted at her husband. "Don't ruin this moment for us, Noah. I'll kill you."

"Wow, already threatening violence in the presence of our child. Very nice."

I just shook my head—this was nothing out of the ordinary for the two of them, especially since I didn't even have to look up to know that Noah was beaming down at his wife with all the love, devotion, and admiration I knew he felt for her. Instead, my attention remained rooted right where it needed to be: on my gorgeous new niece.

"I'm sorry I couldn't get here sooner," I shot Cristina a quick, apologetic glance. "I had to stop at my apartment for my overnight bag and drop off my key for my neighbor," I ignored the way Cristina's eyes flashed at the word *neighbor,* "I think I got here about a half hour sooner because I was driving so fast though."

Noah squeezed my shoulder. "Well, it's good to know you're willing to break traffic laws when push comes to shove, Em."

"Absolutely," I laughed. "Anything for you guys."

. . .

After Noah made a mad dash for some food and a nurse swooped in to check on my niece, Cris patted the space next to her on the mattress and I dutifully crawled into the bed as she laid her head on my shoulder.

"I'm so glad you're here, Em," she whispered. "It's been too long since I've actually *seen* you, you know?"

I pushed out a deep breath and rested my cheek on the top of her head. "I know. I'm sorry."

"Stop apologizing, chica, seriously. You're here now and that's all that matters."

"I suppose...I hope you know you're my hero," I told her. "It's amazing—everything you did, pushing that baby out...you're so strong. So goddamn brave. So much stronger and braver than I'll ever be. I can't even imagine..."

"It's pretty crazy, isn't it? What our bodies can do? I mean, this just gives me a whole other perspective on my body. I don't care what it looks like, bumps, rolls, stretch marks, whatever—every time I look at Maria now, I'm gonna be like—my freaking awesome body *did* that."

And that was why I loved my sister-in-law. Always the eternal optimist.

"It is pretty awesome," I agreed wholeheartedly. "So, what happened? Tell me everything."

Cris just laughed. "Well, it was pretty quick. As soon as my water broke, it was just like…" she swept a hand down the length of her stomach, "whoosh! She just sorta popped right out and I know how lucky I am for that, even though Noah was freaking out that we weren't gonna make it to the hospital in time. Oh…and all I have to say is: epidural. That's it. Epidural. I didn't feel a damn thing once they stuck me with that monstrous needle and it. Was. Beautiful."

"Oh God…and Noah? Did he make it through the whole thing or did he pass out?"

"Surprisingly enough," Cris shrugged, "he made it. There were a few moments where it was a little touch and go, but he pulled it out."

"What a guy."

"Oh yeah…and he's gonna be a great daddy, too. Did you see the way he looks at her?" Cris put a hand over her heart. "I melt a little every time I see it and it's only been a few hours."

I smiled as the memory of the proud papa washed over me. The way Noah's eyes glittered when he saw her, the unconditional love radiating from him…the dude was already a goner.

"And, um, your mom was here before," Cris told me softly, her voice lowering carefully. "Noah told her you were coming and she left about an hour ago. I'm sorry—"

"No," I shook my head to cut her off. "Don't be sorry, Cris. It's probably for the best that we just avoid each other anyway. This is supposed to be a happy day and nobody needs that shit up in here, you know?"

Especially since I had no interest in being in the same room as my mother if I could help it.

Cris smiled wistfully and her fingers squeezed my hand as if she could read my thoughts. "I love you, you know."

"I know," I whispered. "I love you, too."

"So," Cris wiped her eyes quickly and shook off the emotion that had just taken over the room. "Tell me about this neighbor…is this the same one you had over for pizza? And you left him the key for your apartment?"

I winced. I should've known the Puerto Rican Inquisition wouldn't rest just because she pooped out a kid. "Ah...we don't need to talk about that. It's not a big deal. Besides, I want to hear more about the epidural and that monstrous needle."

"Oh no," she laughed. "You don't get to change the subject. Tell me and tell me now."

"Ugh. Really, Cris?" I did my best impression of puppy dog eyes, but she just blinked back at me. "He's just keeping an eye on Oliver for me while I'm gone."

Cris's eyebrows lifted suggestively. "That's awfully neighborly of him. Sounds like a nice guy. So...are you dating him? Seeing him? Screwing him?"

All I could do was squeeze my eyes shut and shake my head. "Come on, Cris."

"What? I just gave birth, okay? My lady parts ain't seeing any action for awhile, so I'm gonna have to live vicariously through you, which, let's face it, is really depressing. *Please* tell me something good. Please, please, pretty please."

"Oh my God," I rolled my eyes up to the ceiling. "We've gone on a few dates, I guess."

Cris's mouth dropped open in faux-shock. "You *guess?* What the hell is that supposed to mean?"

"I don't know," I shrugged. "We're...taking it slow."

My sister-in-law eyed me carefully, studying me with well-practiced scrutiny. "Okay. So, you're taking it slow. That sounds like a good plan. Does that mean you're *not* screwing him?"

"Yes, that's what that means, but," I threw in before I could stop myself, "I *am* kissing him if that makes you feel any better."

"Oh!" Cristina squealed and hugged me to her a little too tightly, shaking and squeezing the breath out of me. "I bet he's a good kisser. Oh...I don't even know what he looks like. Do you have a picture? Can we meet him? Can we visit? Oh, Em, I'm so, so happy for you!"

"Whoa," Noah called out from the doorway with two bags of take-out in his hands. "What's goin' on in here?"

"Emma likes a boy," Cristina informed him in a syrupy sweet sing-song voice.

My eyes must've practically breathed fire because she burst into laughter.

"Thanks a lot, Brett," I muttered under my breath.

"What did you just call me?" she cocked an eyebrow at me.

"Nothing," I waved a hand at her. "Inside joke."

Her mouth quirked up in amusement. "Oh, I see."

Noah, unfortunately, had frozen mid-step with the bags still in his hand. His eyes sparked warily, darting uneasily from me to his wife and back to me again. "Emma likes a boy? Since when?"

"God," I grumbled. "What am I—in middle school or something? Come on. Get a grip, guys. This isn't a big deal."

Noah's eyes narrowed as he set the bags down on the table next to the bed. "Bullshit it's not a big deal. Who's the guy, Em?"

I shifted uncomfortably on the bed and Cristina winced at me sheepishly.

"I'm sorry," she whispered in my ear. "It's the hormones. They're all over the place. I can't control them."

"Don't worry about it."

"Em?" Noah's tense voice cut through the room. "The guy? Who is he?"

My brother's predictable reaction was only indicative of my past—he worried about me, he cared about me, he wanted to see me happy, and most importantly, he didn't want to see me hurt again. But that also didn't mean I was ready for the interrogation just yet.

"Em?"

"He's my neighbor," I finally relented and gave Noah what he wanted. "He's actually, um, taking care of Oliver while I'm gone."

Noah's eyebrows rose dangerously and he hitched both hands on his hips. Uh oh. I'd seen this before. This macho, alpha-male peacocking act would've been hilarious if it also didn't make me fear for Finn's life, too.

"And," Cris chimed in cheerfully beside me. "Emma gave him a key while she's gone. They've been kissing."

"Cris!" I shrieked and swatted her shoulder. "How could you tell him that? What the hell is wrong with you?"

Seriously, did she want Noah to jump in his car, drive three hours to Milwaukee, break down the door, and pummel Finn into oblivion? It's not like it would be the first time...

"Sorry, sorry," Cris held up both hands with a grimace. "Hormones."

Against my better judgment, my eyes skidded to Noah, whose lips had curled back into a snarl. Clearly, he was unamused. And lethal. Luckily, I was saved by the buzz. I dug through my purse for my phone, ignoring the other two people in the room, and praising sweet baby Jesus for the distraction. Swiping across my screen, the only knee-jerk reaction my body allowed was a smile because staring up at me was a picture of Oliver, in all his grumpy, cone of shame-wearing glory, propped up against Finn's chest on my couch.

"Oo, what's that? Did he just text you that picture?" Cris craned her neck over my shoulder to catch a glimpse of the picture.

"Yes," I allowed and begrudgingly tilted my screen to give her a clearer view. "That's Oliver...and Finn."

She bit down on her bottom lip to hide her shit-eating grin and shifted her eyes to her husband, who still observed us darkly with his hands cemented to his hips.

"Look at them. They're so cute!"

"You can't even see Finn," I rolled my eyes.

"Trust me, I can see plenty."

With that, she snatched my phone out of my hand and held it up for Noah to see. To my horror, he leaned down, squinting just enough to make out the image in front of him. And when he straightened back up, that cloudy darkness still hadn't left his eyes. Clearly, he was not convinced and definitely still not amused.

Seeing an opportunity to deflect, I stole my phone back and scrambled off the bed. I'd already made it halfway through the room when I called out over my shoulder, "I just remembered I was supposed to call him when I got here."

When I shut their hospital door behind me, any pressure and any tension fogging my brain thankfully dissipated. Just that little bit of reprieve was enough to let me inhale a deep breath and I hit dial to call Finn.

"Hello?" His deep, husky voice answered and I smiled at the welcome sound.

"Hey, Finn," I hoped he could hear the smile in my voice. "I got here a little bit ago, but I wanted to call you to let you know everything was okay."

"Good," he exhaled. "I figured you would and I guess I just sent you that text to let you know everything was all good on our end, too."

"Thanks. I loved the picture, by the way. He certainly doesn't look worse for the wear."

"Well, that little RB did hit the kitty jackpot when it comes to you, so can you really blame him?"

"No," I laughed. "I guess not. Thank you again for checking in on him. That just made it so much easier to be able to pick up and drive here knowing he was going to be okay."

"That's what I'm here for, Em. Hey, I wanted to ask you—do you think I could crash on your couch tonight? I normally wouldn't ask, but since you're out of town anyway..."

"Sure. Why not? You know, that actually makes me feel better knowing Oliver's not going to be by himself during the night. I'm sure he'd be fine on his own, but you know."

"Yeah, well..." Finn started again a little unsteadily. "There's that and the fact that Sling has a, uh, *guest* in our apartment right now. Your friend and him really hit it off, didn't they?"

My mouth opened to respond, but I shut it almost immediately.

"What was her name? Kara?"

"Mara," I correctly quietly.

There was a part of me that felt insanely jealous of Mara, not because she was with Slinger, but because she was doing all the things I wished I could do with the guy I had feelings for—the intimacy, the normalcy, it was all so *healthy*, even if I couldn't exactly advocate sleeping with someone you've just met, I wished I was comfortable enough to take those steps with Finn, too, albeit at a much slower pace.

"Anyway," Finn went on. "I didn't really feel like subjecting myself to *that* tonight if I could help it, so thanks."

"No problem and feel free to help yourself to anything in my fridge. I don't think there's all that much, but go for it if it's there."

"Sounds good. So, you're officially an aunt now, huh?"

"Yep," I smiled. "I am officially the proud auntie of Maria Owens. She's beautiful, Finn...seriously, the moment I saw her, I think I just burst into tears."

"That sounds about right," he chuckled. "Does that mean I can call you Auntie Em? Please say yes. Please."

"Oh my God."

"Yeah, you know like in *The Wizard of Oz?* Actually, I think you're more like Dorothy. Oliver could be the Cowardly Lion. Sling would be the Tin Man and I'd be the Scarecrow."

"You mean the guy who wished he only had a brain?"

"Hey, he had a brain the whole time. He just didn't know it, okay?"

"Whatever you say," I laughed and shook my head.

And then Finn's analogy started to sink in. So, in his mind, I was some kind of modern-age Dorothy, lost and aimlessly trying to find her way home from Oz, er, Milwaukee? Unfortunately, that analogy had some weight...if I was walking around singing about a place where troubles melt like lemon drops and waking up where the clouds are far behind me. Maybe I'd wake up and this would all have been a bad dream and I could go, "And you were there and you and you and so were you".

Shit. Now I had Judy Garland singing in my head.

It was just too bad that the twister that had bulldozed through my life was very real and the devastation it caused couldn't be magically resolved by clicking my heels together.

"When do you think you'll be home, Em?"

"Tomorrow for sure. I'm probably gonna crash at Noah and Cris's house tonight and head back to the hospital tomorrow morning for a little while before I leave."

"Yeah, I guess that makes sense...I, uh," I could practically see him tugging his free hand through his hair as he spoke. "I miss ya, Em."

I sucked in a deep breath, my chest fluttering and heat flushing my cheeks. "I miss you too, Finn. And I'm really sorry I couldn't stay tonight—I really wanted to. I was having so much fun with you and meeting your friends and your dad and getting to taste all your beers."

"I'm glad, Em and everyone really liked meeting you, too. Hey, we've got that Packer game coming up though, right? You'll see everyone again then."

"Oh, that's right. The Packer game," I looked up just in time to see Noah closing Cris's door behind him and his eyes widened at the words *Packer* and *game*.

He knew better than anyone that I'd never had much interest in the Packers, or going to Packer games for that matter, so this new development certainly wasn't lost on him. But now, unfortunately, his presence in the hallway also meant that I'd probably have to cut this conversation with Finn short.

"Don't worry about the tickets," Finn went on. "I'll take care of it, okay?"

"No, Finn, you don't have to do that. I can pay my own way."

"I know that, Emma, but I'm still taking care of your ticket."

"Ugh," I exhaled and shook my head at my brother, who gawked at me like I'd just said Jay Cutler was the new MVP.

"*What's going on?*" Noah mouthed to me.

"Hey, Finn," I told him and rolled my eyes at Noah. "Can you hold on a second? My brother just came out into the hallway and I think his eyes just about fell out of his sockets when he heard me talking about going to a Packer game."

"Does he like the Packers?"

"Sure," I shrugged. "Of course he does. Cris likes going to the games more, I think, than actually watching the games though."

"Would they wanna come? We didn't buy the tickets yet, so I can easily add in two more no problem."

My brain froze. Oh shit. I felt like the rug just got ripped out from under me and I fumbled to come up with another deflection. "Oh, uh, I don't—"

"It's really not a big deal, Em. If he's right there, why don't you ask him?"

I don't know why I froze. Maybe it had something to do with the fact that my brain completely short-circuited. My eyes flew to Noah, who hovered over my shoulder, eavesdropping like the vigilant big brother he was, and his eyes narrowed.

"Um, Noah?" I started shakily. "Finn wants to know if you want to come with us to the next home game. Him and his friends are getting tickets and he said he can get two more if you guys want to go."

Noah's eyes widened and his head reared back like he couldn't believe what I'd just said.

"Hey, Em," Finn called out to me from the other side of the line. "Why don't you just put him on the phone? It's just easier that way and then I can give him the details."

Almost robotically, I held my phone out to Noah, numb and disbelieving. "Um...Finn wants to talk to you."

How in the hell did this happen? I'd gone from fearing for Finn's life to handing over the phone so they could chat like old friends. It didn't help that my brother was staring at my phone like it had contagions crawling all over it. Finally, some sense of propriety snapped into place and he held out his hand, signaling to me that it was time to relinquish not only the phone, but the control, too.

I really had no choice at this point, so I handed over my phone. Noah brought it up to his ear and it was all over with from there.

"Hello?" Noah started and it was all I could do not to cover my eyes with my hands to block it out. "Really? Well...yeah, I don't see why not...no, I'm sure we could probably have my mom baby-sit or something...yeah, I think so too...nah, you don't have to do that. Thanks though...we can just meet you guys somewhere outside the stadium and I'll have the money for you right away...sounds good, thanks again—I'm gonna hand you off to Em now, okay? Sure, lookin' forward to it, man."

Stunned into immobility, I don't know how I was able to take the phone back from my brother. That just happened. That totally just happened. I couldn't believe it.

I numbly put the phone back to my ear. "Finn?"

"Hey, Em. So, it looks like your brother and sister-in-law are in for the game. Now you can't back out on me, right?"

Well, now it all made sense.

"You set me up," I laughed. Honestly, what other reaction could I have at this point?

"Nah, it wasn't like that. Besides, I think you might have more fun anyway if you know some people at all the pre-game stuff other than just me and Sling."

So any doubt I had about whether or not Finn was clued into my aversion to large social settings was pretty much gone.

"Right."

"Em, you're gonna have fun. I promise. And I'm really looking forward to finally meeting your brother and your sister-in-law...I really am."

And how could I argue with that? I wished I could somehow reach inside my phone and pull him through it so I could kiss him. And then I remembered my brother was still standing right next to me, scrutinizing every word with careful eyes.

"I wish you were here," I suddenly blurted out and then winced. "I mean...I know you couldn't come with me and you were at the party and now you're baby-sitting my cat, but I miss you."

I turned away so I couldn't see Noah's reaction to my words. This was supposed to be a private conversation anyway and the eavesdropping could really only be tolerated for so long.

"I know, Em," Finn told me, his voice warm and just hearing it made me wish I could crawl onto the couch with him tonight and let him hold me for the rest of the night. "I wish I was there with you, too. Look, I know you're still at the hospital, so why don't you give me a call later or something?"

My eyes lifted to the digital clock in the hallway. "Are you sure? It's already 11."

"Yeah, me and Oliver are probably just gonna be watching *Parks and Rec* all night anyway."

"Don't you have to go to work tomorrow?"

"Yep."

"You say that like it's no big deal."

"It isn't."

I pushed out a deep exhale, finally turning to face Noah, who still observed me, but now his lips had quirked up a little. "Alright. I guess I can't argue with the two of you having some man time together."

"Good call, Em. Hey, I'll let you go, okay? *Parks and Rec* is calling and you need to spend some time with your family. I'll talk to you later."

"Okay," I smiled. "Bye, Finn."

"Bye, Em."

I swiped across my screen to end the call and no sooner had I shoved my phone into my back pocket that my brother's quiet voice called out to me.

"Your boyfriend seems okay."

My gaze darted up to him and while I'd expected to find suspicion, darkness, wariness, or *something* along those lines, I didn't see any of that from my brother. In fact, that small smile spread even deeper across his face. I swallowed hard and took a deep breath. Maybe it was time I stopped denying it.

"He does?"

Noah's eyes flashed at my admission that Finn was, in fact, my boyfriend and his mouth quirked up even more. "Yeah. At least from what I could tell over the phone. That was pretty nice of him...inviting Cris and me to the game like that. He offered to pay for our tickets, too, but I wouldn't let him. What, is he loaded or something?"

"No," I frowned. "Well, I guess I don't know. His family owns a brewery in Milwaukee, but I wouldn't say that means he's loaded. I was actually there for the first time today before you called and Finn and his dad did a whole tasting with me. It was pretty cool."

He eyed me carefully. "Are you sure it's a good idea to date your neighbor? I mean, don't get me wrong, you know I wanna see you happy, but if things don't work out...it could get pretty awkward, right?"

Somewhere along the way, I probably should've paused to consider that more thoroughly, but I hadn't planned on Finn worming his way into my life anymore than I'd planned on Oliver.

"I guess it's no different than me wanting to keep a cat I might've been allergic to and technically can't keep in my apartment."

Noah nodded slowly, as if he was taking it all in, step by step, line by line. "He treating you okay?"

I winced—once again, this was just a by-product of my past. "Yeah, brother, he's treating me okay. More than okay. He's...he's the best. I really like him."

"I can see that. Have you told him about..."

He didn't need to finish that sentence and I didn't need to hear it out loud.

"I told him about Justin."

When Noah's eyes widened with surprise, I jumped to explain. "I only told him why we broke up. I didn't tell him anything else."

Noah nodded and scrubbed a hand over his mouth. "Are you going to? Homecoming's right around the corner, you know. If something happens, don't you want him to know?"

That was the question I'd been too afraid to ask myself since the moment I met Finn. I knew that, at some point, I'd have to be honest with him if I wanted him to stay in my life, but would I actually have the balls to go through with it? Would I be able to actually look Finn in the eye and say the words out loud? I'd never actually told the story from start to finish out loud before and even if I wasn't quite convinced I'd be able to do it without turning into a puddle of hysterics, I had to figure out a way to make it happen. And my brother, despite his crazy over-protective tendencies, wasn't wrong in his worries about homecoming. The likelihood of something happening was, well, likely.

"Yeah," I nodded. "I do want him to know."

"Good," Noah told me and wrapped an arm around my shoulders. "That's really good, Emma."

. . .

I sat up from the couch, stretching my hands high over my head to shake out some of the stiffness in my back. It was only seven in the morning, but if I wanted to have enough time to see Cris, Noah, and Maria at the hospital before I had to get back to Milwaukee for my dinner shift at the café, I needed to peel my ass off the couch and get moving.

Because my mind was too preoccupied with warm, happy thoughts of the family that mattered to me—Noah, Cristina, and Maria—and the ones who'd recently entered my life but had just as much of an impact —Oliver and Finn—I think I'd made myself forget where I was.

I wasn't just in my brother's house.

I was in Hickory.

Not a dream I'd wake up from to find that everything was right where I'd left it Dorothy Gale-style. Nope. This was real. I was really here and would have to stay here for at least a few hours longer so I could spend some more time with my niece.

Maybe it was just because being in Noah and Cris's house made me feel too safe. Maybe I'd just let my guard down after seeing my family. Maybe I was just still floating on air after all those "I miss you" declarations with Finn last night.

Whatever the reason, I was unprepared to see my mother let herself into my brother's house like she owned the place with two covered dishes in her hands.

I hadn't seen my mom in over three months, since the disastrous 'dinner' that Noah and Cris had invited me to, the same one my mom had randomly decided she needed to be invited to where she proceeded to treat me like an unholy cross between a pariah and a hooker when *she* was the one who was uninvited. Of course, heaven forbid I should ever mention sex and all things holy in the same sentence.

But I digress.

Even for seven in the morning, Nina Owens was never one to step out of the house without looking her best. Finely coiffed, makeup perfectly in place, not a wrinkle in her pressed, tailored clothes...on the outside, she might have passed for a human being.

Fortunately for me, I knew better.

I knew the exact moment she realized I was in the house because all the air seemed to suck right out of the room. She froze, her face twisting in shocked horror, and she shuffled back a small step, like the short distance might somehow make it so I wasn't in this house with her, like I just didn't exist.

Well, someone had to be the adult in this situation.

"Hey, Mom."

My mom gaped back at me for a moment and then the hardened mask slipped back into place. She ran a hand over her warm brown hair—ironic, of course, because she was anything but warm—and that was all she needed to push away her initial shock and discomfort at my presence. I know...being around me was such a hardship, I didn't know how she could possibly stand it.

"Emma."

Her cool voice reached out to me, wrapping around my spine with its icy spikes, and threatening to pull it out through my throat.

"I didn't realize you would be here."

I huffed a little and shook my head. "Where else would I stay?"

She just lifted a stiff shoulder. "I don't know. I guess I hadn't thought about it."

Of course she hadn't. Why would she give a shit where I slept as long as it wasn't under her roof?

"Well, I was just dropping off some food for Noah and Cristina when they come home from the hospital later today."

"Oh."

What else was I supposed to say? *Oh, that's nice that you actually seem to care about at least one of your kids. You know, the normal one with the wife and kid that you can actually brag about to all your catty, judgmental friends at church?*

"I was going to stop over at the hospital right after I left here."

Right. I knew what that meant. That was her not-so-subtle way of telling me to either make myself scarce or risk creating unnecessary tension at the hospital. It was like no time had passed at all—I'd only been in the same vicinity as her for less than two minutes and she'd already manipulated me into doing exactly what she wanted. Exactly what would make *her* happy and comfortable. Who gave a shit about anyone else?

I didn't want to do anything that would upset Cristina at the hospital and showing up when I knew my mom was already there wouldn't do anything but cause problems. Besides, I knew when I wasn't wanted. This wasn't the first time she'd dismissed me and it wouldn't be the last.

Thankfully, my mom's visit was short. Painful, but short. She discarded those dishes in the refrigerator and promptly left the house without even bothering to ask me how I was doing or if I was okay. Who was I kidding? She didn't care. In her mind, she didn't have a daughter. I'm sure I didn't even exist in her memory.

So, I did as I was told and I waited an hour before texting Noah to see if my mom was still at the hospital. Once I got the all clear, I took my turn at the hospital, held my niece and kissed her goodbye, all the while feeling, once again, like my life had somehow spiraled out of my hands and completely out of my control. It wasn't until I was already in my car and driving back towards Milwaukee that the magnitude of what I'd done hit me.

I'd hidden in my brother's house like a deer in the headlights all because my mom showed up. All because I couldn't stand to spend more than minutes in her presence mainly because I knew she couldn't stand more than minutes in my presence, too. It probably also had something to do with the fact that every vile, hateful thing she'd ever spewed at me ran through my mind the second I laid eyes on her.

I'd let her win. Again.

My hands clenched around my steering wheel until my knuckles turned white and the miles kept right on rolling.

I hated that she got to me this way. It took next to nothing—one cold word, one icy glare—and I was sunk, drowning and flailing in open water while my mom sat in the lifeboat with a preserver clenched in her hand and an evil smile on her face.

There were so many better ways I could've handled that. I could've put her in her place. I could've stood up to her. I could've put my foot down and told her I was going to the hospital whenever I felt like it whether she liked it or not. But I didn't. I couldn't. Something deep-seated inside me pushed back, shoving me even further down the rabbit hole and into a black abyss of my own making.

The problem was that I still had some control. Or, at least, I could if I wanted to take it. Instead, I just handed it on a platter to everyone else because...I don't know why. Was it because I just wasn't strong enough? Was it because I just didn't know how to be strong in the first place? The answers to those questions weren't ones I wanted to take the time to reconcile.

I'd even been too afraid to stop at a gas station outside of town on my way back to Milwaukee for fear of anyone seeing me. The crippling dread, that cold terror at even the *idea* of showing my face anywhere here other than the hospital, which couldn't be avoided...the worse part about it all was that the dread and the terror I felt wasn't entirely misplaced either. Shards of panic splintered down my body as my mind leapt to every ugly, painful possibility of what would happen if I really did stop, if I went into Mike's Market or Jessie's Coffee Shop or anywhere else—the glares, the people shaking their heads in disgust, the whispered sentiments of horror, all with little regard for whether or not I could see and hear it.

I'd been subjected to that enough. I wouldn't put myself through that again if I could help it.

As the miles passed by, the next song on my playlist sounded through my speakers. Damien Rice's heartfelt, passionate timbre sung those familiar words from "The Blower's Daughter" to me and now, the memories washed over me.

I was sick of not having control. Sick of feeling like there wasn't anything *to* control. Sick of being manipulated. Sick of choices being ripped right out of my hands. Sick of being treated as less than. Sick of feeling like my life would never truly get better, that I would never truly heal.

"No love, no glory..."

I wanted to tell Finn. There were plenty of reasons to tell him. I felt like I owed him an explanation. I didn't want him to find out from anyone but me. I wanted to be honest with him. I wanted him to know me, the *real* me. I wanted him to understand why we needed to take things so slow, why I wasn't ready to be the normal girlfriend he deserved to have.

But the bottom line was...I wanted to tell him. I wanted him to know. I trusted him enough to know. He deserved to know.

Maybe it was time I started taking back some of that control. *This* was something I could do and do it on my terms.

"No hero in her skies..."

And then, my mind flashed back to that day, the day I belly-flopped off the deep end and landed face-first on the cold, wet floor of rock bottom…

CHAPTER FIFTEEN

A Year, Six Months, and Sixteen Days Ago

Some days you wake up and you know it's going to be a good, productive day. You can just feel it in the air—you have a little bounce in your step, your routine rolls along without a hitch, you have a few extra minutes to sit down and really *eat* your breakfast instead of resorting to scarfing it down on the ride to work. Everything's going as planned and with a new day, you have the world at your feet.

Other days, whether you slept through your alarm, burned yourself with your coffee, spilled on your outfit, forgot your lunch...whatever it is, you just know the day's going to devolve into shit because it already started out there.

That particular day, I woke up hopeful. Ambivalent and anxious, but hopeful.

A week had gone by since I'd called off my engagement and I remember feeling almost buoyant at the prospect of starting anew. My future had never looked so terrifying and so boundless all at the same time. I could go anywhere, do anything I wanted without having to answer to anyone. I was even considering the possibility of packing up and taking off for the horizon. Maybe I'd teach abroad in London or Paris or even just spend a year traveling around Europe because I was young and because I could. The possibilities were endless—I was a new woman with a new lease on life, unchained, and finally free at last.

I didn't know what the future held for me that morning as I walked into Kennedy High School with my heavy computer bag and my steaming travel mug and maybe, in hindsight, that wasn't a good thing. If I'd known what I was walking into, I might've been able to mentally prepare myself for the shitstorm that was about to rain down on me and I probably would've turned around and ran the other way altogether.

Instead, I walked in thinking it was just another Monday.

It wasn't just another Monday.

Have you ever had one of those dreams where you're walking down a crowded hallway and everyone is staring, pointing, laughing, and whispering...because everyone is wearing clothes except you? You look down, cry out in mortification, one hand flies out across your chest while the other covers your privates, but it's already too late. They've already seen everything there is to see and the damage is done. And you're screwed. Absolutely screwed.

That day, the dream became my reality. While I'd arrived appropriately dressed for the school day, the majority of my students and most of my colleagues had already seen me naked.

I just didn't know it yet.

As I rounded the corner from the usual staff entrance to the center hallway, two girls walking towards me stopped right in their path.

"Morning, ladies," I nodded to them with a tired smile and stifled back a yawn.

I was never much of a morning person and that was probably why it took me so long to realize the root of their baffled silence. The two girls, Lacey and Rae, hesitated, their eyes darting back to one another before Rae muffled a giggle with her hand as Lacey tugged her away, whispering something inaudible in Rae's ear.

"Nice to see you, too," I mumbled under my breath. "Geez."

But as I continued my trek down the hallway, something peculiar was happening around me. Every head turned, whether it was a student or a teacher. Every mouth moved to part in disbelief or to murmur to the person next to them. Every pair of eyes widened. Some even pointed. Most whipped out their phones the second I passed them by.

My lips curled into a tight frown. Was my shirt inside out? Something on my face? I tried discreetly wiping my mouth, my cheeks, and finally smoothed my hair down to make sure everything was in place. Looking down at my outfit, all I could do was shrug. No spills. No weird stains. Nothing in my teeth, as far as I could tell.

I got all the way to my classroom, fumbling with my keys to find the right one and somehow balancing my lunch and my travel mug in one hand while using the other to unlock my door when hushed whispers erupted behind me. One glance over my shoulder told me it was just more of the same, but this time three boys huddled together in one of the desks in the pod, their heads bent close together as one boy pointed to something on his phone and then all three heads whipped up in my direction at the same time.

Coincidence? I think not.

Still, I was willing to shrug off the odd attention for the time being and finally got my key in the lock to let myself into my classroom. I flipped the lights and went about my normal routine: setting my coffee down on my desk, booting up my computer, putting my coat in my closet, and perusing my lesson plans for the day. In an effort to save some time, I grabbed both my lunch and a handout I still needed to make some copies of and headed back out of my room to once again trek down the hallway. Maybe, if I worked quick, I'd have time to squeeze in a bathroom run before the first bell rang.

As I stepped out into the hallway, my eyes fell on one of my department members, Andrew O'Reilly, an older, greying economics teacher nearing retirement and when I rose my hand to wave to him, he gaped as if he'd just realized I, too, was in the hallway and promptly turned on his heel to steer himself the way he just came.

Huh.

I huffed out in annoyance and hitched my free hand on my hip, watching Andrew scamper back down the hallway and disappear around the corner. Was anyone going to invite me to board the crazy train or had they all left without me?

You expect students to act like aliens because, honestly, most of the time they behave like they're from another planet anyway. But that did not explain or excuse Andrew's behavior, someone who'd been a close friend of my dad's when he was still alive and when he worked in this very same department all those years ago.

I'd made it halfway down the hall when another department member, Steph Neilson, sped out of her room and made a mad grab for my elbow, her normal cheerful and peppy demeanor flipped on its head with a frenzied fervor.

"Emma!" she cried out frantically, gripping my elbow in a death-hold to tug me closer to her. "Are you okay?"

My head reared back in confusion. "What are you talking about?"

Steph's free hand flew up to cover her mouth, her chocolate brown eyes wide with horror. "Oh my God. You don't know. You haven't seen it, have you?"

Little pinpricks of heat spread across my lungs. Words strangled in my thick throat. Somehow, my head shook from side to side.

"Oh my God," Steph exhaled, her face chalky and ashen.

She pulled me into her classroom, shut the door just as quickly, and hurried over to her desk, gesturing for me to follow. Steph's smartphone materialized in her hand a second later and I waited, heavy and numb, while she clicked through a few screens and then held her phone out to me with pain etched across her face.

194

At first, I didn't understand what I was seeing. The image in front of me just did not click. Who was that? What was that? Why did it look familiar...and then I got a good look at the Twitter handle responsible for posting the picture: *@JustinVeloso*.

And then the walls closed in on me.

I blinked. It didn't work.

The picture was still there, one that reflected a much-younger version of myself. I was lying on the bed of my college dorm wearing nothing but a lacy black thong, my legs spread wide and the caption read: *Hot 4 teacher or is she hot 4 u?? #kennedyhighwi #iwannabeurcougar #emmaO #open4me*. I blinked again, but my vision had fogged up, clouding the air around me until the image blurred through my stinging tears.

"Emma," Steph's gentle voice called out to me. "I hate to tell you this, but...there's more."

I sucked in a harsh breath, barely getting in enough air to fill my stuttering lungs. "What?"

She nodded and gingerly slipped her phone out of my hand. She swiped down with her thumb and then held the phone back out to me. I didn't want to look. I already knew what I would see anyway. But, being the glutton for punishment that I was, my eyes flicked to the screen. My mouth fell open, but all words died in my throat. It was a wonder air even passed through my lungs.

Picture after picture...and ones I definitely remembered not just taking six years ago, but sending, too. Up until this moment, I'd forgotten they existed in the first place. I couldn't remember if Justin had told me they'd gotten deleted or he'd lost the files, but I did remember him telling me he didn't have them anymore...oh, how foolish I was to have ever believed a word he said.

"I can't believe he would do this to you," Steph whispered. "To use his own screen name and that Kennedy High hashtag..."

He wanted me to know he'd posted the pictures and he wanted to make sure the entire school would get wind of it, too.

"Doesn't Twitter have some kind of policy about this?" I mumbled as I thrust Steph's phone back out to her. I couldn't even look at it anymore. "Don't they have some sort of filter that catches this shit?"

"I think Facebook does," Steph offered helplessly and shook her head, her brows still furrowed into a deep, disturbed frown. "I don't know about Twitter."

Of course. Which explains exactly why he'd chosen this platform to do his dirty work. But who knew where else he'd posted these pictures? Who he'd sent them to? I could almost see it—my mom, my brother, or

Cristina clicking on an email from Justin, not thinking anything of it and bam! Demolition in two seconds flat.

The reality was that even if there was a filter, even if I somehow found a Twitter hotline I could call to file a complaint and subsequently get the pictures removed from Justin's account, and even if, by some miracle, Justin deleted those pictures immediately, the damage had already been done. Those pictures were out there. Those pictures had been *seen* and now, couldn't be unseen.

Life as I knew it was over.

Bile burned my throat, tears clouded my eyes, and the walls charged at me, suffocated me, devastated me.

I don't know how I made to the girls' bathroom at the end of the hallway. That part is still a blank for me. But I do remember skidding into the first open stall, ducking my head into the toilet, and heaving up my breakfast. When my body finished rebelling against me, I picked myself off the floor and opened the door only to find three girls—two I knew and one I didn't—gawking at me like I'd started stripping there right in front of them.

Blinders, Emma, I told myself. *Just pretend they're not there and it'll go away. Please God...make it go away.*

But when I stepped over to the sink so I could splash some water on my face, the three girls huddled together, whispering and giggling and I wanted to put my fist through the mirror.

"I wonder if she's pregnant, too," one of the girls hummed to the others, eliciting a round of muffled giggles behind me.

"I'm not pregnant," I mumbled over my shoulder.

I didn't even bother to stick around long enough to make sure the message had been received. By the time I was back in the hallway, rounding the corner towards my classroom, it was like every person in the building had lined the walls, staring, glaring, whispering, pointing, snapping pictures to tweet...sure, that was an exaggeration, but that didn't dissipate the prickles of humiliation snaking down my chest and the hot sweat pooling underneath my armpits.

To add insult to injury, when I passed by Susan Metcalfe's classroom, my former mentor and favorite teacher from high school shook her head at me, her lips curling with disappointment and disgust.

Feeling that burn following me all the way back to my own classroom, I thought I was safe for a little while. At least, in my own room, on my own turf, I could have a second to catch my breath, to figure out what I needed to do next, to call someone, to scream, to cry, to throw something...wouldn't I?

I stopped short in my classroom's threshold. I was blinded. Gutted. Devastated. Humiliated. Shamed.

Because there, written across every empty space of my whiteboard in bright red marker, was the word: SLUT.

CHAPTER SIXTEEN

Finn

I knew something was wrong the moment Emma opened her apartment door. It was written all over her gorgeous face—there was a weariness, a tiredness there I wasn't used to seeing and I reached for her before I could stop myself. I tugged her into my arms, reveling in the feeling of her smooth skin against my cheek, her warm breath on my shoulder, and her perfume that smelled like musk and sunlight and honey.

I could say I'd missed her, but that would be like saying water is wet. Or that the Seahawks really *didn't* get that touchdown back in 2012—it was an interception, dammit. Everybody and their mother knows that.

"Em," I murmured into her hair, breathing it in and knotting my hands in its softness. "You okay?"

Of course she wasn't okay, but I had to start somewhere, you know?

"I will be," she whispered. "I *think* I will be. Do you wanna come in?"

"Yeah, of course."

Unfortunately, that meant I also had to take my hands off her for the time being and I begrudgingly slipped my hands down from around her waist to shove them into my front pockets.

I got my hands in my pockets and I'm crossing my fingers.

I guess I was always going to feel that way around Emma...out of sorts, a little out of my mind, tossed in the scatter. Man, maybe it was time I switched it up and listened to more than just Kings of Leon for a while. No. I couldn't believe I just went there. If Taylor Swift—good God—spoke to Emma, then Caleb Followill and the rest of his dysfunctional family spoke to me. I'd never turn my back on them.

Emma just had a way of making normal things like brain functioning short circuit. When I was with her, I just didn't see anything else. I just didn't think about anything else. She'd needled her way under my skin, burrowing deep until I'd forgotten where I ended and she began. I'd only known her for two weeks, but it felt like years. I couldn't imagine how I'd feel in a month or six months or a year or...

I'd never known these kind of deep-rooted, soul-jerking feelings could seep in so quickly—a kick in the balls and a shot in the arm all at the same time. It was like my eyes locked on her and my heart went, "*Oh, there you are. I've been looking all over for you.*" It didn't make much sense to me and I guess it didn't have to either.

I wasn't quite ready to throw that L-word out there. Maybe, though. Maybe when the time was right.

When I finally stepped through the door of her apartment and little contraband with his huge plastic cone came running at me, the bell on his collar tinkling, it was weird how much this apartment felt more like mine than, well, mine. I'd only spent one night here on the couch and already, I'd maneuvered around, figured out where everything was and how everything worked, and pretty much made myself at home. The couch wasn't quite as comfortable as I might have liked and the temptation to peek inside her bedroom was a little too enticing, but what else was I supposed to do?

I wasn't planning on stepping foot inside Emma's bedroom until I was asked, or at the very least, shown the way.

"Hey there, RB," I greeted the cat and bent down to scratch the top of his head.

His little white chest jumped a little at the contact and a pathetic mew sounded from his throat. It really was too bad...everything was just a tiny bit more lower pitched before he'd gotten his balls lasered off. Now, all that talking back was high and whiny. Ugh—just the thought of that had me reaching for my package with a wince.

Now, though, as Emma trailed into her living room, my focus was all on her. Something was up. I liked to believe I knew her well enough by now to be clued into her moods and the neuroses I think she'd rather pretend didn't exist. That was pretty much why I'd all but forced her hand with the Packer game in two weeks—she needed a little push, but I couldn't push her too hard.

If I pushed too hard, I'd lose her.

But when Emma set her computer down in front of me, gesturing towards it like I was somehow supposed to know what she wanted me to do with it, my brain couldn't really follow through with its normal functioning.

Emma swallowed tightly and rested a light hand on my forearm. "Hey, Finn?"

"Yeah, Em?"

"You know how I said we needed to go slow?"

I frowned down at her. "Yeah."

"I'm ready to tell you why now."

All I could really do was just stare dumbly back at her. I gestured towards her computer, which was open to a Google search, its cursor blinking up and down manically. "What does this have anything to do with it?"

The edges of her lips lifted up, but it wasn't really a smile. "Google me."

"What?"

"You heard me," she gestured to the computer again. "Google me."

"You're serious?"

"Like the plague, Finn."

I blew out a deep breath, eyeing her carefully. God knew where she was going with this, but who was I to question her methods? And even though I had a sinking feeling this wasn't heading anywhere but bad, the kind of place that would make me need to hit something, throw something, or scream at something, I did as I was told and typed the words *Emma Owens* in the Google search she'd already set up for me.

I hit the search button and waited, not knowing what, exactly, I was waiting for. There were a lot of ways this could play out—there was obviously some secret, something she didn't want me to know. Any idiot with half a brain could've told me that. The cageyness, the way she skirted around the subject of her life in Hickory—all signs pointed to some sort of bombshell I wasn't going to like.

But when my eyes finally landed on the pictures that popped up from that Google search...I don't know what I'd been expecting. It wasn't this. It definitely wasn't this.

My blood ran cold and my mouth dried up like I'd just swallowed a fistful of sand. Tingles of ice slivered down my body, making the hair on my arms stand on end.

Picture after picture...Emma—so much younger than the Emma standing tensely next to me with her baby-faced cheeks and wavy hair flowing all the way down her back—God, Emma.

Emma straddling a pillow in a pair of bra and panties. Emma topless, lying on a bed, both hands drifting lower to the edge of her panties, oozing sex and desire at the camera. Emma cupping herself with both hands, arching her back up against the bed. Emma completely nude, legs open wide, sharing something that only a few people—people she chose—should be able to see.

I scrubbed my eyes with both hands and hoped that would be enough to make this go away. This wasn't how I'd wanted it to happen. Too many days and nights I'd spent daydreaming and fantasizing about what she'd look like when she was ready to let me in, ready to shred both her insecurities and her clothes for me, ready to share the intimacy I knew we both wanted when she was ready.

But this wasn't the way I'd wanted to finally see her. This wasn't just for me. Some motherfucker had done this to her...and then white-hot burning rage splintered through the shock and the horror of what I was seeing.

I wanted to tear her computer to pieces and smash every last scrap into dust. I wanted to flip over her kitchen table. I wanted to rip this counter top off and smash it into the wall. I wanted to scream for her. I wanted to cry for her. And most importantly, I wanted to hunt down the piece of shit responsible for this and tear him apart limb by bloody limb.

"Wha..." I couldn't even form one coherent word, let alone a full sentence. "I don't..."

Emma's aquamarine eyes shone with unshed tears and she shook her head. "I know. It's a lot to take in. I can explain—"

"You don't have to explain shit to me, Em," I growled.

Her eyes widened and I just couldn't take it anymore. I couldn't sit here, in this kitchen, with the most perfect, beautiful, and kind-hearted woman I'd ever met in my life and continue to look at those pictures. My fist closed over the top of her computer and I slammed it shut, shoving it back at her. Just the idea of what still lingered on that screen, of what I'd seen, I didn't know if I could handle it.

Both hands clasped the edge of the counter and I leaned all the way back, desperate to clear my lungs and my head. I didn't know if I'd be able to get through this without throwing open her door and hunting down someone to murder painfully and slowly.

"You remember how I told you about my ex-fiancé? The one I had the pregnancy scare with and then I called it off?"

I nodded. I didn't trust myself to do much else.

"He posted those pictures to Twitter, emailed them to my family, all my friends, my principal, and sent them to just about every online porn site you can think of."

What. The. Fuck.

My face must've said it all because she jumped to continue.

"He was mad about our break-up and my reasons for it, obviously, and I guess I could've handled it better. I could've been nicer, more sensitive to his feelings—"

"Don't make excuses for that fucker," I bit out hoarsely. "You didn't do anything wrong."

She smiled tightly. Neither of us were convinced by it. "Didn't I?"

"What the hell is that supposed to mean?"

Emma lifted a shoulder and stared down at her feet for a long moment. "I took those pictures for him when I was 19—"

"Em," I told her desperately, my fingertips grazing her arm. "You don't have to explain anything to me."

"No," she shook her head, but didn't shy away from my touch. "I want to. I want you to know. You deserve to know and I want to be honest with you, Finn. I don't want to keep this from you anymore."

When she put it like that, the logic was difficult to argue with. So, with my hand planted firmly on her shoulder to remind her that I was here and that I wasn't going anywhere, she delved into the rest of it.

"I was trying to be sexy for him, you know?" she smiled wistfully and took a moment to breath in and breath out. "We'd just started dating and he was only the second person I'd ever been with. He was a year older, so somehow I thought that meant he was more experienced, wiser, too. I didn't think anything of it when I did it all those years ago. I thought I was going to be with him forever. I thought he was my soul mate. And...he just wasn't. And that wasn't my fault either."

"No, Em," I murmured, my thumb rubbing circles soothingly into her shoulder. "It wasn't."

"He posted those pictures a week after we broke up. I hadn't heard from him since then, but I wasn't even thinking about that. I was too busy looking forward to my future, to all the things I'd be able to do that I never would've been able to do if I'd stayed with him, and he'd already taken it all away before I even realized it."

She sighed heavily and lifted her eyes to me for just a second before finding the counter again.

"When he tweeted them, he made sure to include one of our school's hashtags so everyone in the school would eventually see it. I had no idea. I just showed up for school that day thinking it would just be any old Monday. You know how you asked me once about the worst thing a kid ever did in my class?"

I nodded tightly, my hands clenched around the edge of the counter.

"Literally five minutes after I realized what was going on, I went back to my classroom, thinking I would actually be safe there for a little while. Someone had written, 'slut', in big red letters all the way across my whiteboard. I got called to the office not even a minute later, sat down with the principal, and got let go about ten minutes after that."

Holy shit.

"It's not like I had much of a leg to stand on, you know? By then, it seemed like everyone in the school—the students, teachers, librarians, secretaries, janitors, everyone—they'd all seen everything they needed to see and already knew everything they needed to know. And then the rumors started. The comments started. The memes and the videos. All of it. You know, I actually threw up in the bathroom right after I first saw the pictures and then all of a sudden, there was a rumor going around that I was pregnant, too, and then when everyone realized that I wasn't, in fact, pregnant, that I'd had an abortion instead. How's that for irony?"

I shook my head, unable to sift through the torrential horror Emma had just laid at my feet. Maybe if I shook my head enough, the motion would somehow shake out the images, the story, and the devastation of what all this had meant for her life. Everything clicked now—her move to Milwaukee, the need for a fresh start, the reason why she just didn't seem to have any real friends here beyond a stray cat, the reason she'd holed herself up in her apartment with wine, music, and her blog as an excuse to hide, her evasion of social situations, the cageyness and skittishness in those early days of our relationship—it all made sense now. And I absolutely couldn't blame her.

Now, the only coherent thought I could pin down long enough to growl was: "Please tell me that asshole is in jail for doing this to you."

She blew out a hard breath and I knew the answer before she even said the words. "There weren't any laws...nothing anyone could charge him with. Those pictures went up in February last year and there was no actual legislation signed into law until April. They couldn't charge with a crime after the fact, you know?"

My hands clenched around the edge of the countertop until they turned white. My stomach churned, but I needed to put my fist through something more.

"So, you're telling me that *nothing* happened to him? Nothing?"

Emma rubbed the side of her neck and grimaced. "Well...the day he posted the pictures, my brother hunted him down, dragged him out of work, and beat him up. Noah got arrested, Justin pressed charges—I'm sure you're not shocked by that—and Noah did two months for assault."

"I think I like your brother already," I mumbled under my breath, but Emma's head shook furiously from side to side.

"That was the *last* thing I wanted. I didn't need anyone going to jail for me, getting hurt because of me—"

"That asshole deserved a hell of a lot more than what he got," I snapped back.

"I was talking about my brother. He sat in a cell for 60 days, paid thousands of dollars in lawyer fees and—"

"He made a choice, Emma," I argued hotly. "He was defending you."

She opened her mouth to respond, but shut it just as quickly. Finally, after a long moment of awkward silence, she finally spoke again. "All Noah did was just make everything worse."

I wanted to argue, but what was the point? My heart tore at the seams, ripped apart and tumbled to the floor in a tangled mess at my feet. She didn't think she deserved any defense. That's what she really meant. She thought she deserved it—the shame, the humiliation, the loss of her job, the loss of her privacy...I didn't know how to even begin to wrap my head around that.

"So, basically," I clarified incisively, my fingers curling around the counter top to keep myself from latching onto the first thing I could find to smash. "You're telling me that your ex ruined your life, your career, and your reputation and *he's* the victim here? All because your brother beat him up, which he deserved and then some, and that somehow makes it all okay? No charges, no jail time, no fines, no public indictment...nothing."

Emma winced at the bite in my words, but I couldn't apologize for the harsh delivery. There were only a few people who'd earned my unadulterated rage, enough to the point where I've wanted to cause actual, possibly even fatal bodily harm: the punk who beat Sling up my sophomore year of college all because Sling 'looked at him funny', the prick I'd caught Claire with in our bed, Brandon Bostick when he missed that goddamned onside kick, and now, Emma's bastard of an ex.

When she just lifted a shoulder helplessly, I scratched at my beard for lack of anything better to do with my hands. I wanted to pull her to me, but didn't know how she'd take that right now. I wanted to smash her computer into the countertop, but I knew *exactly* how she'd take that right now. Finally, my brain managed to pinpoint a logical question.

"Why are those pictures still out there, Em?"

She pushed out a shaky breath and glanced at me with that smile that was more like a wince. "It's not as simple as you might think. After a little while and a lot of begging on my part, Justin deleted the pictures from his account, but they'd already been online for a week. That was more than enough time for any sites that he hadn't emailed to pick them up and post them and anyone else to at least download them."

"But there are companies that specialize in this shit, right? Ones that can clean all that up?"

"Sure," Emma just shrugged. "I did that as soon as I was coherent enough to start making some decisions and not even five hours later, they were all all out there again. I think every student and their mother had at least one picture downloaded to something by the end of the first *day*, let alone week. I tried a different web service about a week later and it was the same thing. Noah and Cristina did it too, same result. After a little while, I think Justin started to feel bad enough to realize what he'd done to my life and he tried to have all the pictures removed. He even went as far as emailing the porn sites he'd originally sent the pictures to, but it was the same thing. At a certain point, there's only so much money you can spend on something that you know is only going to matter for days, maybe a few weeks if you're lucky."

I wasn't going to dignify her asshole ex's lame attempt at fixing the damage he'd done.

"But, I mean, there are other things you can do, aren't there? Some kind of law out there about online sexual harassment...*something*?"

Emma winced at the words *sexual harassment*, but that's what it was. All I'd done was state the facts. She sighed heavily and I reached up to wipe a stray tear from her cheek.

"We tried claiming copyright on the pictures since I was technically the owner. I took them, I sent them, so they should be mine, right?"

I nodded. That sounded about right to me. The only people who should've ever seen them were people she *chose* to see them.

"I couldn't prove that they were actually taken on my phone because, of course, I didn't have the phone anymore. Justin was the only one who actually had the copies on his computer and by that point, he'd deleted them from his hard drive so that was that. I sent letters and I don't even know how many emails to all the porn sites that still had my pictures up begging them to take them down—some of them did, some of them didn't. Freedom of speech, right? Anyway, if I'd been able to copyright the pictures, I would've been able to take action against the kids who downloaded and reposted the pictures, but other than to ask the school to take action, there wasn't much else I could do about that part of it because, well...freedom of speech. There was nothing the union could do to help me because, well, there isn't much of a union left anymore. I barely had enough money to pay to get those pictures taken down, let alone even think about hiring a lawyer. At some point, it just sorta took on a life of its own and I didn't know how to stop it."

I couldn't believe what I was hearing—it sounded like her and her brother took all the steps that needed to be taken in order to get those pictures taken down at the time, but now, the current 'owners' of those pictures were probably a pack of horny, infantile high school kids who thought they were the shit because they had naked pictures of their former history teacher.

"And the school—they just did nothing?"

"The only kids they could really discipline, if that's what you want to call it, were the ones that were stupid enough to comment and share the pictures at school for violating the school's internet use policy. But for everyone else, the ones who weren't using the school's network, there wasn't much they could do other than to ask them to delete whatever they'd posted, whether it was a comment, a picture, or a meme. Nothing like this has ever happened there before, so they didn't really have any protocol for what to do. Besides, it wasn't exactly a surprise—a few years ago, a student tweeted a picture of a guidance counselor with just the n-word next to the picture. Just that one ugly, terrible word, you know? All the school was able to do was ask him to delete it, which he didn't, and as far as I know, his parents touted the freedom of speech argument just as much as he did. I doubt that kid ever deleted the tweet, too."

That was the biggest pile of bullshit I'd ever heard. Who in their right mind would ever think it was actually acceptable to allow fucking teenagers to run wild with something like this? Hiding behind freedom of speech—it was just an excuse.

"You have to understand, Finn, Hickory is a really small town. Everything about it is small—the population, the stores, the school district, the church, the ideas. I think the teachers, principals, and school board were just as scandalized by it as everyone else."

"I honestly don't give a shit, Emma," I shook my head. "That's the worst thing I've ever heard."

"Finn," she sighed, but I just lifted up both hands against the countertop and sawed down on my bottom lip.

I couldn't sit here and listen to her make excuses for these people anymore. I didn't care how small their town or their minds were—this was the 21st century. People had sex. People enjoyed sex. Sometimes, people even took pictures of themselves having sex. Big deal. Did these people in Hickory have their heads buried in the sand or something? Jesus, next she was going to tell me they'd outlawed dancing and that the kids weren't allowed to hold hands until they were engaged or some shit like that, too.

With that thought, I snapped her computer back open and tilted it so we both had a good view of those pictures. "Emma. Look at me."

Her shining eyes lifted up, brimming with fresh tears and just a hint of fear that broke my heart. Maybe she didn't expect me to walk away from her completely now, but it was like she was waiting for the other shoe to drop, too—waiting for something to fracture between us.

"Em," I jerked an index finger at the screen. "The people who downloaded these pictures and kept them up on the internet—they're cunts. I don't care who they are, where they're from, or how old they are. They're the lowest scum of the earth. They're selfish, immature hypocrites, and what did you say? It should only be said when someone is a complete, no-holds-barred, insensitive, and all-around asshole douchebag. It might be the worst word ever, but what they did is just as bad if not worse. And what does that make them, Emma?"

I waited as her mouth curled up ever so slightly. She nodded.

"Cunts," she whispered.

"Good," I told her with a tight nod. "I told you I'd get you to say it, didn't I?"

Somehow, she still managed to huff out a laugh even as I pulled her into my arms. She leaned into me and I gladly beared the brunt of her weight, holding her close and kissing the side of her head as wetness pooled into my shoulder. My fingertips lifted to her caramel-colored hair and swept her bangs out of her eyes.

"Being back there just brought everything back," she murmured into my shoulder. "I felt like I was reliving it all over again. I couldn't even make it all the way back into town without having to pull over and dry-heave over the side of the road."

"I'm sorry, Em," I smoothed her hair down and pressed my lips into her temple. "I wish you'd told me sooner. I would've went with you yesterday."

"It's okay. I wasn't ready anyway and it was just so much *harder* than I thought it would be. I hadn't been back there in months and yet, the second I passed that welcome sign, it was like all the walls were closing in on me again. And...I saw my mom. Well, it was an accident that we ran into each other. She purposefully left the hospital before I got there so she wouldn't have to see me, but she didn't even think about me long enough to consider the fact that I would have nowhere else to stay in town except for Noah and Cristina's."

"I'm so sorry, Em."

She blew out a heavy breath and pressed her cheek deeper into my shoulder. "We don't talk. I'm sure you figured that out already."

I nodded into her hair. I'd figured as much when she'd been open about her dad the night of our first date, but hadn't said a word about her mom. The only reason I knew her mom was even still around was because her brother mentioned her in passing when we'd spoken on the phone last night.

"I think that out of all the people who hated me, were disgusted with me, and were disappointed in me...she was the worst. She wouldn't speak to me for days after it happened...wouldn't even look at me when Noah sat us all down to try to come up with a plan. I guess in order to really get it, you have to understand that my mom is probably the most religious person I know. She's the person sitting in the front pew every Sunday so everyone can see her, she's the one running the Bible studies and vacation Bible school in the summer, she's the one organizing the events and fundraisers so she's front and center of everything. When my dad died, she just sort of threw herself into her church because I think that was the only way she was able to really deal with it."

The way she said *her* church—her mom's church—instead of *our* church wasn't lost on me, but I'd be an idiot right now to interrupt her. She was purging and I had to let her do it.

"Right away, it was *what will the congregation think?* and *How am I supposed to show my face at church on Sunday when everyone knows my daughter's a whore?* and *People think you had an abortion, Emma! An abortion! How am I supposed to look our pastor in the eye?"*

"Whoa," I pulled her head back from my shoulder so I could get a good look at her. "Wait a minute, did she actually say all that? To your face?"

"Pretty much."

Jesus Christ. No wonder she'd run away. No wonder she'd felt like she couldn't stay. Of all the wolves that descended on Emma to rip her apart, her mom's teeth were the sharpest.

"I think she was happy when I left last year because that just makes it easier for her to pretend I don't exist."

All I could do was tug her tight against my chest and tangle my hands in her hair. At this point, it was for me as much as it was for her—I needed to touch her so she would know I was there and so I would know she wasn't running away from me.

"I'm pretty sure her exact words to me were that she couldn't believe any child of hers would participate in something as immoral as pornography. She said I'd debased myself and that I'd brought everything on myself by taking those pictures in the first place."

Words failed me and I squeezed her shoulders, trying to convey everything I needed to say to her in my touch. I just couldn't find the words to properly articulate how I felt about this monster—Emma's mom. That's what she was. A hypocritical, judgmental, cold, and insensitive monster.

She unearthed her face from my chest and looked at me. "Isn't it ironic that the people who throw the first stones are the ones who are supposed to be the most compassionate? The most forgiving and the most understanding?"

My thoughts exactly and I was glad she'd been the one to come to that conclusion herself, instead of through me. I tucked some stray hair behind her ear and leaned forward to press my lips into hers.

"There's something else, too," she swallowed tightly and looked down at her feet. "Noah's really worried about homecoming in a few weeks. And, I guess, considering what happened last year, he has every right to be."

I frowned back at her and ran my thumb over her cheek. "What happened last year?"

Emma pushed out a heavy sigh. "The senior class wrote me into their senior skit. It's…it's not worth saying anything else about, but Noah's worried something like that is gonna happen again."

If I didn't already have my hands around her face, my fingers would've curled into a tight, white-knuckled fist.

"I wish there was something I could say or do that would make this better for you, Em," I whispered to her as I brushed some of her bangs out of her eyes.

"You're doing it, Finn. You really are."

"What made you decide you were ready to talk about this?" I murmured as both my hands closed around her cheeks.

Emma squeezed her eyes shut and took in a deep breath before finally opening those beautiful green-blues back up again. "I want to be with you, Finn, and that means I can't keep anything from you either. I wanted you to know."

I swallowed hard and let my thumb rub soothingly into her cheek. "I want to be with you, too, Em. None of this matters to me. You know that, right?"

Her eyes slammed down to my chest, but my hands lifted her chin back up so I could look her in the eye.

"Emma, I don't care about any of this. Well, I *care*. Trust me, if I could hunt down that asshole and every single one of those little shits and beat them to within an inch of their life, I would."

She winced and bit down on her bottom lip. "Don't say that. Please don't say that. I don't want you to ever do anything that would—"

"If someone disrespects you, I'm not gonna stand by and let anyone walk all over you if I can help it."

That was a warning as much as it was a promise. If push came to shove, I wouldn't hesitate to do exactly what her brother did and then some. She was worth it. Absolutely worth it.

"Em," I pushed on. "What I'm trying to say is that what you showed me on that Google search tonight doesn't change the way I feel about you. Besides, you weren't the one that did anything wrong. Everyone else? They're the ones who have something to answer for, not you. All you did was take some hot as shit pictures for your boyfriend when you were 19. That's not wrong, Em. All you did was trust the wrong person with them and even then...what he did to you wasn't your fault. Please tell me you know that."

She nodded quickly, but I didn't believe her. I'm pretty sure she didn't even believe herself.

"So..." she chewed on the inside of her cheek a little. "We're really doing this? We're going to be together?"

"Emma," I laughed. "We've been together this whole time. The only one who didn't see that was you."

"Okay," she lifted her eyes to the ceiling and then eyed me carefully. "So, I have a question for you. And I think I already know the answer, but I'm going to ask it anyway."

"Go."

"Will you stay tonight?"

I sucked in a hard breath. This was the question I'd been hoping for, but never wanted to push for...and now that it was finally out there, there was no way I could deny her.

"Of course I'll stay."

Her eyes grew rounder and I pressed a quick kiss into her lips.

"We'll take it one step at a time, okay, Em? Me staying over tonight just means we'll be sleeping in the same bed. That's as far as it has to go. Whatever you want, whatever you need, Em—we'll go at your pace."

Her lips curled up into the happiest, most beautiful smile I'd ever seen and I almost said it. The words almost left my lips, but I stopped them right in their path. Too soon. Even though I felt them, it was just too soon. One step at a time...I just had to make myself remember that.

.   .   .

I rummaged around my messy room for something I could sleep in tonight and ignored Sling's presence lingering in my doorway. It was my own fault—I should've shut my door and locked it behind me, but it was a little late for that now.

"So," he tossed out lightly and right about now, I was really glad his overnight guest, AKA Emma's co-worker, was currently using our bathroom and wouldn't hear this conversation. "I take it you'll be spending the night elsewhere again?"

I didn't even spare him a glance as I lifted up a pile of clothes. "Yep."

Slinger rubbed his hands together and shook his shoulders to the music only he could hear. "Yes! I knew it! Ah...I figured it wouldn't take long. You know what? I have a present for you, bro. Just hold on, okay?"

He disappeared from my doorway and I took that opportunity to step out of my jeans to slide some mesh shorts over my hips. I was already eyeing my laptop when Sling materialized in my doorway again and tossed me a long sleeve of Trojans.

"Jesus, Sling! What the hell?" I flung the condoms onto my bed angrily.

"What?" he frowned back at me. "You're sleeping at her place tonight again, aren't you? And she's back now, isn't she? You need those, Finnegan. Trust me. And you can thank me later when those come in handy for you tonight."

I rolled my eyes up to the ceiling. "We're not gonna go there tonight."

Disappointment dimmed in his eyes and I couldn't help but laugh. "Aw...shit. That sucks. Here I thought you were finally gonna get laid. I was so happy. Really, I was. What's goin' on? She lay down the law with you just now or what?"

"No," I shook my head. "I'm not gonna let it go that far tonight even if she wants to."

Sling gaped at me like I'd just told him Brett Favre was coming out of retirement. Again. "Wha...?"

"Don't ask."

"So..."

"We're taking things slow," I shrugged. "That's all I'm gonna tell you."

No way I would betray Emma's confidence, especially given the magnitude of what that confidence was. Sling would just have to deal with it because he wasn't getting anything from me.

His shoulders slumped in defeat. "Well, will you just take *one?* Better to be safe than sorry I always say. And, between me and you, Emma doesn't really seem like the type of girl that's got condoms just lying around, you know?"

I smiled ruefully. If Slinger knew the details of the conversation I'd had with Emma tonight, I really hoped he'd still feel the same way. *I* still felt the same way. If anything, it just made the feelings I already had sink that much deeper and my protectiveness that much fiercer.

Still, I figured it was better to appease Sling and, like he said, it was probably better to be safe than sorry. Maybe, if I was prepared, I wouldn't need it anyway. And...I think that was the first time in my entire life where I hoped I wouldn't need a condom.

"Alright, alright," I held a hand up in the air and promptly ripped the top foil packet off so I could tuck it into my wallet.

"You're gonna get something tonight though, right? Please tell me this isn't one of those platonic sleepover things where she's scared of the dark or some stupid girl shit like that."

"No, no," I laughed. "I wouldn't exactly call it a platonic sleepover and like I said before, I'm not telling you shit."

Slinger pressed a hand into his heart, his head falling back with a wince like he'd just been shot. "You're killing me, Finnegan."

I pointed a finger at him. "I don't care. Now get out."

He held both hands up, his green eyes wide with surprise, and finally, just shrugged, waved his hands at me, and shut the door on his way out. At least we'd lived together long enough by now that Sling was very aware when I needed some space and right now, I needed peace, quiet, and room to feed a few demons before I could go back to Emma.

With my computer open and sitting in my lap, I scrubbed my face with my hands and got down to business. I repeated the same easy search I'd done on Emma's computer before and winced at the images filling my computer screen. This was bullshit. Complete bullshit. And against my better judgment, I clicked on one at the top of the search and then clicked over to the 'host' site for that particular image.

Sure enough, it brought me to a Twitter account using the handle @bigcasey_14. I shouldn't have been surprised, but the account still had me shaking my head at my computer...until my eyes landed on the comments underneath Emma's picture.

The first one, from another handle similar to the original poster's, read:

All my dreams just came to life. Don't have to imagine it anymore. B back after I bust a quick nut.

* * *

My teeth were already grinding into my jaw when I read the next one:

Always knew she was a dirrrrty little slut #kennedyhighwi #iwannaburcougar

Followed by, obviously:

Ms. O can be my cougar any day #kennedyhighcougar

And another:

Ms. O makes good O face

And this one:

Do u think she takes requests? Id like to see 1 from behind #doggystyle

And this one too:

2 many pics to decide which 1s going in the spank bank first #decisionsdecisions

Oh, and this one:

Do u think this was b4 or after that dude got her pregnant?? #lucky

Mob mentality at its finest.

Then another comment, this time, judging by the account's picture and handle, was obviously from a girl:

This is what happens when ur easy and take pics like this. Bound to happen eventually. Don't feel bad 4 her at all.

Out of all the comments, that one pissed me off the most. This stupid girl, too stuck in the kind of backwards, idiotic, and cruel thinking that makes the recipients want to kill themselves, was just as bad as the boys. The idea that Emma had somehow brought this on herself, that calling off her engagement because she realized she didn't want to have kids with that dipshit had given anyone license to do this to her—I couldn't

213

even see straight.

Everything in my room blurred. Red streaks fogged my vision. The walls inched in closer. It was all I could do not to rip my computer off my lap and slam it into the wall.

Because I just couldn't stop myself, I clicked over to another picture, which took me to yet another Twitter handle with more comments all too similar to the ones I'd just seen. So I did it again. And again. It was just more of the same hateful vitriol.

I just wanted to reach through my computer screen, strangle these little fuckheads, and scream at them, "She was your *teacher*, for Christ's sake! What the hell is wrong with you?"

Maybe if I shook them hard enough and slammed my fist into their faces enough times, it might knock some sense into them.

Then again, probably not. For whatever reason, these shitheads felt entitled to those pictures. Like they owned them. Like they owned *her*. And those spineless pricks at her school hadn't helped matters by just firing her instantaneously.

That sparked yet another search and I typed in *Emma Owens Kennedy High Hickory WI*. The news articles were well over a year old, but there they were for anyone to find. My eyes skimmed the first article, ironically enough from the *Hickory Press Gazette*, and my fists clenched when I read the line: "The district would not comment directly on Ms. Owens's dismissal from her position, but Dr. Rebecca Leonard, Hickory School District Superintendent, stated that 'the district does not tolerate inappropriate and lewd behavior of any kind from our students or our staff'. An open records request for Ms. Owens revealed the official reason for her termination was inappropriate conduct..."

That was as far as I got. I couldn't read anymore.

From what I could tell, there'd been no investigation, no mediation, no effort to actually educate their students about this kind of shit, no protection for Emma's privacy, and zero sympathy towards an employee who'd been violated in public. And thanks to the powers that be, there also wasn't much of a union left to help Emma either. She'd had no support other than from her brother and sister-in-law.

I felt sick to my stomach just thinking about it.

And the worst part about it all was how accepting Emma seemed. Not that she wasn't upset, but she wasn't as angry as she should be. How could she not want to slap all these kids into next year after seeing this? Why didn't she try to do more? Even if she'd been able to actually file charges against her ex, those pictures were still out there. They were still being posted and she could still take action, especially now that there was a law in place…but she didn't.

She wasn't angry. She was defeated and exhausted. I couldn't blame her for feeling that way, but it seemed like she hadn't even really tried to defend herself either. Like she felt she deserved this, that she'd earned it somehow by taking those pictures and sending them to her boyfriend in the first place.

Two thoughts popped into my head at once and I got to work on the first one, typing in a new search on Google to take care of the problem. After a few minutes of digging, I settled on one possible solution that would take some time and effort on my part, but it was free and effective. My next step was to test it out to make sure it actually worked, so I copied the url of the first picture I'd found of Emma and pasted it into Google's url removal tool. After selecting to remove the entire page from a search, I hit the request button.

Well, it was worth a try. I'd have to check back in a few hours to make sure it actually worked, but it was something. Even if I had to manually enter every single one of these urls by hand, I'd do it if it actually worked.

Now, my next order of business was Emma herself. She didn't have to tell me how all this had destroyed every shred of self-worth, dignity, and confidence she had before this all went down…everything I knew about her leading up to the bombs she'd dropped on me tonight was proof enough.

We would take it slow, I promised myself, and everything would have to be at her pace.

Emma clearly didn't believe she was worthy of just about anything good anymore and she'd taken great pains to punish herself when she wasn't the guilty party in this mess.

I was just going to have to change that.

CHAPTER SEVENTEEN

"Come on, buddy," I knelt down on all fours, trying to coax my cat out from underneath the kitchen table. "I have to give you your pain meds. Oliver, you have to take them!"

He just dipped his striped head down until the white plastic cone hid his eyes, but I knew exactly what I would find if I had a clear view of him—the kitty stink-eye. Instead of seeing him, I heard him: *maawhr.*

That high-pitched mewing tore at my heart, but I couldn't give in. The poor little guy needed some relief and it didn't help that trying to force that liquid medication down his throat was just as bad as trying to herd him into his carrier. God, he really could be a little rat bastard when he wanted to be.

"You know, if he had the view I've got right now, he'd probably come running right out of there," a familiar deep, throaty voice chuckled from behind me.

I glanced over my shoulder to find Finn standing in my open doorway, a change of clothes and his guitar lodged underneath one hand and the other hitched onto his hip.

"Shut it," I threw back and tilted my chin up to him. "And you wanna shut the door, too, while you're at it before Mrs. Johanssen realizes I've got contraband in here? She's already pissed enough at us, so I'm pretty sure she wouldn't think twice about ratting me out."

"Right, right," he laughed, shaking his head at me and promptly followed my instructions.

He set his clothes and his guitar down on my kitchen table then lifted the edge of the table up with his fingertips, shaking it up and down until Oliver scurried out from underneath it, knocking himself sideways a few times when his cone caught on the edge of a chair on his way out.

"Hey!" I scolded him. "That wasn't very nice. You scared my baby."

Finn just rolled his eyes and glanced back at Oliver, who sat about 10 feet away from us on his haunches and stared back at Finn as if to say:

216

What? Bring it, asshole. I might've lost my balls, but I still got my claws.

"He's gotta get his meds somehow, doesn't he? You just gotta do what I did last night. I held his ass down and shoved that syringe down his throat."

My mouth dropped open in faux shock. "You did what?"

Finn shrugged and crouched down, patting the carpet to get Oliver to come closer. "You know he's not an actual human baby, right?"

When I shot him a withering glare, his lips curled up into a sly smirk. "He's not gonna break, Em. He'll be fine and so will you."

There was probably a double meaning in that, but I wasn't exactly up for decoding tonight.

"If you say so. I guess that means you're gonna help me?"

His lips spread apart even wider into a warm smile that hit me all the way down to my knees. "You say jump, I say how high."

"Oh boy," I lifted my eyes to the ceiling.

"Let's tag-team RB and get it over with, shall we?" Finn called over his shoulder as he advanced on Oliver, whose sweet, sea foam eyes rounded with alarm.

He scooped my cat up into his arms like he'd been doing it for years and carried him over to the couch. I scrambled into the kitchen to grab the needle-less syringe the vet had given me and the little vial of liquid kitty morphine—or whatever it was—and joined Finn on the couch. With Finn holding my cat in a vice-grip, I pried open Oliver's jaws, who clenched down with the strength of about 20 cats, and when I had an opening, I shoved that syringe in and squeezed the pain meds down his throat.

True to form, Oliver squirmed out of Finn's grasp, leapt off the couch, sputtering, spitting, and *meh*-ing all the way into the bathroom.

"He's probably gonna sulk in his litter box for a little while," I laughed. "That's nothing new."

Finn cocked an eyebrow at me. "Well, what do you say we order a pizza and then as soon as RB decides to make an appearance, the three of us park it out on your patio for awhile tonight?"

"I think that's the best idea I've heard all day."

So, an hour and a half later, Finn, Oliver, and I parked it out on my patio. The pizza box was already demolished, two empty Matthews Brewing Co. beers already sat at our feet, Finn had his guitar in his lap, and a cone-less Oliver sat in mine. Finn picked away at the strings and it took me a second to get the melody.

The song didn't fully click until Finn's soft voice sang out to me about how I should excuse him for forgetting and I laughed when he sang,

"You see I've forgotten if they're green or they're blue."

"Oh, I know this one now," I smiled and helped him finish the rest of the lyrics. *"Yours are the sweetest eyes I've ever seen."*

Finn kept strumming away, finishing up the next few bars of the song with its sweetly sincere lyrics and I smiled at him, even as Oliver rolled on my lap to reach a white paw out to my chest.

"Aw...is this my song, now?" I laughed.

He just nodded, flashing me a wide grin and kept on playing until my cat blinked up at me, yawned, and let out a long *meh*.

Finn abruptly drummed his fingers on the neck of his guitar and grinned down at Oliver. "You know, when he does that, it sounds an awful lot like he's saying, *Mom*."

I arched an eyebrow at him and huffed out a laugh. "Okay. Sure."

"No, I'm serious. It's like this..." he proceeded to do his best RB-impression, *"Moooooommmmm."*

My head dipped back into my chair as my shoulders shook with laughter. Oliver, however, was not amused and curled the side of his upper lip up at Finn in response.

"Oh, the stiff upper lip! Good one, contraband," Finn chuckled, shaking his head.

Oliver responded by crawling up on my lap until both front white paws latched onto my collarbone and he settled his head on my left boob, purring and *meh*-ing the whole time.

"Wow," Finn's eyes widened and he nodded to my cat. "You sure know how to hit me right where it hurts. Well-played, RB. Well-played."

My cat responded in turn by taking his sweet time to blink at my boyfriend and nuzzled his head into my boob once again. I wrapped both arms around him, hugging his furry body to me and thanking whoever controlled things like fate and circumstance for bringing the little furry man on my lap and the larger, human man seated at my elbow into my life. I honestly didn't know what I'd do without them.

"Hey," Finn called out to me softly. "You ready to go inside now? Head to bed?"

I swallowed tightly. This was the part that had me shaking with jittery excitement. Finn might have promised me that we'd take things slow, that nothing had to happen, but I just wasn't sure what I wanted tonight. Did I want to 'go slow' or did I finally want to attack the fine piece of man-meat sitting next to me?

What did 'taking things slow' even mean? It was my own fault for leaving those terms so undefined...I guess I was going to have to clarify those terms tonight.

. . .

We did all the normal, end-of-day couple things: cleaning up from dinner and putting away the dishes, brushing our teeth, putting our pajamas on, which, incidentally, we did in separate rooms, kissing Oliver goodnight—well, I did that; Finn made fun of me while I did it— and by the time he crossed the threshold of my bedroom, Finn wrapped an arm around my shoulders and kissed the top of my head.

The fact that I was even referring to us as a couple was a victory in itself, but still...this nervousness, these butterflies playing hopscotch in my stomach, my chest heaving in and out...I couldn't remember if this was normal or not. It'd been so long since I'd been in this position. God, what had it been—seven years since I'd done this whole new-relationship thing? It didn't help that my fingers wound around themselves until I was practically wringing my hands in front of my bed.

I lingered at my usual side of the bed, glancing up at Finn with the best imitation of a smile I could muster. I knew what I wanted to do; I just didn't know how to get myself to do it. Pesky things like nerves and hesitation kept me from moving much closer.

"Hey," Finn called out to me as he rounded the other side of the bed. "I'm nervous too, Em. It's been awhile since I've slept in the same bed as someone who wasn't Sling."

A laugh escaped my throat.

"Don't ask," he pointed a finger at me as he tossed the edge of my comforter off to the side. "I'm scarred for life and I'm not ready to talk about it yet."

I scrunched my nose at him, holding up both hands. "I won't say a word. Promise."

Finn waggled his eyebrows at me as he slid into my bed and all I could do was follow his lead. I trusted him not to take me anywhere I wasn't ready to go yet, but I still needed him to show me the way. Shit, too bad I didn't keep my turntable in my bedroom—I could totally play Peter Frampton right now and that would totally be weird, if not completely inappropriate.

Oliver chose that particular moment to hop up onto the bed, plastic cone of shame and all, purrumbling his way around our legs, not caring if he stepped on either of us, and did a little circle in the middle of the bed before finally settling right in between us.

Finn let out one long sigh and sat up to lift my cat high in the air until he deposited Oliver right at the foot of the bed.

"There you go, contraband," Finn mumbled to him. "Right where you belong."

My shoulders started shaking, but the laughter died in my throat when Finn's fingertips brushed my cheek. I shivered under his touch and let him me pull in closer until my chest pressed up against him. His thumb traced circles into my skin and my eyes flitted shut, reveling in the way the light sensation lit tiny fires in his wake.

My breath seemed to leave me all at once when his lips sealed over my mouth, begging my lips to part, and finally slid his tongue in between the open space.

Finn pulled away abruptly and pressed his forehead into mine. "Em?"

"Yeah?" I didn't know how I had any breath left to answer.

"You trust me, right?"

I didn't even need to think about it.

"Yeah."

Of course I trusted him. How could I not?

"Good," he murmured as he leaned in to kiss me again.

This time, he didn't stop. My eyes closed, wanting to savor this moment, and he really did take it slow, moving his lips gently against mine, tasting and taking the way I needed him to. One of his hands slipped underneath the comforter, trailing down and reducing me to a shivering mess until his fingertips curved around my hip. He pulled me tighter against him and now, I suddenly didn't care too much about the cat nestled in between us at the foot of the bed.

The cat would survive on the floor for a little while and sure enough, about a second later, he hopped off the bed, mewing and grumbling all the way down the hallway.

My fingers closed around Finn's overgrown scruff and I tugged on it playfully to somehow bring him in deeper. As if my limbs had a will of their own, my right leg lifted up and curled around his waist, squeezing him in just about as close as I could get him. His hand glided all the way up until it closed gently around the base of my thigh, his fingertips lightly trailing circles up my skin. Needless to say, I was pretty grateful I'd decided to wear the skimpiest, laciest scrap of underwear I owned when he groaned into my mouth the second his fingers came in contact with the material.

It was lazy now, easy and slow as his hands drifted up and down, slipping underneath my oversized T-shirt, and at no point did I want to stop him. At no point did I freeze up and try to push him off me...I didn't want him to stop. I *never* wanted him to stop. I think I could spend the rest of the week like this with him, wrapped around him and tangled in my sheets. Here I'd been so nervous and so worried about how I would feel when all I'd needed to do was trust him.

My hands fisted into the hair at his nape and I shivered at the heady sensation of his long, wiry scruff tickling the side of my face. Suddenly, the temperature in the room hiked up about 10 notches when he pulled away from my mouth to leave feather-light kisses on my neck and my collar bone, only removing his mouth long enough to jerk the T-shirt over my head and send it flying to the carpet. His lips started their descent now, taking careful inventory of the space in between where my bra ended and began, and moving down to cover my stomach.

When he finally found the top of my underwear, he pulled the material down and kept kissing each new area of skin exposed to him until he finally slipped my shorts and my underwear down my thighs and sent them both flying over his shoulder.

I wanted to laugh at the gesture to lighten the mood a little, but I could feel myself tightening up, pulling back just enough to suck in a hard breath. My body tensed underneath his touch and Finn didn't miss a beat, lifting himself up to hover over me again to kiss me.

"Em," he whispered. "Look at me."

My eyes lifted up to him and found him smiling down at me, his thumb brushing the side of my cheek again.

"You're the most beautiful thing I've ever seen. You're sweet and funny and kind and I..." he swallowed tightly as he trailed off, looking down in between us. "I'm so lucky I found you...did I mention that you're sexy as hell?" he shot me a sly grin and a breathless laugh escaped my lips, "I'm not gonna let things go too far tonight, but there is one thing I wanna do. Do you know what that is?"

I think I had a pretty good idea and so I nodded. I didn't trust my voice to work properly right now.

"Good," he nodded down to me and pressed a quick kiss into my lips. "I wanna make you feel good tonight, Em. It's not wrong to feel that way and we've got all night. We don't have to rush and I wanna spend my whole night right here if you'll let me. Is that okay?"

How in the hell could I argue with that? Because my voice died out on me, Finn must've taken my silence as answer enough and he grinned at me. Suddenly, I was wondering what that scruff would feel like on places other than my face. He wouldn't get any protesting from me.

The rest of my night rolled out in a Finn-fueled haze. True to his word, he dipped his head back down and my eyes just about rolled into the back of my head. Little tremors of warmth pricked the entire length of my body, starting up at my ears and snaking all the way down to curl my toes into the mattress.

Complete ecstasy. That's what this was. It coiled and twisted, turning tighter and tighter until my head fell back against my pillow and I gripped the sheets, finally letting out a low moan in response to his ministrations. Even just letting that noise free felt good.

I didn't care that he was seeing everything up close—everything those pictures had shown him just a few hours earlier—and I didn't even care if anyone heard me as another low moan sighed from my lips.

When my finger tips tangled in his overly-long hair to keep him right *there*, it was brazen and wanton and everything I hadn't let myself feel in so long, but it just felt *so good*. I could feel myself beginning to let go and finally, something else I'd been needing for too long coiled tight and flung free.

My whole body seemed to shatter underneath his touch, splintering right across the room. Part of me was on the pillow, another part landed at the foot of the bed, and I'm pretty sure the rest of me scattered around the carpet.

I'd sort that out later because right now I was free-falling, slipping down into the hazy fog Finn created for me, pulsing over the edge, and spreading my arms out wide across the bed to take it all in.

I was still coming down from that high when Finn fell back against the bed next to me. Seeing him in my bed, still fully clothed even after what he'd just done for me...it just wasn't right. In fact, I needed to rectify that problem immediately and reached out to tug on the waistband of his shorts, but his hands shot out to my wrists to stop me.

"What—"

"Em," he murmured. "I don't need you to do that for me. This was about you. I already got everything I needed tonight."

My laugh came out breathlessly and I suppose that was just because I didn't have much air left in my lungs. "Tomorrow night then?"

He flashed me a wolfish grin. "I think I could handle that."

"Will you at least take off your shirt? I feel really exposed right now and I think it's only fair you get at least a little naked too, don't you?"

"You know if you wanted me naked all you had to do was ask," he smirked and promptly tugged at his T-shirt's neck to pull it over his head.

As soon as bare skin and hard muscle appeared on my bed, my fingers just had a mind of their own. There was no stopping it. They trailed up and down the hard planes of his chest before finally drifting down to the defined six-pack I found on his stomach. I loved the way my touch had his breath coming in harder, faster, and the way his smooth skin jumped at the contact—*I* was the one doing that to this gorgeous Browning Adonis...

"I can see this is going to be a problem for you tonight," Finn pushed out hoarsely. "Maybe I should put my shirt back on."

"You put your shirt back on and I kill you."

Even in the darkness, I could still see Finn's eyes widening playfully and he crossed his index fingers in front of him as if that would somehow save him from my touch tonight. I was still laughing as his arms wound around me, tucking me against his bare chest, and smiled into his skin when his lips found my hair.

CHAPTER EIGHTEEN

Two Weeks Later

Pandemonium. That was the only word my brain could latch onto. I just couldn't believe *this* many people showed up to see a bunch of guys running around in tight pants, kicking, and throwing balls to each other. Let's not forget the tackling and all the slapping each other on the butt on and off the field. But who was keeping track?

Our little caravan parked about three blocks away from Lambeau Field right on some random family's lawn. They had a whole system down too—someone, decked out from head to toe in green and gold, stood at the end of the driveway waving a sign that read, *$15 Parking*, and after you pulled in to pay, another person, again decked out in assorted Packer gear, waved you in and directed you which way to go, and then yet *another* person met you at your designated lawn space to make sure you parked where they wanted right down to the inch.

With two hours until kick-off, the modest-sized yard was already almost packed full. These people seriously had to make a killing every season. I guess there had to be some sort of silver lining for living so close to such a crazy, mob-infested part of Green Bay.

"I still can't believe you've never been to a game before," Finn murmured in my ear as he draped a jersey-clad arm around my shoulders and led me off the random stranger's lawn.

"I guess I just never got around to it," I laughed.

"Well," Slinger chimed in from behind us as we stepped out onto the street. "Someone had to pop your Packer cherry. Might as well be Finn."

Finn jerked around to smack Slinger on the chest with his free hand and pointed a finger at him. "Watch yourself."

Slinger's hands flew up in the air, but that knowing smirk didn't slip off his round cheeks as he put an arm around Mara, who was just shaking her head at the whole scene. We fell into step with the rest of our party—all the friends I'd met at Finn's party two weeks earlier—and I finally took in the festivities surrounding me.

The houses that weren't capitalizing on their close proximity to the stadium were still packed full of people. Some lingered on the sidewalks, high-fiving people that walked by, others camped out in driveways, lawns, garages, some wore face paint, most sported various Packer jerseys, others proudly donned green and gold striped bibs, and a few brave, chubby souls ran around the street shirtless with numbers like 12, 52, 27, and 87 painted onto their chests to correspond, I assumed, with popular players.

Of all the celebrating and tailgating around us, they all had a few very important things in common: the smell of charcoal and grease wafting from the driveways, beer bottles clanking, pre-game shows and/or loud music blasting through their speakers, and everyone, I literally mean, *everyone*, was celebrating and the game hadn't even started yet. I could only imagine what the mood would be like post-game if the Packers won, or heaven forbid, if they *lost*.

Wasn't there a study done once about how domestic violence always increased in Wisconsin right after the Packers lost?

Probably not the time or place to think about something like that.

Besides, focusing on my surroundings rather than the eyes boring holes into my jersey-clothed back was a welcome distraction. Throughout our entire journey from Milwaukee to Green Bay, the majority of which was spent stuck in traffic on Highway 41, I'd had the misfortune of also being stuck in a car with Chase, Finn's friend and the same friend who'd eyeballed me at the party two weeks ago.

From the moment we got in the car, I'd felt his eyes on me, snaking over me, penetrating me. Little pricks of awareness slithered down my spine and caged me in. Even sitting in the passenger seat right next to Finn, who'd been our driver, wasn't enough to create any semblance of safety for me. I'd tried to busy myself with listening to the small talk around me and even participating in it every once and awhile, but nothing worked. Those two hours on Highway 41 felt like the longest two hours of my life.

Up until now, these last two weeks had mostly been spent basking in my new relationship with Finn. It was just so *easy*, so *fun*, and he was everything I'd always hoped I would find. We spent most of our nights sitting on my patio with Oliver in my lap, listening to music, drinking Matthews Brewing Co. beer, and talking until the sun went down.

After righting the great wrong I'd committed when I'd left Finn's family business without a tour of the brewhouse, we'd made the most of our time together. Finn had even treated me to a trip to the Milwaukee Public Museum to 'indulge my inner history nerd and visit with local historical heroes', as he called it and together, we'd discovered the joys of *Drunk History*, binge-watching every episode in just three days and laughing our asses off together. Sometimes we'd have a movie night with Slinger and Mara, sometimes we'd even go out to dinner with them too, but every night since the night I'd divulged the full details of my past, Finn slept in my bed.

Everything hadn't snapped back to the way it'd been before I left my hometown, but in some ways, my life was better. *I* was better...happier, calmer, and more at peace, which was a two-week miracle in the making. Life with Finn, and Oliver, too, wasn't something I'd ever planned on, but I couldn't imagine either of them disappearing.

So, I hated the paranoia creeping its way into my happiness now. I hated that Chase couldn't seem to tear his eyes away from me, even if that was all in my head. I hated that the fear of being discovered, of being recognized, of being shamed all over again threatened what was supposed to be fun. After all, I was about to get my Packer cherry popped—wasn't a girl's first time supposed to be something she'd never forget?

Here I was, ruining my first time. The story of my life...implosion after implosion by my own doing.

It was one thing for Finn to know...but his friends? I wanted them to like me and to approve of me and because of that, they'd never know, at least not if I could help it.

Ear-splitting hollering filled my ears and yanked me right from those dark thoughts. Thank God.

"Whoo!" some random person decked out in Packer-themed pajamas yelled out as he proceeded to high-five every single person that passed by.

Finn didn't hesitate, jerking forward to slap hands with the crazy drunk guy, and then the guy held his palm out to me, waiting and yelling, "Go Pack!" I didn't have much choice and tapped his hand with my open palm. When in Rome, you know?

We made our way to Kroll's, an old-fashioned restaurant where we would commence our true tailgating festivities and meet up with Noah and Cris. According to Finn, Kroll's was a Green Bay institution, known just as much for its location as its greasy cheeseburgers and fries and as Finn paid my cover to get us inside the packed parking lot, I could see why: the restaurant was located directly across from Lambeau Field, a prime, no-brainer location for a pre-game blowout.

The whole parking lot was fenced in and we had to push our way through the throngs of tailgaters, the majority of who, let's face it, were already shit-faced at 10 o'clock on a Sunday morning. A band played "Don't Stop Believin'" on a makeshift stage in the far corner of the parking lot and we had to weave around a few booths of people, naturally decked out in green and gold, selling everything from overpriced jerseys to cheap Mardi Gras beads. Somehow, in between getting some beers and finding a place to camp out, I caught sight of two long arms waving at us.

"Oh, hey!" I tugged on Finn's sleeve and pointed. "There's Noah and Cris!"

Cristina was already practically stampeding towards us, sidestepping through the pack, pun intended, of tailgaters and she threw her arms around me when we met her in the middle.

"Em!" she yelled in my ear above the music. "I'm so happy to see you! I never get to see you this much!"

"I saw you two weeks ago," I laughed. "I wouldn't exactly say that's a lot."

"Oh, whatever," she batted a hand at me, but then her attention moved to the action next to us, where Noah and Finn were interacting for the first time.

This was the real moment I'd been dreading: the inevitable meet and greet. For obvious reasons, I legitimately feared for Finn's life. The way I saw it, this could only play out one of two ways. Noah would size Finn up, gruffly shake his hand, and make small talk for the rest of the day, barely tolerating who he would undoubtedly view as a guy who could potentially hurt me. Or Noah would take one look at Finn, hate him on sight, and spend the rest of the day shooting not-so-subtle daggers at Finn's unsuspecting and well-intentioned head. Either way, I didn't necessarily see this ending well for anyone involved.

That was why when Finn thrust his hand out for Noah to shake, I had to fight the urge to watch the whole encounter through my fingers. Noah, in full alpha-peacock mode, glanced down at the outstretched hand and then back up at Finn with calculating eyes.

"Hey, man," Finn greeted him good-naturedly. "It's really great to finally meet you."

My brother eyed my boyfriend carefully, sweeping his gaze over every inch of Finn's face in search of some sign of duplicity from him, but nothing about Finn was fake or dishonest. Noah had to see that and sure enough, not even a moment later, he thrust his hand out to shake Finn's still-outstretched hand.

I blew out the breath I definitely knew I was holding and even Cris exhaled loudly next to me. Then she reached around me, laying the charm on thick to make up for her husband's frosty reception, and smiled wide at Finn.

"Hey! I'm Cristina!" she told him as Finn shook her hand. "You have no idea how excited we are to meet you! Em's told us nothing but great things."

At that, Finn's eyes flew to me and even in the presence of my family, that lopsided grin crinkling his sky-blue eyes hit me right in between the legs, sending hot tingles all the way down to my toes. This was probably a bad time to reminisce about the night before in bed when he'd...Finn winked at me as if he knew exactly where my dirty mind went, right in front of my brother and sister-in-law no less, and it was right about then that my eyes flicked back to my brother in a panic.

Noah had observed our entire exchange with narrowed eyes, but when Finn threw an arm around my shoulders and tucked me in a tight, protective embrace, that stormy expression gathering in his eyes lightened considerably. Cristina, on the other hand, looked like she was having a hard time keeping from clapping her hands together in glee.

Thankfully, the rest of our tailgate experience flew by with a few more beers, more loud music and unfortunately the return of "Green and Yellow" by Lil' Wayne blasting from the speakers, and Slinger and Cristina grooving their hips in ridiculous unison with each new song leading up to our departure from Kroll's. When it was time to head across the street to the stadium, we waited our turn to cross the street with the help of our friendly neighborhood Green Bay police officers waving the traffic through.

I didn't even really have much time to let all the people I was literally rubbing elbows with needle any anxiety because there was just so much going on...so much to look at, so many drunk people to laugh at. Because of the sheer size of the clusters of people flocking towards the security line, I'd even been able to put Chase's lingering ominous presence out of my mind, which was really saying something. Any jitters I might've had flew to the wayside because here in Lambeau Field, all you had to do to blend in was wear the home colors.

As we stood in the snail-paced security line, Cristina treated our entire group to the latest pictures of my beautiful little niece and I could feel Noah's eyes on us the entire time while Finn, hopefully none the wiser, stood behind me with his hands resting over my shoulders.

"Oh, Em," Cris called out to me when she swiped past a recent picture I'd sent her of Oliver. "How's your little kitty doing? Is he feeling okay?"

"Is everything okay?" Heather asked.

"He's gonna be fine," I told them firmly, telling myself that if I said it enough times, I would have to convince myself it was true.

"What was that thing he has called?"

I knew Cris meant well, but referring to it as Oliver's 'thing' ruffled my feathers a little. Luckily, I had some backup.

"It's FIV," Finn answered for me from over my shoulder and when Cristina's eyes widened in melodramatic horror, he jumped to the rescue yet again. "It's not as bad as it sounds. I mean, it's not *great*, that's for sure, but he's got a great owner who's watching him like a hawk, so he'll be absolutely fine."

Cristina's gaze flipped back to me for just a second and then her eyes settled on her husband, who still observed in scary silence.

"I've never heard of that before," Heather mused as we moved a hair up in line. "Is he gonna be sick all the time though?"

This time, I jumped in to answer. "The vet said he needs to stay stress-free as much as possible, but as long as I bring him in immediately when I notice something's not right, keep him on a good diet and give him his multivitamin treats, and make sure he's healthy, he should be okay."

I know *should* was a relative term and that even the suggestion of giving a multivitamin to an animal might seem a little over-the-top, but I'd gone on full helicopter mom mode when it came to Oliver. While the vet tech had told me Oliver probably wouldn't be an 18-year-old cat, I still found comfort in the notion that if I continued being attentive, if I was diligent and always did what was best for him, my cat would have a happy life—however long it lasted.

"Aw," Heather smiled at me. "So you're still keeping him?"

"Yeah," I nodded. As if there was any other option.

Finn pulled me in a little bit closer and, despite the crowd and the presence of my brother, pressed his lips to my temple. But when I dared a glance at Noah, I found him watching us with quirked lips, that stormy glint in his eyes almost diminished completely.

It wasn't until we breezed through security and crossed the threshold of Lambeau Stadium that I had the sudden urge to cut and run. Only, this time, it wasn't because the crowds made me feel like the walls were closing in on me.

It was because of my boyfriend. Might as well throw the rest of his friends in there, too.

In unison, every single guy in our party—save for Noah—raised their green and gold clad arms high in the air and howled at the top of their lungs.

"I'm here!" Finn yelled out to no one in particular. "I am *here!* Whoo!"

High-fives were handed out all around and even Noah got in on it with the help of Finn, but all I could do was gape at the scene, frozen in shock at the display in front of me. The rest of the girls with us laughed and shook their heads, clearly well-versed in their significant other's insanity, but this was a first for me. Cristina, unsurprisingly, threw her head back in laughter and joined right in.

Finn found me easily after the initial craziness and wrapped me up in a tight bear-hug. "How does it feel to be inside the greatest place on earth, Em?"

"Oh boy," I managed to croak out, despite how tightly he squeezed me against his jersey-covered chest. "Um, good. I guess."

"You guess?" he chuckled and closed both hands around my cheeks to give my forehead a quick peck.

"Uh huh."

"Oh, Emma. I have so much to teach you."

I laughed as he tucked us in with the rest of our group. When we turned the corner, falling in step with the rest of the crowd moving towards their respective seats, it was just sensory overload. I could barely even see two feet in front of me as we tramped through the cement hallways, dodging people with every step. Finn had to grab hold of the back of Slinger's jersey to keep him in line when he snarled at a person wearing a Favre Vikings jersey—the nerve!—but we mostly survived the trek from the entrance all the way through the mob of Packers and Bears fans, even if the opposing side's cheering section seemed to be few and far between.

But when I stepped through the walkway and that 'hallowed' field came into view, even I had to suck in a sharp breath. Suddenly engulfed in the organized chaos that was Lambeau Field, I was momentarily blinded by the glare of the sun beaming down at us. The people on the other side of the stadium looked like little green and gold ants and stadium workers dressed in yellow jackets directed people where to go, but it was more than that.

There was magic here—something in the air, something about the camaraderie between all these people, tens of thousands of them, coming together for one sole purpose to cheer on these gladiators in our modern Colosseum...it stunned me. Awed me. So much to the point that Finn had to practically push me forward to get me up the stairs.

So yeah. Not even a minute in the stadium and I was already a convert.

We climbed the ridiculously high cement stairs—seriously, how did people not hurt themselves on a game day basis here?—and found our seats, settling into the cold cement bench with Finn to my left and Noah to my right.

"See that over there?" Finn pointed to a long green tent-like structure protruding from the bottom of the field to our right. "That's where all the players run out from. And we've got the end zone right in front of us, so we'll be able to see all the Lambeau leaps...these are freaking great seats."

Well, seeing as how we had to climb up about 40 rows, I didn't really see how they were all *that* great, but I wasn't about to ruin this moment for either of us. Now that we were settled, everything happening around me started to sink in. Everywhere I looked, people were high-fiving, sipping on a beer, munching on a skinny, foot-long hot dog, leaning their heads down to speak warmly to their children, taking selfies, clapping along to the warm-up music, and generally doing everything you'd expect to see in a place like this. Somewhere to my left, a group of guys sang off-key, "The Bears still suck! The Bears still suck! The Beaaaars. Still. Suck!"

My initial assumption about this place wasn't wrong: there really was some kind of magic here. What I had been wrong about though was the people—they weren't a mob. They were a community. There was a fellowship here unlike any I'd ever seen at my mom's church. Here, the Packers were the religion and Mike McCarthy, Aaron Rodgers, and Clay Matthews stood at the pulpit ready to deliver, not a sermon, but a win. Nearly every person in this stadium had come to worship and you could feel it in the air.

There was a spark here. Electricity crackling in the air as the players prepared for kick-off. Palpable energy blanketed the entire stadium.

I got it now. I understood the craziness, the face-painting, the Vince Lombardi pope, the basement shrines, and the frenetic worship.

Here, everyone was the same and green and gold served as the equalizers. Everyone was part of the fellowship—just as long as you weren't wearing a navy and orange jersey. Here, I truly could get lost in the crowd, but feel like part of it all the same.

And, just a few minutes into the first quarter, when Rodgers found James Jones in the end zone, every member of the community leapt to their feet, green and gold arms lifted high in the air, screaming at the top of their lungs, clapping along, and singing loudly as Jones jumped into the crowd just beyond the end zone to receive his glory and slaps on the back.

Now, I clapped and sang along too, one with the crowd.

"I don't wanna work...I just wanna bang on this drum all day..."

.   .   .

We were back in my apartment a few hours later and while part of me hadn't wanted to leave Noah and Cris, especially since I wasn't sure when I'd get to see them again, the other part was happy to be home. Oliver greeted us at the door, rubbing up against our legs and stretching up on my shins to reach one tiny white paw up to me.

"Hey, buddy," I murmured to him. "Did you miss us?"

"What are you talking about?" Finn laughed. "He probably had a raging party while we were gone. You know, inviting all his cat friends and maybe even a few dogs, too," he bent down to scratch the top of my cat's head, "Good thing you got everything all cleaned up before we got home, huh?"

"Wow," I muttered under my breath and reached down to scoop Oliver up into my arms so I could give him a kiss on his little striped cheek.

Finn's eyes glittered with amusement. "And you think *I'm* the one with the problem. You should see yourself from my end."

Just as I opened my mouth to respond, he jerked his head towards the living room.

"Hey, Em, you got your computer handy? I wanna show you something."

I cocked a wary eyebrow at him, but just shrugged, set Oliver back down on his feet, and padded over to the living to grab my laptop for him. When I brought it back into the kitchen and set it down on the counter in front of him, Finn tilted his chin towards the screen with a small smile.

"Google yourself, Em."

I reared back a little and frowned. "I feel like that could be taken a couple of ways."

He barked out a laugh and shook his head, gesturing yet again to my computer screen. "I'm serious, Em. Google yourself."

I blew out a deep breath and figured the only thing I could do was just go with it. So, I opened up a new search and typed in my full name, something that I hadn't actually done on my own in a long time. Just the physical act of typing in the letters was enough to conjure the kind of memories that would have my head in the toilet pretty soon, but today had been a good day—one of the best days I'd ever had with Finn. I didn't want to ruin it so soon.

But when I hit search, my mind couldn't process what it was seeing. In the past, Googling myself would've rounded up pages and pages of obscene pictures, courtesy of my ex-fiancé and my former students, but now...there were only six full pages of pictures.

My eyes flew up to Finn, who was still watching me with that glittering smile. "What...?"

He just shrugged. "I found a work-around on Google."

"I don't understand."

"Google's got this tool that lets you delete urls from any searches, so I went through and started entering all the urls that had your picture attached to them. It's still a work in progress, but it's something."

While I'd heard the words, they still just did not make any sense. He'd actually went through and deleted everything...well, not *everything*, but he'd still whittled 20-plus pages down to just six. My mind went blank. My throat went dry. And my heart...my heart screamed for joy.

"It doesn't delete the pictures from the internet," Finn explained, hands on his hips and brow creasing a little with worry. "It just removes the url from popping up in a search, so say some idiot posted one of the pictures on their Twitter account, it just deletes the url that hosts the tweet, but doesn't delete the tweet itself from the person's account. Right now, it's just a search through Google, so technically, anyone could still find them. They just have to do a little bit more digging, which, let's face it, will probably happen, but it's better than nothing, you know?"

Yeah. I did know. And now, I felt a little stupid, too, that this option was out there and I never knew about it. I'd been so preoccupied by getting the pictures removed all together that I hadn't really looked into other alternatives to reducing the traffic. At a certain point, I think I'd just given up hope that it was even remotely possible.

He sighed again and rubbed the back of his neck. "It's not an easy fix. Hell, it's not even that great of a fix. Some of the pictures have been retweeted, reposted, that sort of thing, which creates a new url, so it's...complicated, to say the least. At one point, I had the search results down to two pages, but then the next day it was back up to ten. There's probably a better way, but this was the first solution I could find, so I went with it."

I didn't care about any of that because I knew, just as well as anyone, that those pictures would always be out there on the internet in some form. What mattered to me was the steps Finn had taken to help me.

"But you went through and entered all that? That had to have taken you—"

Finn just shook his head to shut me up. "It doesn't matter, Em. Do you think I could really just sit here knowing all that shit was out there without even *trying* to do something about it?"

I bit down on my bottom lip, but my mouth still curled up into a hesitant smile. I knew I shouldn't have been all that surprised, but I found my eyes stinging with fresh tears all the same. That he would take the time to do this for me, that he cared enough to sit at his laptop and enter in all those urls one after the other...I reached for his neck and pulled his lips to mine, kissing him long enough to tell him everything I couldn't find the words to say.

Finn pulled back a little, dipping down with both hands closed around my face to look me in the eye. "Em, I didn't do it for...*this*. I did it because—"

"I know," I murmured breathlessly and sealed my lips back where they belonged, wrapping my hands around his neck to pull him in deeper.

Then the awkward shuffling began. Step by step, we trekked around my counter and headed for my bedroom. We'd barely made it halfway down the hallway before I felt him pulling me closer and a hand snaked around my waist, just barely skimming the space between my jeans and my borrowed Rodgers jersey. I shivered into him and it was difficult to keep my entire body in check, to keep from trembling after just one brief glimmer of contact.

I pulled away for just a moment to watch him as he edged us closer and closer to the doorway of my bedroom and the intensity darkening his normally light eyes just about knocked me sideways. I'd seen that before whenever we'd gotten tangled up in each other all the previous nights he'd spent in my bed, but there had been some restraint there as well. There was none of that pooling in his eyes now. The sheer force of his eyes, which took on an even more magnetic force in the dim hallway light, pushed me deeper until I was crossing the threshold to my bedroom. There was no going back now, even if I wanted to.

I didn't want to go back. I just wanted to keep moving forward.

Just as my hands wound around his neck, his lips descended on me and I felt his hands burning into my waist as he pressed me more closely to him. He was still walking me backwards, closer and closer to the bed, when my hands took on a mind of their own and tugged Finn's jersey up and over his head. They didn't stop there and reached around to lightly skim up the hard muscles of his back. He leaned back, a grin dancing on his lips, as he lifted his arms so I could pull his T-shirt off, too.

Biting my lip, I trailed a hand lightly down his bare chest, gently tracing the muscles I found there, marveling in the way his skin jumped taut at the contact. My fingertips continued their explorations and trailed down his rippled stomach, feeling my breath quicken at the sensation of his skin. When I tugged my gaze back up to him, his eyes were closed. Deciding to test out just how much I was affecting him, my hand drifted a little bit lower and gently skimmed over the section of skin that led directly to his belt buckle. When I heard him take a sharp intake of breath, I grinned slyly.

I hadn't forgotten this after all. Somehow, after being so out of practice, my body still knew what to do.

Feeling a newfound sense of empowerment, I yanked him closer to me by his belt buckle and his eyes shot open as his muffled laugh tickled my ear. His hands were tugging up my jersey now and I said a silent prayer of thanks that I'd decided to wear one of my sexier pairs of bra and underwear today.

While my shirt floated to the carpet at our feet, Finn's mouth captured my lips and this time, his tongue darted in and out of my mouth as his hands trailed up the sides of my back until he had both hands full and kneaded them roughly. A moment later, he reached around and made quick work of unclasping my bra, shoving it to the side and onto the floor. He gently nudged me closer to the bed until my calves hit the edge.

I scooted backwards, with Finn in hot pursuit, and settled back against the pillows, allowing him to move in between my legs. This was what I'd been waiting for and now that this moment was finally here, it just felt surreal. I had a rough, tousled, unshaven Browning Adonis in between my legs and I wanted to savor every single moment of it.

Of course, savoring the moment would only take me so far. I needed him closer and he was still wearing too many clothes to get as close as I wanted. Before I could stop myself, my fingers worked on his belt buckle and he reached down to help me, shoving his jeans down and kicking them off to the side, his attention never leaving my lips.

By the time I kicked off my own jeans, my patience had started to wear thin. I didn't want to wait anymore. But when he lowered his head and placed a light trail of kisses from my collarbone all the way down to the edge of my lacy boy-shorts, I knew what was coming next and I'd had every night for the last two weeks to prepare myself for it.

I almost couldn't take it anymore. I just wanted him closer, deeper.

I had no idea what I'd been waiting for...all this time, we could've been doing this and I denied myself for no good reason. Why the hell had I ever wanted to take things slow with him?

His head jerked up when another unabashed moan fell from my lips and Finn grinned back at me. Then he was scrambling over the side of the bed, rifling through his discarded jeans for his wallet. When he came back up with the foil package in his hand, he wasted no time to simultaneously rip it open with his teeth and kick his boxers off. He propped himself up on an elbow as he hovered over me and I could feel the tip of him pressing into me.

"Finn, please..." I pleaded breathlessly.

He kissed me again and when he pushed himself inside me, my body tensed at the invasion as I inhaled sharply. Catching the pain in my voice almost immediately, Finn froze and broke away from my lips to look in my eyes.

"You alright, Em?" he asked softly, concern shining in his eyes in the moonlight.

I nodded quickly. "I'm fine. It's just...been a little while. Just give me a second."

He nodded, bending down to suck softly on my neck, helping me relax and I ran my hands up his arms until they were tangled in his hair to pull him down closer, to draw him in deeper. He took that as his signal and began moving, slowly at first, and then picking up speed until he gripped my hips to pull himself in deeper with a deep groan.

I gasped at the sudden motion and ground my hips up to meet him halfway until I was pulling lightly on his hair with each thrust of his hips, his hands still viced tightly around my hips, bringing me up to meet his rhythm.

Everything started to get hazy and I could feel myself getting closer and closer to the brink of coming undone beneath him. I had to move a hand down to his back to hold on because he just kept moving faster and faster, both of us too caught up to slow down, too entangled to break away and when it started, my head fell back into the pillow, my nails dug into his back, and my back arched against the mattress as my entire body surrendered, crying out at the release.

Little tremors shot all the way to my toes as I convulsed against him and then, in a brief moment of awareness, I felt Finn shudder against my skin and he let out a low groan as his body went rigid. I could've sworn I heard him stop breathing completely.

We stayed like that for a moment, each of us trying to get a hold of our breathing and some of my focus returned as he pressed his forehead against mine.

He grinned lazily before leaning back down to kiss me softly on the lips, moving to both my cheeks and then my forehead. With a deep, relaxed exhale, he pushed himself back on his knees and hopped off the bed to head into the bathroom. I leaned up on my elbow to watch him with a small, satisfied smile as he quickly tossed the condom in the trash and rubbed his face with a nearby towel. When he appeared in the doorway of my bedroom, he grinned at me as he rested his hands on the edges of the doorway, completely stark naked in front of me.

With an easy, sly smirk, Finn sauntered back to the bed, taking his sweet time so I could drink in the hard planes of muscles, the smooth, polished tanned skin, and that little trail of dark hair leading right to all the places I wanted to keep playing with. Exhaustion was the only thing keeping me from pouncing on him again when he collapsed on the pillow next to me, so I snuggled up to him and he tucked me under his arm, squeezing me into him about as close as I could get.

I rested a hand gingerly on his chest, watching it rise up and down with a labored hitch and listened to his heartbeat, which still drummed unsteadily in his chest. Grinning into his skin—after all, I'd been partly responsible for the state he was currently in, I reveled in the feeling of him still lingering in between my legs...it had never felt that good before. While I wasn't completely inexperienced in the bedroom, it had never been like that—the intensity, the way I just let myself go and give in...it wasn't even close to being on my radar of what was possible in bed.

He shifted around and hitched my leg up and around his hip, pulling up the sheet around us that had pooled to the bottom of the bed. When my breathing started to feel a little more normal, everything else slipped away...Noah's concerns about the upcoming homecoming, Chase's leering, those pictures still out there for anyone to see...I didn't want to think about any of that right now because I was in pure, blissful heaven.

As my eyes fluttered to a close, somewhere I felt Finn's warm lips press into my forehead before he settled back into his own pillow.

Life was good.

CHAPTER NINETEEN

I knew it was going to happen. I'd expected this—Noah had expected this, Cristina had expected this, Finn had expected this. So when my sister-in-law called, I should've known.

Wishful thinking had just gotten the best of me.

Today was the day before Matthews Brewing Co. had their rollout at the Bluestone Lounge and I wished that event was the one I could spend my energy focusing on.

Today was also the culmination of Hickory's week-long homecoming celebration, starting with a half-day at the high school, a pep rally immediately after the school day, a parade through the streets of Hickory, which would take about five minutes, and finally, the homecoming football game against Hickory's arch nemesis, the Kohler Ghosts.

The whole process was one I knew well. As a high school student, I'd loved every minute of it, reveling in the festivities and participating along with my classmates...you know, being a normal teenager with a normal life. As a teacher, seeing it from a different perspective was another beast entirely—the kids were always out of control during homecoming week and forget trying to do anything meaningful in your classes because you'd just end up beating your head against a wall by the time the week was over. Between dress-up days, class competitions, float decorating, and senior pranks, it was all one headache after another and I found myself counting down the minutes until the stupid week was over—a huge change in perspective from my high school days.

The problem I saw as a teacher was exactly the reason I'd loved homecoming week as a student—you pretty much had free reign to do just about whatever you wanted as long as no one got hurt and nothing got damaged.

Needless to say, we all had every reason for concern because the following year, the first homecoming since my firing, I'd been an easy target. How could they resist using me as their personal punching bag? I wasn't there anymore and it was well-documented within the school that most teachers and administration alike didn't necessarily disagree with my treatment following the 'scandal'. If you throw raw meat to a pack of rabid dogs, they're going to attack. That's just all there is to it.

Still, I'd exercised a sliver of hope that somewhere, somehow, someone would come to their senses and intervene this year.

I was wrong.

When I got the call, Finn and I were working our way through a season of *Arrested Development* on my couch. The second I saw Cristina's name on my screen, I knew. Finn must've felt me tense next to him because his eyes flashed to me, wide with concern, and his fingers squeezed my shoulder. Part of me didn't even want to answer, but I knew Cris would just keep calling until she talked to me. So, with a heavy heart, I swiped across my screen to answer.

"Hey, Cris. What's up?"

The brief, albeit weighted pause on the other line told me everything I needed to know.

"Hola, Emmie," Cris greeted me softly and I wished she would just get it over with already. "Look, I wish there was an easier way to tell you...I don't know *how* to tell you...but there's a video that just popped up online. Noah's texting you the link right now. I know you won't want to watch it, but I think you should or at least let Finn see it so he knows what's going on. I'm so sorry, Em. I wish this would just go away...I'm so sorry."

I swallowed hard and glanced at Finn, who'd since paused the episode and was leaning forward with his elbows on his knees, watching me intently as concentration creased his forehead.

"Okay. Thanks for letting me know, Cris."

"Love you, Em."

"Love you too."

I blew out a heavy breath as I swiped across the screen to end the call. Sure enough, not even a second later, Noah's text came through with that dreaded link. My finger hovered over the link and I wavered between clicking it and deleting the text altogether when Finn's voice called out to me.

"Emma? What is that?"

Another labored breath pushed through my lips and I knew I couldn't lie, even if I wanted to. "I don't know....but something happened today. It's only 4:00, so I'm guessing it was during the pep rally."

Finn was already leaning into my shoulder to peer at my screen and the mounting fury clouding his eyes had me squeezing my eyes shut.

"Open the link, Emma."

I shook my head furiously. "No, I don't wanna see it. Can't we just —"

"No," he cut in sharply. "We can't. Open it."

Seeing as how I didn't really have any other options, I opened the link, which sent me to a Youtube video. I wanted to bolt. I wanted to hide. Unfortunately, Finn had an arm around my shoulders to support me and to keep me in place all at the same time so I couldn't bolt, so I couldn't hide, so I had to sit down and face it. He did the honors for me, reaching forward to hit play on the video, and my heart flapped wildly in my chest when Kennedy High's gym came into view.

As the first few seconds of the video played out, a group of students huddled right in the middle of the gym as the rest of the assembly looked on in anticipation. The video was up close enough to see all the faces clearly, so whoever had filmed it was probably sitting in one of the bottom rows in the gym.

Yeah. This looked familiar.

The senior skit. I should've known.

It started out just like all the other senior skits I'd ever seen when I was a student *and* when I was a teacher, too. Each senior class had the opportunity to perform a supposedly staff-approved skit during the homecoming pep rally and each senior class, just like the one before it, always did a variation on the same idea. Apparently, none of the senior classes ever cared too much about originality.

Three senior boys, ones I recognized as former students, stood off to the side and took turns with the microphone as they introduced each section and performed all the voices. The rest of the students in the middle of the floor emulated a typical school day with various students taking roles as teachers in the school—all a ploy to make fun of the school and their teachers. As a student I'd found it hilarious. As a teacher I'd found it mean-spirited and disrespectful.

They started out how all the school days at Kennedy High started: with a brief announcement from Principal Denfield and the pledge of allegiance, only the student with the mic did his best mockery of the principal's delivery, making sure to make fun of the school's new dress code policy as a 'first day of school' announcement.

Then, after that was all said and done, they moved into first period, which found all the students scurrying across the gym to their respective places as a student stepped in front of a makeshift whiteboard wearing a sign that read "Mr. Hamilton" as everyone else gathered around like they were in class.

The boy with the mic then proceeded to mimic Mr. Hamilton, a much-maligned chemistry teacher, while the boy wearing the sign mimed the movements and mouthed the lines. It was all the same bullshit they did every year—making fun of Hamilton always showing up late to class, being unprepared, and losing everyone's papers. As far as I knew, most of that was exaggerated and it wasn't any less funny now as it'd been the first time I heard it as a teacher.

Next, they moved on to mocking a popular Spanish teacher as the pack scampered over to the other side of the gym, where yet another student wore a sign that read "Mrs. Allan-Perreault". This time, the student with the mic read his lines in a high-pitched girly voice and the student playing her waved his hands manically in the air to demonstrate that she was over-caffeinated and overzealous. Pretty tame, all things considered, and probably indicative of the fact that most students liked Mrs. Allan-Perreault anyway.

Next up was an English teacher, with the students once again flocking over to the side of the gym to signal a change in class periods and another student stood in front of the mock class wearing a "Mr. McLean" sign. This time, they weren't so kind and skewered the teacher, who had a reputation for being a hard-ass and the kind of English teacher that rarely gave out As on anything. They pitched McLean as a drill sergeant and throwing things like pencils and pretend staplers at kids when they answered a grammar question wrong and at times, suggested that McLean was related to Adolf Hitler. Nice, right?

Now, as they moved once again to the other side of the gym to another class change-up, my palms got clammy. I knew what was next: me.

Unlike all the 'impersonations' before it, the student playing me was dressed in a button-up shirt and a black pencil skirt. It looked like they'd taken great pains to make this particularly demeaning, even more so than the year before. As the students gathered around this fake-me, I glanced at Finn out of the corner of my eye and found his chest heaving and his face darkening with each second. I wished I could just stop the video right there, but I knew Finn would never let that fly.

Another student with the pic read his lines in a high-pitched voice, mimicking me and thinking he was funny as the student playing me started unbuttoning his shirt.

"Now, class," the student with the mic started. "We're going to play a little game. For every question you get right, I'll undo *one* button and if you get one wrong, back up the button goes."

The whole gym had already descended into a fit of laughter and cat calls and someone yelled, "Ms. Owens is hot!" from somewhere in the audience.

"Why the fuck is no one stopping this?" Finn muttered under his breath.

I just shrugged, turning my attention back to the video.

"Okay, here we go," fake-me went on in that high-pitched, nasally voice as the student playing me kept unbuttoning his shirt. "Who was the first president of the United States?"

He pretended to call on another student in the 'class' who'd raised his hand. "Oh, hey there, Tommy. How you doin' hot stuff? What are you doin' later? Oh...you wanted to answer? Okay, go for it—I gave you an easy one to make sure you'd get it right, big boy."

More roars of laughter. More cat calls. No adults intervened.

When the student answered correctly, fake-me took off his button-down completely to reveal a lacy bra and he wound the shirt over his head like a rodeo cowboy before tossing it into the screaming crowd like he was some kind of rock star. Just as fake-me reached for the zipper on his skirt and started to do a little dance with it, the pretend bell sounded, signaling it was time for yet another class change-up.

I'd seen everything I needed to see and promptly hit the stop button so I could toss my phone onto the coffee table.

Finn, on the other hand, opted to plant his foot against the edge of the table and furiously pushed it aside as he leapt to his feet. He crossed the short distance in between my living room and my kitchen, stopping short at my table and pacing in front of it. Both hands pushed back his hair and he'd let out a low growl by the time I had my hands on his chest in a futile attempt at calming him down.

"Finn—"

"How the hell does something like that happen? Doesn't anyone check their scripts before they get up in front of the whole school and taunt their teachers?"

I heaved out a loud sigh and pressed my fingertips into his chest to get him to listen. "They're supposed to, as far as I know. It's always been that way. The senior class advisers are supposed to review the script ahead of time and sit-in during the practice, but once they get on the floor, I guess all bets are off. They could go off-script as much as they wanted and deal with the consequences later."

Finn barked out a bitter laugh. "Consequences? What fucking consequences? They think they can do whatever the hell they want."

I ignored that last comment and moved forward with the rest of my explanation. "All the teachers are supposed to sign-off on the script and give their permission to be included."

"Except for you," Finn spat hotly. "Right? No one gave a shit if you gave them *your* permission or not."

"I'm sure that part wasn't in the original script," I murmured.

Finn's hands tore at his hair again. "I can't believe this bullshit. This is such...fuck! What are you gonna do about this, Em?"

Another sigh pushed its way from my lips. "I don't think there's much I can do."

His eyes widened in horrified disbelief. "What do you mean there isn't much you can do? There's a helluva a lot you can do."

"I don't—"

Finn abruptly pushed past me and stalked back into the living room until he swept my phone up in his hand. "I'm calling your brother."

"What? Finn, don't. Please."

His eyes snapped back up to me, flashing dangerously. "If you're not gonna do anything then I will."

I watched helplessly, wringing my hands in front of me, as Finn called my brother. Whatever happened from here on out was probably going to suck in epic proportions and just make all this that much worse.

"Hey, Noah, it's Finn," he started, his voice tight and barking out the syllables in rapid succession. "Yeah, we just watched it....yeah, I know, I'm right there with you. So what can we do to get that shit taken down? We can delete the url, but...right, I figured that wasn't the only link out there...it's got how many shares? Jesus fucking Christ. I can't believe this. Yeah, I'll do that, too. I'll follow-up with some emails too and I'll just keep doing that until someone talks to me. I'll let you know as soon as I hear something. Sounds good. Bye."

He furiously swiped across my screen to end the call and his eyes flicked up to me yet again. This time, his light eyes softened, his face twisting in pain.

"Noah said that video has more than 700 shares in less than two hours and that's just for that link. Apparently, there are at least 10 other links out there with that video and those are just the ones Noah and Cris were able to find," he explained quietly.

Two seconds later, my phone buzzed in his hand from a text message and Finn's eyes skimmed over the text, pressed something on my screen, and brought my phone back up to his ear.

"Finn," I whispered and swallowed heavily. "What are you doing?"

"I'm doing something about this," he informed me and then his eyes flicked to the wall as he spoke into my phone again. "Hi, my name is Finn Matthews. I'm calling because I want to know what you're doing about that senior skit video that's been circling around social media. It's disrespectful, inappropriate, and cruel and if you're *not* doing anything about it *or* disciplining the students responsible for it, I'm just going to keep calling until you do. And then I'm calling every news station in the area and telling them that your school district allows its students to participate in sexual harassment, bullying, and verbal abuse. You can call me back at 414-555-6727. Thank you."

He swiped across my screen again and tossed my phone onto the couch before tugging his hands through his hair. I was still frozen to the carpet, unable to believe what I'd just heard. Everything fogged up around me and I felt dizzy enough that I had to put a hand on the back of my couch to keep myself upright.

"Finn," I tried again. "Please...just let it at that, okay? You said what you wanted to say and now just leave it alone."

His eyes flashed wildly. "Leave it alone? What are you talking about? How are we supposed to just leave it alone and let those idiots run wild with this?"

"They're just kids," I sighed. "They don't know what they're doing."

"Just kids? They're fucking animals, Emma. And clearly everyone at that school doesn't know how to do their jobs because none of those animals obviously know right from wrong."

"Finn—"

I stopped short when Finn abruptly kicked over one of the chairs at my kitchen table, sending Oliver scurrying for the bathroom. Finn's chest heaved wildly and he paced around my tiny kitchen, hands in his hair, and finally scrubbed both hands over his face.

"Finn, you need to calm down."

His steps stalled and he whipped around to face me. "I'll calm down when that video is off the internet and every single one of those little bastards involved with it gets their asses suspended."

"That's not up to you to decide, Finn."

Now, he stalked towards me until both his hands settled over my shoulders. "How are you not angry about this, Emma? I don't understand why you're not tearing this place apart right now."

"Of course I'm angry," I whispered. "How could I not be?"

It was just more complicated than that. Anger wouldn't help me. Anger wouldn't remove that video any faster. And anger wouldn't erase the last year of my life.

"I don't believe you," Finn murmured and he gave my shoulders a little shake. "Get angry, Emma. You have to get angry. Goddammit, get angry!"

"I am angry."

Clearly, neither of us were really convinced by that and Finn released my shoulders, taking a few steps back as his face twisted with pain and disbelief.

"I can't understand how you can be so passive about this, Em."

"And I don't understand why you're overreacting like this," I shot back hotly, finally exhibiting some of that anger Finn wanted to see.

Finn's hands swept up to his hair. "I think my reaction is completely appropriate given the situation. *You're* the one who isn't reacting the way you should."

My breath whooshed out in one huff, but Finn just shook his head.

"You know what, Em? I think I do need to cool off. I'll just..." he sighed and scrubbed his eyes. "I'll call you later, okay?"

I watched, my feet rooted to the carpet, as Finn shot me a weak smile and walked out the door.

Once again, my life was crumbling over things I couldn't control and now it was happening all over again...the devastation, the humiliation, the fear, the panic, the paranoia...it was never going to stop.

And here I was. Still helpless. Still powerless.

· · ·

A few hours later, I sat on my couch with my computer on my lap and a half-empty glass of wine resting on the coffee table. In between keeping tears at bay, fielding text messages from my brother and sister-in-law making sure I was 'okay'—as if I'd ever be—and checking my phone every two seconds to see if Finn had reached out like he'd said he would, my attempts at distraction and deflection were failing.

My fingers rested on the keys, but I just couldn't conjure any words. Writing a blog post about which moisturizer to use for winter just seemed so trivial compared to the way my life had once again imploded because of my own actions seven years ago. It was so stupid—how could I possibly expect to write even one coherent sentence about something as irrelevant to my life as *moisturizer* right now?

So, in an effort to distract myself, all I'd done was make everything worse. Go figure—the story of my life, right?

Maybe I would just get drunk. That would at least numb everything that wasn't already paralyzed with fear. With that thought, I snatched my wine glass from the coffee table and downed the rest of the contents.

My phone rang and my heart leapt at the sound, only to plummet back down to earth when I realized it wasn't Finn calling, but Cristina. I figured voicemail could take care of that for me, but I guess I should've known Cris wouldn't take being ignored lying down and my phone buzzed a second later with a new text from her.

Please call me back. It's really important.

I blew out a breath and muttered, "Fine...you win. I guess."

But as soon as Cris picked up, panic prickled up yet again that something else had gone very wrong.

"Em?" Cris answered, but her voice wasn't distressed the way I thought it would be. Instead, her tone had a breathy liveliness that caught me off guard.

"What's up, Cris?"

"Have you looked at the comments under that video Noah sent you?"

I frowned into my phone. "No. Why?"

"Just...just do it, okay? Read the comments."

"Cris," I sighed and rubbed my forehead. "I really don't want to. What I want is for all this shit to be over."

"I know, chica, I know. But do yourself a favor and read the comments, okay?"

I huffed out a sigh. "Fine."

"You won't be sorry. Just do it."

"Whatever you say. Bye, Cris."

After Cristina echoed my goodbye, my fingers swiped through my phone to find the link Noah had texted—and incidentally, Principal Denfield's office number at school, too—and I opened the video, quickly clicking over to open the comments before the video could start playing again. I scrolled and scrolled, skimming through the various comments I'd already expected to see: I think we should start a petition to bring Ms. O back so we can make that a reality and Sexy striptease...fuck yeah! and I bet that really happened to! Everyone knows the senior skit always speaks the truth and Best. Skit. Ever. and Next year we should make Ms. O the principal. She could teach the whole school all her moves.

Then my eyes flicked to another comment: When is this video going to be taken down? Seriously. You guys are stupid.

My heart twisted a little and I shook my head.

"Oh, Luke," I whispered to my screen. "Why do you even bother?"

Luke was one of the few students who'd actively spoken out against all the pictures, videos, memes, and comments and, it seemed, he was still doing it. He was always one of those students who made you actually like your job—happy, friendly, funny, smart, willing to participate in class, and an overall decent human being. I'd had him in class two years in a row and when his dad passed away last year right before the first round of pictures hit the internet, I'd made a point to attend the wake.

Sometimes, you look at a student and their antics in class, whether it's disrespect towards you or another student—it was always the boys that caused the most trouble in class, too—and you think to yourself, *This kid is an asshole and he's always going to be an asshole.* Sometimes, you look at a student and you think to yourself, *This kid is an asshole now, but maybe he'll grow up and figure it out.* And sometimes, you look at a student and you think to yourself, *This is a good kid and he's going to grow up to be an even better adult,* and you feel like maybe your job isn't so pointless after all.

Luke was one of those kids who made me feel like maybe there was still some hope for humanity left. Contrary to Finn's belief, they weren't *all* animals. Some of them were actually pretty great to be around; it was just too bad that by the end, the number of decent ones at that school seemed to be few and far between.

When I found yet another comment from Luke asking his peers to 'grow up and take the video down because it wasn't funny', tears stung my eyes.

Defending me was just a wasted effort.

But when I read a comment just a few lines down from Luke's most recent one, my eyes just about jumped out of their sockets.

Hey, Matt? You think it's cool to make fun of a woman who's been sexually assaulted? I feel really sorry for your girlfriend. She must be miserable.

The commenter, naturally, was Finn, who'd logged-in through Facebook, probably so everyone would see it was him.

The student, Matt, who Finn had directed his first comment to, responded with:STFU man. Who the hell are you anyway?

Finn: I'm the guy who actually knows how to treat a woman with respect.

Matt: Fuck off loser.

Finn: How am I the loser in this scenario? You know what? Maybe we should talk about this face to face. You're at Jason's house right now playing CoD, aren't you? I'll swing by.

Matt: How do you know that stalker

* * *

Finn posted a screenshot of Matt's Twitter profile in response highlighting the tweet, *Going to @jasonclearmen for a CoD war tonight. Gonna get an ace! Die crawlers die!*

Finn: 127 Field Ct, Hickory, WI. Right? Doesn't feel so good knowing people can find out whatever they want to know about you, does it?
Matt: How do you know that?
Finn: Google.
Matt: What the hell is your problem?
Finn: My problem is dipshits like you who think you can do whatever you want because you can hide behind your smartphone and your computer when you do it. You shouldn't be allowed to use it if you don't know HOW to use it.

Then Finn moved on to his next target, the poster who'd commented about starting a petition.

Finn: Hey Brady?

Then he posted yet another screenshot from Twitter that featured Brady with his arm around a girl I recognized from one of my classes last year, both of them drinking out of a red solo cup, a cluster of empty beer bottles visible on a table to their left, and a crowd of kids behind them.

Finn: How much will you pay me to keep me from sending this to your athletic director at school? How about your football coach?
Brady: Who the hell is this guy?
Finn: You know what? Never mind the money. I'll send it anyway just for fun.
Brady: Already deleted it asshole. Nice try.
Finn: Already saved the screenshot to my phone, dickhead. Nice try.

At that point, Finn was clearly ready to move on and he fired at his next target:

Hey Jesse? I see you've been accepted to UW-Madison. Congratulations. Do you think the admissions people would be interested in knowing you've participated in documented sexual harassment? Maybe I'll email them a running doc of all your comments on this video and the sexually explicit pictures you posted last month of your teacher without her permission so we can find out.

He didn't wait for Jesse to respond, instead moving on to Luke's comment, and said:

It's nice to see there's at least one person at that school who's a human being. I'd say I'd find you so I can shake your hand, but I respect your privacy too much. Stop by Matthews Brewing Co. when you turn 21 and I'll buy you a beer.

I couldn't believe this...what right did Finn have to pull this kind of shit? All he was doing was stirring up more trouble and causing more problems to an already shit-smeared mess. He'd gone too far, pushed the whole thing over the edge and I'd already snapped my laptop shut and was stalking out of my apartment before I could stop myself.

When I pounded furiously on Finn and Slinger's front door, the wrong roommate answered. Slinger's eyes widened almost instantaneously and he stepped aside as I blew right past him with just a muttered, "Hey, Slinger", in greeting. I ignored Mara on the couch and marched right up to Finn's bedroom door so I could pound on it too.

Finn flung the door open, his lips set in a firm line like he'd been expecting me, but I didn't give him a chance to get the first word in.

"How could you do that?" I demanded as I stormed through the threshold, brushing past Finn's shoulder on my way.

I obviously didn't need to explain because Finn just shrugged and shoved his hands in his pockets.

"I'm not gonna apologize to you, Em. If anything, those stupid shits should be apologizing to *you*, but fat chance of that ever happening."

I shook my head furiously at him and crossed my arms over my chest. "I can't believe you did that. You just made everything worse!"

A slow, bitter smile spread across Finn's handsome face. "It's good to see you're finally angry. It's just too bad you're angry at the wrong person."

"I think I have every right to be angry at whoever I want to be angry at!"

Even as the words left my lips, I knew how ridiculous they sounded. I just didn't care.

"You just made everything worse, Finn," I told him. Now it was my turn to pace in front of him. "You shouldn't have talked to them...used your real name...what was the point of doing any of that?"

"The point is that someone needs to teach those pricks that the stupid shit they post online follows them around just like it does everybody else. They're not immune and they can't do whatever the hell they feel like doing just because they feel like it."

I huffed out a deep breath and squeezed my eyes shut. "Why can't you just let this go?"

Finn's face twisted. "Let this go? Are you kidding me?"

"In a few years, everyone will forget all about it and they'll have moved on to the next scandal. It'll run it's course and then it'll be over."

Now, his face contorted into barely-bridled fury. "Let it run it's course? Do you hear yourself, Emma? Did you really hear what you just said?"

"Yeah, I did and you wanna know something else? Now you're no better than the rest of them. You're just like them...hiding behind your smartphone and your computer, right?"

Finn barked out a bitter laugh. "Yeah, well, if I got out from behind my computer and hunted them down, things wouldn't end so well for any of us."

My mind flashed to an image of Noah sitting in lock-up with his knuckles bloodied and torn and the exact same unapologetically murderous expression on his face that I saw mirrored on Finn right now.

"Please promise me you won't do anything else. You called the school, you called out some kids...can you please just leave it at that before you make things even worse?"

His eyes darkened. "Right, so *I'm* the problem now? *I'm* the one who's really making this worse? You know what? *You're* the one with the problem. You being passive like this, Emma? You just letting people fucking walk all over you? *That's* the problem. Not me."

"You know what?" I flung my hands in the air. "I'm done with this right now. I'm leaving."

"Fine," he snapped. "I'll walk you out."

"I'm pretty sure I can find my way out on my own," I retorted as I yanked Finn's door open only to find Slinger and Mara camped out just a few feet away and gaping at me.

I froze mid-step, jerking forward when Finn all but crashed into my back. His hands slipped to my waist to steady me, but I pushed him away.

Slinger tilted his head to the side, his green eyes still wide with bewilderment and disbelief. "Wha...?"

"Leave it alone, Sling," Finn grunted roughly from over my shoulder.

"No, seriously," Slinger shook his head and held out a hand towards us. "What the hell is goin' on here?"

I opened my mouth, but then snapped it shut just as quickly. The words were right there, but I couldn't do it. There was no way I could handle the look I'd see in both Slinger and Mara's eyes the second the words left my lips.

Slinger turned his impatient gaze to his best friend. "Finn? You gonna tell me what's goin' on?"

My head whipped around to face him and my heart just about leapt into my thick throat, searching his eyes wildly and silently pleading with him to keep my secret.

"I'm not gonna say anything, Em," Finn told me, his eyes soft with remorse and defeat. "I'd never hurt you like that."

"Not gonna say what?" Slinger demanded again, but both of us ignored him.

"Thank you," I whispered to Finn and he shot me a weak smile in response.

His fingertips ghosted down my forearm even as I moved back to step around both Slinger and Mara, who still stared at me like I'd suddenly sprouted a peg leg or something.

Even as I walked through the doorway, I could still hear Finn telling Slinger, "I can't tell you, Sling. Stop asking."

I almost turned around, but I just couldn't bring myself to do it. We both needed some time to cool off and calm down. This was just the worst timing ever—the Bluestone Lounge rollout was tomorrow and I was supposed to be Finn's date. Go figure...when life decided to give you lemons, it pelted those lemons right at your face.

And now, for the first time in nearly three weeks, as I closed my apartment door behind me and felt Oliver rubbing up against my legs, I was almost grateful to be alone again.

Almost.

CHAPTER TWENTY

The Bluestone Lounge was exactly what I'd expected: covered in blue stone and a lounge. Go figure, right? It was, however, way swankier and more upscale than I thought it would be...dim blue lights, granite bar tops, large pane glass windows facing Water Street with unobstructed views of Milwaukee's downtown scene, navy blue leather couches lining the walls, contemporary decor, elegant, and pretty damn high-brow all the way around.

When I stepped inside the lounge, it took my eyes a few moments to really drink everything in. This was the complete opposite of the dive bars I was used to both when I was in college and living back in Hickory. I'm sure it had something to do with the fact that when I was in college at UW-La Crosse, I didn't want to spend the money—if I even had it in the first place—on fancy cocktails because I was all about quantity over quality. After I graduated and moved back from college, I had a little more money—emphasis on *a little*—but Hickory only had bars sporting names like *The Country Bar* and *Jim's Place*. Original names for an original town, right?

Music played in the background, but it wasn't overpowering and just mellow enough to keep the mood up but maintain the 'chill' atmosphere. From what Finn had told me, the Bluestone Lounge was more of a cocktail bar, so the fact that they'd agreed to partner with the brewery was a huge get for Matthews Brewing Co. and signaled a shift in business for the lounge, too. Overall, everyone here had something to celebrate tonight.

I just wished I was in the mood to celebrate.

I might as well walk in and introduce myself saying, *Hey, everyone. My name's Debbie Downer. I'd ask yours, but I really don't care.*

The source of my downer mood lied in my still-unresolved argument with Finn and it didn't help that I hadn't seen him since I'd left his apartment yesterday. We'd texted cordially a little today throughout our respective shifts at work, mainly to confirm the plans for tonight, but that was it. Finn had even offered to pick me up, but since the lounge was literally right down the street from the brewhouse, it just didn't make sense. Besides, if I came on my own, then I could leave on my own if I needed to.

So, while part of me felt just a tiny bit pathetic by taking extra pains tonight at trying to be the hottest girl in the room, I decided that for once in my life, I'd just own it and strut my stuff, so to speak. Even though I'd had to buy the navy racer-back sheath dress I was wearing right now especially for this occasion, I *did* have a mini-Sephora in my bathroom, so it was nice to be able to actually have a use for all those products in real life instead of just trying them out in the solitude of my apartment and reporting about them on my blog.

I tucked my bright yellow clutch underneath my arm and blew my bangs out of my eyes so I could more easily scan the lounge for that familiar head of floppy chestnut hair. It only took me a few moments before I spotted him—well, I spotted Slinger's orange hair first, but that was pretty hard to miss, even in the dim lights. With my heart pounding in all its anxious idiosyncrasies, I wove through the crowd of people already assembled by the bar and placed a careful hand on Finn's back.

He jumped a little at the contact, but when he shifted around, his arm was already lifting over my head to settle around my shoulders and tuck me in tight. His lips curled up into that sweet, familiar smile I knew so well and he leaned forward to press a quick kiss into my lips, lingering just long enough to tell me everything was going to be okay now.

"It's good to see you, Em," Finn murmured in my ear when he pulled away from my lips.

I smiled back, finally releasing that breath I'd been holding since I stepped foot inside this place. Maybe now I'd actually be able to enjoy the night and celebrate my boyfriend's accomplishments like a normal person. But first, I needed to say a few things.

"Finn," I whispered to him, grateful that everyone around us was too wrapped up in conversation and alcohol to notice us. "I'm sorry I freaked out on you like that yesterday."

His lips pulled into a tight line and he shook his head. "It's not like you were the only one who freaked out. I could've handled my shit better, too, and I didn't. I'm sorry, Em."

"You weren't wrong though," I reminded him with a rueful smile and his arm slipped down to my waist to tuck me in closer.

The problem, though, was that I didn't know what to do with all the truth he'd bared down on me yesterday. I knew I needed to be angrier than I was...I just couldn't summon the emotion the way he wanted me to.

"We'll get it taken care of," he promised me and kissed the side of my head. "I still haven't heard back from the principal after I left that voicemail yesterday, but we'll keep trying, okay? Noah's on it, I'm on it, and we won't stop until the people at that school start doing their jobs."

I swallowed hard, my eyes darting around us to make sure no one was listening in. "Do you think we can talk about this later?"

Finn smiled tightly, but he relented. Then he leaned forward to kiss my temples again. "You look beautiful, Em."

"Thanks," I grinned and gripped his tie with both hands to tug him in closer, taking in the slightly rumpled white button-down with its sleeves rolled up to his elbows and the black pants that I was already fantasizing about taking off him later. "And *you* don't look half-bad yourself."

He shrugged and glanced down at his attire before finally cocking an eyebrow my way. "I figured I might as well clean up for the occasion. I wish I owned a decent shirt that wasn't wrinkled to high hell though."

"You know ironing is still a thing, right? People do that to get the wrinkles out of their clothes."

Finn just batted a hand out. "That sounds like it would take work and effort, two things I just don't really care about when it comes to clothes...or grooming."

His fingertips fluffed up the dark bushy scruff on his face to prove his point and I reached up to give his unkempt beard a playful tug.

"Promise me you'll never shave? I don't think I'd survive if you did."

His lips spread apart into a slow, knowing grin. "You like the scruff, huh?"

"I don't mind it."

With that, he pressed his face close to my cheeks until his whiskers tickled my skin. "You like the way it feels right here?"

I nodded helplessly, a rush of heat flooding all the way down from my ears to my knees. Suddenly, I was hyper-aware that we were standing in the middle of a crowded room and I was too busy contemplating how long we could disappear somewhere dark and quiet before anyone noticed we were missing. I must've squeaked in response because Finn's voice dropped an octave and his husky breath in my ear sent my knees rattling underneath me.

"You like the way it feels other places, don't you, Em?"

My head bobbed up and down, my lungs wiggled for air, and thankfully, his arm wrapped around my waist to steady me. Finn's head dipped down even lower so he could catch my gaze and he winked at me deviously.

"Maybe we should hold that thought for later?" I exhaled breathlessly.

"Okay," he grinned slyly and bit down on his bottom lip. "Later."

At that point, the rest of his friends decided to make their presence known and I found myself wrapped up in hugs from Heather, Amanda, Megan, and Mara, which surprised me, and an awkward side-hug from Slinger, which didn't really surprise me all that much. The rest of the guys nodded and waved in greeting and then it was back to normal again, where I could slip back underneath the safety of Finn's arm and hide a little more.

Conversations carried on easily around me and—wonder of wonders —I found myself actually joining in every once and awhile, laughing along with something somebody said, adding in a little commentary to a story Slinger was telling, and even gave them all a quick update on Oliver. For all intents and purposes, I'd found myself enfolded in a group of friends again. It'd even gotten to the point where Mara and I had gone out to lunch and a few shopping trips together without our guys...and I felt like I could finally, actually, call her my friend without any twinges of guilt.

I was in a crowded bar in downtown Milwaukee with my boyfriend's arm wrapped around my waist, laughing with friends, and...I felt normal. It felt so good to just feel normal, like this was where I was supposed to be—here, with these people, with Finn's warm breath humming in my ear.

"Hey," Finn whispered in my ear. "You need a drink. Let's head to the bar, huh?"

Finn's fingers closed around my hand to lead me through the crowd, weaving in and out, until we finally stopped right in front of the bar. He raised a hand to call the bartender over and kept his other hand planted on the small of my back.

"I'm assuming I should probably order one of your beers, right?"

He flashed me a wide grin and leaned in to whisper in my ear, "Get whatever you want."

I eyed him warily and when the bartender waited for our drink orders, I diplomatically ordered the honey ale since they'd opted to keep my personal favorite, the vanilla porter, exclusive to the brewery. It didn't seem right to order anything tonight *other* than Matthews' beer and Finn winked at me when I gave my order, telling me I'd probably made the right choice.

Just as the bartender stepped away to grab our drinks, someone brushed up against my right shoulder and I felt it before I saw him. That little prickle of awareness sliding down my spine, my breath lodged in my tight throat...I knew what that was before I even turned my head.

"Hey, man!" Finn called out to him over my head and reached around me to shake Chase's hand. "I didn't think you were coming tonight."

Chase just lifted a shoulder. "Where else would I be? This is your big night!"

I wanted to roll my eyes, but that would give away the fact that I was on to Chase just as much as he was on to me. Luckily, the bartender reappeared with our drinks and I could distract myself with sipping on my beer. And then everything seemed to happen all at once.

Chase leaned forward on his elbows, angling himself so he could smirk at both Finn and me. "How long you guys been together now? A month?"

Finn shrugged and the hand on my back slipped to my hip. "Closer to two months."

"Good to see you're keeping track," Chase laughed, his eyes darting to me for just a moment, but it was long enough for that paranoia to slip right back into its old familiar place.

"You know," Chase shook a finger at me now with that smirk that made my breath hitch in my throat. "I've been trying to figure out where I've seen you before. Ever since that night at the tap room a few weeks ago, I just *knew* that I recognized you from somewhere."

Finn frowned at his friend, but when his gaze shot down to me, I could feel his entire body tense, tightening, and readying himself for a fight.

"What are you talking about?" Finn shot back, his face just as hard as his tone.

Chase, on the other hand, didn't seem to notice and I watched, frozen to the ground, as he unearthed his phone, swiped through a few screens, and then held it up for us to see. Everything shifted in that moment— the air ran cold right along with my blood, the hand at my hip tensed into a fist, and all the people around us might as well have just disappeared.

I should've known. I should've seen it coming, but that still hadn't prepared me to see one of those familiar, humiliating pictures flashing across Chase's screen.

"Chase," Finn murmured lowly and even in the dim light, his face had turned a dangerous shade of crimson. "Get that shit off your phone. *Now*."

"Whoa," Chase held up both hands. "Did you know about this? Shit...I didn't know you were into this kinda thing. Good for you, bro."

I read somewhere that flight or fight aren't the only two reactions you can have in a tense, potentially dangerous situation. While flight or fight are the most common responses, there's a third response, too, that's just as likely and it was the response that had my body in a hold right now: I froze. I couldn't move. I couldn't think. I couldn't breathe.

All I could do was stare at that picture on Chase's phone and my world crumbled all over again.

"Didn't you hear me?" Finn shot back. "Get that off your phone. *Now*."

Chase's eyes widened and he immediately set his phone down, but didn't bother even closing the screen. That picture still stared up at me, taunting me, haunting me...

"Sorry," Chase shrugged again. "I guess I see why you'd wanna keep it a secret. But I gotta say, all my buddies at the office are gonna shit themselves when I tell them..."

The moment Chase's hand connected with my shoulder, Finn whipped around me, shoved me behind him, and stood just inches away from Chase's face.

"Don't touch her," he growled.

Chase's hands immediately flew up in the air. "Okay, okay. Sorry, bro, I didn't realize you wanted to keep her all to yourself like this. I thought...I don't know, if this is some kinda escort thing, I thought you wouldn't care if I stepped in when you were done and—"

Finn's hands shot out to shove Chase right in the chest, sending him stumbling back into the person next to him.

"Hey, man!" Chase yelled. "What the hell? Back off, Finn!"

Finn gripped Chase by the collar and shoved him backwards again. "You fucking back off! You don't know what you're talking about!"

"I don't, huh?" Chase huffed before shoving Finn right back in the chest and jabbed a finger at me. "All I know is that I've seen your 'girlfriend' or whatever she is—but I've seen her, and I mean *all* of her, on more triple-X sites than I'm willing to admit. I'm not the problem here, Finn. Don't blame me because your girl's been jacked off to more times than—"

Finn's fist flung out, connecting with Chase's jaw and sending him flying backwards, and everything dissolved around me in a blur. Someone yanked me back, pushing me away from Finn, and several pairs of hands held me in place so I couldn't even step forward. From around the bodies descending around the scene in front of us, I could see Max pushing his son back and Tyler in between them with his hands on Chase's shoulders.

"It's not my fault your girlfriend's a fucking porn slut," Chase hollered from over Tyler's shoulder, pointing a finger at Finn, who's face had distorted into red, murderous rage.

Despite Max yelling at Chase to shut up, he couldn't keep hold of his son. Finn shoved and jerked his way free from his dad's grasp and sprung forward, pushing Tyler into the crowd of people surrounding them, and slammed his fist into Chase's face twice before Max managed to grab hold of him long enough to yank him away.

Everything had devolved into chaos now. People were scrambling to either move away from the fight or towards it, the bartender leapt over the counter to yell something in Finn's face, someone's hands shot out to keep me out of the fray, and the whole time, Finn just leaned his elbows on the back of the bar, his eyes boring maliciously into Chase, who spit a tooth out on the floor.

"Hey, Sling!" Max yelled out and jabbed a finger in my direction. "Get those girls out of here."

It was only then that I realized it was Slinger who'd held me back this entire time and Mara whose hands had settled firmly over my shoulders to keep me from moving any closer. Suddenly, Slinger was jerking me aside so two police officers could move through the crowd where Finn waited patiently for them. He didn't look surprised to see them at all and he just shrugged when Max murmured something in his ear.

"Slinger, let me go," I pleaded, but his grip on my arm just tightened.

"I can't," he murmured as he pulled me back towards the main exit with Mara coming in behind me to keep me from bolting back towards Finn.

I don't know how my limbs carried me to Slinger's car parked a block away. Everything was numb. Somehow, probably with Mara's help, I slid into the backseat and shut the door behind me. Fog clouded my eyes...I couldn't see anything around me. It was all just one thick, red haze.

It wasn't until we'd driven in silence for a few minutes that Slinger's tense voice finally called out to me from the driver's seat.

"What happened back there, Emma? I saw you guys talking to Chase and then...what happened?"

Mara twisted around in the passenger seat, her bright blue eyes wide with worry and confusion. "I heard Chase say something about you and he called you a..."

She trailed off, unable to say the words out loud, and looked down at my feet.

"What?" Slinger asked tensely. "What did Chase say?"

Mara's eyes flew back up to me and she opened her mouth to answer, but just couldn't bring herself to do it, so I did it for her.

"He called me a porn slut," I answered. Even to my own ears, my voice sounded hollow. Dead.

"What the fuck?" Slinger jerked around in his seat to face me despite the fact that he was still technically driving. "No wonder Finn beat the shit out of him. I don't get it, Emma. Why would he...?"

I only got a moment of reprieve when Slinger's phone rang. He answered it, listened for a few moments, said a few 'okays' and 'yeahs', and promptly swiped across his screen again to hang up.

He blew out a deep breath and ran a hand over his face with the other still on the wheel. "Max said both Finn and Chase were taken in for disorderly conduct. He's following them there so he can bail Finn out as soon as he can."

My eyes squeezed shut, but I was too far gone to feel anything but numb.

"Emma?" Slinger asked me again. "You wanna tell me why Finn got arrested for disorderly conduct tonight?"

I should've known I'd have to do this eventually. Secrets rarely ever stay that way for long and sooner or later, everything you bury in the dark always comes to light. My secret was no exception to that rule. So I went on auto-pilot, dutifully and numbly relating the events that had led to Finn punching one of his oldest friends in the face, starting with me calling off my engagement to Justin and ending with our confrontation with Chase at the bar.

Mara and Slinger sat in the front of the car in complete silence, listening with rapt attention, and finally, when I had nothing left to say and spilt all my dirty secrets out into the open, I blew out one long, heavy sigh.

There was no relief here. Not the way it'd been there when I'd told this exact same story, albeit with more details, to Finn a few weeks ago.

Now, I was reliving it all over again. I was suddenly back in Principal Denfield's office, listening to him explain why he just couldn't 'in good conscience' keep a staff member who'd behaved 'that way'. I was suddenly back at my mom's kitchen table, trying in vain to explain to my family why they'd all gotten emails from my ex-fiancé that day with those pictures attached, and watching my mother coldly, systematically, close the door on our relationship. I was suddenly back in Hickory, at Mike's Market with my grocery cart, trying to ignore the whispers behind my back, the patrons glaring at me with disgust. I was suddenly back at Jessie's Coffee Shop, there for my usual vanilla latte, but met with stares, whispers, and a phone number written on my cardboard cup as everyone else around me snickered.

It didn't matter that Slinger and Mara were looking at me now with only pity and sympathy. It didn't matter that I didn't find any judgment in their eyes.

Their pity was just as humiliating.

． ． ．

A few hours later, I jumped at the knock on my door. Oliver leapt off my lap and I sprung towards the door, breathlessly pulling it open to find a tired, disheveled Finn staring back at me. With one hand planted into my doorframe, he reached for me with the other, but I stepped aside to give him room to pass through the threshold.

When he stepped inside, he shut the door behind him and bent down to scoop Oliver up in his arms. His torn, bloodied knuckles were all I could see.

I took that opportunity to put even more distance between us and moved into the kitchen to get Finn something for his hands. I held up a bag of frozen vegetables and he promptly set Oliver down on the kitchen table, so he could catch the bag I tossed his way. He pressed the ice into his knuckles and leaned his hips into the table before finally searching me out.

"You okay?" Finn's hoarse voice called out to me.

I huffed out a laugh. "*You're* asking *me* if I'm okay?"

"Come on, Em. Tell me you're okay."

My eyes flicked up to him and found him watching me with soft, worried light eyes. I couldn't lie to him.

"No," I whispered. "I'm not okay."

Finn's face twisted and just as he moved to rise up from the table, I shook my head at him, finally heaving with all the emotions I'd numbed myself to before.

"You got arrested tonight, Finn. How could I possibly be okay?"

He sighed heavily. "I know what you're thinking and it's not gonna happen. I told the cops everything they needed to know and they know Chase harassed you *and* provoked me just as much next as the next person. I'll have to go to court, but all I'll get is a fine. That's it."

That didn't make me feel any better. Somehow, it just made me feel even worse.

"Em," he called out to me again, but this time, his voice had a harder edge to it. "Don't ask me to apologize because I won't do it."

"I'm not gonna ask you to apologize. I know you're not sorry. I just...I just wish you wouldn't have done it."

A hard line ticked down Finn's jaw and he slammed the bag of frozen vegetables down on the kitchen table, sending Oliver scurrying for the bathroom.

"I'm not gonna do this with you, Em. We went through all this yesterday already and I'm not doing it again."

My breath came out in one hard huff and tears stung my eyes. "Maybe you should've thought of that before you got yourself arrested tonight."

"Don't do this," he shook his head furiously and shot to his feet. "I never knew Chase was such a scumbag...and, well, I'm glad I know now because if I never see that asshole again it'll be too soon."

I squeezed my eyes shut and rubbed my face with my hands to scrub the tears away. "That's not the point. I mean, what's gonna happen with the Bluestone Lounge now? I can't imagine they'll be very happy with you because you started a fight in their bar the night you rolled out your beer there."

Finn just shrugged like it was seriously no big deal and I gaped at him.

"We'll have to meet with them on Monday. They'll probably drop us," he lifted a shoulder again the way he might if we were talking about which *Arrested Development* episode to watch tonight.

My life felt like it was on continual repeat, like a broken, tattered record cemented to my turntable and no matter what I did, no matter how hard I tried, I just couldn't yank it free.

"Finn," I whispered, my breath stuttering in my throat and now I couldn't stop the tears from slipping down my cheeks. "I'm so sorry. I —"

The second the word *sorry* fell from my lips, Finn sprung forward to reach for me, but I shoved his touch away.

"Emma," he stared me down with his hands on his hips and despite the fact that his chest heaved, his voice was calm. "This was not your fault. Nothing that happened tonight was your fault. Chase is a bastard. That's on him. I punched him. That's on me. None of this falls at your feet."

I was so sick of hearing him tell me it wasn't my fault...maybe I hadn't provoked Chase tonight, but did Finn actually believe that if Chase hadn't seen my picture on some porn site, that he would've *still* punched his friend in the face not just once, but three times tonight?

Finn's face twisted like he'd just heard every sad but true thought and his jaw set in a tight line as he tentatively took a step towards me. "You don't believe me, do you? That's what this is really about. You don't want anyone doing anything that might actually help you because you don't think you deserve to be helped."

I backed away from him until my hips hit my kitchen counter. "Stop it, Finn."

"You don't want anyone defending you."

He said it like no truer statement had ever been uttered and that just sent another wave of tears flooding down my cheeks.

"Well, you know what, Emma?" Finn moved even closer and folded his thick arms across his chest. "Someone has to do it because you obviously have no interest in doing it yourself."

He'd boxed me in now as both arms descended on either side of me. I had nowhere to run. Nowhere to hide.

"The people who care about you, Em," Finn's voice lowered an octave and my breath hitched in my throat. "We're never gonna stop protecting you and defending you *because* we care about you. It's my right to throw a punch if someone disrespects you just as much as it is your brother's. I'll never apologize for it and I'll never stop protecting you because I...I love you, Em."

Everything stopped. All I could think was: *How? Why?*

Finn's hands moved from the countertop to my shoulders and I winced at the contact.

"Look, this isn't the way I wanted to tell you, but it doesn't make it any less true. And...honestly? I fell in love with you the moment I saw you. It just took me a little while to figure out what it was. I'd told myself I was done with everything—relationships, commitment, all of it—and then I met you and I forgot why I'd made that promise to myself in the first place. I just wanna be with you, Em, in any way you'll let me...but you gotta let me in."

I swallowed hard as his words swum around in my head. He was saying everything I should want to hear, everything that should have me screaming those three words back to him, and then leaping into his arms so he could carry me to bed.

I pushed him away instead.

Alarm bells sounded in my head. Red flags waved across my eyes. My throat closed. My eyes watered. My hands pressed against Finn's chest to shove past him and put more distance between us. Finn, however, had no interest in taking this lying down and stalked after me, spinning me around to face him.

"Emma," he pleaded desperately. "Don't do this. Don't run away from me. Don't push me away. Come on, just talk to me."

Even if I knew what to say, the words wouldn't come anyway. Even if I knew what to say, there was no point in talking anyway. It would just make all this so much worse.

"I know what's holding you back," Finn pressed on even though I'd backed away. "And I get it, Em. I really do. I'll do whatever I need to do to help you get over this and then we can—"

That was where I had to draw the line. The words *get over this* had me bristling up like a porcupine and I knew he was trying to help. I knew that. But that didn't mean I wanted or needed to hear it.

"Stop it, Finn."

He reared back, gaping at me as if my words had slapped him right in the face, and then, in a flash, a hard mask slipped over his features, clearly gearing up for the fight to come.

"No, Em," he stared me down. "I think you need to stop it. You're the one that's had to live with this and it's time for you to stop. You can't keep doing this to yourself...punishing yourself this way. You don't deserve it and I don't know what it's gonna take for you to understand that."

Hot tears stung my eyes, but I ignored them.

"You have no idea what I've had to live with," I whispered.

Finn swallowed hard and his head tilted a little to the side as his eyes filled with sympathy and pain for me...more emotions I just couldn't deal with. More emotions I just didn't understand.

"Then tell me."

I didn't know what he expected me to say, so I just said nothing.

His hands tugged through his hair in frustration and then he scrubbed both hands over his face. "Or, you know what? If you won't talk to me, then maybe you should start seeing a therapist or something. I mean...I fucking love you, Emma, but I don't know how to help you if you won't even talk to me."

It tumbled out of me before I could think twice: "I don't think we should do this anymore."

I'd felt myself pulling away from him the second I opened the door for him tonight and now, I ejected myself completely. I just needed this to be over. I just needed to go back to what I knew. I'd been fine that way. Being with Finn had just caused more problems and more headaches and I didn't need that in my life right now.

Finn frowned back at me. "What do you mean you don't think we should do this anymore?"

I lifted a shoulder and took another step away from him. "You heard me. I just...I can't do this with you. I'll never be what you want me to be. I'll never be able to do the things you want me to do and I'm sorry you've had to put up with me for as long as you have. It's just better this way...better if we just end it now before..."

His face twisted angrily and red spots splotched his cheeks. "Before what? Before we get too attached? It's too late for that shit. I told you I *love* you tonight and somehow that means we should break up? That's bullshit, Emma, and you know it."

"I'm not gonna sit here and argue with you about this all night. This," I gestured between the two of us, "is over and it never should've started in the first place."

"Don't say that, Em. Don't stand there and tell me I haven't made you happy because you've sure as shit made me happier than I've ever been in my life."

Even now, I still couldn't lie.

"Yeah," I whispered in spite of myself. "You've made me happy. And I think you should be with someone who can give that back to you and I mean *really* give that back to you. I'm not that girl, Finn."

His face hardened and he tugged his hands through his hair again before shifting those shards of blue ice back to me. "I think you are. I just told you—"

"I know what you just told me and I don't know what to tell you other than that this is over. I think you should leave now."

"Just like that?" Finn spread his hands out wide in front of me to illustrate the massive distance I'd just lodged between us.

"Just like that," I nodded. "Please go. Don't make this harder than it has to be, Finn. Please...just go."

His eyes rounded, but just as quickly, that light I loved so much went out. Finn's eyes grew hard, his body went rigid, tense with the weight of the splintering fracture between us. He ran a hand over his face one last time before walking towards my front door.

When his hand closed around the doorknob, Finn turned back to me, his eyes flaring with determination. "This isn't over, Emma. I'll give you what you want right now, but I'm coming back."

With that, he stepped out of my apartment and shut the door behind him.

CHAPTER TWENTY-ONE

Finn did come back. And he came back again. And again. And again. And again.

I just never let him back in.

It started the morning after I'd all but kicked him out of my apartment. I woke up to knocking at my door, a flurry of text messages begging me to open the door and when I didn't respond, finally to at least text him back. I didn't. He waited a few more hours that Sunday morning and then it started again, the knocking, the texts, the calls, and then the cycle just continued on that way until I finally relented at the end of the day and responded with a simple and succinct message: *Please just stop.*

To his credit, Finn still had a key from when he'd kept an eye on Oliver for me all those weeks ago, but he never used it. He wanted me to *choose* to let him in, not to force his way back, and in a brief moment of weakness, I almost opened the door that Sunday night.

I'd stood in front of my door, listening to Finn on the other side, hearing him tell me how much he loved me, how much he wanted to make it work, how he knew I felt the same way, but was just too scared to admit it, and he wasn't wrong about any of it either. My hands had tingled at my sides and I'd sucked in a harsh breath when I heard him whisper through the door: *Please, Em. I love you. I know you love me, too. Just let me back in.*

My fingers reached for the doorknob, but then I heard yet another voice in the hallway.

"What are you doing out here, making all this racket?" Mrs. Johannsen yelled at Finn.

"I'm sorry, Mrs. Johannsen. It's just that—"

"You don't need to tell me. I've already heard everything and I'd like to get some sleep tonight. I think it's pretty clear she's not opening the door for you right now. Why don't you just call her or text her like a normal person?"

"I've tried that already, Mrs. Johannsen, and I'm really sorry I'm disturbing you. That's not what I'm trying to do. I'm just trying to——"

"Win her back. Yes, I understand. I just don't care. What I care about is getting to sleep tonight."

My hand squeezed the doorknob, but I just couldn't force myself to turn it. I wanted to set Mrs. Johannsen straight, to tell her *I* was the one who'd messed up, not Finn...but my body just wouldn't follow-through.

Finn sighed loudly and the echo bounced off the hallway walls around him. If I looked through the peephole in my door, I knew I'd find him tugging his hands through his hair, but doing that would just be self-inflicted torture.

"Alright," he told our neighbor. "I'm sorry. I really am. I'll go back into my apartment now."

"Good," I heard Mrs. Johannsen yell back as she went back inside her own apartment, slamming the door on her way.

"Em," Finn told my door softly. "I gotta go back inside now before Mrs. Johannsen comes at me with a steak knife or something, but this doesn't mean I'm giving up. I know you have to work at the café tomorrow, but I'd really like to talk to you when you get home. Please call me or text me back. I love you."

Every time he said those three words it was just another knife twisting my heart. One of these days that knife was going to twist too hard and I'd be left with my heart in my hands...on second thought, I had a feeling that had already happened. I just hadn't realized it yet.

The next day, I found him leaning against my door, waiting patiently for me to come home from my shift at the café. I had no idea how long he'd been standing there, but he was still wearing work pants and a button-down, so he'd clearly stood here since he got home from the brewery. When he heard the heavy door to our shared entryway open, Finn straightened, standing at attention now, and met me halfway in the hallway.

It wasn't lost on me that he'd effectively blocked my path so that my only way into my apartment now was through him.

"Em," Finn's soft voice called out to me and even as he reached for me, desperate to touch me, I still backed away. "It's good to see you."

I sighed wearily and despite my better judgment, my eyes flicked up to meet his gaze. His light eyes watered at the sight of me, his face twisted in pain, and it seemed like every muscle in his body tensed because I'd shied away from his touch. Tears burned my eyes, but I just shook my head. The last thing I needed to do now was let him see me cry. That would only fuel his determination to prove to me that our separation was temporary—it was anything but.

"Will you *please* talk to me?" Finn implored. His eyes crinkled up at the sides, but this time, it wasn't from laughter or happiness or that playfulness I loved about him so much. When he reached for me again, pure weakness held me in place, and his fingertips skimmed my forearm, sending a trail of goosebumps in his wake.

His fingers slid around my arm to tug me closer and I felt my resolve waning for just a moment. I squeezed my eyes shut as his thumb brushed my cheek. Never one to miss an opportunity, he pounced and wrapped both strong arms around me, holding me as tight as he could without suffocating me, his hands tangled around my nape, and his lips found my temples, pressing sweet, gentle kisses into my skin.

I did my best to push him even further away. "What happened with the Bluestone Lounge? You met with them today, didn't you?"

He pushed out a rough breath and scrubbed a hand over his eyes. "They dropped us."

My heart twisted. Of course they'd been dropped. Why would a classy lounge like that want to do business with anyone who'd start a brawl on the very same night they were supposed to be rolling-out their product? As far as business decisions went, it was a logical, if not practical one. And it was all my fault.

As if he could read my thoughts, he stepped forward and closed both hands around my face to force me to look at him. "I already told you—it's not your fault. Just...*talk* to me, Em. That's all you have to do. We can fix this, okay? These last few days have been complete shit for both of us and neither one of us has been thinking clearly. Just *talk* to me. Tell me what's going on."

I squeezed my eyes shut again and gave myself one last moment in his arms. My senses fanned out, spreading up and down to memorize this feeling, this safety I'd always found in him, the musky, earthy scent he always brought home with him from the brewhouse, and finally, I pulled free of his arms.

"I said everything I had to say last night, Finn. Nothing's changed since then and it never will. You're just wasting your time on me."

He scratched his scruffy beard in thought, squinting a little as the wheels in his head turned, and suddenly, his head dipped back and shook from side to side. "It's because I told you loved you, isn't it? That's what this is really about?"

I frowned back at him. "I don't know what you're—"

"I got too close, didn't I?" His soft voice cut in gently. "And now you're scared and you're pushing me away."

One traitorous tear trailed down my cheek, but I furiously wiped it away. I found myself backing away until my back hit my apartment door.

"I'm sorry," I whispered and bit down on my trembling bottom lip to keep from weeping in front of him. "I wish I could—I just can't, Finn. I'm so sorry."

He nodded carefully, his eyes still squinting at me, still seeing right through all my defenses despite the fact that I might as well be running away from him and screaming my head off.

I couldn't get my key in the door fast enough.

That was almost a week ago and since then, it'd just been more of the same. Finn blowing up my phone. Finn waiting outside my door when I came home from the café. Finn knocking on my front door *and* my patio door. Finn begging me to listen. Finn pleading with me to just let him back in.

I evaded him at every opportunity. I ignored his texts and sent his calls to voicemail. When I found him waiting outside my door after work, I listened politely for a few moments, backed away when he reached out to touch me, and told him I couldn't talk to him before letting myself inside my apartment.

By the end of the first week, I knew how much I was hurting him—I wasn't a good enough liar to convince myself otherwise...I could hear it in his hoarse voice, see it in his watery eyes every time he managed to catch me coming or going from my apartment, and every time he reached for me, I wanted to reach right back.

I just didn't.

By the end of the second week, I'd become so detached, so numb that I managed to convince myself that I really *didn't* care anymore when or if Finn called, that my heart really *didn't* tug and leap into my throat at the sight of him waiting by door or camping out on my patio, even though I'd long closed the blinds so he couldn't see inside. Even when he left me a voicemail to tell me he'd finally spoken with Principal Denfield and that the major players involved with the senior skit had been suspended, I just felt nothing.

All I knew was that I just wanted my life to go back to how it'd been pre-Finn. Post-Finn was painful, agonizing, and swallowed whole by tears and regrets. Pre-Finn I'd been alone, but at least the only person I'd been hurting was myself...there was no one else to bear the brunt of all my issues. Finn didn't need that. He deserved to have a girlfriend who hadn't been seen naked countless times on the internet. He deserved someone clean, someone good, and someone who was capable of giving him a long-term commitment.

Maybe I didn't know how to do casual, but I didn't know how to do commitment anymore either. Anything that involved leaving myself so bare, so vulnerable...I just couldn't do it.

I couldn't let him in.

By the time the third week rolled around, I gradually heard from Finn less and less. He hadn't given up necessarily, but the calls and texts were fewer and farther in between and he only knocked on the door once when he knew I was home from the café, waited a few minutes, and then left.

Every night I cried myself to sleep. Every night I wished I could be different, that I could really be the girl Finn thought I was...he was right though. I was too scared to try and there was nothing I could do about it. And now, I was sitting here on my couch, living in agony knowing that Finn was just feet away, but I was just too stubborn to put one foot in front of the other.

Every night I came home from work and tried to resume life as normal, pre-Finn. Blogging, listening to music, Netflix, wine...it wasn't enough to distract me. Finn was right. He'd gotten too close and now, that closeness suffocated me. I couldn't get away from him...everywhere I looked, everywhere I turned, Finn was always there. I saw him on my couch. I saw him in my kitchen, on my patio, in my bathroom...and especially in my bed.

I'd tried sleeping on the couch, thinking that maybe that would solve my problem, but all I got was a stiff back and an annoyed cat, who was more than disgruntled that there really wasn't enough room on my couch for both of us to sleep through the night comfortably.

Now, Noah's warning echoed in my head: *"Are you sure it's a good idea to date your neighbor? If things don't work out, it could get awkward..."*

This wasn't just awkward. This was agonizingly painful. Every time I caught a glimpse of Finn, whether he was coming or going in our shared parking lot, my heart twisted and throbbed, screaming at me to either put it out of its misery and just cut it out of my chest or stop being so stupid already and talk to him. Sometimes Finn stopped to try to talk to me and sometimes he didn't.

Slinger wasn't much better. During that first week, he'd wave grimly with a tight smile on his face. After that, the cordial niceties stopped and I was lucky if he even made eye contact with me in the parking lot or the hallway.

So, I did something drastic and if I was being completely honest with myself, really cruel...but the idea of being cruel to be kind...that resonated. I felt that. And so, I found a new apartment. At this point, it was really the best thing for all parties involved.

If I moved, Finn would have to leave me alone—he might still be able to call and text, but I wouldn't find him standing outside my door anymore, wanting to talk and wanting to fix someone who couldn't be fixed. If I moved, we could all just move on with our lives and forget this ever happened. Finn could forget he'd ever known the crazy, neurotic girl across the hall and I could forget I'd ever had a chance at...well...a second chance.

I told myself that I probably would've had to move eventually anyway because of the cat, but even I knew that excuse didn't fly. Here I'd thought having an 'illegal' cat or contraband as Finn so fondly put it, would be more of a problem, but in reality, I'd never gotten so much as a letter or a phone call for a 'random' inspection that obviously wouldn't be random. If anything, all my worrying about my landlord was just an excuse to keep from doing something that scared the hell out of me.

The problem was always in my head, just like the real reason I wanted to move lied just beyond the door right across from mine.

Luckily enough, all I needed to do was give my landlord a 30-day notice and I could get out of there. Even though I was the only one who could easily leave, given that Finn and Slinger had only been in their apartment for about three months, it was only fair that I was the one to go. I was the one who'd made it awkward. I was the one who wouldn't talk to him. I might as well be the one to bite the bullet and move first.

Finding a cat-friendly *and* a budget-friendly apartment in Milwaukee wasn't an easy feat, but I'd managed to find a decent and clean one-bedroom about 10 miles away from Finn, which meant I'd have to sacrifice the ability to walk to and from the café—a small price to pay for the distance I so desperately craved.

Oliver and I could be happy there if only I could actually figure out how to let myself be happy.

.   .   .

By the one-month mark, I hadn't heard anything from Finn all day. Granted, I was working a shift at the café and he probably knew that, considering he seemed to be more in-tune with my schedule now than he'd been when we were still together. My heart seized at that thought. *When we were still together...*

So, even though I shouldn't have been surprised, I still stopped right in my tracks when Finn stepped through the café's front entrance. My breath hitched in my throat and my hands shook so badly I thought the tray in my hands might come crashing down at my feet. Gone was the brilliant, bright smile I used to know and in its place, a grim, tight smile forced its way across Finn's beautiful face.

I did that. My fault. My goddamn fault.

Finn waved weakly and he sank down into the same booth he'd sat in nearly three months ago. Mara materialized at my side a moment later and promptly slid the tray out of my hands before it tumbled onto an unsuspecting customer. She took charge, while I stood numbly by, and made sure my table got their food before yanking me into the kitchen.

"Emma," Mara told me desperately. "You have to talk to him. Look at him…"

She trailed off, gesturing out to the floor and my eyes, as if they had a will of their own, flicked to Finn and found him sitting stiffly in the booth with his hands folded in front of him. But it was his eyes…God, his eyes…that yanked me off-kilter. So hollow. So exhausted. So devastated. I did that.

"He's miserable," Mara murmured to me. "And so are you. These last few weeks…I don't know what you've been doing and I don't understand—just go talk to him."

"How did he—?" I started, but the guilt in Mara's eyes told me everything I needed to know. "Right. It all makes sense now. That's how he always knew when I was working. You."

She just lifted a shoulder. "He asked me, so I told him. How could I not feel sorry for the guy? He's crazy about you…he *loves* you. And he's been going out of his mind. Slinger had to practically lock him in his room last week to keep him from breaking down your door…"

This would probably be a bad time to tell her Finn still had a key or that in two weeks, Finn having a key wouldn't matter anyway.

"He's been absolutely miserable," Mara pressed on, her voice taking on a more urgent tone. "That's why he's here. Just…please. Take your break. I'll cover your tables. Just go talk to him."

She pushed me out onto the floor and in a daze, my feet somehow carried me across the café until I stood in front of Finn's booth. His sunken, mournful eyes observed me every step of the way and his expression never shifted when I slid down across from him in the booth.

His lips lifted for a moment then fell back down. "Hey, Em."

His voice sounded different than I remembered, but maybe that was just because it'd been almost a month since I'd really heard the deep timbre I'd grown so familiar with...or maybe...maybe he'd changed. Pale skin, dark circles around his eyes, even his clothes seemed to hang more loosely and I wondered if I wasn't the only one who'd forgotten about eating these last few weeks.

"Hi, Finn."

Finn's lips curved a little now. "It's really good to see you."

I swallowed tightly. "You too."

It was the truth, but that knife in my heart twisted all the same.

He leaned forward on his elbows and for a split second, I thought he would reach for me, but he didn't. Part of me wished he would.

"Look, I know you're on your break right now and you don't have a ton of time, so I'll make this quick," Finn paused just a beat to make sure I was listening, but my attention had never waned for a moment. How could it?

"I miss you, Em. I know I probably don't have to tell you that, but I wanted to say it anyway. This last month..." he winced and shook his head, "it's been really hard for me. I've been trying to respect your space, trying not to give up on us, and I feel like I've just been chasing my tail here. That doesn't mean I wouldn't do anything you asked, anything you needed if it meant we could figure our shit out and make this work...you know I'd do it. But I can't keep running around in circles if you won't even meet me halfway."

I nodded slowly. I knew what he was doing and I couldn't blame him for grasping for some self-preservation. Granted, I hadn't encouraged him or given him false hope, but he'd suffered for a month. Hell, we'd both suffered, but at least my suffering was self-inflicted. Finn's heart had shattered across my apartment floor and we both knew who was to blame.

Then, his next words practically jolted me right out of my seat.

"Are you really moving?"

I sucked in a harsh breath and squeezed my eyes shut. "How did you —"

"Mrs. Johannsen," Finn answered before I even had a chance to finish. "She saw our landlord show someone your apartment yesterday."

Of course. The whole apartment showing had been a stressful fiasco —I'd had to scrub the whole place clean to make sure there was no trace of a cat, hide every single scrap of evidence, smuggle both the litterbox and the cat out of my apartment, and drive around town with a grumpy, howling Oliver until enough time passed when I'd just have to do it all over again in reverse.

Mrs. Johannsen had always had a chokehold on the pulse of all the goings-on in our building and while it was no surprise that she knew, it was, however, a shock that she'd go as far as to tell Finn. Clearly, my tolerance of her Estelle Getty addiction had done me no favors in the end because in the end, she still sold me out anyway.

So, I couldn't lie even if I wanted to. "Yeah. I'm moving."

His jaw hardened, but his light eyes held only remorse and devastation. "When?"

"Two weeks."

"What day?"

His motive was clear—if he knew the exact day, he'd also know exactly what day to be as far away from our building as possible.

"The 28th."

He nodded stiffly, almost robotically, and I didn't like this new, colder version of Finn in front of me. It was all just one more reminder of the damage I'd left everywhere I went...destruction after destruction in my wake.

A few moments of awkward silence passed between us and finally, Finn put us both out of our misery by leaning forward once again.

"I don't want you to leave, but I'm not gonna try to stop you either if this is what you really want. I'm not gonna plead. I'm not gonna beg. I've done all that already and it hasn't worked. I want you to stay, I want you to talk to me, I want you to..." Finn trailed off, his voice thick with emotion and he glanced over his shoulder for a moment. When he shifted back to him, his eyes were swimming again. "I just want you to be okay, Emma. I just want you to be happy and...if moving away, if us not being together, if that's really what you wanna do, then I don't know what else I can do or say that I haven't already to make you see that you're making a mistake."

My chest heaved violently and I had to look down at my hands. This was it. I knew that. This was where we'd either try to fix things or shatter completely. He was giving me one last chance after almost 30 days of chances. And because I had no other options, I set out with my hammer, ready to start smashing.

"I know you love me, Finn," I whispered and I hated the hope that crept into his eyes. I didn't want to see it, didn't want him to feel it. There was no point. "I don't understand how or why that's even possible."

That did it. All the hope in his eyes died out.

"If you didn't love me, you wouldn't have tried as hard as you did and even though I wish you hadn't bothered, I understand why you did," I pushed on, desperate to just get this over with already. "But I think we can both agree that this isn't helping either one of us. I don't want you to keep chasing after me because we're over. I'm gonna move in two weeks and then...then that'll be it, okay? We'll both be able to just move on."

His face twisted and his eyes flicked to something over my head, his head shaking tightly. "You're right. I can't keep chasing after you like this. So, I'm gonna get up and I'm gonna start walking towards that door. And if I walk out that door, that's it. We're done. I can't keep doing all the work here if you can't even sit down and have a real conversation about why you're pushing me away. I love you, but I don't know what else to do...this is so one-sided it's not even funny, but if you tell me to stay right now, I will. We'll figure it out, but you gotta give me something, Em."

We'd both suffered in silence for a month and it was time to end that suffering.

When I didn't respond, Finn winced and scrubbed his face with both hands. Then he slid out of the booth. He stood at the table for a few beats, waiting for me to give him something that would make his wait worthwhile—I couldn't give him that and instead, my eyes bored a hole into the cracked table in front of me.

"So this is where it ends? Right where it started?"

I looked up to see Finn standing in front of me, hands spread out wide, and his gorgeous face twisted with an agonizing mix of heartache and frustration.

"This is what you really want?"

My eyes flicked back to the crack in the table because I just couldn't bring myself to see the pain in his eyes anymore.

"I really do love you," he murmured one last time. "I wish I didn't have to walk away."

Through my tears, I let myself glance up only once and it was long enough to see him grip the door handle, look over his shoulder as he waited—my final and absolute last opportunity to keep him in my life. Finn gave me two more moments. Two more moments to jump out of this booth and run to him. Two more moments to at least do *something*. But I didn't.

And so, as tears streamed down my cheeks, I watched Finn yank the door open and walk right through it.

I thought I'd feel relieved when it was finally over, when I knew the calling and texting would stop, when I knew he wouldn't be waiting for me at my door when I got home later...I felt gutted instead. Raw. Like my insides had been ripped out and splayed across the table. Wrung out

K. Ryan

and wrenched tight.

Mara was walking towards me now and it was only then that my feet jerked themselves free. I sprung past her and didn't stop until I pushed through the café's back door. My back slid down the brick wall as I convulsed and sputtered into sobs with my head in my hands and my heart at my feet.

I cried for Finn. I cried for everything I'd put him through and the pain I'd brought to his life. I cried for my own stupidity. I cried because seeing him walk away was like getting run over by a train.

But I'd be lying to myself if I said that this was the moment I shattered beyond repair. I'd been broken a long time ago.

The real lie was ever telling myself I'd be able to put myself back together in the first place.

CHAPTER TWENTY-TWO

Six Weeks Later

The R+Co Mannequin styling paste is perfect for achieving that tousled, textured, I-woke-up-like-this hair for any length, not to mention the fact that it smells like a day at the beach with its fresh aromas of coconut and sea salt. This product will transport you back to those warm summer months that seem so long ago, especially now that Wisconsin's brittle winter is upon us. You'll love using this everyday just as much as I have.

I sighed at my computer screen and fought the urge to roll my eyes. This November favorites post was a few weeks overdue, but...could you tell I was past the point of caring? I hadn't even really loved a few of the products I currently toted on this post, which was normally my main criteria for a product making it on a post like this in the first place. I'd just tried them once, liked them well enough, and that was that.

For the first time since I'd started it almost 10 years ago, writing on my blog felt like a chore. I felt like a fake, feigning cheeriness and enthusiasm, especially when I made it seem like I used those products in my everyday life, too, when in my *actual* everyday life, I just pulled my hair up into a top knot and swiped on some mascara before I left for the café.

My appearance was the least of my problems.

As I set my laptop down on the coffee table, Oliver took that as his cue to slink over from his spot on the end of the couch and hop right into my lap. He circled around twice before deciding to crawl up my chest instead and stretched his front paws up to my collarbone, settling right across my chest and nuzzling my chin.

"Hey, buddy," I murmured into his fur as my fingers scratched the space in between his ears.

One white paw stretched up to tap my chin, flexing his claws just once, and making me wince at the sharp pricks.

"Ow. That hurts...thanks a lot, RB," I grumbled. "You know, you and I are dangerously skirting Lucille and Buster Bluth co-dependency territory here."

Meh.

He went right back to purring and purrumbling, so I shifted him down a little and wrapped my arms around his furry body to hug him to me. These days, the only thing that seemed to put me in a good mood was black and grey tiger-striped fur, which sounded about right, all things considered.

I'd been in my new apartment for almost a month and in that time, life had more or less returned to what it'd been pre-Finn. The only real difference, I supposed, was Oliver. I worked. I blogged. I listened to music. I drank too much wine. I binge-watched too much Netflix. That was about it.

What a fulfilling life I led.

At least I hadn't made the mistake of trying to convince myself that everything was 'back to normal' now and that I was actually happy this way. The only person I enjoyed spending time with these days was my cat and yes, I knew exactly how pathetic that sounded. Lucille Bluth, here I come...at least I didn't get off on being withholding the way she did.

"Just wait," I informed my cat dryly and gestured to my TV, where Buster Bluth dutifully zipped up his mom's dress, albeit with some difficulty considering one of his hands was technically a hook. "Pretty soon, that'll be us. I'll be the boozy helicopter mother and you'll be the needy, overgrown child who should've moved out years ago. Well, come to think of it...we're not that far off from that reality, are we? It's a good thing they don't let cat moms and their cat sons go to that Motherboy convention, otherwise we'd be first in line, my furry child."

Oliver's little white chest bumped in response. *Meh. Just as long as you don't start calling me Buster, we'll be good.*

I really needed to start watching something other than *Arrested Development* for awhile, but when I did, I switched right over to *Parks and Recreation* and started where Finn had left off when he'd cat-sat Oliver for me, which had inevitably sent me plummeting down to the depths of despair yet again. It seemed all I wanted to watch on Netflix were the shows that reminded me of Finn.

Today was Christmas Day and all I really had going on was finishing this stupid blog post—I wasn't going to post it today since people would be too busy doing things like spending time with their families, eating home-cooked meals, and opening presents to read an entry I should've posted three weeks ago.

Noah, Cristina, and Maria had come for the day yesterday and while I'd enjoyed going out to dinner and exchanging presents with them, being alone today was fine by me. Noah was worried—that was nothing new—but he knew well enough not to even suggest I come to Hickory today. Making that trek meant spending the day with my mom and I think I'd rather stick hot needles in my eyes than have to spend more than two seconds in the same room as that woman.

Oliver nuzzled my chin again as if to say, *Hey, lady. You still feed me, so I still like you.*

At least I wasn't completely alone on Christmas. At least someone liked me.

"I'm glad you're still here," I told him. "Love you, buddy."

He pressed the top of his head into my cheek to say, *Yeah, I guess I love you too.*

"Well," I shrugged. "It's Christmas. Maybe we should do something Christmas-y and I don't know, watch *Elf* or something."

Meh.

"Yeah, well, it's my favorite, so deal with it."

The side of Oliver's face curled up into a tiny snarl. *Oh, the stiff upper lip!* My eyes squeezed shut as the memory of the last time I'd heard that flashed through my mind. It wasn't the first time and it most certainly wouldn't be the last a not-so-distant memory assaulted my mind. Today would probably be the worst day of all, seeing as how it was Christmas Day and all I had to keep me company was my cat, a bottle of wine, music, sappy holiday movies, and leftovers.

By the time Buddy the Elf was picking off gum underneath railings, I was just about done. In Christmases past, I'd giddily looked forward to watching this movie, so much to the point that I rearranged plans specifically so I could watch this movie whenever it was on TV this time of year. Now, the movie's cheery mood had me snarling at my screen.

"Screw you, Buddy," I grunted and Oliver tilted his head back to look at me, purrumbling his agreement. "You know what? Spaghetti and maple syrup makes me wanna puke!"

This movie was just too cheerful and joyful for me right now. I didn't really feel like laughing today, but then again, it *was* Christmas, so I toggled over to *Love Actually* before I could stop myself. What followed was nothing short of a descent into wine-induced madness.

I'd downed my second glass of wine when the prime minister did his little 'jump for my love' dance through his house and it was around this time that I started tossing popcorn at my TV screen.

"Screw you, Hugh Grant!" I spat. "Your charming little dance doesn't change the fact that you were an asshole in *Bridget Jones' Diary!*"

Feeling proud of my outburst, I rewarded myself with a third glass of wine and I sank back down into my couch, ready to continue my Christmas insult-fest towards a movie I used to really enjoy watching this time of year. Now, that kid who looked like a baby-faced version of a young Dwight Schrute was watching *Titanic*, mimicking that famous bow scene like pretending to fly on a doomed cruise liner from 1912 would somehow give him the courage to win over the girl he loved.

Fuck that.

"Screw you, Leo!" I cried as I chucked another handful of popcorn at my TV. "Do you just go to those stupid Victoria's Secret runway shows and go, *I want that one and that one and that one!?* You probably wouldn't even date Kate Winslet in real life even though she's probably perfect for you...stupid jerk. All you do is date models! You don't know a good thing when you see it."

I sucked in a harsh breath as my words caught up with me. The impact hit me harder than I was willing to admit, surging through like a freight train and seeping through my alcohol haze to knock me sideways. Luckily, that dude from *The Walking Dead* was creeping on his best friend's wife already and holding up those ridiculous signs...

Just because it's Christmas
(And at Christmas you tell the truth)
To me, you are perfect

I officially hated this movie.

"Screw you, dude from *The Walking Dead*!" more popcorn flung at the screen, "and you too, Keira Knightley! That dude and the dude from *12 Years a Slave* love you *and* you look just like Natalie Portman? Spread the wealth, huh? What's wrong with you?"

To congratulate myself on that eloquent barb towards an actress playing a fictional character, who was probably very nice in real life, I poured myself my fourth glass of wine.

"Good thing I sprung for the value size," I muttered under my breath.

Yep. I was pathetically alone *and* sloppy drunk on Christmas.

Whatever.

As if he could read my thoughts, Oliver jumped back onto my lap and *maawhr*-ed right in my face. *Excuse me*, he was trying to say, *and what the hell am I? Canned tuna?*

"You're right," I nodded, my head jerking up and down drowsily.

"I'm not alone. I've got you. My little buddy...but not that elf though. I used to like that movie, but Will Ferrell annoyed the shit out of me today."

My breath hitched at the words: *used to.*

So many things I *used* to do. So many things I *used* to feel.

I squeezed my eyes shut just as Emma Thompson locked herself in her bedroom after she realized that ugly necklace wasn't really for her...which, in reality, her husband did her a favor because who would really want that fake gold piece of crap anyway? I guess I shouldn't say that, seeing as how Professor Snape in nerd glasses probably cheated on her. Okay, he most definitely cheated on her with that slutty secretary of his.

Once again, my breath hitched in my throat. *Slutty.* Why had I used that word? I hated that word. I might as well have called her the c-word.

Around the time the strains of that hauntingly depressing Joni Mitchell song filled my living room, the alcohol-haze really started to catch up with me. I didn't know how much more of this I could take, so I hit pause on my remote to rid myself of barely-intertwining stories and unrealistic circumstances. I mean, come on. All the characters in that movie were loosely-connected at best and I still didn't really understand how Laura Linney's character was related to any of the others. Was she someone's co-worker? Sister?

Ah. It didn't matter. It was just a stupid holiday movie that had no emotional resonance with me whatsoever.

Nada. Zero. Zip.

I sighed into my wine glass and took another gulp of that cold, sweet grape-flavored alcohol. Maybe more wine would make my disillusionment easier to swallow. Then again, maybe not. I didn't want to watch Emma Thompson stare catatonically around her bedroom after finding out her husband cheated on her, whether it was emotional or physical, but I still couldn't tear my eyes away when I hit play again. My body sat rooted to my couch, my eyes fixed intently on my screen as Emma gazed sadly at all the family pictures on her vanity, wringing her hands and playing anxiously with her bracelet.

And as Emma Thompson wiped her eyes and pulled herself together before going back out to her family, my eyes watered and my face burned. All I could think about was how brave she was. She walked into that bedroom a victim of her husband, of circumstance, of life and somehow, in those three short minutes, she managed to grieve the life she'd known and lost so suddenly *and* find the strength to carry on. It was Christmas, after all, and she had a family who was counting on her.

Maybe she wouldn't call out her douchebag husband right then because it wasn't the time or the place, but you knew she'd do it eventually. You knew she wouldn't take that shit lying down and allow her spineless husband to walk all over her. She was stronger than that.

She walked into that room a victim and left it a survivor.

I wished I could do that.

I wished I knew *how* to do that.

One more gulp of wine later and I'd paused the movie again so I could focus on my computer screen instead. I chewed on my bottom lip in thought as I perused my library.

"Hmm," I murmured. "Joni, Joni, Joni...where are you? I know you're here somewhere."

I was positive my dad had had at least one of her records, but I was also too lazy to peel my ass of my couch to look for it. This was way easier.

"Aha!" I cried out, startling the cat in my lap and I clicked on the first Joni Mitchell song I could find, which just happened to be "River".

When Joni's voice, hoarse and exhausted with heartache, sung out through my speakers, I was too drunk to stop my eyes from rolling up to my ceiling.

"*It's coming on Christmas/They're cutting down trees...*"

"Ugh," I mumbled. "Screw you, Christmas."

But as I sat there, rigid on my couch and clutching my sweaty wine glass for dear life, the rest of the song washed over me...was someone messing with me? What were the odds that *this* song, on *this* day would be the one I chose to listen to? Alcohol-haze and lowered inhibitions had pretty much set me up to fail today and now, I felt the brunt of that failure. As Joni crooned with longing and regret about wishing she had a river she could skate away on, my emotions swept away with the lyrics and that sweetly melancholy piano accompaniment.

When the lyrics shifted to talking about her ex-lover, how he tried to help her, put her at ease, and loved her naughty, that was it...the waterworks started and now that they were turned on, I probably had no hope of turning them off tonight, too. Fresh, mournful tears leaked out of my eyes and slipped down my cheeks.

I curled my legs underneath me and took another long gulp of wine. It didn't make me feel better.

A loud sob hiccuped from my lips as I listened to Joni sing about being hard to handle, selfish, and sad, and how she'd lost the best baby she ever had and I covered my mouth with my free hand, squeezing my eyes shut tight at the lyrics. I hated those lyrics. Hated the honesty and the truth and the way it all sliced right through me. That was exactly what I'd done...next to the cat still perched on my lap, Finn was the best thing that had ever happened to me. To say I'd been hard to handle was probably the understatement of the century. He'd been nothing but supportive, understanding, patient, and loving, and all I'd done was skate away.

I'd been so unfair to him. Unfair and pointlessly cruel all because...why?

Why did I do it in the first place? Why had I put both of us through that when he clearly wanted to be with me, when he clearly didn't care where I'd been or what had happened to me, when he'd been willing to throw caution aside to protect me and defend me, almost to a fault? All he was guilty of was loving me and I'd punished both of us for no good reason.

What the hell was my problem?

Finn was everything I'd never even known I'd wanted before I met him and I'd tossed it all down the toilet because...why?

With a frustrated huff, I stopped Joni from singing to me—there was just too much truth there for me to handle right now—and hit shuffle on my library instead. Just as I was contemplating the pros and cons of getting a fifth glass of wine, the words of the next song slammed into me, running me right over, and left skid marks down my face.

"It must have been love/But it's over now..."

Screw this song. Screw it and it's heart-achingly truthful lyrics. Screw it all the way 'til Sunday.

I hated it, but I listened anyway, wallowing in wine and tears and all the ways I'd willingly destroyed the one good thing I ever really had.

As far as pity parties went, I had to say this one was pretty epic. And pathetic. And depressing. Pretty soon, I'd be wailing on my couch to "All By Myself" in typical, lonely girl fashion. God, I was an idiot. So, so completely stupid. And stubborn. And selfish. And sad.

Finn was willing to give me everything and I ran away instead.

I'd loved him. I *still* loved him, but instead of facing what that meant, I ran away instead. Why did I do it? Why did I push? Why did I run? The words were right on the tip of my tongue, but they just wouldn't come.

Then my thoughts caught up to me. I loved Finn. I think I'd loved him the moment he brought Oliver back to my old patio; it'd just taken months of denial, miles of distance, and too many glasses of wine to get me to realize it.

Something so obvious shouldn't have taken me this long to figure out.

The problem was that I'd put a barrier up and even though I'd let Finn into my apartment, my bed, and my life, I'd still held him at arm's length. I still hadn't really let him in. I'd had every opportunity and I just couldn't do it.

I was drunk and alone on Christmas and I didn't really have to be.

Self-inflicted emotional harm was a bitch and I knew that first-hand. All the heartache, regret, and longing I felt now...I'd done that to myself. There was no point in denying it anymore.

I was almost 27-years-old with next to nothing to show for it. I had a cat, who I loved, a one-bedroom apartment, which was tolerable, a blog where thousands of faceless women flocked everyday to get recommendations on products, a brother and sister-in-law who tolerated my drama because they loved me, a mother who wouldn't speak to me, a ruined teaching career, a useless degree in broad field social sciences, and a dead-end job waitressing at a café.

Not exactly Disney material.

Screw Disney. Wasn't he a racist or something like that anyway? Probably a misogynist, too.

Ugh.

This was bullshit. Complete bullshit. I was so sick of all this bullshit. And I was crying now. I'd shoved my computer aside, buried my face into a pillow, and sobbed until my entire body convulsed and finally relented. At some point, Oliver crawled back into my lap and I curled my arms around his furry body, finally letting it all pour out of me, and taking comfort in the only good, real thing I had left in my life—my cat.

His head nuzzled my neck, flexing his paws against my collarbone, and he stayed right where he was, purring away and flicking his tail on my waist, letting me purge through everything I'd held inside for too long. Everything twisted and coiled, expelling from me like my body physically rejected the notion of spending one more day cemented in place and spinning my tires.

I was so sick of this. I hated feeling this way. I hated that the only defense mechanism I had was just to shut out the people who loved me. They didn't deserve that and neither did I.

"You can't keep doing this to yourself...punishing yourself this way. You don't deserve it and I don't know what it's gonna take for you to understand that."

I squeezed my eyes as his voice flooded my mind. All he'd wanted to do was protect me, love me, and help me.

Then, Finn's voice grew angrier, darker as he yelled at me, *"You're the one with the problem. You being passive like this, Emma? You just letting people fucking walk all over you? That's the problem. Not me."*

He was right about everything. I just wished I knew what to do about it...how to be stronger, how to be braver. I wanted to be; I really did. Getting there, though, that was the real problem. With that bleak thought, I peeled myself off the couch and padded into the bathroom. My face felt sticky from my tears and splashing some water on it might help. But after I wiped my face clean with a towel, I dropped it onto the sink and leaned forward, glaring at my reflection.

"I'm so sick of you," I whispered into the mirror.

I didn't recognize the girl staring back at me with her swollen eyes, splotchy skin, and tangled hair. It wasn't even just the appearance that I didn't recognize—it was the way I felt, too. Hating myself, blaming myself, punishing myself...I was so sick of it. I'd become everything I always thought I'd never be: weak, passive, and a victim.

I was so *sick* of being a victim. So *sick* of feeling unclean and unworthy. So *sick* of letting other people dictate how I saw myself. So *sick* of living in fear of other people. So *sick* of letting other people define me.

I jabbed a finger at the mirror as another tear slipped down my cheek. "You're better than this. You've always been better than this. How did you let it happen?"

My jaw tightened as I glared at my reflection.

"Get it together. I'm serious. Get your shit together. Now."

More tears ran down my cheeks, but I furiously wiped them away with the back of my hand.

"No. You're done crying. When you walk out of this bathroom, you're done crying. You're done being weak. You're done being passive. You're done being a fucking victim. *You* let it happen and now *you* have to make it stop."

My breath surged in and out, heavy with the weight of this moment, and I could feel the change before I saw it.

"You pushed him away because you thought you didn't deserve him. It was all bullshit and it was all in your head. You thought you weren't worthy of him because of those fucking pictures," I pointed at my reflection again just to reiterate my point. "Well, guess what? You're not a slut. And even if you were, he would've loved you anyway. Why shouldn't you be happy? Why shouldn't you be with someone who loves you back? You deserve it. You really do."

That was it. The reason why I'd pushed Finn away and tore our relationship apart.

There were no explosions or fireworks. No standing on a rooftop. No screaming or wailing. No magic wand waving up and down to transform this sad, pathetic girl into the survivor she needed to be.

When I looked in the mirror, I was still me. I was just a different me. The girl I was before those pictures set my life on fire just didn't exist anymore and sooner or later, I needed to make peace with that. The life I'd had in Hickory was over and so was the life I'd had when I lived across the hallway from Finn.

Up until this moment, those changes to my life had been nothing but devastating and destructive. I couldn't stop Justin from posting those pictures on the internet anymore than I could stop those kids from commenting on them. But I could've done something. I could've fought harder.

I didn't though. *That* was the problem.

So, I splashed some water on my face one last time, wiped my face, and took a deep breath.

Then I walked out the door.

. . .

The next morning, I felt like I had to physically pry open my eyes just so I could see. My throat burned like someone had shoved gravel down it and I gasped, probing the coffee table for the first thing I could get my hands on even though I was still face-down on my couch. God, this was probably the worst hangover I'd ever had in my life. It felt like someone had taken a sledgehammer and pounded it into my head until all that was left was just a flat sheet teetering on top of my neck.

In my blind attempt at groping for something to drink, which, let's face it, there probably wasn't anything there besides warm, stale wine anyway, my fingers closed around my phone instead. It buzzed in my hand, signaling that I had a text message I'd yet to read and I groaned. Probably just a message from Noah or Cris to wish me a merry Christmas...not that I was all that surprised, but it was also probably for the best that I'd missed it.

Texting and drinking did not mix. Who knows how I would've responded?

I stretched my neck from side to side to shake out the stiffness and when I hit the home button on my phone, my heart shot up into my throat.

Finn: *I miss you too. Merry Christmas, Em.*

My eyes widened and I couldn't breathe. I swiped my index finger across my screen, panic seizing just about every working faculty I had left, and I swiped to my text messages. When my eyes skimmed what I'd texted him, my entire body crumbled in mortification.

Three messages. Each one just as pitiful and poorly-timed as the last.

Just because it's Christmas.

And at Christmas you tell the truth.

I miss you.

This was a new low. *Hello, rock bottom. Nice to see you again. How've you been?*

Note to self: Do not, I repeat, do not under any circumstances allow yourself within 10 feet of your phone ever again while drinking.

Texting and drinking. There had to be some statistics out there detailing all the carnage it created or some sort of lame public service announcement declaring its evils and all the harm it could potentially cause your life. Hell, I could be the face of that public service announcement if I wasn't already the perfect candidate for a different one.

There was a tiny part of me that felt a sliver of hope. He'd texted me back...he told me he missed me too, hadn't he? Wasn't that a sign that maybe—nope. Not going there. I drunk-texted him on Christmas. He didn't know about the drunk part, but still...it was Christmas. People were always a little bit nicer, a little bit more civil on the holidays.

Telling me he missed me didn't mean he was telling me he wanted to try again or even that he'd be willing to talk to me beyond that brief exchange. I was the one who'd pushed him away and because of that, I had no business trying to push my way back in.

At this point, I was more embarrassed than hopeful, which should probably tell me something.

But that still didn't change the fact that every word I'd said was true. Even though I quoted that stupid, God-awful movie...it was all true.

I missed Finn.

I missed the way his eyes crinkled up when he smiled. I missed the way he laughed—his whole body seemed like it was in on the joke. I missed that crazy obsession with the Packers. I missed watching games with him and cheering with him. I missed going to bed with him at night and waking up with him in the morning. I missed the way everything seemed a little bit brighter because he was there with me. I missed sitting on my patio with him and listening to him strum along on his guitar. I missed the way he touched me, how I felt it all the way down to my toes, how it felt like everything else around me could fade away as long as his hands were somewhere on my body. I missed the way he understood me, even if I didn't understand myself...he took one look at me and he knew everything I couldn't say.

I loved him and I'd thrown it all away.

Finn had left this giant, gaping hole in my life. I hadn't even realized what I'd been missing until he found me. And every day, I found myself falling deeper and deeper into that hole, flailing head-first to the bottom.

Finn deserved someone who wasn't a mess. Someone who could actually say 'I love you' without running for the hills and smashing everything in her wake. I just wasn't that girl.

This wasn't going to get any better. Trying to forget Finn was like trying to get Oliver *not* to spend his whole day sleeping. Or Aaron Rodgers to quit football. It just wasn't going to happen. Lately, I felt like I sucked at just about everything in my life—blogging, maintaining relationships, texting and drinking responsibly—and there was nothing I sucked more at than trying to forget Finn. Maybe it was for the best that I just call this what it was, think realistically, and focus on what I could control.

So, a few hours later, after a shower and some greasy food to combat the effects of my massive wine hangover—seriously, wine hangovers were the worst—I once again found myself sitting in front of my computer. This time, I'd decided to forego the glass of wine and settled on caffeine instead, but I scrolled through my music library, looking for something that could settle my mood.

Ugh. Everything just sounded so stupid. Nothing fit. Nothing worked. Nothing would really make me feel better.

I clicked over to a search and before I even really knew what I was doing, I typed in Kings of Leon. This wasn't going to end well, but I just couldn't help myself. My lips quirked up when I found that the first songs listed in my search as the most popular were "Use Somebody" and "Sex On Fire". I could practically see Finn rolling his eyes and hear him grumbling, *"Go figure."*

All my admissions and declarations in front of my mirror last night didn't mean that I couldn't mourn Finn, so I decided to do a little experimenting. I went down the line until I landed on "Supersoaker" and listened with a small smile on my face, bobbing my head to the buoyant beat and wistfully imagining Finn listening to this same song at this exact moment, even if I knew just how stupid that was. Then I moved on to "Molly's Chambers", laughing at the euphemism about Molly's 'chambers' having a hold on his 'pistol'. It was funny how "Supersoaker" sort of sounded like if "Sex On Fire" and "Molly's Chambers" had a baby, meshing their old stuff with their newer stuff to create one coherent sound.

Yeah. I could see why Finn loved this band so much. I'd only heard a couple songs and I was already a convert.

Next, I moved on to "Ragoo", a Rasta-inspired jam that had me bobbing to the music all the way into my kitchen as I filled up my coffee and I'd even laughed in spite of myself as the lead singer crooned about being caught with his pants down. By the end, I was singing along and I'd never felt so close to Finn, but so far away all at the same time. I wished he was here right now...he'd probably launch into the behind-the-music story of how all those songs came to be and throw out factoids about the band that probably would've been as weird as they were entertaining.

When "Charmer" started playing, the rollicking, furious guitar riffs caught me off-guard. When the lead singer screamed before even singing a line, my head reared back in shock, my eyes wide, and for a second, I had to double-check that something hadn't gotten messed up on iTunes...nope, this was still the same band. It sounded different than any other song I'd listened to so far and there was something almost sinister about the guitar progressions, combined with the screaming that held me at rapt attention.

Maybe the music hypnotized me. Maybe it was just exactly what I needed to hear. Either way, while I nodded along to the beat, my blood began to simmer. At first listen, from what I could tell, it sounded like a preacher's wife was acting a little like a creeper, touting the line, *"She's aaaalways lookin' at me."*

But on second listen, after I immediately downloaded it of course, I found myself Googling the band and through a quick skim of their Wikipedia page—a great source for legit information, I know—I learned that the band, three brothers and a cousin, were actually raised in a devout Pentecostal environment and that the three brothers were, literally, sons of a preacher man. They'd even went to parochial schools growing up, too, just like me. The basis of the song, and the name for the album the song came from, revolved around experiences from church conferences they'd attended as kids.

What a strange little coincidence that was—the band I was currently listening to had rebelled from their religious upbringing through sex, drugs, and rock and roll. I couldn't exactly say I was a rebellious child growing up, but I'd more or less been trying to shake my own religious upbringing for longer than I cared to admit, not to mention the fact that my non-existent relationship with my mom was primarily due to differences of spiritual opinion.

And when the singer sang with that tinge of paranoia, *"She's aaaalways lookin' at me,"* I murmured right back, "Yeah, you creeper, stop lookin' at him." As the song went on, I was like a woman possessed and "Charmer" was my theme song. My fingers flew over my keys until I found what I was looking for and I hit play on that nefarious video before I could stop myself with "Charmer" still playing in the background.

That cruel and insensitive senior skit played back for me and that simmering turned up to a boil as the song reached it's crescendo of ominous guitar riffs. The laughing, the jokes, the fact that *no one* even attempted to stop it...it was all bullshit. Every single second of it and every single person involved with it was a heartless asshole. How the hell did those little shits think that was okay? Why would they even think that was funny? To publicly humiliate me all over again...especially since I wasn't even there to defend myself?

Maybe the answer was in the question—I wasn't there to defend myself and even if I had been there, I probably wouldn't have defended myself anyway.

That video, those pictures, those kids...they'd ruined my life. Ruined what little joy I'd had in my job. Ruined any hope I had of a normal, stable life. Ruined my reputation....everyone thought I was a slut and why? Because I'd taken some sexy pictures for my boyfriend when I was 19? Because I'd sent him those pictures?

The pictures weren't the problem.

"Stop looking at me," I murmured to my screen as the ferocious beat surrounded me. "Stop fucking looking at me."

I closed out of my still-unfinished November favorites blog post and opened a new document instead. With my cursor blinking back at me and the strains of "Charmer" still blasting through my speakers, I began to type:

Motherfuckers.

That felt good. So I did it again:

Motherfuckers. Motherfucking assholes.

I started typing that four letter c-word, but quickly deleted it. Even in my flurry of rage, I still couldn't bring myself to use that word. Now, the words flowed out of me, streaming from my pent-up frustrations and everything I'd never allowed myself to say:

My mom, those stupid kids, the administration, the town, the internet···they're the problem. I'm the problem, too.

My attention shifted to my music library for just a moment and I hit shuffle just to see what would happen. When "Teenagers" by My Chemical Romance started playing, I burst out laughing. Oh, the marvelous irony of the lyrics, *"Teenagers scare the living shit out of me."* When they all got together and conspired against someone or something, they were a force to be reckoned with. They did have power, but that power also should've been reined in the first time someone commented on my pictures. And now, all the internet did was give them more power. With that thought, I clicked on another song and let the strains of "Virtuality" by Rush set the tone for my next rant.

"Net boy, net girl/Let your fingers walk and talk…"

Then I just kept on writing:

These stupid kids don't really know how to use the power they have. There's no accountability there if they don't have to say it to someone's face. They think they're indestructible. Whatever they tweet or post, that somehow makes them a god if it gets enough retweets or likes. Who gives a shit about anyone else?

Nothing I did makes me a slut.

My breath hitched in my throat as I stared at what I'd just typed. There was that word again and all it's inevitable variations: Slutty. Easy. Whore. Nympho. Ho. My fingers flew across the keys:

Why is it that a guy can turn around and do exactly what I did and no one cares? Why do girls get that scarlet letter 'A' written into their chests and scrawled across their whiteboards and all guys get are high-fives?

What's the big deal with sex? Nobody cares what you do behind closed doors, but as soon as those doors open and your sexual habits are out there for everyone to see, suddenly everyone has a right to pass judgment on you when they're just doing the exact same thing, albeit behind the safety of closed doors.

I should've sued the school district's ass off. I should've reported every last one of those little jerks. Instead, I laid down like a good little girl and took my public whipping because that's exactly what I was raised to do. I hate myself for that. Other people's opinions about me was never worse than the way I thought about myself. I accepted the blame for something that wasn't my fault...not for one second.

My blood boiled over, churning and bristling, until white-hot rage engulfed every single one of my senses. Suddenly, I lurched forward and sent my coffee cup flying into the wall with a sick crash. Oliver went running, but I was past the point of caring.

I was angry. So fucking angry I could barely see straight. How had this happened? How had my life gone so dramatically off the rails like this?

And better yet...what could I do to get it back?

They didn't get to win. They didn't get to continue ruining my life over and over again, taking what little good I had and crumbling it before it even really had a chance to get started.

I was a victim no more.

Then the change really began. Following the coattails of my written rant, I found myself standing in the middle of my walk-in closet, staring at all my old teacher clothes with my hands on my hips. These were the clothes I'd worn in my past life, but I wasn't a teacher anymore. I would never be a teacher again and it was time to let that go.

It was almost a new year and it was time for a new me. I was sick of the old me, the pathetic me, the depressing me, the self-destructive me, and now, I needed to shed the old me like a snake sheds its skin.

But I couldn't do it when I was hanging on to all these skeletons in my closet. So, I systematically went through each article, hanger by hanger, and tossed everything the old me used to wear into a pile. That pile grew exponentially by the time I'd finished, but the purge was rejuvenating...and now, I felt like I could finally breathe. I couldn't keep hanging on to all these ghosts, dragging them around, and beating that same old dead horse over and over again. All it'd gotten me was loneliness and more heartache. All I'd done was push away the best thing that had ever happened to me.

I hung on to a few blazers and dress pants for practicality purposes and threw everything else into a garbage bag. Goodwill could thank me later. Next, I hopped into my hairstylist's salon chair for the first time in way too long.

"Chop it all off," I told her. And she did.

Now, I stood in front of my bathroom mirror, staring at my reflection, and I liked what I saw. My hair sat just a few inches below my chin, styled in beachy, fresh waves, and luckily, my bangs had grown out enough, so the style looked more chic than awkward. It was a good change—a change I'd needed for a long time. A change that felt like I'd finally taken a few steps in the right direction to becoming the person I wanted to be.

It was crazy how a wardrobe change and a new hairstyle could make you feel like you had a new lease on life, but that's exactly how I felt. I'd embraced the change and embraced the new me, even if I was still working out who that girl really was.

I wasn't fully healed yet. That would take more time and I wasn't naive enough to believe that one written rant, a new wardrobe, and a new haircut would be enough to get me there, but it was a start. I wasn't completely okay, but now, I felt like maybe I could be. The potential was there. The anger was still there. The drive to move forward was still there.

But what was that next step? Where did I go from here? I was still living in my one-bedroom apartment with Oliver, still blogging, still working at the café…

I had a college degree, didn't I? I could probably do more with the degree I had, but I'd gravitated towards a job like waitressing primarily because I knew the odds of my boss, Marcus, caring about my past were slim to none. I mean, I knew for a fact that Joe, one of our line cooks, had been in jail for petty theft and Marcus *still* hired him in spite of Joe's arrest history. I figured I was pretty safe there and it was that sort of hiring behavior that had sparked my ability to move in and out of each shift with ease and without too much attention on myself.

I had a degree in broad field social sciences. There had to be something I could do in Milwaukee that would utilize my degree as much as possible…I had skills, didn't I? Communication skills, interpersonal skills, presentation skills, teaching skills…wouldn't someone pounce on that? I could be doing more, but I'd hidden behind the general privacy I'd gotten from my job at The Corner Café. My waitressing job had just been another crutch. Maybe it was time to leave that behind, too.

It had taken losing Finn to see what had always been right in front of me—the only thing holding me back was me. Finn wasn't like my mom or Justin or anyone else from my old life. I think I'd been so afraid of letting him in because letting him in meant giving him an opportunity to hurt me. The people who I'd trusted to love and protect me hadn't done that and that was why I'd been so scared to open myself up to that again. I'd lumped Finn in with anyone who'd ever hurt me and it was so unfair. I didn't want to be that scared little girl hiding in the corner anymore.

From here on out, I would be a survivor.

I might have lost Finn, but somewhere along the way, I think I also might have found myself.

CHAPTER TWENTY-THREE

Two weeks after my eventful and highly productive Christmas, I found myself passing that 'Welcome to Hickory' sign again. This time, however, I hadn't needed to pull over and dry heave on the side of the road halfway there. This time I made it all the way to town without stopping once. Sure, my heart drummed in my chest, my sweaty palms gripped the steering wheel like my life depended on it, and my breathing was a little sketchy, but who was keeping track?

I had some business to take care of and I wasn't leaving this town until I did it.

I'd decided somewhere in between drunk-texting, throwing out three-fourths of my wardrobe, and chopping off my hair that this was the next logical step. There were things that needed to be said, air that needed to be cleared, and it wasn't the kind of thing I could do over the phone. This was the kind of thing I needed to do in person.

When I pulled into my mom's driveway, I froze for just a moment. My hands cemented to my steering wheel and sweat dripped down my back and pooled underneath my armpits as my body readied itself. This was it. Now or never. With a heavy inhale for strength, I slid out of my car, walked the short distance from the driveway to my mom's front door, and knocked.

I knew she was here because I'd texted Noah to do some discreet reconnaissance for me and when I got the go ahead, I made my move.

She couldn't hide from me because I wouldn't let her.

The door opened and my mom blinked back at me, surprise flickering across her face. Just as quickly, suspicion replaced that surprise and her icy green eyes narrowed at me. She ran a hand over her carefully coiffed and styled brown hair and I knew what was coming next.

"Emma," she greeted me coolly. "What are you doing here?"

I didn't miss a beat. "I'm here to talk to you, Mom."

She glanced over her shoulder as if that would somehow make it so I wasn't standing there and then when she finally spared me another glance, her tight eyes trailed up and down the length of me, taking shrewd inventory of my appearance. I could practically hear her thoughts, *What did she do to her hair? My God, it's dreadfully short.*

"Well, I really wished you'd called before just coming over here," my mom told me in her familiar clipped tone. "I was just about to leave to run some errands."

Sure, you were, Mom, I thought ruefully. *Nice try.*

"Mom," I tried again. "I just need 10 minutes. You can wait to run errands for 10 minutes."

She blinked back at me, most likely stunned by the fact that I hadn't asked her, I'd *told* her. But when she disappeared into the house, I knew what was happening here. She was heading right for the garage to evade me and planned on leaving before another word could be said. That wasn't going to happen. I flung the door open and tracked through the house, following her footsteps, and gaining ground before she even realized I'd advanced on her. Even though she'd already slid into the driver's seat and had her key in the ignition, I didn't hesitate. She didn't get to leave until I said what I'd come here to say.

I opened the passenger door, sat down, and slammed the door shut before she could even get a word in.

"Emma, what are—"

"What the hell is your problem, Mom?" I cut in harshly and stared her down. "I'm your daughter. You running out on me like this, trying to sneak away without even giving me a chance—what's wrong with you?"

She reared back like I'd just slapped her and I guess I might as well have.

"How dare you speak to me like—"

"Mom," I cut her off yet again and shook my head. "Just let me say what I need to say and then I'll go and you can run your fake errands like you fake planned."

My mom opened her mouth to speak, but quickly shut it. I took that as my sign to push forward.

Time to bury some demons.

"Mom," I started again, my heart already pounding with the weight of what I needed to say. "I have some things I want to say and all I'm asking is that you listen. I don't need you to do or say anything. Just listen, okay?"

Her jaw clenched and both hands turned white-knuckled as she gripped the steering wheel, her gaze focused directly ahead of her. Well,

I didn't need her to look at me in order to do this, so she could stare blankly ahead all she wanted.

"I'm really disappointed in you, Mom," I told her and for a moment, I almost didn't recognize my own voice. "I've felt that way for a long time. I just never figured out how to tell you until now. When everything happened last year, I can understand you being embarrassed and even a little disappointed in me. But once the shock wore off, you should've been on my side."

I paused long enough to gauge her action, but her face remained a cool, impassive mask. If she was feeling anything right now, she didn't show it.

"You were too busy worried about your own reputation and what your friends at church would think to care about what was happening to me. You made it about *you* when...honestly, it had nothing to do with you. You should've went on a rampage trying to protect me and help me. Instead, you made me feel like it was my fault."

At that, my mom finally came alive and whipped around to face me. "Do you mean to tell me it *wasn't* your fault? That you honestly believe you didn't do anything wrong? Emma, everyone in this town has seen more of you than anyone should ever see and you're *not* to blame?"

Normally, this would be the point where I'd shut down and surrender to guilt. Tears would already be flowing down my cheeks and I'd be consumed by humiliation and shame. Not today.

"Yeah, Mom," I nodded tightly. "That's exactly what I'm saying. The only thing I did wrong was trusting Justin with those pictures. You thought Justin was the end all to be all and he just wasn't. He planned everything he did to me and he knew *exactly* what would happen the second he did it. He used those pictures to publicly humiliate me and ruin my life. Some people would call that sexual assault, Mom. It's a crime now to do what he did to me. Did you know that?"

She barely even flinched.

"I would've given anything to make those pictures go away, to go back and make it so I'd never taken them in the first place. But you wanna know something else, Mom? It's taken me a long time to realize this, but...I'm *not* sorry I took them. I'm sorry I sent them to someone who couldn't be trusted with them and I'm sorry they were used to hurt our entire family, but I'm not sorry I took them."

Still nothing.

"I know you don't wanna hear this and I know it's gonna make you uncomfortable, but I'm gonna say it anyway. I've had sex before, Mom, and I've enjoyed it before, too. Many times. There—now it's out there,"

I laughed a little in spite of myself and for some reason, it felt really good to say it to her face. "I was with someone a few months ago. I don't know if Noah told you about him or not, but I loved him, Mom. I *still* love him and...I pushed him away because I wasn't ready to deal with all the things I'm talking to you about right now. He was...everything. He was sweet and kind and patient and understanding and funny and all the things Justin wasn't. He loved me, too, Mom, and I had sex with him because I loved him, because I wanted that physical connection with him, too. I'll just come right out and say it—he was the best I ever had. And I think it made me love him even more. Why is that wrong, Mom?"

Instead of answering, she sucked in a heavy breath and her hands dropped into her lap. I just lifted a shoulder—it wasn't like I'd expected anything less from her once the topic turned to sex.

"It's not," I answered for her softly. "But after everything happened, I felt so dirty. Like I couldn't let myself enjoy something our bodies are naturally supposed to do. I couldn't even handle anyone looking at me for too long because I was so scared they'd seen my picture somewhere. I felt like a slut. I felt like a whore. *That's* what's wrong here. I never should've felt like it was wrong because it's just not. And if you feel like it is then that's your problem, not mine."

I figured she wouldn't have much of a reaction to that, but that impassive mask slipped for just a second to reveal an emotion that looked a little like anger and frustration. She could be angry and frustrated with me all she wanted. God knew I was angry and frustrated with her, too.

"And you can throw the whole 'no sex before marriage' thing at me until you're blue in the face, but Noah and Cris lived together before they got married and you never said a word to them. You know, I don't remember much from Sunday school—I think I've blocked most of it out—but I do remember something about judging others and all that. I had to look it up online, but the Bible verse goes something like, 'You have no excuse, you who judges, because in passing judgment on others, you pass judgment on yourself because you, the judge, practice the very same things.'"

I left that hanging there for a few moments to see if that would garner some sort of reaction from her, but if anything, that mask didn't move.

"The only reason you cared in the first place was because everyone knew about it, right? That's what it's always been about. Everyone knowing our business. And those horrible, ugly rumors about me having an abortion...you *knew* it was a lie, but you treated me like it was the truth just because other people thought it was. And even if that's what actually happened, it would've been *my* choice, *my* business, not yours. Justin committed a crime and I was the one who got punished. How is that fair, Mom? How could you stand there and let people treat me that way without even once stepping in?"

Now, I paused because I needed to wipe my eyes free of the tears clouding my eyes.

"The only reason those pictures had any power was because we gave it to them. I'm not gonna say I took all my cues from you because I need to be responsible for my own actions, but I will say that, out of all the people who hurt me, you were the one who hurt me the most."

I sighed heavily and glanced one last time at my mom, whose gaze was still fixed in front of her. I shrugged just once and shook my head.

"If you want to talk, you know my number. Until then, I don't have anything else to say to you."

Then I opened the passenger side door and slid out of her car. I got into my own car without so much as a glance over my shoulder and when I backed out of her driveway, she was still sitting in her own car with her hands clenched around the steering wheel.

It didn't matter. If she never came around, if our relationship had been severed beyond repair, that was something I could live with. At this point, the ball was in her court. If she wanted to talk, we would. If she didn't, I didn't feel like I'd lost anything that wasn't already gone.

There was nothing more to say and for once in my life, I'd stood up to my mom without backing down.

.   .   .

After stopping in by Noah and Cristina, relating the details of my conversation with my mom, and kissing my niece, I was back on the road. Now, as I drove through the familiar streets of my former hometown, I didn't feel any of the anxiety and panic that used to plague me. No feeling like the walls were closing in on me. No feeling like I had to constantly look over my shoulder.

I just drove right through.

But just as I neared the outskirts of town, I took a quick detour. I wasn't hungry and I'd never really cared for the cheeseburgers dripping with grease from the Burger Bar, but I knew some people who did. Or rather, a certain *kind* of people who did. Putting the word 'bar' in any place that didn't actually serve alcohol made it catnip for the kids here in Hickory. They felt cool and sort of hip, or as hip as you could be in a town called Hickory, and the owners cashed in on that feeling like nobody's business.

Since it was a Friday afternoon and just a half hour after school let out, I knew exactly what kind of patrons would be in the Burger Bar right now and as I pulled into the parking lot, I was counting on it. I'd already exorcised one demon today. Might as well make it two.

My plan, or the spontaneous, probably reckless idea that sort of resembled a plan, was to just walk inside and order something to go. I wouldn't stay there and eat. I'd just stay long enough to make an impact and then I'd leave.

The second I stepped into the restaurant, that old familiar panic slipped down my back in cold beads of sweat and I almost turned right around and walked back out. I needed to be strong now and I needed to stop running.

My feet carried me all the way to the counter and I did my best to ignore everyone else inside. It didn't matter if anyone was looking at me or whispering about me. If I didn't see or hear it, then it wasn't happening, right? Well...it *was* happening. It might have taken them a few seconds to not only realize I was there, but realize who I was, too, but as soon as they did, the assault of stares and the flurry of whispers started.

It doesn't matter, I told myself, *they're just teenagers. Nothing to be scared of. You're the adult here. Now act like it.*

So, I straightened my shoulders and held my chin high. I easily recognized the employee at the counter as a former student from a U.S. history class last year and smiled at him.

"Hey, Mason," I greeted him. "How's it going?"

Mason blinked back at me for a moment and then his eyes darted to something, or probably someone, behind me. When his eyes flicked back to me, he pressed a hesitant, slightly flustered smile on his face.

"Hey, Miss Owens," Mason finally acknowledged me as he swallowed tightly. "I'm, uh, I'm good. How...um, how 'bout you?"

"I'm good," I told him warmly. "I'm actually living in Milwaukee now, which is a lot better than this place, you know? School going okay this year?"

He seemed a little taken aback that I'd continued the conversation, but nodded anyway. "Yeah, school's...school, I guess."

"Fair enough," I laughed and figured it was about time to put the poor kid out of his misery. "Alright. So, I should probably order something here, huh? I'll take a number seven with no onions and a

Mountain Dew. And that'll be to go, too."

His fingers flew across the screen to enter my order and after I paid, I quietly took my leave to the side of the counter to wait for my food. By that point, it was very clear the majority, if not all, the teenage patrons inside the restaurant were well-aware who was standing at the counter and those little pinpricks of awareness snaked right down my spine—just like old times. My palms felt clammy, but I rubbed them on my jeans to wipe it away. No point in ruminating on something I couldn't control. No point in worrying about what a bunch of teenagers thought of me.

Out of the corner of my eye, I watched the booth directly to my right. This was exactly what I was counting on and probably more than I ever could've hoped for...because that booth held nearly every single boy that had led the student body's charge in obnoxious, demeaning, and sexually explicit comments directly right at yours truly and sandwiched right in between them was Luke, one of the only students who'd vocally advocated on my behalf.

They were nothing if not predictable creatures of habit.

I'd probably never get this opportunity again, so as soon as my to-go order was in my hand, I went for it before I could talk myself out of it. As my gaze scanned the wide eyes and blank stares gaping at me, part of me wanted, once again, to cut and run. They'd gossip about my little appearance here at Burger Bar anyway, so why not give them some more fodder? But that wasn't why I was here.

You're the adult in this situation, I reminded myself.

My eyes landed right on Logan, the boy who'd 'played' me in the senior skit, and it was right on the tip of my tongue to say something along the lines of 'you're quite the actor', but my life had been ruled by negativity for too long and now, I needed to focus on the positive. Now, I needed to move forward.

"Hi, Luke," I smiled and waved a little with my free hand. "It's good to see you. How are you?"

Surprise flickered over his freckled face for just a moment, but he quickly recovered. "Oh, hey, Ms. Owens. It's good to see you, too. I'm good...just chilling. Eating some burgers before we head over to the basketball game later."

"Figures," I laughed and kept my focus directly on the boy speaking to me, rather than the other boys in the booth, who were pretty much white as sheet. "How's your mom doing?"

Luke's face dropped for just a second, which was understandable considering he'd just endured his second round of holidays without his dad, but once again, he wiped the wistfulness from his face just as quickly. He really was a great kid.

"She's good," he answered with a tight smile. "Thanks for asking."

"Would you tell her I said hello?"

"I will," Luke nodded. "I appreciate that, Miss Owens."

There was so much more I wanted to say to him, but I couldn't do it here in front of all his friends. I'd probably never get this chance again, but my hands were tied. I wanted to hug him and tell him how proud I was of him, how proud his dad would be, how he was one of the few boys in that school who gave me hope for the future, but I didn't want to embarrass him or cause any problems for him.

But as I waved goodbye and turned on my heel to head back to the parking lot, I abruptly shifted back to the table. My eyes found Luke one last time and while I didn't want to make him the butt of a joke, I needed to do this and I couldn't leave until I did it.

"Hey, Luke?" I called over my shoulder and squared my shoulder to the table.

He frowned back at me. "Yeah, Miss Owens?"

I swallowed back the tears stinging my eyes. These kids wouldn't see me cry, not even because of this.

"Thanks," I nodded to him with a tight smile.

It took him a second, but the moment he realized the weight of what I was saying, a small smile crossed his face and he nodded back, even though the other boys around him snickered and elbowed him.

"Anytime, Miss Owens," he called back to me as I turned to leave once again.

This time, I didn't look back. With my to-go order in one hand and my dignity in another, I walked out of Burger Bar and headed to my little beat-up Corolla. On my trek from the exit to my car, I walked right past a group of girls on their way in.

"Miss Owens?" A familiar voice called out to me.

I frowned and whirled around to see Lacey, one of the girls I remembered seeing at school on that fateful morning. She looked almost exactly the way I remembered her: dark wavy hair, worn jean jacket, and jeans rolled-up at the ankle, but she was smiling and waving now instead of whispering behind my back.

"Oh, hey, Lacey," I waved back. "How's it going?"

Despite the fact that the other two girls she was with stopped right in their tracks and stared me down like I was an animal at the zoo, Lacey didn't miss a beat.

"Oh, you know, same old, same old."

I smiled at her, glancing briefly at the other girls who still stared right back at me. "Good to hear. You must've heard back from some colleges by now, right?"

"I did. I got into UW-Milwaukee and UW-Green Bay."

"That's great, Lacey! Congratulations! Have you decided on a major yet?"

"Yeah," she laughed a little unsteadily. "I'm actually going to be a teacher."

I couldn't stop the wince. Part of me wanted to scream, *Don't do it! Run while you have the chance!* But I wasn't exactly in a position to be handing out life advice either.

"That's really great, Lacey," I told her instead. "What do you wanna teach?"

She smiled softly. "History. Just like you."

Anything I might've said died in my throat.

"You were a really good teacher, Miss Owens. The *best*," Lacey pushed on. "I just wanted to tell you that."

Tears stung my eyes once again and it took all my remaining strength to hold back them back.

"Thanks, Lacey. I really appreciate that."

She smiled back at me with a stiff wave as she continued on the path towards the restaurant's entrance, both of us satisfied with the exchange. I guess there wasn't anything else to say and as I drove out of the parking lot and back onto the road that would lead to the highway, the tears I'd held at bay broke free, flowing with abandon down my cheeks and dripping onto my lap.

I'd always known I was a good teacher, even if I didn't particularly enjoy it the way I should have, but knowing I'd played a part in her life…it was a gift. I'd made an impact and that had to be enough.

That part of my life was over and I needed to let it go. It wasn't all clouded in painful memories…but teaching was my past. I needed to look towards my future now.

A future that needed to be fulfilling. A future that needed to make me happy. Even if that future didn't include Finn, I needed to figure out how to feel whole again. I needed to start practicing what I preached, so to speak, and finally heal.

Now, as miles of distance separated me and my hometown, I felt purged. I felt free. And I supposed it was only fitting that the first song I found on the radio was "Shake It Off" by Taylor Swift. Having drank the Taylor Kool Aid a long time ago, I embraced my Jerry Maguire moment and sang along at the top of my lungs. There was no one else here to care and I just let it fly, shaking my shoulders, dancing in the driver's seat, and singing along as Taylor shook off the haters and the players.

There were tears in my eyes, but these were the good kind of tears. The tears that meant there was no more humiliation, no more devastation, and no more shame in my life. Everything was literally in my rearview mirror now and I'd never felt more alive.

I was finally free.

That peace and happiness followed me all the way down Highway 41 and back into Milwaukee, my new hometown, until I sucked in a deep breath and abruptly took the next exit before I could stop myself. This was a bad idea and probably a bad idea that wouldn't end well either, as most bad ideas were wont to do, but this couldn't be helped and I pulled into my old parking lot at my old apartment building before I could stop myself. I was probably only going to end up hurting myself, but it was too late now and I still had some more things I needed to say.

I hit the buzzer at the shared entryway, but the voice that answered wasn't the one I wanted to hear.

"Hey, Slinger," I murmured into the speaker. "It's Emma. Is it alright if I come in?"

"Sure. Why not?"

A second later, he buzzed me in and I stepped inside the old familiar hallway, smiling wistfully at Mrs. Johannsen's doorway. When I ventured further down the hallway, my eyes flicked to the left and landed on my old door. My heart lurched and churned...if things had been different, if *I'd* been different...

The door flung open to reveal Slinger, who was really a sight for sore eyes, and Mara appeared at his side a moment later, surprise and a little bit of happiness flickering across her face. Any initial hope and whatever expectations I might have had went right out the window the second my eyes flew to the duo sitting on the couch.

There was Finn, dressed in those worn jeans I knew so well and a rumpled Youth and Young Manhood T-shirt, which I now knew was a reference to the first Kings of Leon album, but his attire wasn't where my attention landed first. All my focus lied on the girl sitting on the couch with him, who at first glance, with her easy and open demeanor, seemed to be everything I wasn't and everything Finn deserved. They were laughing about something and he had his arm thrown around the back of the couch, as close as he could be to having his arm around her without actually touching her, and my throat burned.

He looked happy.

And just as suddenly, the laugh died on his lips and Finn's face

303

dropped when he realized I was standing in the doorway.

I don't know what I was expecting. Of course he was here with another girl. Of course he'd moved on. Why wouldn't he? Why *couldn't* he? We'd broken up almost two and a half months ago and he had every right to find someone who could give him what he needed, especially after what I'd put him through for an entire month. I was kind of surprised he wasn't storming over here and slamming the door right in my face.

Instead, he swung his arm away from the couch and stalked over to the doorway, slipping in between the space left vacant by Slinger and Mara, who'd immediately stepped aside for him. He promptly shut the door behind him and I gave myself this moment to drink him in, to inhale his musk and oak scent, and to wish things were different.

"Em," Finn started finally and raked a hand through his hair, a familiar gesture that made my heart ache. "What are you doing here?"

I froze and just as suddenly, I backpedalled.

"I'm sorry," I shook my head and moved backwards. "I shouldn't have come here. I didn't mean to interrupt and I...I should leave."

His hand reached out, skimming my forearm until his fingers finally closed around my wrist to pull me back. My eyes shot down to where our bodies were connected, my skin practically leaping off the bone at his touch, and he immediately dropped his grasp, shoving his hands in his pockets before either of us could do or say much else.

Finn pushed out a rough breath. "Why are you here, Em?"

I squeezed my eyes shut and when I opened them again, I found light eyes imploring me, but I didn't know what he was asking. Did he want me to stay? Did he want me to go? I didn't know...so I just said what I'd come here to say.

"I went home," I told him quietly. "I talked to my mom and I pretty much told her she's a horrible mother and that she hurt me. It felt really good to say that to her."

I paused for a moment to gauge his reaction. He didn't say anything, but his eyes crinkled a little in concentration as he listened intently, so I just pressed forward.

"I don't think it made much of a difference, but at least I said what I wanted to say to her, you know? She didn't really say a word to me, but that was okay because she listened. That's all I wanted. And...I guess I just wanted to tell you that, but I didn't mean to come over here and disrupt—"

"It's okay, Em," Finn cut in quietly, his eyes still fixed on me with an unfathomable expression. "That's...that's really good."

"And," I went on. "When I left town, I stopped at a burger joint and the whole place was pretty much crawling with former students. I talked to them like nothing ever happened and I saw Luke…do you remember him?"

Finn nodded tightly.

"I said thank you to him. That felt really good. And I saw another girl told me I was a good teacher. That felt really good, too. I didn't…" I shook my head. "That's all I wanted to say. I was just driving home and I wanted to tell you."

He nodded again, his face twisting with pain, and he opened his mouth to reply, but shut it just as quickly.

"I'm gonna leave now," I told him with a tight smile. "I really should've called or texted or something before coming over. I'm sorry about—"

"You don't have to be sorry," he murmured and his left arm lifted for just a second like he wanted to reach for me, but his arm dropped back down to his side. "I'm glad you got what you wanted. I'm really happy for you, Em."

"Thanks," I whispered, tears burning my eyes, and I took a step backwards. "I didn't mean to—well, what I mean is, I miss you. I really do. And I'm…I'm so sorry for everything, Finn. I told my mom that she'd made everything about her and I realized that I did the exact same thing with you. I made our whole relationship about my drama and my bullshit instead of actually letting myself be happy for once and…what were you getting out of it anyway, right?"

I laughed a little in spite of everything, but Finn clearly didn't see the humor here. Instead, his face twisted with that familiar heartache I'd grown so used to seeing at the end and his jaw set in firm line.

"You were right about everything," I told him softly. "You got too close and that scared the hell out of me, but I shouldn't have pushed you away. I should've talked to you instead of running and I'll never forgive myself for throwing away the best thing that ever happened to me. That's my fault and I wish I could take it all back, but I know it's too late. I'm sorry for that, too."

There was nothing more to say. Telling him I loved him right now wasn't fair to either of us, especially him. I could stand here for a little bit longer and add to our discomfort or I could just cut my losses and save us both the trouble. I opted to just cut our losses.

"I should go," I told him and smiled sadly.

I left Finn standing in the hallway again and once again, I was the one walking away. This time, though, I didn't feel like I was running or hiding or any of the things that had kept us apart to begin with. This time, it was just over and I had to find a way to live with that. I didn't want to be without Finn, but I'd have to figure it out. What did I really expect? Finn to just be waiting around for me to randomly stop at his apartment to beg forgiveness so we could run off into the sunset together?

Life didn't work that way. I knew that better than anyone. Maybe I shouldn't have stopped in today, but it was just as cathartic as driving into Hickory today. And maybe I needed to let Finn go now too—I'd already put both of us through enough and I'd had plenty of chances to set things right. If we were meant to be, we'd figure out a way to be together, wouldn't we? With some time and some distance, maybe we'd cross paths again someday, but until that day came, assuming it ever did, I needed to figure myself out first.

It was time to start accepting responsibility for the things that were my fault and letting go of the things that weren't.

And as I crossed town, I took yet another exit to take me to my last destination of the day. Unlike my last impromptu stop, this one I'd planned ahead of time and had taken the necessary steps to fully prepare. I had things to offer the world—all things I'd wasted since my teaching career ended and it was time to rectify that.

So, I walked into the Milwaukee Public Museum, pushing aside the fact that the last time I'd been here was with Finn, and didn't stop until I reached the main office. After a few minutes of waiting as the receptionist disappeared down a hallway, I straightened my shoulders when the human resources director stepped outside of her office.

"Hello," she greeted me. "What can I help you with?"

With my resumé in hand, my reply was short, simple, and heavy with long-lost power: "Hi, my name is Emma Owens. I was wondering if you were hiring?"

CHAPTER TWENTY-FOUR

A few days later, I woke up with a smile on my face. I stretched my arms up over my head, trying not to jostle Oliver too much. He'd taken to sleeping right in between my legs, whether it just made him feel safer or he liked using my shin as a pillow, which was fine and sweet, but uncomfortable as hell for me. I literally couldn't roll over or even really move all that much unless I wanted to roll right on top of my cat.

Let's face it, the little dude owned me and he knew it.

Despite a stiff back and my foot falling asleep, that smile on my face stayed in place. Life felt okay now and the smile on my face only widened because I knew it would still get better, too. During my brief meeting with the museum's HR head, she'd taken one look at my resumé, saw the words 'broad field social sciences' and 'educator', and she immediately sat me down for an impromptu interview. While any positions in curating would require a master's degree, which I didn't have, she informed me that I was a perfect candidate for the museum educator position they had available, which I'd already deduced myself.

After some standard questions about my teaching experience, she quickly scheduled me for a second interview with the Director of Education the next day. That interview went just as well as the first one did until it hit the inevitable snag:

"So, Emma," his voice had taken on a more serious tone and that was how I knew what he was going to say next. "I contacted your former principal and he had an, uh, *interesting* explanation for your termination."

I'd anticipated that. I'd mentally prepared myself for that. Hearing it out loud, though, still caught me off-guard and still brought heat flushing my cheeks. I'd pushed it away and spoke the truth.

"I understand, Mr. Newman, and I appreciate that you were still willing to speak with me after your conversation with Principal Denfield. The best explanation I can give you is that the administration decided to let me go without investigating the circumstances of how those pictures got online, which they deemed inappropriate behavior. Had they investigated, they would have learned I was the victim of a crime. My ex-fiancé posted those pictures without my permission to hurt me and at the time, it ruined my life. I didn't do anything wrong and yet, I was the one who was punished. I'm still working through the damage, but I want to put that behind me and move on with my life. I hope you understand that."

The words hung in the air, but I'd had nothing left to say and really, nothing left to lose. What was the worst that could happen at this point?

Mr. Newman had studied me quietly, taking in my words, judging the sincerity of them, and weighing just how much the circumstances surrounding my termination mattered to the job at the museum. I never flinched, never once shied away from his scrutiny, and maybe, in the end, that was enough. Finally, he'd nodded tightly and pressed a cool smile on his face.

"Alright then," he'd told me. "Let's continue, shall we?"

A day later, he'd called to thank me for applying, but said the museum had passed on hiring me. When I asked him why he'd made the decision, he'd skirted around the issue with as many vague deflections as possible before finally admitting that he just didn't feel comfortable hiring me given my 'history'.

Maybe I was the only one who saw the irony in his use of the word 'history', but what can you do?

So, the museum was a dead end and that was just the way life worked —figuring out where to go next was never going to be easy and I knew that. As frustrating as it was that my past had outweighed my qualifications, just walking inside and turning in my resumé was enough for me. It wasn't fair that I'd been turned away for something so out of my control, but it was still a first step towards reclaiming some sort of career again. While I knew I'd have to answer for my 'history' at every job interview I ever went on again, now I had that answer well-prepared. I didn't know where that path would lead, but I knew, with time, I'd figure out that part of my life, too.

At some point, I wanted to be in a position that would let me quit the café and really leave that last reminder of the scared, pathetic girl I used to be behind.

But now as I sat in front of my computer, it still didn't quite feel like enough. I wanted to do more, but I just didn't know what that *more* was. On pure reflex, I opened up the rant I'd written the day after Christmas and skimmed through it. The anger, the pain, and the frustration I'd felt then—and still felt—slammed over me yet again. I hadn't forgotten about those feelings; I'd just set them aside for the time being, but now I was ready to revisit them.

In my rant, I'd laid out the groundwork and it was time to keep building. There were obviously more women out there like me, who'd had their privacy ripped away and posted on the internet for everyone to see, but I'd just never felt strong enough to actually dig deeper and see what those women had to say.

After a quick search, I read story after story about women who'd gone through and were still going through circumstances similar to mine. Every story had its own variation, but what we all had in common was the way it'd made us feel: humiliated, scared, violated, and stripped of our power. Most related feeling betrayed by their ex—someone who was supposed to love them, but turned into a tormentor instead. There were plenty of resources out there now; one in particular that caught my eye was the Cyber Civil Rights Initiative, which seemed to be one of the driving forces behind recent legislation in the country and even had a hotline you could call for legal advice.

I even came across a story about a teacher in Indiana, whose experience was nearly identical to mine right down to being unable to report her ex for his crime because of nonexistent laws, except for the fact that she had the full support of her school district behind her.

God, I thought, *what would that have been like? Everything would've been so different if they'd just listened to me.*

But the story that really resonated with me the most was the woman who described feeling as though she'd been sexually assaulted over 30,000 times, which was how many times her picture had been shared online. I pushed further in my search and found similar testimony, women who'd said they'd felt raped, women who said commenters online had even went as far as to threaten to hunt them down and actually rape them, and women who were too afraid to even step outside for fear of being recognized.

At the end of the day, it all came down to control. I'd ended our relationship and Justin had wielded his control and his power over me by taking his revenge just because he could...wasn't that what motivated most rapists anyway? Control? Power?

Tears stung my eyes and I furiously wiped them away with my thumb. I didn't want to cry anymore. Justin and every single person who'd seen, downloaded, and commented on my pictures didn't deserve anymore of my tears.

I clicked onto another article describing a woman who'd been drugged by her ex-boyfriend, who later sexually assaulted her, filmed it, and posted the video online to over 35 porn websites. For reasons not outlined in the article, the police failed to prosecute him even after she charged him with rape. However, the woman took further action by filing charges against him in Britain because that was where he'd been when he initially posted the video, where her ex was about to be brought to trial. It wasn't the full charge he deserved, but it was something—some sort of justice for the crime that had been committed against her.

Every single instance I'd read about that mirrored my own were all non-consensual. Every woman had been violated when her body was put on display without her permission as a means to exploit and humiliate her.

With that thought, I opened up a new tab and did a quick search for Wisconsin's new law. I knew it existed, but since it was pretty much useless to me, I didn't even really look into it when the bill was signed well over a year ago. The language was muddled and just vague enough to allow for interpretation and that in itself was infuriating. But when my eyes fell on the punishment, all I could see was red.

A misdemeanor? That was it? Up to nine months in jail and a $10,000 fine?

Now, I was sitting here, glaring holes into my computer, and seething. It wasn't fair. The punishment just didn't fit the crime and I was just as angry with myself. I'd lost more than just my privacy and deep down, I'd always known that—I just hadn't allowed myself to see it until this moment. My eyes flicked back to my holiday rant and I squinted in thought, my mind flying back to the woman who'd had to go all the way to Britain to even attempt to get justice for herself.

Where was my justice? The simple answer was that it was nowhere to be found. All my aggressors, every single last one of them, were walking around with no consequences and with no true understanding of the damage they'd left in their wake. It didn't matter that Justin had eventually apologized and tried to get the pictures removed—he was the one who'd started it and he'd deserved more than just the beating he'd gotten from Noah. They needed to know what they'd done. They needed to understand how they'd made me feel.

But how would I—ah. That was it. The answer was so simple. I'd had a platform this whole time and hadn't even realized it.

My blog.

Thousands of hits a day of people reading about moisturizers and dry texturizing sprays...why couldn't I use my blog for something personal, too?

I knew what I needed to do now. I needed to tell my story. I needed to take back the control and the power that had been ripped right out from under me.

Everyone around me had always wielded the power—my mom, Justin, the school, the students and staff, the town. Now I needed to take it back.

I had nothing left to lose and so, with "Shake It Out" playing in the background, I started typing:

I know I don't normally post much personal information on here and many of you have asked why I've chosen not to include video tutorials or even pictures of myself other than my hand for a swatch or close-ups of parts of my face. The problem is that I've been hiding behind my computer screen. I haven't wanted anyone to see my face or know my name. In reality, I'm no different than the thousands and thousands of people everyday who use online anonymity to achieve a purpose.

For some, it's completely innocent. For others, a screen name signifies a power you wouldn't have otherwise. Abraham Lincoln once wrote, "Nearly all men can stand adversity, but if you want to test a man's character, give him power." How we use this power online defines us. It illuminates us. It shields us. It empowers us. It excuses us. It defiles us.

For years, I've hidden behind the anonymity this blog provided. It was my shield, my platform to write about a sort of guilty pleasure that, honestly, I'm still a little embarrassed about even though I know I shouldn't be. This blog gives me the means to indulge those guilty pleasures without the responsibility and the accountability attached to giving you my real name.

But through this last year, I've learned that the things we do online can follow us around like a ghostly cipher, sucking away at real life and threatening our actual lives. It's easy to forget and even easier to hide behind.

Today, the hiding stops. Today, I want to use this incredible platform you've given me for a different purpose.

If you Googled my full name, Emma Owens, you'd see some images that might shock you, depending on your opinion about racy photography. Well, racy isn't really the right word. Let's just call this what it really is, shall we? It's porn. You heard me. P-O-R-N. But there's an adjective we're missing too: revenge. Put that together and you get revenge porn.

I never knew that term existed until it happened to me. I took those pictures for my then-boyfriend, who later became my fiancé, and then my ex-fiancé. The circumstances involving our break-up aren't important. What's important is that we broke up and he posted those pictures online as a means to punish me.

I'm not sorry those pictures exist. They're hot as hell, aren't they? They represent a time in my life when I was uninhibited and experimenting with my sexuality in a safe environment with someone I thought I loved. It's taken me longer than I care to admit to feel that way.

I am sorry, however, for my response to the posting of those pictures. I wasn't strong enough to stand up for myself. I wasn't strong enough to defend myself. Instead, I remained passive. I let it happen to me and I didn't fight back. In fact, I took it one step further: I ran all the way from Hickory to Milwaukee to hide and lose myself in the big city.
I'm done with hiding. I'm done with passivity. Today is the day I start fighting back.

If you dug a little deeper in your Google search, you'd probably also find that I used to be a teacher, too. The day the school and the student body got wind of those pictures was the day I also lost my job. And that day I learned just how cruel teenagers can truly be when I walked into my classroom and found the word, "slut", written on my whiteboard in red letters. There's no coming back from that. No excusing it away. Even now, I'm sure they don't see the damage their words did.

I can't blame the administration for letting me go. If I'd been in their shoes, I would've felt like my hands were tied and that I had no other choice, but they also never once asked me for my side of the story. The online chaos that followed was predictable. The student body had a field day with this one—my pictures and various memes of those pictures popped up on Twitter, Snapchat, Facebook, Instagram, and any other social media platform you can think of.

Thousands upon thousands of comments later and I was a 21st century Hester Prynne, wearing a self-inflicted scarlet S online for the masses to see (S, of course, for slut). Or even better yet, I'd suddenly morphed into Blanche DuBois, whoring myself out for free and somehow expecting people to sympathize and show mercy when the court of public opinion never stoops low enough to exude an emotion as human as mercy. Those comments ruined my life. Ruined doesn't even completely cover it. Demolished is probably a better adjective. Decimated might be better even yet.

A teacher ruined by her students. Is there anything more ironic than that?

What infuriates me now is the response to those pictures. The adults in the situation, namely myself, the administration, my fellow teachers, and the community members—all of us dropped the ball. Nobody stood up and told the herd they were wrong. That they were cruel. That their actions could have lasting consequences. That their actions had destroyed not just my life, but my career, too.

Silence is validating and by remaining silent, every single adult involved sent the message that 1) it's okay to shame a woman for her sexuality 2) it's even more okay to make that woman feel as though she's worthless, dirty, a slut, and a pariah 3) blaming the victim is socially acceptable 4) by taking those pictures, I'd somehow brought it on myself and 5) it's totally fine to write vulgar, immature comments about someone online because you can hide behind your smartphone when you do it.

Like I said, we dropped the ball.

As educators and adults, we are responsible for teaching children the right way and the wrong way to deal with real-world crises. We are supposed to be the example and the models. The day those comments were allowed to flow freely through the school and the day I was released from my position...all of us failed. We're supposed to teach the future leaders and citizens of our country how to act like decent human beings who care about others, who defend others, and who are able to walk in someone else's shoes. We lost a valuable opportunity because we're supposed to be the moral compass, but on that day and all the days that followed, there was no moral compass to be found.

If you're wondering what happened to my ex-fiancé, I can honestly tell you that I don't know other than that he was not charged with a crime. When this happened over a year ago, Wisconsin still did not have legislation regarding this type of cyber crime. We do now, even though it was already too late to help me. The legislation itself, if you really study the fine print, will probably leave you just as frustrated as I am. The wording is vague, messy, and almost indecipherable because it's muddled in political jargon that just doesn't get the job done. Someone convicted of revenge porn in Wisconsin currently could face up to a $10,000 fine and/or nine months in jail in exchange for ruining someone's career and reputation and causing severe emotional trauma to the victim.

Those terms are not acceptable.

Now, we are one of 25 states that actually has any sort of revenge porn legislation, which is progress in itself, but what we currently have is not enough. While this bill stipulates that a person cannot post anything online of a sexual nature without the other party's consent, this bill does not cover the intent to humiliate and demonize the person, usually a woman, represented in the picture through the person's sexuality. Our legislation needs to be re-evaluated and re-drafted so that the punishment fits the crime.

The problem here is that revenge porn is a sex crime and should be treated as such, but it's not. The pictures that were posted of me online were of a sexual nature with the purpose to humiliate and punish me, to make me feel ashamed of my body, and to get revenge. If that is not sexual violence then I don't know what is.

Some people might say that if I had never taken those pictures in the first place, I wouldn't have found myself in that position. I reject that. All that statement does is validate rape culture. Why should I just 'expect' that those pictures would've shown up online? Just because I'm a woman, because I'm young, because I was a public figure in my community, doesn't mean I asked for this.

Based on my understanding of the law, the first stipulation surrounding sex crimes is that it must be a non-consensual act.

I did not consent to have my entire hometown see pictures I took privately for my boyfriend, who I trusted and who I thought I loved. I did not consent to be humiliated. I did not consent to be a laughingstock and a social pariah.

I did not consent.

It was, however, my choice to exercise a healthy sexual relationship and I have the right to decide who, where, when, and how. The fact that the choice was taken away from me is absolutely disgusting. Anyone who looked at those pictures, commented on those pictures, and downloaded those pictures is perpetuating a sex crime. It's as simple as that.

There are only two people who I've actually given permission to view those pictures: the first, my ex-fiancé and the second, the man I've been waiting my whole life to meet who I loved and who I pushed away because of my stupid insecurities, because I didn't believe I was worthy of the kind of pure, whole-hearted love he offered me.

Why is it so difficult to remember that I'm a human being? That I was somebody's teacher? That I'm somebody's daughter? Somebody's sister? Somebody's friend? Why is it so difficult to understand that, first and foremost, I belong to myself and nobody else? Why am I not entitled to privacy? Why does society believe it can shame, disgrace, and embarrass women for doing what men have always done—enjoy sex?

It's not dirty. It's not indecent. It's just life.

I wish I could tell you that I've moved past this, but I'm not quite there yet. I'm still angry. I'm so goddamn angry. And that's okay. I think that's a perfectly acceptable response to the situation and for a long time, I blamed myself for allowing this to happen to me. I bought into what people were whispering about me behind my back and shouting in my face. I allowed other people's opinions of me to shape my opinion of myself.

That also stops today. I'm strong, resilient, funny, talented, shy, beautiful, unique, and none of those things have anything to do with the pictures of me online, as it should be. They are all separate entities and one does not necessarily preclude another. I'm not a slut and I'm not a whore. I'm a woman and that's all you ever need to know.

Before I wrap this up, I have one more thing I need to say to anyone who's ever been victimized: never remain silent. Don't make the mistake I've been living with for more than a year. The only person who can truly defend you and tell your story is you and if you don't do it, you can't expect anyone else to do it for you.

You are your fiercest ally, your most valuable asset, and your loudest advocate. Never underestimate the power of you.

Thank you for allowing me to use this platform for a different purpose today. If you choose to share this post on your own social media platforms, I only ask that you use the picture I've included below. I think it's about time a picture of me was posted online of my choosing, don't you?

I read through the entire thing twice, left it open on my computer for about 10 minutes as I ran to the bathroom, grabbed some food, and threw a scoop of kibble in Oliver's food dish. The whole time, my heart thundered in my chest, butterflies bounced around in my stomach, and when I finally sat back down in front of my computer, I blew out my breath in a slow, controlled stream.

Control. That's what this was.

I took in another breath as my index finger hovered over the button that would send my story out into the online world and beyond. It was only fitting that my platform was the very same one that had been used against me in the first place.

I nodded to my computer screen.

Then I hit submit.

. . .

Finn

Call me a glutton for punishment or whatever, but I never took Emma off my Google alerts. I'd set it up right away when I figured out that the url removal tool actually worked so I could keep an eye on anything new that popped up about her. I just hadn't been able to force myself to turn it off.

Almost two months later and I still couldn't let go. It didn't matter that she'd shredded my heart, not to mention smashed what was left of it when she moved out of our building, because I just couldn't shake her. Not that I didn't want to—what was the point of hanging on to something that didn't want to be kept?

I wanted to move on. I wanted to forget her, but that was easier said than done. You can't just make yourself forget about the person you know you should be with until the day you die because it just doesn't work that way. When you love somebody, you don't let go, even when all you're doing is just kicking yourself in the balls, even when you know the odds of things working out in your favor are slim to none.

That was probably why I was sitting in front of my computer right now, obsessively copying and pasting links to those goddamn pictures into that url removal. Yeah. I knew exactly how masochistic and just incredibly stupid that was, but nothing and no one could stop me from continuing to do the only thing I had left to help her.

I might have been able to force myself to walk away two months ago...what else was I supposed to do? She'd pushed me away, wouldn't talk to me, and hid in her apartment until she ran even further away from me. My hands were tied. It's not like I could force her to talk to me or to stay in our building.

I'd learned from experience that I couldn't tell Emma to do anything she didn't want to do. She was difficult, skittish, and terrified of just about everything around her, especially me.

Unless something changed, I just didn't see how we could ever figure it out. I wanted to figure it out, but like I'd told her that day at the café, I couldn't keep doing all the work. She needed to meet me somewhere in the middle and who knew when she'd ever be ready to do that?

Of course, her random materialization out of nowhere a few days ago hadn't helped matters. Just when I thought I was rounding the corner, just when I thought I might've found a way to move on, Emma showed up and blew it all away again. In retrospect, it really wasn't that different from the first time I ever saw her—I'd been content in avoiding monogamy, commitment, and relationships, but lonelier than I was ever willing to admit—and then bam!

What happened a few days ago just threw me into the deep end of the pool again. Flailing my arms, barely keeping my head above the surface, and sucking in water—I was pathetic and I knew it.

To make matters even worse, I technically had a date tonight, too, and here I was, compulsively deleting urls that linked to nude pictures of my ex-girlfriend, who really should still be my actual girlfriend. God, I was even annoying myself—I honestly didn't know how Sling had put with me post-Emma. He'd only had to physically intervene once and that was to confiscate my laptop long enough to delete the entire Bon Iver's "For Emma, Forever Ago" album from my music library. I'd been listening to it with the volume cranked up to def con levels for longer than I cared to admit and at some point, someone had needed to step in and save me from myself.

There had to be some sort of meeting I could go to, like an Ex-Addicts Anonymous or something. Anything to kick the habit, especially since I needed to pretend to be a normal, single, well-adjusted guy tonight.

I had about 10 minutes before I had to leave with Sling and Mara to meet Hayley downtown, which I figured was plenty of time to check my Google alerts one last time before finally stepping away from my computer tonight.

Huh.

It looked like Emma added a new post to her blog tonight. She hadn't posted anything since right after Christmas and curiosity got the better of me—it was all I really had to feel close to her. But when my eyes landed directly on the title of her blog post, "My Story", I thought my heart might have stopped altogether.

I clicked the link and jumped to the first line, "*I know I don't normally post much personal information on here...*". At first, it took me a moment to really understand what was happening, but as I read through each new paragraph, my lips curled up the side of my face. My heart pounded, heat spread through my chest and rushed down my shoulders, and I found myself nodding at my screen when I read the words, "*I did not consent*".

"Damn right," I muttered.

I couldn't believe it...she was really doing this. She wasn't holding back either and between the scope and the depth, she was saying everything she needed to say.

And at the end, when she included a picture of herself and asked readers to share her story with a picture of her choosing, I laughed at my screen and shook my head, collapsing back into my chair.

Wow.

That took balls. Huge, massive balls. I always knew she had it in her; I just never knew what it would take for her to realize it and I wasn't about to take credit for it either. This was about her—it had nothing to do with me, just as it should be.

"*I made our whole relationship about my drama and my bullshit instead of actually letting myself be happy for once...*"

She was right. She had made it all about her, but I understood why. I was willing to work through it with her as long as we were on the same page...which just wasn't in the cards at the time.

"*What were you getting out of it anyway, right?*"

Her. It'd always been her. That's what I was getting out of it and that's all I needed.

My eyes flicked back up to her essay, landing easily on the only mention I'd received, which to be fair, was probably one too many…*"the man I've been waiting my whole life to meet who I loved."*

Who she loved. I would've waited the rest of my life to hear that if it meant I'd still be able to have her in it.

Loud banging on my door jerked me out of that reverie and about a second later, the door swung open to reveal Sling, his eyebrows lifting expectantly into his forehead and his hands spreading out wide in front of him.

"So…are we gonna go or what?"

My eyes still hadn't left my computer screen. "What?"

"You know we're meeting Hayley downtown, right?"

I blinked and shook my head. "Huh…oh, right. Yeah."

Sling just frowned back at me and crossed the short distance between my door and my computer desk. "What're you doing? We gotta get our asses on the road. Mara's getting a little bitchy about the whole thing and you know I need to keep that shit on lockdown…"

He trailed off when he finally got a good look at what was on my computer screen. As he crouched down to read through Emma's blog post, Mara appeared in the doorway.

"Guys? What's going on? We have to leave…like, two minutes ago."

Sling batted a hand at her. "Hold on, woman. Give us a second here."

That didn't appease her and soon, she was squinting at my computer screen right along with the rest of us and after she got through the first paragraph or so, her hand shot up to cover her mouth.

"I can't believe it," she murmured and shook her head. "This is…"

"Wow," Sling exhaled. "I don't really know what to say here, Finn."

It's not like there was much to say. The blog post spoke for itself. Pretty epically, too. Unfortunately, now that the two of them were finished reading it, they were also now staring at me like they half-expected me to leap right out the window or something, which didn't matter much anyway because we lived on the first floor.

"So…" Slinger started again. "Are you coming with us or should we tell Hayley you bailed?"

I pushed out a deep breath and tugged my hands through my hair. Hayley was a nice girl—funny, pretty, smart, good head on her shoulders…everything I knew I should probably want. Mara had started pushing her on me about a month ago, stating that her friend was, like, perfect for me. I'd went along with it out of obligation and because I thought it was what I was supposed to do in order to move on with my life.

The problem was that I didn't want to move on, but I also couldn't just set aside the fact that Emma had torn everything to pieces for no good reason and had continued tearing everything to pieces for even worse ones.

I didn't know what else to do, so I just nodded and stood up from my chair, leaving Emma's essay staring back at me from my screen.

The whole ride to Water Street was a blur. My mind just kept replaying it all in my head.

"I'll never forgive myself for throwing away the best thing that ever happened to me."

"You got too close and that scared the hell out of me, but I shouldn't have pushed you away."

Somewhere along the way, she'd figured it out. All the things that were keeping her from really letting me in, that had her frozen in place and holding me at arm's length, she'd figured it out. But she'd also owned up to the way she'd needlessly thrown our relationship in the trash. When she'd texted me on Christmas, I'd almost called her. I'd almost interrogated Mara, on Christmas Day no less, to give me Emma's new address, so I could at least...I didn't know what I'd even thought I would do.

I'd held back because I didn't want to wind up hurt again. Because I'd done everything I could think of to keep her from walking away and none of it mattered. She'd just walked away anyway.

But when I slid into a booth next to Hayley, everything just felt off. Sitting across from Sling and Mara felt right, but when I glanced at Hayley, who smiled back at me with excitement and hope glimmering in her pretty brown eyes, the best I could muster was a pained smile back.

I pretended to listen as Mara and Hayley chatted about something I didn't really care about and perused the beer menu as Sling mimed holding a gun to his head and fake-firing.

"Hey, Finn?" Mara called out to me.

My eyes lifted from the beer menu just long enough to find her gaze shifting expectantly from me to Mara and back to me again.

"What's up?"

"Don't you have another pitch meeting coming up soon?"

I pushed out a sigh. Her motive was clear and one sideways glance at Hayley just confirmed it. Mara was nudging and in the process, giving Hayley some false hope. Shit. I felt like a massive asshole now.

"Uh, yeah," I shrugged nonchalantly and did my best to just focus on the menu for as long as possible.

This time, the nudging came from Hayley's direction. "So, who are you meeting with?"

"Just some bar a few blocks away. Should be an easy get for the brewery."

"They always have a little celebration after a pitch meeting," Mara informed Hayley and my eyes flicked up to her, narrowing ever so slightly. "If everything goes well next week, you should come too, Hay."

I swallowed tightly, glancing around for our goddamn waiter already. I needed a drink. We'd only been here for five minutes and already, my leg bounced underneath the table to keep myself from bailing. That would be a real dick move, but still, a move I could live with.

When I made the mistake of glancing up from the menu yet again, I found Slinger's bright green eyes scrutinizing me carefully and I think he knew exactly what was going through my mind right now. I scrubbed a hand over my face and turned my head towards Hayley, who was still smiling at me with that earnest, albeit clueless, grin on her face.

My heart just wasn't in it. Frankly, my heart had *never* been in it.

The problem here was obvious: she just wasn't Emma. It didn't feel right to sit here without her next to me and until she was, nothing would feel right again.

So, I sat through drinks and small talk, doing my best not to be an antisocial prick. Hayley didn't deserve this—she deserved someone who was free to really be with her, instead of someone just going through the motions. This wasn't where I was supposed to be and she wasn't who I was supposed to be with.

It wasn't until the three of us were back in the car when they finally called me on it.

"Dude, what the hell was that back there?" Sling shifted around in the driver's seat to crinkle his nose at me. "You sick or something?"

No. I wasn't sick, but I knew what I needed to do in order to finally feel better.

"Hey, Mara?" I leaned forward so she could hear me better. "Where is she living now?"

I knew I didn't need to elaborate and honestly, this shouldn't have been a surprise to either of them.

Mara pushed out a quick sigh and glanced at Sling, who just shook his head. "Finn—"

"Look, I think we all knew things weren't gonna work out with Hayley and I honestly didn't mean to lead her on. I'll talk to her; I'll let her down easy, I promise, but please, Mara, just tell me where Em's living now."

Mara groaned and ran a hand over her face before finally huffing out a breath. "I honestly don't know, Finn. She's been really quiet at work ever since...well, you know. She doesn't talk to me much anymore."

Fine. I couldn't say I was exactly shocked by that development.

"When does she work next?"

"Come on, Finn."

"No, you come on, Mara. If you don't know, find out for me. Please. I just wanna talk to her. I *have* to talk to her."

Sling shrugged from the driver's seat. "I don't know, babe. We all read it, didn't we? Can you really blame the guy right now?"

"Ugh," she sighed again. "Fine. I'll find out, but after that, I'm staying out of it."

"Thanks, Mara."

That was all I needed anyway. I just needed to talk to her and find out where we stood. I didn't think I'd be able to do much else until I did. There was always a way. *"I wish I could take it all back, but I know it's too late..."* Even when time, distance, and everything else tossed every obstacle out there in our way, it still wasn't too late.

We loved each other. I knew it and now, she knew it, too. The only thing standing in our way now was us.

CHAPTER TWENTY-FIVE

"More coffee, Ed?" I asked, lifting the coffee pot up to him.

My gruff, yet ever-regular customer, just grunted in response and held up his empty coffee mug. Given how many times we'd done this, we had this little routine down pat. I quickly obliged him by filling the mug to the brim and shot him a quick, knowing grin.

"Food should be out shortly."

On any other normal day, Ed would grunt and shove some more food in his mouth. Instead, he pointed his fork down at the newspaper on the table and garbled, "This is you, isn't it?"

I glanced at the picture next to my story and shrugged. Not much can prepare you to see your personal and highly emotional words printed in a newspaper and the best reaction I could come up with was as little reaction as possible.

"Yep. That's me. Can I get you anything else?"

Ed studied me carefully for a few moments. His eyes drifted back to the paper and then flicked to me again. Then he shrugged, throwing an easy nod my way. "Good for you."

"Thanks," I murmured, a slow smile slipping across my lips. "Did you, um, need me to get you anything else right now?"

He just batted a hand at me. "Nah, Emma. I'm good for right now."

I blinked back at him in shock. Since when did he actually bother to remember my name? Since when was he actually sort of polite? For lack of a better response, I just nodded and walked away from the table. When I glanced over my shoulder, he'd folded the paper over so he could grip it in one hand to continue reading as he took a sip from his coffee cup.

Hitting the submit button was one thing because while I knew people were still going to read it, I wouldn't actually have to *see* them reading it. This was a different story. I wanted to duck into the kitchen and hide until he was finished for reasons I didn't quite understand. No part of me was ashamed of what I'd written or held any regrets, but watching someone actually read my words made my palms sweaty and my throat itchy.

With only an hour left of my lunch shift, I still had a little side work to finish and since Ed was currently the only customer in my section, I'd probably be heading home as soon as Ed finished up here. I glanced over my shoulder one more time at my customer, who was still reading the article, and swallowed hard.

In the span of 72 hours, my whole life had shifted on its axis. Within hours of hitting the submit button, my blog post had been shared thousands of times, a number which only multiplied by the hour, starting with my initial blog readers and trickling down through the blogosphere and the Twittersphere, or whatever it's called, at warp speed. So, basically, I went viral. Again.

I hadn't planned on it and I'd definitely never expected it. Even though this was the first time in a very long time I'd ever received any sort of positive attention online, trending on Twitter wasn't exactly my intention. All I'd wanted to do was make an impact. All I wanted to do was come out of hiding and finally exude some real honesty for once. It looked like I'd accomplished all that and then some.

In the short time since hitting that submit button, I'd heard from just about everyone I'd ever met in my entire life—some I remembered and some I didn't. Within about 20 minutes, Noah and Cris called. After that, the floodgates opened and it hadn't really ever stopped. Everyone saying how proud they were, how brave I was, and how they just *'couldn't believe I did that'*. Whatever that meant.

Regardless, my blog post brought everyone out of the woodwork: I'd heard from long-lost friends from college that I'd completely forgotten about, nearly all my former 'friends' from my past life in Hickory, former colleagues from school, former students, old neighbors, my old babysitter, a few people from my mom's church, Principal Denfield, Mara, just about everyone at the café, and even Slinger, the last person I thought I'd ever hear from.

And that was even before I'd gotten the call from an editor at the *Milwaukee Journal Sentinel.*

Of course, the only person I'd actually *wanted* to hear from hadn't called, texted, or commented on my blog post, as opposed to seemingly everyone else who had internet access.

I'd even heard from my mom.

I know. For a second there, I thought hell might have frozen over, but she hung up before I even really had a chance to realize what happened.

What a shocker, right? Considering we hadn't spoken since the day I'd shown up uninvited at her house and barricaded myself in her car, my mom's reaction was the last thing on my mind.

Maybe that was why, when the café's front door swung open, the plate in my hand nearly tumbled down to the floor. It was amazing how you could survive for weeks, even months, and convince yourself that you're not starving. That you're not deprived. That you're not dying. Because the second Finn walked through the door, the weight of those hours, days, weeks, and months I'd somehow survived without him hit me like a freight train.

Pre-Finn me was hardly even awake, let alone a functional human being. Post-Finn me was stronger, wiser, and more resilient, but still wasn't completely whole. Now, I shoved pre-Finn me to the curb, that long-lost part of me finally jerked alive, finally free, finally complete with the missing piece of the puzzle...and we hadn't even said a word to each other yet.

I could only stare, my heart and my breath tangled up in my throat, as Finn stood in the doorway, a folded up newspaper in one hand and unzipping his thick winter jacket with the other, revealing a wrinkled grey T-shirt that read *Aha Shake,* and his lips curling up in that warm grin I knew so well. He waved the newspaper in the air and gestured with his head towards the empty booth right next to Ed, the very same one he'd sat in both times he was here in the café.

Unlike the last time I saw him, well over a week ago when I'd went on my purge-and-catharsis-spree, this time, he wasn't angry. This time, he wasn't staring at me with hard eyes and keeping himself from reaching for me. This time, he looked like he knew I was finally ready to talk.

With no other options available to me, I just nodded. I didn't trust myself to do much else. While I was too busy blinking back the shock of this ghost's appearance in the doorway, the plate in my right hand jerked to the side. I glanced down to find Ed pulling on the plate with a grunt.

"I got it," he huffed in exasperation when I finally let the plate slip through my fingers. It was probably for the best I wasn't holding it anyway...if I waited much longer, it probably really would tumble to the floor.

"Go."

That shook me out of it a little and my attention, or what was left of it, shifted momentarily to my cantankerous customer.

"What?"

Ed rolled his eyes up to the ceiling, shooting me a quick glare as he scooped up a fork, and then swept it out in front of him to gesture towards the near-empty café.

"I'm good," he groused. "And it's not like this place is exactly hoppin'. Go on now. Talk to your fella."

Your fella.

My heart danced in my throat, heat coloring my cheeks and flooding down my limbs. The last time Ed had said that to me, I'd balked, terrified that Finn heard it, terrified about what that would mean if it was true, terrified of letting Finn get too close. I wasn't scared anymore, but that didn't mean I approached Finn's booth with any less hesitation.

I didn't know what was going to happen next, but I'd never find out if I didn't get my ass into that booth.

When I slid in across from Finn, that grin on his handsome face only widened and his light eyes softened.

"Hey, Em," he murmured.

"Hi, Finn."

Somehow, my lips curled up, but I think it was the sound of his voice more than anything. That deep, robust timbre wrapped around me, pulling me in, and holding me tight. Just like every other time I'd heard it. I opened my mouth to speak, but he pointed down to the newspaper on the table, his eyes crinkling up at the sides a little.

"I read your article," he informed me. "Well, if I'm being completely honest, I read it as a blog post first."

Of course he'd read it on my blog. I probably shouldn't have been surprised that he still read it even after I'd put as much physical and emotional distance between us as possible. Again, because I didn't trust myself to do much else, I just nodded.

His eyes flicked back down to the newspaper and he shook his head. "That's...seriously, Em, that's the bravest shit I've ever seen."

I laughed lightly and finally tore my eyes away from him so I could slide the paper towards me. This was the first time I'd ever really seen it in print, I mean, *really* looked at it, and seeing my words staring back at me in black and white in the *Sentinel* was a surreal experience, even in front of Finn. I'd never set out to be a writer, never even thought of myself as a writer despite the fact that I'd been writing a blog for years, but the evidence was here. My work, my words, my life...in print.

"It wasn't brave," I shrugged. "It was just the truth and It was just the right thing to do."

"Yeah, well," he grinned. "It takes balls to do the right thing and Em, you've got the biggest pair of I've ever seen."

I cocked my head to the side. "How many pairs have you seen?"

"Ah, I'm not at liberty to say. Enough to know what I'm talking about though."

"I see."

He flashed me a quick smile, but it dropped just as quickly. "I bet things have been a little crazy lately, huh?"

I just lifted a shoulder. "A little bit. Mostly just emails, texts, that sort of thing. My mom called me, actually, too."

His eyebrows leapt up into his forehead. "Really?"

"Yeah," I huffed out a bitter laugh. "She said it was, and I quote, 'very well-written' and that was pretty much the end of it. But it was something, I guess, and if that's all our relationship ever is then that's something I can live with."

Finn nodded somberly.

"Anyway, this legal group, the Cyber Civil Rights Initiative, emailed me yesterday and they want me to join this task force that meets in Madison. They've been active all around the country, trying to get movements started in each state. I guess it would involve, at some point, going in front of the state senate to talk about my experience with other women from the state who've gone through this. They're pushing for...pretty much everything I wrote about. Stronger and clearer laws, redefining the crime, harsher punishments."

"Wow," Finn's eyebrows rose. "Are you gonna do it?"

"I don't know," I shrugged and tried to brush it off like it wasn't as monumental as it actually was. In all the comments and emails I'd received since my story went viral, the ones from all the women out there who were just like me, who were just like all the stories I'd read, those were the ones that resonated the loudest.

On second thought.

"Well," I smiled softly. "Maybe I will."

He nodded, his eyes crinkling up again at the sides, and I hadn't forgotten how much I'd missed this. Just sitting here like this, talking to him, being with him...I could stand on my own two feet without him. I knew that now. I just didn't want to.

"So, from waitress to political activist, huh? I think that'll be a good look for you."

"Yeah, well, I *did* teach civics once upon a time. So I guess I have that going for me."

And just like that, the final piece clicked into place. Maybe I was never meant to be a teacher or a historian or an educator at a museum. Maybe I was meant to take the cues from my historical heroes and fight for my rights and the rights of others. Maybe that broad field social sciences degree would come in handy after all. Maybe all these terrible, life-altering events had happened in my life to lead me here, in this city, to that cat, on that patio, to finally end up in this booth. Maybe fate had me on the right path all along.

Nah.

I'd gotten here on my own. Fate, circumstance, and maybe even God, too, if you wanted to get all spiritual about it, had played a small hand, but the cards were always up to me to play. I could've folded altogether. I could've taken my money, so to speak, and run. But I was here. I was still standing. I'd picked myself up and put myself back together again. I'd become the hero of my own story.

Okay. Maybe I had a little help from a stray cat.

But now, the ball was in Finn's court. He'd shown up here at my work, after all, uninvited and unannounced and I still technically had a customer to handle, too.

So, I swallowed tightly, pulled on my big-girl pants and asked him point-blank, "Finn, what are you doing here? Are you just here because you read the article?"

He opened his mouth to answer, but my compulsive need to explain myself got the better of me.

"Before you say anything, let me be clear: I didn't write that article for any purpose other than to tell my story and to take my life back. That's it. I didn't do it because I wanted it to go viral, I didn't do it for attention, and most of all, Finn, I didn't do it for you."

Finn didn't miss a beat and his lips curled up into the sexiest grin I'd ever seen.

"I know. So—"

"I'm so sorry," I cut in abruptly, unable to hold it in anymore. "I know I've already said it, but I wanted to say it again. I wish I could take everything back...I wish I'd talked to you. I just wasn't ready."

He nodded tightly. "Are you ready now?"

There was no question about it. "Yes."

"Is it okay if I talk now?"

He paused for just a second to gauge my reaction and then pushed out a rough breath.

"I tried really hard to forget about you, Em," Finn started and ran a hand through his hair. "I *wanted* to forget and I'm sure you remember the girl that was in my apartment that day you just showed up out of the blue?" He waited long enough for me to nod tightly at the memory. "I went out with her a few times...well, *tried* to go out with her is probably a better way to describe it. The problem was that I just kept thinking about you instead. The problem was that I'm in love with you and that's not something I ever want to shake. Something really terrible happened to you, Em, and I didn't handle it very well."

I opened my mouth to add to that last comment, but he jumped back in before I got the chance.

"I've had a lot of time to think about it and I know you're going to say that it's all because you pushed me away and wouldn't talk to me, and all that's true, but I pushed you too hard. I wanted you to just get over it and I thought me telling you it wasn't your fault, that I love you anyway, I thought that would be enough. I never stopped to really think about what that must've been like for you and how you really felt about it and it wasn't until after you stopped talking to me that I realized my own part in all that shit. I never should've tried to push you into doing something you weren't ready to do."

"I was terrified," I whispered.

He nodded tightly. "I know."

"You scared the hell out of me."

"I know."

I sucked in a harsh breath. "I should've let you in, but I just couldn't."

"I know," he nodded.

"I felt like I didn't deserve you...like I didn't deserve anything good in my life after doing something so terrible."

"I know."

My eyes squeezed shut when I felt his fingertips brush the top of my hand. "It wasn't terrible. *I'm* not terrible and I should've let you love me."

"I know."

"I don't expect you to forgive the way I hurt you. I made everything so much more complicated than it had to be. I was so stubborn. So, so stupid. And selfish. And I didn't stop to think about your feelings at all. I'm so sorry."

"I know."

Tears stung my eyes. This was it. I was going to say it. And I wasn't terrified at all.

"I love you, Finn."

He smiled and his fingertips finally closed around my hand.

"I know."

. . .

I did my best to ignore the pair of strong hands skimming up my waist as I tried and failed to get my key in the door. Lips and warm breath brushed my neck and I shivered underneath his touch.

"Need some help?" Finn laughed against my skin.

"Well," I huffed playfully. "If you'd just keep your hands to yourself for a second and let me concentrate, I could…"

My words died in my throat when he reached around my waist, plucked my key chain right out of my hand, and shoved my key in the lock without any further obstacles.

"There."

"I could've done it on my own," I grumbled under my breath, despite the fact that his mouth had found my neck again.

"I know," he murmured. "But that wasn't gonna get us in the door any faster."

"I see your point."

My neck muffled his laugh and we pushed through the door, shutting it behind us just as quickly. That familiar tinkling echoed from the hallway and I heard the *mehs* and the *maahwrs* before I even saw the four little white paws and dark pointed ears.

"Contraband!" Finn called out to him, momentarily releasing me so he could bend down and scoop my cat up in his arms. "I missed ya, buddy."

"Hey," I corrected sternly, but my tone softened the second I saw the two most important men in my life cuddling with each other. "He's not exactly contraband anymore, you know."

Finn just shrugged and kept right on scratching the top of my cat's head, chuckling as Oliver craned his neck up even further as if to say, *Oh yeah. Right there.*

"That may be true," Finn announced as he set Oliver back down on all four legs. "But he'll always be contraband to me."

I could only laugh as Finn winked down at my cat, shrugged his coat off, and then turned to survey the rest of my apartment with his hands on his hips.

"So this is the new place, huh? Cat-friendly and everything?"

"Cat-friendly and everything."

He chewed on the inside of his cheek, his eyes still roaming around. It must've been a little like deja vú for him—same furniture, same decor, same cat, just a different place. Different girl, too.

"Well," he announced as he gripped the neck of his wrinkled grey T-shirt and yanked it over his head. "I've seen enough."

While I laughed, he was already unbuttoning his jeans. "Just like that?"

"Yep," he told me with a wink and shoved his jeans down. "Just like that."

So, I shrugged and followed his lead. I kicked off my work shoes, ignored the fact that Oliver had parked it right in the hallway and watched us with wide, sea foam-grey eyes, and jerked my own T-shirt over my head. Finn's light eyes darkened as I unclasped my bra and let it dangle from my fingertips playfully before tossing the lacy material at him. He just flipped it over his shoulder, waiting patiently for me to catch up to him, his eyes following my every move.

By the time he advanced on me, there was nothing separating us anymore. No more clothing. No more distance. No more vulnerability. No more insecurity. No more hesitation. No more painful pasts.

His hands closed around my face and he sealed his lips over mine. I breathed him in, my senses filling with his earthy musk, his heat, his love, everything that I loved and everything that I'd taken for granted. And when our bodies and everything else in between finally found each other again, this time there was no holding back.

This time I let him in.

"What greater gift than the love of a cat?"
—Charles Dickens

EPILOGUE

Nine Months Later

"Ah! Watch it, contraband!" Finn yelped. "Goddammit, we need to trim your claws or something. Shit, that's sharp!"

"Oh, don't be such a baby," I laughed from my chair next to him. "It's not that bad."

"Uh, yeah, I think it is. RB's got some serious talons on him right now."

I just rolled my eyes and tucked my Matthews Brewing Co. beer bottle underneath my chair on the patio. All I had to do was hold my arms out and my cat obliged, leaping from one lap to the other, and I hugged him to my chest.

"Hey, buddy," I murmured into his soft fur. "Daddy's being a jerk right now. And a grump. You just stay right here for awhile."

Finn huffed out a laugh and shook his head at us. Oliver, naturally, responded by nuzzling my neck before scooting down my lap to tilt his head right into my left boob.

"Jesus," Finn muttered under his breath. "It's a good thing I actually like that damn cat or else I'd probably be out on my ass by now."

"That's only sort of true," I shrugged diplomatically. "I love both of you equally and differently."

"Yeah, I know where I rank. Pretty soon, *I'm* gonna be the one sleeping at the foot of the bed," Finn glanced over his shoulder at Oliver and jabbed a finger at him. "I know all your tricks, buddy."

"Oh boy," I sighed and gestured with my head towards the grill in an effort to distract him. "How're those brats coming? Slinger and Mara are gonna be here soon and we can't miss the pre-game now, can we?"

Finn shot me an exasperated, albeit playful, glare but eventually gave in and stood so he could check on our tailgate food.

The crisp September breeze curled around us, lifting up the edges of Finn's overly-long, floppy brown hair and making me wish I'd worn something other than just a Packer jersey outside. It was amazing how

332

much difference a year could make—the different twists and turns that made up a life, that took you to unexpected places, both good and bad, and the people who helped you get there.

Regardless of how I'd gotten here, I was right where I was supposed to be. Less than two months after Finn came to the café, he moved in with Oliver and me, and we'd never looked back.

Life had settled down since the initial outpouring after my article went viral. Finn put in his hours at the brewery, but practically ran out the door the second his day ended to come home to us. I'd cut back my hours at the café so I could devote more of my time to working with the Madison chapter of the Cyber Civil Rights Initiative, which meant I had to travel from Milwaukee to Madison at least once a week, but the time was worth it. The work was worth it. And in a month, I'd get to speak in front of the state senate along with 14 other women, putting a real voice and a real face to the crimes committed against us.

The past was behind us now. We could only move forward and I'd never felt happier in my entire life.

Finn's hand closed over my shoulder and I tilted my head back to find him grinning down at me.

"I gotta run inside quick to grab a plate for the brats," he told me warmly. "You need anything?"

"Nah," I shook my head. "I'm good. Hurry up so you can come back out here by us."

He chuckled and then his lips grazed my neck, trailing all the way up along my jawline until he found my lips, pressing a hard kiss there that told me to expect more of that later tonight after our game day guests left.

"Love you," he murmured against my lips.

I reached up to tangle my free hand in his hair. "Love you too."

"I'll be right back."

"Okay."

He slid the screen door open so he could step through and retreated inside our apartment. I glanced down at my cat, smiling as "Let My Love Open The Door" played softly from my turntable inside our apartment, and he blinked at me before burrowing even deeper into my lap, his little white paw stretching up to give my cheek a light tap.

"Love you too, buddy," I murmured to him.

Meh.

Oliver nudged his cheek into my neck, but saved the theatrics for when Finn came back out so they could resume their little competition over me, and I kissed the top of his soft, furry little head.

I guess I never thought I'd get here, never knew it was even *possible* to be in a place where I'd feel this safe, this loved, and this happy. And I guess that was before I looked out my old patio door at my old apartment and saw those streaks of grey and black and those little flashes of white.

I'd always known I was lost. I just hadn't known how lost I really was until he found me.

So, like I said, it all started with a cat.

Author's Note

Calling this book semi-autobiographical is a huge stretch. Loosely inspired by real events and real people is more accurate. So, let me help you sift through fact and fiction. Oliver is very real. In fact, he's trying to walk all over my computer right now as I type this. The journey that Emma takes with him in this story is nearly identical to the one Oliver and I are still taking together, save for a few minor adjustments. Everything else...that's not me.

I have, however, drawn on an aspect of my life that I've since put behind me. My reasons for leaving teaching were boring things like budget cuts rather than the nightmare Emma experienced. My goal in choosing to include that aspect of my 'former' life, my teaching career, is not to vilify anybody or anything related to education (okay, maybe one person), but to simply express a perspective rooted in my personal experience in that field.

The inspiration for what happened to Emma came about last year during one of my (former) classes. We were discussing society's double standard when it comes to the genders and sex related to A Streetcar Named Desire. I brought in an article detailing Jennifer Lawrence's phone-hacking scandal and the nude photos that leaked onto the internet as a result, asking the class to consider things from her point of view. Was it wrong for the pictures to exist in the first place? Is it wrong for anyone to look at the pictures now that they're out there on the internet? A heavy topic for juniors in high school, I know, but it was still a valid one considering nearly 99 percent of them view their cell phones as another appendage.

I remember very clearly that the girls in the class were screechingly, almost annoyingly vocal about the invasion, and about how it should be considered sexual assault, while the guys were sitting there going, What's the problem? One boy in particular unknowingly drove the point home—I called on him and his response was, and I quote, "Sorry, I didn't hear what you were saying because I was staring at this picture of Jennifer Lawrence." The frustration I felt towards the boys in my class kind of came out of nowhere for me because they were just seeing her as an object and not as a person. I thought to myself, What if this was me? What if someone had done this to me...how would you be looking at me now? That experience was something that stayed with me and ultimately, served as some of the inspiration for writing this book.

I know my book isn't the first book to tackle this issue, but given my experience and my own feelings on the subject, I felt like I had something to add to the discussion and wanted to offer another point of view.

I honestly believe that what happened to Emma could easily happen to anyone. She could've been me. My friends. My cousins. My co-workers. Any of my former students. Hopefully, this book provided some comfort to all the girls like Emma out there who've made mistakes, but who've yet to figure out how to forgive themselves as well as some insight into an aspect of education that isn't really discussed openly, but should be.

If you'd like to learn more information about the Cyber Civil Rights Initiative, you can visit their website, www.cybercivilrights.org.

Thank you for reading.

About the Author

K. Ryan is a former English teacher, who graduated from the University of Wisconsin-Stevens Point in 2009. When not writing, she's either binge-watching something on Netflix, running, reading, or cheering on the Packers. She lives in the Green Bay area with her crazy-supportive boyfriend and the best decision of her adult life, a not-so-stray cat named Oliver.

Follow her on Twitter @authorkryan, visit her Facebook page or visit her website, authorkryan.com, for updates and news.

Other Books By K. Ryan

The Carry Your Heart Duo
Carry Your Heart
Carry You Home (TBA)

Acknowledgements

Like I've said before, I think a book is really only as good as its cover, so I owe a huge thank you to Christa at Paper and Sage. When I first saw this cover on your website, I just about fell out of my chair because it was like you'd gotten in my head and created exactly what I wanted.

To Mia at IndieSage PR, thank you for all your advice and your support through the release of both my books. Your encouragement and your friendship has been invaluable to me through this process. Thank you for always being my cheerleader!

To Ali, Nikki, and Krista, my awesome betas—I can't tell you how much easier the editing process was this time around, but it went so smoothly because I had you wonderful ladies in my corner. Thank you for giving up some of your free time to help me. Let's do it again.

To Mike, Mom, Dad, and Matt—thank you for your unwavering support and making me feel like I was getting it right every step of the way.

To my readers—thank you for letting me close a chapter in my life through writing this book and thank you, again, for reading.

Songs In Order Of Appearance:

1. "Come and Get Your Love" by Redbone
2. "Like a Rolling Stone" by Bob Dylan
3. "Start Me Up" by The Rolling Stones
4. "Green and Yellow" by Lil' Wayne
5. "Mama Said Knock You Out" by LL Cool J
6. "Country Girl (Shake It For Me)" by Luke Bryan
7. "Just What I Needed" by The Cars
8. "Runaway Train" by Soul Asylum
9. "Proud Mary" by Creedence Clearwater Revival
10. "Hotel California" by The Eagles
11. "Baba O'Riley" by The Who
12. "Moondance" by Van Morrison
13. "Go Your Own Way" by Fleetwood Mac
14. "Any Way You Want It" by Journey
15. "Closer To The Heart" by Rush
16. "Hey Jude" by The Beatles
17. "That's All Right" by Elvis Presley
18. "Hold On Loosely" by .38 Special
19. "Stand By Me" by Ben E. King
20. "Under the Boardwalk" by The Drifters
21. "Sex On Fire" by Kings of Leon
22. "Back Down South" by Kings of Leon
23. "Snow (Hey Oh)" by Red Hot Chili Peppers
24. "Californication" by Red Hot Chili Peppers
25. "Sitting, Wishing, Waiting" by Jack Johnson
26. "The Pretender" by Foo Fighters
27. "Afternoon Delight" by Starland Vocal Band
28. "Skinny Love" by Bon Iver
29. "Fake Plastic Trees" by Radiohead
30. "Karma Police" by Radiohead
31. "High & Dry" by Radiohead
32. "Temple" by Kings of Leon
33. "Fans" by Kings of Leon

34. "Here I Go Again" by Whitesnake
35. "Yellow" by Coldplay
36. "Why Should I Worry?" by Billy Joel
37. "Long-Legged Guitar Pickin' Man" by Johnny Cash and June Carter Cash
38. "Begin Again" by Taylor Swift
39. Theme from *Mission: Impossible*
40. "Everything Has Changed" by Taylor Swift feat. Ed Sheeran
41. "Give Me Love" by Ed Sheeran
42. "Taper Jean Girl" by Kings of Leon
43. "Always Alright" by Alabama Shakes
44. "Maria" from *West Side Story*
45. "Somewhere Over The Rainbow" by Judy Garland
46. "The Blower's Daughter" by Damien Rice
47. Theme from *The Twilight Zone*
48. "Your Song" by Elton John
49. "Show Me The Way" by Peter Frampton
50. "Don't Stop Believin'" by Journey
51. "I Don't Wanna Work" by Todd Rundgren
52. "Both Sides Now" by Joni Mitchell
53. "River" by Joni Mitchell
54. "It Must Have Been Love (Christmas For The Broken-Hearted)" by Roxette
55. "Supersoaker" by Kings of Leon
56. "Molly's Chambers" by Kings of Leon
57. "Ragoo" by Kings of Leon
58. "Charmer" by Kings of Leon
59. "Teenagers" by My Chemical Romance
60. "Virtuality" by Rush
61. "Shake It Off" by Taylor Swift
62. "Shake It Out" by Florence + The Machine
63. "Let My Love Open The Door" by Pete Townshend

www.ingramcontent.com/pod-product-compliance
Lightning Source LLC
Chambersburg PA
CBHW030557180626
46816CB00005B/1573

* 9 7 8 0 6 9 2 5 4 8 4 9 3 *